As *the* Tide Comes In

New York Times and CBA Best-Selling Author

CINDY WOODSMALL

& ERIN WOODSMALL

A Novel

As *the* Tide Comes In

WATERBROOK

As the Tide Comes In

All Scripture quotations or paraphrases are taken from the Holy Bible, English Standard Version, ESV®
Text Edition® (2016), copyright © 2001 by Crossway Bibles, a publishing ministry of Good News
Publishers. All rights reserved.

Trade Paperback ISBN 978-0-7352-9101-0
eBook ISBN 978-0-7352-9100-3

Published in the United States by WaterBrook, an imprint of the Crown Publishing Group, a division
of Penguin Random House LLC, New York.

WaterBrook® and its deer colophon are registered trademarks of Penguin Random House LLC.

Library of Congress Cataloging-in-Publication Data
Names: Woodsmall, Cindy, author. | Woodsmall, Erin, author.
Title: As the tide comes in : a novel / Cindy Woodsmall, Erin Woodsmall.
Description: Colorado Springs : WaterBrook, 2018.
Identifiers: LCCN 2018007644| ISBN 9780735291010 (softcover) | ISBN 9780735291003 (electronic)
Subjects: LCSH: Female friendship—Fiction. | BISAC: FICTION / Christian / General. | FICTION /
    Christian / Romance. | FICTION / Contemporary Women. | GSAFD: Christian fiction.
Classification: LCC PS3623.O678 A9 2018 | DDC 813/.6—dc23
LC record available at https://lccn.loc.gov/2018007644

Printed in the United States of America
2018—First Edition

10 9 8 7 6 5 4 3 2 1

To Chutinun Muelae:
You've been a part of our lives for a long time
although an ocean separates us once again.
I pray we share a home together one day soon.
I love you beyond words, dear one.
Cindy

To my mother, Norma Rainwater:
Thank you for raising me "wild" in the outdoors,
from running trails
and splashing in mountain streams
to the many summer weeks spent roaming St. Simons Island on bikes.
Thank you for the gift of an adventurous childhood.
Erin

July 2, 2005

T he canvas painting on the wall called to Tara as she walked back into the kitchen, this time her arms filled with rock-climbing gear. She set everything on the table and went to the painting. Once again her heart beat faster, and whispers from a past she didn't remember haunted her. It was the sole remaining object from her childhood. The day social services arrived at the trailer to take her away, Tara begged to take the painting with her. After all, it had been given to her . . . maybe.

The painting was of a lighthouse, beach, and ocean, as if the artist's view was from the ocean. Deep red and gold reflected off the water as though it was depicting sunset, or maybe sunrise, but those colors were usually brighter and lighter. That painting and the woman who painted it seemed connected to Tara somehow. At the bottom the artist had signed it "To my Spunky Boo ~ Love you, Nana." Tara had no recollection of anyone named Nana, but she did recall her mom calling her Spunky Boo at times, so the artist either knew that or also called Tara that. As a child abandoned to the foster care system by a drug-addicted mother, she liked to daydream that someone somewhere loved her.

A noise from the bedrooms in the small apartment pulled Tara from her thoughts. Why was she marinating in old hurts? After months of working two jobs, she had the entire day off, and she would not spend another second thinking about sad things.

She sat in a kitchen chair and put on her athletic shoes. She'd restocked the grocery store shelves until midnight, so she'd slept late. As good as that felt, she knew the best part of the day was still ahead. Her gear was spread across the small table: dynamic ropes, various sizes and shapes of carabiners, and a climbing pack with power snacks and water. Her TomTom was on the table too. It had nothing to do with climbing mountains, but it got her to the agreed-upon destinations to gather with other climbers.

"Oh, thank goodness." Hadley's voice carried down the short hallway. She stepped into the kitchen, wearing a robe, her hair wrapped in a towel. "I smell coffee."

"Tara,"—Elliott was behind her, already in her hospital uniform—"please never quit your job at the grocery store." Her roommates made a beeline for the coffee maker.

Hadley and Elliott had worked second shift last night and then stayed for some overtime hours, so they'd slept in later than Tara.

"The good news is we have coffee." Tara picked up the TomTom and began entering the address of today's destination. "The bad news is we only had enough money for either coffee or milk, not both."

"As always, T,"—Hadley put the mug to her lips, closed her eyes, and took a sip—"you made the right decision."

"Yeah," Tara scoffed, "it's almost as if I'd spent years under the same roof with you two while growing up or something."

Hadley and Elliott chuckled. The three of them had shared a foster home for several years. That's when the feeling of sisterhood began, and even though Hadley and Elliott had quit high school and run off to work and live in Georgia until they were legal adults, they had continued the bond with Tara through phone calls and emails, so very many calls and emails.

Tara shoved the TomTom into her backpack. "Be sparing with the sugar. It doesn't go on sale until next week."

Maybe when they had college degrees, they'd make decent money, but for now they eked by on minimum wage jobs, sharing the bills and saving every penny for their education. Tara had graduated high school a couple of months ago, and with some help from the state, she'd begin college this fall, although she was unsure what her major would be. Was there a degree that could mix her two favorite things: food and outdoor life?

Hadley and Elliott knew what they wanted degrees in, but right now they were working toward getting their GED.

"Oh, this came for you yesterday." Elliott pulled a letter out of the pocket of her scrubs.

Tara took it from her. "A real letter?" She glanced at the return address. There wasn't a name on it, and what little Tara could make out, she didn't recognize. But it was to Miss Tara Abbott and had her address. "Who even sends these anymore?"

"That's exactly what I thought." Elliott opened the fridge and grabbed the carton of eggs. "Have you eaten, T?"

"Yeah." She glanced at the clock on the stove. "I need to leave in a few." Her climbing buddies would be gathering at a specific parking lot in ninety minutes, and it'd take Tara more than an hour to drive there. She and her climbing buds had been planning quite a while for today—Saturday, July 2. They'd climb the face of a mountain long before sunset, waste time until dark, and watch fireworks. Afterward, using flashlights, they would hike down a clear trail on the slope of the mountain.

Tara pulled the letter from its envelope. The notebook paper looked as if it'd been jerked from a three-ring binder. She glanced at the signature. "It's from Patricia."

"Who?" Elliott asked.

Tara looked up, surprised by the question. On the other hand, Tara had met the woman only once, four years ago when she'd brought Sean and Darryl to the foster family and biological family picnic. It was the first and last time Tara had seen any of them. "She's my half-brothers' grandmother."

"Ah." Elliott slid her hands into the shirt pockets of her scrubs. "I'm not sure I even knew her first name. You say little about her, and when you do, you usually call her Mrs. Banks."

The three of them had no real family, so it seemed that the name of Tara's almost relative should be etched in Elliott's mind, but she had a reasonable point. Tara nodded and turned her attention to the note.

Hi, Tara.

I know it's been years since the boys and I have seen you, but I have good memories of that day. I'm hoping you'd be willing to reconnect. I have some important matters I need to talk to you about—they are rather urgent, but they are also familiar ones.

Could you come for a visit in the next few days?

Warmly,

Patricia

It ended with the woman's address written in large letters.

Hadley sat in one of the kitchen chairs. "Anything important going on?"

Tara passed her the note.

"Interesting." Hadley held up the letter and pointed. "Is that word *familiar* or *familial*?"

"I wondered the same thing, but my guess is it's *familial*, as in a family-related issue." Tara shrugged. "My mom probably showed up on her steps, looking for shelter—and money—and that very kind, sweet old woman has no idea what to do about it. I have good advice for Mrs. Banks. Tell her, 'This isn't your house. Now get out.'" She shrugged. "If that doesn't work, she should call the police."

"Maybe she needs you to say that for her."

"Maybe so." Tara had no burning desire to see her mom, and maybe that wasn't what was going on, but she was curious. Why was Mrs. Banks reaching out? Were the boys okay?

Memories of the day she met Mrs. Banks and her half brothers were more like snapshots than a video clip. Tara had been fourteen at the time. Sean was the older of the boys, and he'd been five. Despite the awkwardness of having just met and the nine-year age gap, they'd had fun, even won a three-legged race and came close to winning the watermelon-eating contest. The younger one, Darryl, hadn't been quite a year old then, and he'd been whiny or asleep the whole time.

Hadley studied the envelope. "And there's no chance that Patricia Banks is your nana, right?"

Tara's attention moved to the eleven-by-fourteen canvas painting. "No." She fidgeted with the rope, uneasy with any talk of unearthing a maternal or paternal family member. It was never going to happen, and she didn't like entertaining the false hope that it would. She'd not seen her mom since she'd abandoned her ten years ago. Within a day of her mom walking out, Child Protective Services showed up and took Tara away, allowing her to take the painting with her. After hightailing it elsewhere, had her mom called CPS and left an anonymous tip?

It didn't matter. For Tara, foster care was definitely the better place to grow up. "No way. Mrs. Banks is Sean's and Darryl's paternal grandmother. My mom met her after we moved to North Carolina *and* after I entered foster case. I'd had that painting for years by then."

"Okay." Hadley rapped her fingers on the table again. "I figured as much, but it was worth a shot."

Tara used to dream of finding the woman who'd painted the picture, but how did one search for an unknown place where a "Nana" may or may not live?

Elliott cracked an egg into a bowl. "How old are the boys now?"

"Nine and almost five."

Hadley pointed at the letter. "How did Patricia even know where you live?"

Tara put the ropes and carabiners into her backpack. "Maybe she got our address from Dianna."

"Our last foster mom?" Elliott asked.

"It's possible." Tara shrugged. "Mrs. Banks and Dianna talked a good bit the day of the picnic. When Mrs. Banks needed my new address, my guess is she called Dianna. She's made a reasonable request, and I'm pretty curious about what's going on." Tara opened the short letter. "It says they're in Sylva, North Carolina. Either of you know how far that is from Asheville?"

"Sure." Hadley opened Tara's backpack and pulled out the TomTom. "It's about an hour west of us here in Asheville, not far from my dream school of Western Carolina University. I think the best way to get there is on the Great Smoky Mountains Expressway, but your TomTom should take you right to it."

"Okay. Good to know. I'm not changing my plans today. If it's that urgent, she can call the police." Besides, if Tara kept her plans in place, she could show the note to James and get his opinion. He was close to thirty, a bit of an older-brother type, and he'd taught her how to rock climb and rappel. She didn't see him outside of group gatherings for hiking or rock climbing, but he and his longtime girlfriend were always willing to listen and offer some helpful life tips. "And I gotta be in the bakery department at four in the morning. I work until noon on the Fourth, but I could go that afternoon."

～～

Tara drove up a long gravel driveway, hoping she was at the right place. About two miles back her GPS claimed she was on unverified roads, so it was useless at this point. That didn't stop it from suggesting two dozen times that she turn around at her earliest convenience.

She felt out of sorts about this whole thing, which made her agree with the device. She was tempted to make a U-turn and go the other way, but after coming this far she'd stay the course. She hoped to be on the road back to Asheville within the hour, but it might take a little longer than that to send her mom on her way or to sort through the issues with the police.

An old cabin on a hill came into view. A short set of rock steps was on the far side, and split railing ran across the front of it. The house itself was tiny and probably seventy years old. She imagined it'd been built as someone's weekend fishing cabin.

Did the occupants constantly trip over one another? Or maybe it wasn't as small on the inside as it appeared from the outside. The yard was nicely mowed, and the bushes lining the porch were trimmed.

Tara parked the vehicle and stared at the cabin, her heart pounding. The full impact of her awful plan hit her—to reintroduce herself to two half brothers, send her mom packing, and leave.

The front screen door flew open and stayed there, but she saw no one. She got out of the car, carrying a container with homemade cookies. *Look, kids, our mom has to go, but I brought cookies! And there's a watermelon on ice in my trunk.*

Just how insensitive and self-absorbed could she be?

A horizontal silvery, pipe-looking object edged out of the shadow of the doorway. Soon an elderly woman appeared. She hardly resembled the woman Tara had met four years ago. This woman was skin and bones and hunched over a walker as she shuffled onto the porch.

Tara took a deep breath and closed her car door. "Hi." She went toward the stairs.

Mrs. Banks stopped walking, raised a shaky arm, and waved.

Was she managing to take care of the boys, or were they tending to her?

"Hello." The woman smiled. "Tara?"

Tara remained at the foot of the steps. A whisper inside her said this visit had nothing to do with her mom. Something far more difficult than facing a deadbeat parent was happening here. In that moment her mouth went dry, and her heart pounded. "Yes."

Two shadows peered from behind the woman. The bigger boy seemed to be supporting the woman, and the younger appeared curious.

"You've grown up." Mrs. Banks motioned. "Come."

Tara climbed the steps and held the plastic container out in front of her. "Cookies."

The woman wavered as she released her walker and accepted them. "This was very kind of you."

Sean gently lifted the container from his grandmother before he guided her hands back to the walker. He studied Tara with a gentleness in his dark brown eyes.

"Boys,"—Mrs. Banks gestured toward them—"this is Tara. You met her a few years ago."

"Hi." Tara smiled, but the warnings inside her rumbled like thunder.

"I don't know you." Darryl narrowed his eyes. "But you look familiar." He held out his small hand.

Tara put her hand in the little boy's and squeezed it gently before letting go and turning her attention to Sean. "Win any three-legged races lately?"

He shook his head, stone-faced as a con man playing poker, and she had no idea if he remembered their fun at the picnic.

Darryl snatched the container of cookies from Sean's hand and lifted it to his nose. He breathed deeply. "Didja make these?"

"I did."

"Are they for me too?" Darryl's eyes were big with hope.

Why wouldn't they be for him too? Did he have food allergies?

Mrs. Banks glanced at the little one. "Yeah, for you too." She nodded toward the front door. "Sean, take your brother inside and get him a glass of milk. Two cookies each." She paused. "How many?"

"Two each, Granny," Sean repeated. "Come on." He cast a wary look Tara's way as he motioned for Darryl.

Darryl clutched the container close, as if hugging a bear. "Two *whole* cookies each?"

"Yeah." Sean opened the screen door and waited for Darryl to go inside first. Sean studied her again, appearing unsure whether she was friend or foe.

Mrs. Banks turned, shifting her walker. "Go. This ain't for children."

Sean lingered another moment. "You look like her."

Tara nodded, trying to hide her embarrassment. "I do." Their mother was pretty enough, she guessed, but she wished she didn't favor her. How could he remember what their mom looked like? At the picnic Mrs. Banks had said that Tara's mom left the boys right after Darryl was born. Maybe he had a picture of her, or maybe she'd come back for a visit.

"Scan." Mrs. Banks twitched her head toward the door, a clear signal she wanted him to make himself scarce.

"Sorry, Granny."

Mrs. Banks gestured toward the only decent chair on the porch, a rocker. "Sit, please."

"Has she been back?" Tara refused to say the word *mom* out loud, but Mrs. Banks had to know whom she meant.

Mrs. Banks shook her head. "I've not seen or heard from her." Her eyes held sympathy, but she pointed at the rocker again. "Sit."

Tara started toward the rusty folding chair, wanting to leave the good one for Mrs. Banks.

"Nah." It was more like a squawk from an angry goose than a word. "Not there." She pointed at the rocker.

Tara went to it and sat.

Mrs. Banks shuffled, using the walker. "I remind myself of that nursery rhyme. 'There was a crooked man, and he walked a crooked mile,' but that's not who I was until recently." She eased into the weathered chair, wincing. "I was healthy and strong until a few months ago, but I started hurting deep inside, shooting pains that stole my breath."

Tara could hardly breathe as she pieced together why she was here. "You're sick."

"I am. I thought the pain and tiredness were just part of the normal process of aging. Then I fell ten days ago, and while taking an x-ray of my ankle and foot, they found tumors. I have bone cancer, spread far and wide in my body, and the doctor has no idea how I'm not already dead. He says I shoulda been bedridden long ago. That's what he says, but I say that God's given me the strength to tend to my boys. And now He's giving me time to sort through this mess the boys are in."

Tara's head spun from the news. "I . . . I'm sorry."

"Death comes to us all." Mrs. Banks pursed her lips, nodding. "But God is good. Still, I got no time to waste, so I'm gonna get right to the point. My boys need you, and maybe you need them."

Tara's thoughts twisted into knots. "Wh . . . what?"

"I know this is a shock, and no girl your age wants to be a guardian, but—"

"How are Sean and Darryl taking this news?"

"Sean knows I'm sick and getting weaker by the day, but neither one knows I'm dying."

Tara's world spun with anger and disbelief. "Why? What on earth are you waiting for?"

"A miracle."

"Wait." Tara raised her hands, giving herself time to piece together what was happening. "Are you suggesting *I'm* that miracle?"

"You could be. The three of you have the same mother, and they need you."

Tara's heart raced. "Look, I don't mean to be disrespectful. You're clearly in an awful predicament, but the idea of me being their guardian is crazy. And you can't keep putting off telling them. Imagine the shock they'll feel to lose you without warning."

"I was hoping to have a bit of good news to go with the bad. They'll take the news a lot harder if they know they've got to go into foster care. They could be separated, you know."

"I'm sorry. I really am, but I'm just eighteen."

"You don't got to worry about your age. The law says you can't be a foster parent until age twenty-one, but you're their sister, and if you'd move in before I die and make sure they attend school, the state won't have no reason to come poking around here as long as you don't go to them for financial support."

Tara wished she could give the woman the comfort she longed for, but everything within her was screaming *no*. "That's not what I meant. I just can't. I'm sorry. Truly."

Mrs. Banks's eyes filled with tears, but she nodded.

Tara's hands trembled. Mrs. Banks and the boys were in a horrid predicament, but Tara wasn't the answer. She had dreams of her own, and she had no experience, not even of taking care of a kitten or a puppy. "You need to tell them what's going on, Mrs. Banks."

"Patricia, please."

Tara nodded. "Patricia."

Patricia ran a loose thread over her frail fingers. "Can I count on you to come here when I pass, help them through that time? Maybe just a couple of days?"

Tara's boss at the grocery store would let her off for a few days, maybe a week, if she explained the situation. "I can do that. I'm sure of it. But they'll be in a home by then, right?"

"Maybe so." She sounded resigned.

"I'm barely out of high school."

"I know, child." She tugged on the thread. "But you gotta let me tell you everything so I know I did my best."

Tara could give her that much. "Okay."

"This cabin is old, but it's sturdy. My daddy built it in 1939 as his fishing cabin. It has a pond and a little over three acres. Most important, it's paid for, and there's money in an account to cover property taxes for five years, assuming they don't go up too much. I got a car, six years old, and there's money set aside for day-to-day living that ain't for my funeral or taxes, about ten grand. I know it's not much, but it's yours. All of it if you'll keep them."

"It's not about money."

"There's a community college less than six miles from here. You could go there," Patricia said. "I know the dean, and he'd help you get a scholarship. The town's nice, real nice. I've lived here all my life, and I have friends who'll help you get a job and look in on you and the boys."

Tara's heart ached. "I know what you want, but—"

"I call them *my boys.*" Her weathered hands shook as she wiped away a tear. "They're good boys, Tara, and nothing like their dad. He was difficult most of his life. Argue with anyone about anything. Not just normal stubborn, but mean stubborn. By the time he turned eight, I took him to be seen. The doc said he had oppositional defiant disorder. His dad and me kept trying to work with him, but he got into drugs, swearing there was nothing wrong with it. And then he married your mama, and they fed off each other's worst traits. He ran off to who knows where a few months before Darryl was born, and I ain't heard a word from him since. But like I said, the boys aren't like their dad. They're good boys, but it'll break their tender hearts to lose me and then be put with strangers, shuffled from one home to another until they break and turn mean. It'll ruin them."

Tara had little else to say, and she needed to be on her way. "I'll return in a week or so, after you tell the boys the truth of what's going on, and I'll help them adjust to the idea of foster care." She stood. "But I need to go. I'm sorry."

The door flew open, banging against a nearby chair. "Those cookies was so good!" Darryl stumbled to a stop in front of her. "You're gonna do it again sometime, right?" He held out his hand as if wanting to shake her hand.

Sean was behind him, his face blank as he studied her.

She put her hand in Darryl's.

He shook it, smiling up at her. "Then it's a deal!"

Tara made a mental note to bring fresh cookies when she returned after Patricia passed. "Sure."

Should she call social services and explain the situation? She didn't want Sean and Darryl waking one morning to find Patricia dead.

"You're stayin' for supper, right?" Darryl asked. "Granny has a big roast in the oven, and she don't do that unless someone's staying. Will ya be here for the fireworks?" He made a blasting sound and spewed his hands out. "I love fireworks. Could you take us with you? Granny says town is too crowded for her on nights like this, but we can't see them from here. Last year I could hear them and see the smoke. That was cool. Oh, and we saw a few fireworks." He made the whispery sound of an explosion again.

"Darryl, stop," Sean fussed. "She ain't staying. Can't you see how she's standing there, angled toward her car, ready to hurry off?"

Sean was observant and sharp, and he reminded her of herself at his age.

Darryl shook his head. "Tell him he's wrong. He thinks he knows everything, and don't nobody ever tell him he's wrong."

Did anyone correct their grammar? Dianna wouldn't have put up with that poor grammar for two seconds. But that was the least important concern here. "I can't stay."

The hurt on Darryl's face sent a dagger through her heart. She wanted to scream, *Look, kid, I don't know you, and you're not my responsibility!*

"I'm sorry." Since arriving Tara had apologized enough to last a lifetime. Couldn't she at least take the kids to see the fireworks before hurrying back to her own life?

Sean walked to her. "You were nice at the picnic all those years ago. I remember having fun. But we're nobody to you. I get it. Darryl will too in time. But we got Granny."

Tara looked at the old woman. In that moment she understood. Patricia Banks wasn't just hoping for some good news to add to the bad. She didn't have it in her to break their hearts.

Sympathy for what the coming weeks would bring worked its way into Tara's heart and out of her mouth. "I could stay for a few hours."

"And take us to the fireworks?" Darryl sounded so hopeful.

She nodded. "Why not?" What could it hurt to give them a really nice memory to look back on?

"Yes!" Darryl jumped around clapping. "Real fireworks!" He ran to her and grabbed her hand. "Come see our pond. I'll teached you how to throw a rock so it skips. I can make a rock skip two times." He held up two fingers. "But Sean, he made one jump twenty times."

"Six, Darryl," Sean said. "Just six."

Darryl was an enthusiastic ball of energy, and Sean was a reserved realist. It seemed odd, but she saw parts of herself in each boy. Tara had a lot of energy, but she was a realist like Sean.

"I've never skipped a rock," Tara said.

"Never?" Sean sounded appalled.

"I rock climb," Tara said, "so remove the shock from your face. I *am* familiar with rocks." Did he know she was teasing?

"But you could fall off." Darryl raised one hand high and slammed it into a clap. "Granny says so."

"We wear harnesses, use ropes, and have carabiners to anchor them into the rock, keeping us safe."

Darryl ran full force from the porch, but since neither Patricia nor Sean said anything about it, she didn't either.

She reached for Sean's chin. "You favor her too." She shouldn't have said that. Why had she? Maybe because it was clear they were siblings, no matter how much she wanted to use the word *half* to describe their relationship. "Not as much as I do, and you won't when you're a man."

He shrugged. "My plan is to grow a beard and shave my head."

The words of a wounded child. "It doesn't matter what's here." Tara jiggled his chin. "Or here." She put her palm on his head. "It only matters what's in your mind and heart." *Where did those thoughts come from?* They were freeing as she spoke them, and she gently squeezed his shoulder. "Her leaving wasn't about us. You have to hold on to that truth. She's broken, not us."

Sean's face clouded, and he swiped at his eyes, nodding. His dad left. Months later his mom did the same. Soon his granny would die. What would it do to him if his sister callously disappeared, leaving him to live with strangers, maybe in a separate home from his brother?

Darryl ran up the steps, tossed a rock near her feet, and jumped on it. "I can rock climb too!" He held out his hands. "Look, Granny, no biners or ropes."

Granny laughed, but Tara couldn't budge as a desire to protect the little boy's sense of humor and innocence captured every thought. She couldn't stand the thought of Darryl's losing his enthusiasm and it being replaced with hurt and anger.

God, just stop it! You stop it right now! Would He listen to her?

"Boys." Patricia lifted a shaky hand. "Wash your hands and set the table."

"You won't leave, will you?" Darryl's eyes betrayed his fear that she'd drive off and he wouldn't get to see the fireworks.

"Not until after the fireworks. I promise."

"Yes." He jumped up and down. "Hear that, Sean! You is wrong. Wronger than wrong."

Sean pursed his lips and nodded. "Good." He opened the screen door. "Now let's go inside."

Darryl skipped toward the door, singing, "I'm gonna see fireworks. I'm gonna see fireworks."

Tara melted against the rocker, trying to stay in the moment and not worry about tomorrow or next week. A cool breeze roused from nowhere, and despite the heat a chill ran down her body. A feeling eased over her, as if God was more than inside her heart and in all of nature. It was as if He were there beside her. And she felt love as she'd never felt it before, and in that moment she had nothing but love to give. No reservations. No dreams that mattered beyond sharing His love.

She turned to Patricia. "I . . . I'll be here for them. For your boys. And raise them."

Patricia drew a sharp breath, staring at her, and soon tears rolled down her cheeks. "Thank you. Oh, dear child, thank you."

Tara looked across the yard, seeing a pond at the side and the long gravel driveway that led to here. What was she doing?

Dear God, help me raise them right. Let love and joy mold them, not hurt and anger.

2

Twelve years later

Tara stood in the parking lot of Western Carolina University, near her car and outside of the Ramsey Center, waiting for Sean to put on his socks and shoes.

Butterflies flitted about wildly in her stomach. Was Darryl prepared? He loved spontaneity, but surely he would stay on point tonight. "Weren't we just here yesterday for your high school graduation?"

"You're funny." Sean stood, towering over her by six inches. "Still cracking jokes as we approach what is bound to be the most embarrassing night of your life."

"I should've entered you two boys in a weird-off contest back when you were young and cute. I know you'd have won, and I could've held it over your head anytime I wanted to."

Sean pulled a crumpled tie out of his pants pocket.

"Sean Banks." Tara clicked her tongue. "I asked you if you needed anything ironed."

"It's fine." He looped it around his shirt.

Tara tried smoothing it. "Maybe you should go without one."

"Or . . . I could use this one." He pulled a neatly rolled, wrinkle-free tie from his other pants pocket.

Tara clicked her tongue again. "I started out in this relationship praying, 'Dear God, help me raise them right. Let love and joy mold them.'" She jerked the wrinkled tie off him. "Now I just wish I could figure out how to stop the pranks." After looping the smooth tie around his neck, she began making a Windsor knot. "Any chance Darryl is pulling a stunt of some kind and he removed his rock from the windowsill?" She'd been looking for it for two weeks now.

"I don't think so. I looked him in the eye the other night and asked him straight up. He said no. Later on I saw him sweeping the floors, trying to find it for you. Like I told him, it'll show up. If it doesn't, it's just a rock."

She nodded, but it wasn't just any rock. It represented their beginning. It was the one Darryl had thrown on the porch and stood on, claiming he could rock climb too. She'd used red fingernail polish to put the boys' initials on it, and her plan had been to mount it and send it with Darryl when he went off to college. Over the years she'd often teased him that the stone was their first rock climb together. It was her fault it was missing. She should've done something permanent with it long ago. But for twelve years she had kept it in an antique dish on the kitchen windowsill over the sink, only taking it out to think and smile before returning it to its place.

Sean put his hands on her shoulders. "He'll be fine at college."

She shook her head, biting back tears. "He's not ready for this step, not like you were." She straightened the tie, trying to make it look as it should. This wasn't her forte. She still worked at a grocery store and an outfitter store, only here in Sylva rather than Asheville, and she'd been promoted to a department manager at each place.

She grabbed his jacket out of the back seat and began brushing and picking lint off it. "He'll move into his dorm room in seven weeks."

"If that's nagging at you like this, let's make the most of this summer. Take off work tomorrow and go with us."

"Don't be silly. We've been working on these plans for two years. You and your brother need a road trip, just the Banks men off to explore at will. I'll meet up with you in St. Simons Island next week. Why are we going to that island again?"

"Ha . . . Ha . . . Ha." Sean faked a laugh, spacing out each syllable, his low voice dry.

"I try to be amusing." She held out his jacket.

"We'll be at the airport to pick you up. It's all arranged. I'll have alarms set. No way we can forget. I'm excited. I know we can find out something about your roots. I may even have a lead."

"Or not," Tara mumbled.

"I think I do, and I feel good about it. You deserve to at least know something about your roots, and my leads indicate you have relatives from there. Maybe it's your nana."

Tara nodded. "You keep telling me the same information over and over. Did you know that?"

"Yeah, I keep hoping you'll believe me one of these times."

They began walking toward the Ramsey Center. "What I believe is that we'll have a *great* time. Our first real vacation."

"Hey," Sean fussed, "we go hiking and camp out somewhere fun every summer."

"As I said, it'll be our first real vacation. Hotels. Restaurants. A bed. Air conditioning. No cooking over a campfire."

"And finding your roots."

"You and Darryl *are* my roots." She paused, looking at the double doors leading into the building. "I'm not ready for him to graduate from high school and for both of you to leave for college in August." Because he'd taken off a couple of semesters to earn money, he was a year behind. But he'd graduate next spring.

"The cabin will be quiet during the week, and that'll take some getting used to. You might even have time to think or, heaven forbid, date. But Darryl will be home every weekend with loads of laundry. He'll be hungry and need someone to talk to, and every third weekend I'll join you guys. We'll hike and rock climb and—"

"Stop." She bristled. "I was just having a moment. I'm not some desperate old mom who needs her kids." She walked toward the center's door.

"No, you're not." Sean stayed in step with her. "You're a desperate *young* mom."

Before she could retort, Collin, a young man a grade below Darryl, touched her elbow and spoke. "Ms. Abbott." He'd never called her that before. He pulled a red carnation from behind his back and bowed. "Compliments of the valedictorian."

Tara's heart fluttered. "Thank you, Collin."

He opened the door, and there was a row of boys and girls on each side of the entryway, twenty or so total. Joy bubbled inside her . . . and a bit of embarrassment. They were all juniors from Darryl's school, but she knew most of them by name. Every one of them held out a carnation for her, creating a beautiful multicolored bouquet. She wanted to ask Sean if he'd known about this, but she wouldn't right now. These kids were doing as Darryl had asked. She thanked each person as she took the flowers, her cheeks burning, but she smiled and nodded and kept going.

She knew this building well. Hadley had attended school at WCU for six years until she graduated three years ago. The two of them would occasionally come to Catamounts basketball and volleyball games inside this building. The Ramsey Center could seat more than seven thousand people, but the high-school graduating class was under two hundred, so the school had sectioned off a small part of the seating area. She led the way, climbing the arena steps.

"Tara." Pastor Mike spoke from one of the seats. After twelve years of being in his church, she'd recognize his voice anywhere.

She glanced around and soon spotted him. His wife was next to him, smiling. Pastor Mike waved.

"Thank you for coming. It'll mean a lot to him."

"Of course. We knew the minute we received an invite that we wouldn't miss this."

"I'm glad."

Sean nudged Tara from behind, clearly encouraging her to continue onward. A line must've formed behind them. "I better keep it moving."

"See you Sunday, T." Patti barely moved her fingers as she waved.

Tara went to the area that she knew would have the best view. Sean moved in beside her.

"You knew about this"—she held the flowers up to her face and breathed in the scent—"didn't you?"

"It's why I wasn't dressed on time. I was sticking to the plan Darryl gave me."

"Putting on your socks and shoes once we got here," she mumbled.

"It slowed you down and gave them time to get their flowers and line up."

People continued to pour in, and soon the sounds of "Pomp and Circumstance" filled the air. The faculty and graduates filed in. It seemed no time passed before Darryl was behind the podium, standing tall. He welcomed the graduates and those attending. "Every one of us graduating here tonight has at least one person who helped along the way. For me that person is my half sister, Tara Abbott, but I usually call her T-Mom."

Darryl's classmates clapped, and the applause spread throughout the arena. Tara's cheeks burned.

"I call her that because she's been raising me since I was five years old." He paused and cleared his throat. "I think most people here tonight can imagine some of the sacrifices an eighteen-year-old girl made to accept the responsibility of raising two wild and rowdy boys. Well, actually she had to tame only one wild and rowdy boy. My brother is the good one." He made a face, and the audience chuckled. "For those of you visiting from out of town, T-Mom is the barely thirty-year-old, cute, *single* blonde sitting right there"—he pointed—"holding a lap full of flowers. I leave for college in August, and someone should date her."

The crowd broke into laughter. Tara smiled and waved. She leaned toward Sean. "I will make him spend the rest of his days paying for this."

"I look forward to watching that," Sean mumbled back.

He held up both hands. "I'm kidding. I'm just kidding. Settle down . . . before she comes out of those stands after me. Any of you ever been grounded by a sibling?"

The crowd laughed again.

Darryl grasped the sides of the podium. "We're having fun here tonight, and that seems to be everyone's end goal in life, but life is about doing what it takes to get to these moments. I'm teasing my sister because that's what we do. Some of you feel sorry for me because my mom skipped out. But I had a good granny. When she died, Tara took over raising us. I can't imagine how terrifying that must have been for her or all she gave up to be here for us. Some of us will go off to college. Some of us will even graduate from college. But the power of who we are isn't in the education or golden opportunities. Our power is inside the sacrifice of loving and giving, and it doesn't matter if you're the valedictorian of a class or the last in the class. It doesn't matter if you go to college or go to work at a local store. What matters is your power to love when it's not easy and give when you're empty and believe in God's goodness when you've lost your granny or your mom or dad. I know learning is important, and I encourage everyone to do what you need to in order to learn all you can, but remember that knowledge and earning good money aren't the most important things. Love, sacrifice, and respect are the most important things . . . and harassing your sister." He grinned. "Let's pray."

Tara bowed her head, grateful that God had opened her heart all those years ago and helped her take the best route, not the easiest one.

Carrying her running shoes, Tara walked out of the cabin and moved to the old rocker on the front porch. After putting on and tying her shoes, she stood and breathed deep. Warm winds rustled through the treetops. Clouds were gathering and thunder gently echoed.

She went down the steps and began her slow run around the pond and toward the mountain path. Was anything more beautiful than her neck of the woods? She didn't think so. Rain or shine, hot or cold, green leaves or fall's brilliant foliage or barren trees—it didn't matter. She loved taking a run or hiking in all of it, and with some patience and humor, she'd taught her two younger brothers how to enjoy the outdoors too, just as they'd taught her how to be part of a family. But she hadn't been able to rouse them this morning. Both had mumbled as she woke them, begging her to let them sleep.

Joy fluttered through her as her feet hit the path, and she quickly found her stride as she put distance between her and the cabin. Memories came at her from a gazillion directions, covering tidbits from the last dozen years. She grew miserably out of breath, and all thoughts slipped from her except the focus of continuing to run when her body didn't want to.

The sky darkened and the wind picked up. Rain began pelting her, but she never minded running in the rain. Still, she came to a halt and turned toward home. She was a good two miles from the cabin, and if lightning soon accompanied the rain, there were better places to be than in the woods.

She kept her pace as she went toward home. A gust of wind knocked her off the trail. She grabbed a tree and righted herself. The treetops were bending and bowing northeast as if straight winds were fierce, and those could precede a tornado. But tornadoes were rare. The county averaged one a year, and fatalities were unheard of. Still, she'd feel better if the boys got out of the loft. She pulled out her cell and called Sean.

The call immediately went to voice mail.

She dialed Darryl. Same thing.

She tried again. If they had their phones on Do Not Disturb, her call would ring through if she called twice.

Still no answer.

Thunder popped, and rain fell as if someone overhead were throwing buckets of water on her. Her gut said she had to make sure Sean and Darryl were out of the loft. She tucked her phone away and ran down the trail, but this time her gait wasn't even or pretty, only desperate. A siren shrieked from her phone.

Dangerous weather.

She pulled the phone out again and ran harder. The phone jiggled and jerked in every direction, but she dialed Sean again. "Pick up!"

But he didn't.

Somewhere behind her she heard the cracking of a tree splitting. She could only hope the path of its fall didn't connect with the one she was on. She had run in rainy weather for years, both here and in Asheville. Never in all that time had a storm sneaked up on her.

Her phone screeched again, warning of dangerous weather. Her lungs ached, but she kept pushing to get to the cabin, and finally it came into view.

"Sean!" She drew a breath. "Darryl!" She ran, and when she came to the opening where trees gave way to cleared land, she saw nearby clouds swirling. "Boys!" She screamed with all she had, running as fast as she could. "Get out of the loft!" She peeled around the side of the cabin, slipping in the wet grass, but finally crawled to the stairs and got her footing. "Boys!"

The air thundered, and she knew a nearby tree was breaking. She jerked open the screen door and kicked the front door open. "Boys! Now! Out of the loft!" She ran toward the stairs to the loft. "Sean!"

The air ricocheted like a high-powered rifle going off. The roof moaned and debris fell.

Something knocked Tara off her feet, and warmth covered her head. She tried to muster the strength to yell, but the room grew darker until it was black.

3

Gavin scrawled his name across the last of the paperwork, grabbed his phone and keys off the desk, and headed for the firehouse door. Why was there always last-minute work to do when he had somewhere to be? It wasn't that he had many appointments, but when he did, getting away on time seemed impossible.

A vacuum cleaner rumbled against the floor down the hallway, and the smell of burned popcorn hung in the air. He put on his sunglasses and left the building. June's heat and humidity fell over him like a wool blanket, and it wasn't yet nine in the morning.

Three bays were open. Fire truck seven was out of its bay as a crew washed it and two members checked off the equipment. The rear-entry doors to ambulance three were open, and two EMTs were taking inventory and restocking it—another check-off task. When firefighters and EMTs weren't out on a call, they seemed to spend half their time doing checkoffs.

"Have a good shift, boys." Gavin inwardly smiled at his calling them "boys." At twenty-eight he was younger than most of the men here. He went toward his pickup.

"Lieutenant?"

Gavin knew Bryan's voice well. He was the captain's kid, a fresh-faced fifteen-year-old who longed to become a firefighter. Gavin pulled his phone from his shorts pocket and pressed the Home button, checking the time. The information verified he was already fifteen minutes late. There was no way to know if Bryan was here of his own accord or if some of the men had sent him to keep Gavin from getting to his destination. Still . . .

Gavin turned. "Hey, Bryan. What's up?"

Bryan seemed to want this life every bit as much as Gavin had when he was young. But Bryan was far more qualified than Gavin had been. It'd been a battle for Gavin to earn a spot as a firefighter. He'd been obese and clumsy. Sometimes that unhealthy kid version of Gavin seemed like a stranger he'd once met, and he ran about five miles daily to stay ahead of him.

Bryan rubbed the back of his neck, taking his sweet time before answering. "I'll finish my first aid and CPR courses next week."

Gavin knew what he wanted. "Yeah? The courses will be done, but the real question is, Will you pass the tests?"

Bryan laughed. "I'll pass."

"Then, yes. Once you've successfully completed the courses, you can shadow me. Okay?"

Gavin started for his truck again.

Bryan kept up. "I need you to sign this."

"Can it wait?"

"No, I was supposed to have it signed last week. If I don't have it ready to turn in first thing tomorrow, I'm booted from the class."

"Come on, Bryan. You're full of beans, man."

"No, really. Please." Bryan looked innocent and sincere, but Gavin glanced at the crew in the driveway doing their work. They appeared to be focused on their jobs, but were they really? The whole lot of them lived to harass one another. However, he didn't have time for their pranks right now.

But on the chance he was being unfairly suspicious of what was going on, he nodded. "Fine. I'll sign it." He took the pen and put the sponsor card against his palm, but the pen didn't work. He shook it and tried again, cleaned off the end of it and tried again. It still wouldn't work. He looked at the pen. "I need to go. I'll stop back by here after the meeting at the lawyer's."

"No! You'll get busy and forget. Just wait. I'll get a good pen."

"Bryan, I have to go."

"I'll grab a pen and be right back." Bryan ran toward the fire station door.

Gavin stood there, holding the card and useless pen. Jimmy glanced his way, and despite wiping down the fire truck and such, the other men seemed to have an eye and ear out for what was going on, although that was just Gavin's gut feeling.

When Jimmy glanced his way again, amusement tugging at the lines in his face, Gavin knew for sure what was happening. Apparently he was looking at the reason behind his inability to get out of the station when he had appointments. Gavin realized they'd also planned the stack of last-minute paperwork that only he could sign. Of course they had. How gullible was he, anyway? And how many times had they caused him to run late?

He walked toward the lieutenant on duty, holding up the pen. Jimmy kept a straight face, but most of the other men were chuckling.

"How's your hand, Lieutenant Jimmy?" Gavin asked. It felt good to be the target of harassment. During the first year after his dad died, Gavin was exempt from all pranks. Maybe now, eighteen months after his dad's passing, the men were determined to make up for lost time. If so, Gavin had a target on his back, and just the thought of it made him want to laugh. It should make for some interesting pranks over the next few months.

"What?" Jimmy cupped his hand to his ear.

"Did your hand cramp up while you doodled until this pen ran out of ink?"

"Now that you ask"—Jimmy slung his hand as if it hurt—"it is bothering me, and I don't think I can work today."

The men broke into laughter as if they were at a live comedy show. Despite wanting to keep a poker face, Gavin slipped into a smile before regaining control. He pointed at them, refusing to look amused.

But firefighters, EMTs, and paramedics needed to mash—to laugh and joke and become like brothers—because no one knew what they'd face during the next call. This Glynn County station was one of nine firehouses, and it averaged nearly four calls every twenty-four hours, seven days a week, fifty-two weeks a year.

Foolishness, merciless teasing, respect, trust, and love kept them sane and functional for the next call.

"It's not all *that* funny."

"I agree. It's not." Jimmy grinned. "But we're laughing more about what will happen next. 'Cause the Glynn Girls will have a dozen bees in their bonnets when you're late, especially if they learn it was due to a pen." Jimmy used two fingers to imitate a person running. "Better run along, Sonny Boy, or the next call for help the department gets will be from you as you're being flogged by your mamas."

Bryan held out a new pen. "I hear having four mamas is tough stuff."

"You have no idea." Gavin took the pen and clipped it on his shirt before shoving the card against Bryan's chest. "But I will get you for this." He pointed at the men in the driveway. "All of you."

The men guffawed.

"Yeah." Gavin pulled his keys out of his shorts pocket. "It's all fun and games until the genteel Southern women come after *you*." He pointed at Jimmy and then swooped his hand across to include the others before he turned toward his truck.

"True," Jimmy said, "but it'll be quite hard for you to convince them that I used all the ink in a pen, and if you can convince them of that, they aren't going to believe something as small as a stack of paperwork or an empty pen caused you to be late."

Gavin chuckled. He'd lost this one. Somehow he needed to up his game.

"Is that what the Glynn Girls are really like?" Bryan asked. "Your mom taught my Sunday school class the whole time I was growing up. Miss Julep seemed real nice. A little fussy, but she made us cookies."

"She is real nice, but when the four are banded together without Sunday school restrictions? Hoo boy."

The captain came out of the firehouse, spotted Gavin, and strode across the lot. "You're still here?"

The men broke into laughter again.

"Things happen while you have that infernal vacuum cleaner running. Your son can fill you in since he's part of the cause."

"You're just joking about the Glynn Girls being mean, right?" Bryan's eyes moved back and forth as he looked from his father to Gavin and back again.

"Maybe." Gavin wasn't letting Bryan off the hook that easily. He got in his truck and turned the key, letting the air conditioner run.

"Nope." Captain Dan clapped his son on the shoulder. "You better watch out once Gavin tells them what held him up." Captain pointed at Gavin. "His mamas—the Glynn Girls from Glynn County, Georgia—are sweet and salty, certain and muddled, gentle and fierce."

"Yeah, that's it. Sunday school teacher and Mr. Hyde," Gavin teased. He pushed the button that lowered his window, and he closed the door.

Bryan held up the card. "I really do need this signed. The bad pen was their idea."

"Later, Son. Give us some space." Captain nodded toward the firehouse. Bryan and the others slowly scattered, returning to their work. The captain knew Gavin was running late for an appointment, so if he wanted to talk anyway, Gavin would give him a few minutes. Worst-case scenario, his mamas and the lawyer would need to reschedule. But could the law office work them in later today or tomorrow? He hoped so.

Captain put his hands on Gavin's truck door near the open window. "I won't keep you, but my wife and I happened to be on the marina yesterday with some friends, and being there got us to talking about your dad's death and the stress it caused your family, financial and otherwise. She made me promise to prod you for some answers, and then she texted me while I was vacuuming, asking if I'd spoken to you privately yet. You know my Millie; she's cared about you since you were a teenage junior fireman, and she wanted to check on you. It's so hard to believe your dad's been gone eighteen months."

Gavin nodded. "Sometimes it feels like yesterday, and other times it feels like I've been without him for a decade."

"That's rough, Gavin."

"Yeah, but it's also life. I'm fine." The words felt funny coming out of his mouth. It wasn't a lie. His words just held more hope and determination than reality. They would be fine *if* his and the Glynn Girls' plans actually worked out.

"The rebuilt part of the marina looks great."

"Yeah?" Gavin chuckled. "It's only been a year since I helped finish the repairs."

"That's me, a year late and a grand short." Captain looked down, a lopsided smile on his face. "I was outside shooting off firecrackers with the grandkids that New Year's night, and I saw your dad's fireworks. Did I ever tell you that?"

"I don't think you did." But there was so much to process during that time that Gavin had a hard time remembering who said they'd seen the grand display.

Captain chuckled. "I know the accident was a tragedy, and I'm not making light of it, but your dad went out in a blaze of glory."

A smile tugged on Gavin's lips. "He did that. No doubt."

It helped soothe his and his mom's grief to know the accident spared his dad from being bedridden and dying of lung cancer. When he was diagnosed in November, the doctors had given him only months, and that wouldn't have been the way Dad wanted to go. But if he'd known what his final *"Hey, y'all watch this"* act on this earth would do to his family, he wouldn't have bought the fireworks in the first place.

"And the lawsuit from the injured bystander?" Captain asked. "Is it still an issue?"

Gavin shrugged. "We settled . . . more or less . . ." They'd had to take out a balloon loan.

His mom hadn't been anywhere near the marina that night, but as a co-owner of the boat—a boat without insurance—she was on the hook for damages to the marina and the personal injuries of a man who was standing nearby. The man's injuries healed within a month, but because of Gavin's dad's negligence, the injured man had hired lawyers, and he intended to take Gavin's mom to court. He would've easily won what he was suing for. But Gavin met with him and said that once a jury was involved, there was no guarantee that the person suing would win, and he'd have steep legal fees. Gavin convinced him that a bird in the hand was worth two in the bush. The man settled outside of court for a fourth of what the lawsuit asked for, but it was still a hefty amount.

Soon after the incident Gavin sold his home in Brunswick, moved in with his mom, and put every dollar from the sale toward the debt. His mom mortgaged her house to the hilt and pulled all equity out of her business. Of course, they'd also used up every bit of his dad's meager life insurance. The huge balloon payment for the loan they'd used to settle the lawsuit was due in July.

But as far as the marina and the injured man were concerned, they'd paid the debt.

"More or less?" Captain asked. "'Cause if you need money, we could do a chili cook-off at the station, and—"

"I appreciate the offer, but no thanks." Not only would that be completely inappropriate, but also it wouldn't be a drop in the bucket of the money he needed. But he had a solid plan, and it would be all right.

"Your mom is still living in the house she and your dad built before you were born, right?"

"Yeah." Gavin tapped the gearshift. "This stuff we're discussing is why I'm supposed to be at a meeting right now with my mamas and the lawyer."

"Oh." His captain's eyes grew wide. "That's where you're going. Go. We'll talk later."

Gavin waved and drove out of the fire station parking lot and onto the main road. He glanced at the clock on the truck's dashboard. He was now twenty-five minutes late. The upside of living on a tiny island is he never had far to go. The downside was that the tourist traffic in June was as thick as the air. Both would be worse next month.

He didn't like to talk about the accident or the financial issues it caused, especially to coworkers. People wavered between being sympathetic for the Burnsides' loss and feeling angry because of the senselessness of it.

Those things pulled at him like the swirling currents pulled at the sand on the island. He was an only child, and his mom had lost so much within a few months' time. How could he not do everything in his power to save her home and to keep her business alive? He could fix everything, even if he had to do financial gymnastics to make that happen.

If things went as planned, he would have all the money necessary to pay everything off without his mom losing her home or business. All he had to do was remove a historic home piece by piece, subdivide its plot of land, and sell both, even though none of it actually belonged to him.

What could possibly go wrong?

———

Tara tried to move. Why was her body unbearably heavy? High-pitched beeps were echoing. Muffled voices droned on just outside Tara's darkness.

She struggled to pull free of her nothingness, free of what seemed like a deep sleep, but each time something dark and heavy fell over her. Pushed against her. Pulled her down. She rolled in it, black tar clinging to her heart. Its fumes were toxic and suffocating. How many times had she tried to wake, but this thing—this weight of a mountain—had taken up residence inside her, and from her feet to her knees seemed mired in thick mud. Her mind felt warped and damaged from the viciousness growling at her, threatening to devour her.

What was happening? And what was that thing, that unfamiliar, God-forsaken thing?

"Tara . . ." A deep, soothing voice called to her, and soon other voices joined in—young and old, male and female voices—calling her.

The weight of the mire and darkness lifted. The heaviness of the earth's pull and that of her own body released her. A small light on the horizon drifted toward her, growing larger, and as it did, the toxic fumes dissipated, and a lovely scent of flowers filled the air. The black tar seemed to glide off her skin. Was she dying?

Wispy rays of white light gently touched her, and she felt a peace unlike anything she had ever experienced. Sean and Darryl came to mind, and the light seemed to want to permeate every thought with peace and hope and joy.

An inkling of fear for them edged in. They'd lost so much already. She fell to her knees. *God, am I dying?*

4

Gavin pulled into the parking lot of the lawyer's office, hopped out, and went inside.

"There you are." Sue Beth's Southern drawl was clear, and her long platinum hair with pink streaks stood out among her three fifty-two-year-old peers. "We were gettin' worried that you'd taken a wrong turn."

The women laughed as they approached him. He'd lived on the island his entire life, all seventeen square miles of it for twenty-eight years.

He breathed a sigh of relief that the lawyer hadn't called them into his office yet. Walter was probably running behind.

His mom straightened the collar of his polo shirt. "Maybe I should've brought you a sport coat."

"The heat index is over ninety already today," Luella said. "Are you hoping to render him unconscious or something?"

"But he'd look good in a jacket." Dell winked and held out her to-go cup of lemonade. "Take a sip. It'll help."

He was thirsty, and she probably saw it written in the sweat across his forehead, but the straw had lipstick on it, so he shook his head.

"For goodness' sake, Dell." Sue Beth sighed. "Julep doesn't actually have a jacket for him to put on, and we're in an air-conditioned room."

His mom scanned him from head to foot. "Seems to me if he's running this late, he could've taken the time to put on dress pants. After all, part of why we're here is so Gavin can imbue the lawyer with confidence in his savviness as a property business tycoon."

Gavin glanced at his shorts and running shoes. It was summertime on an island, for Pete's sake. After returning from a fire call at seven thirty, he'd taken a shower and put on street clothes instead of his uniform, but he wouldn't waste his breath defending himself. His mamas were wound tight about this meeting, and he'd never convince them that the way he was dressed wouldn't matter one iota.

Sue Beth dabbed gloss across her lips. "*Imbue* the lawyer?"

"Fill. Instill. Saturate," Dell said. "I think it's a befitting word. We are here to convince the lawyer that Gavin should be allowed to begin the process of moving Sapphira's house almost two months before it's legally his."

"Ah, yesss"—Sue Beth returned the lip gloss to her purse—"that *is* what *you're* here to do. So why didn't you at least come in your fireman's uniform instead of looking like you're going to the beach?"

There they were—all four women dressed in their Sunday finest while fawning over him and fussing at him—Sue Beth Manning, Dell Calhoun, Luella Ward, and his mom, Julep Burnside. There wasn't enough real estate on St. Simons Island to contain their personalities, and yet he seemed to be stuck trying to appease each of them—his true mom and his adopted mamas. Why him? He could see Luella wanting to adopt him. She didn't have children of her own. But Dell and Sue Beth did, and they hadn't adopted each other's children. Just him . . . Why him?

"Stand back." Gavin spread his arms and used his best authoritative voice as he did when necessary as an EMT. "Let the man have room to breathe."

The women chortled.

"Isn't he the cutest thing?" Sue Beth elongated the words while pinching his cheek. The scary part was she meant it, as if he were a five-year-old wearing a Halloween costume. "Once we get this legal stuff handled and Gavin digs his mama and us out of the financial hole, we need to set our sights on finding him a girl."

Gavin pointed at her. "Don't even start." He knew every local girl in the county, and very few had been friendly to him when he was overweight.

"Don't worry, sugar." Dell grinned. "The girl doesn't have to be from here. The internet can locate someone perfect."

That was Dell, the mind reader. But she'd tell anyone there wasn't anything supernatural about it. She was simply skilled at picking up on body language that others didn't notice.

The other women gasped, turning a sharp eye to Dell.

"Dell Calhoun," Sue Beth said, "don't put ideas in his head or promise things we will not do. We need him here. He's the only one of my kids that doesn't rush off ten seconds into a conversation, and he's Julep's only child, period. How would she—"

"Mamas, please." Gavin backed up. "Can we focus on why we're here rather than picking me apart?"

Luella pursed her lips. "Where's the fun in that?"

Gavin suppressed a chuckle, unwilling to encourage further harassment.

"Julep,"—Luella tucked her salt-and-pepper curls behind one ear—"did you think to bring your lease for Blue Sails?"

Sue Beth's eyes grew wide. "Oh, Julep, you didn't—"

"Hush it." His mom sighed. "Of course." She reached into her purse and pulled out a folder marked "Blue Sails Casual Living."

"Excellent." Luella's expression didn't change when his mom snapped at her and Sue Beth.

"I also brought Sapphira's will and a plat of the land."

Gavin wouldn't mention it, but the lawyer already had all the estate information.

His mom jerked the file open. Her movements used to be gentle and kind, but she'd been defensive and edgy since losing his dad. She looked up, catching Gavin's eye. A gentle smile lifted her lips as her eyes misted. "Look, kiddo." She pulled out a few pictures. "You and Sapphira when you were about five."

Gavin took the one photo she held out. He and Saffy were walking toward Gould's Inlet hand in hand. He was looking up at her, and she was looking at him. His mom passed him the other photos. "Good pictures, Mom. I remember this." He turned the one of Saffy and him making ice cream toward his mamas.

"It was your birthday." Mom smiled. "She always loved coming up with fun things for you two to do together."

"I remember." Gavin chuckled. "The best Saffy ever." When he was in high school, he'd begun calling her Sapphira, so he didn't usually think of her as Saffy anymore.

Dell traced a photo with her finger. "She was a good friend to all of us girls, despite being thirty years older."

"Friend, mentor, entrepreneur, and art teacher extraordinaire," Luella said. "But let's not get too mushy here. We've respected her wishes concerning her house even after the hurricane hit. It's been nearly two years since she died, and if Sapphira had an inkling Gavin needed the house to settle the debts Mitch left on Julep, she'd give it to him even if she were still alive."

His mom smiled at him, nodding. "I think so too . . . with all my heart."

Gavin passed the picture back to his mom. He hoped so.

Dell leaned in. "Are you okay with starting now?"

He half shrugged while nodding. "I'm fine with it." Did he sound as unsure as he felt? "Let's sit." He gestured toward a group of chairs and a small sofa.

There was no choice about starting the work. He'd held off too long as it was. Saffy's historic home was valuable, and taking it apart piece by piece to sell to the highest bidder would take time, a lot of it. If he didn't start that process soon, he'd never have the land cleared, surveyed, and divided into two parcels in time to sell it by July 21, when the balloon payment was due in full to the bank.

Sue Beth sat next to him. "Whatever it takes to get this financial burden off you and your mom, we're behind you."

His mom raised a brow, not a hint of humor on her face. "Just be aware, Son, that when she's behind us, we can't see what she's doing."

Dell put an arm around his mom's shoulders. "Be nice," she whispered. "We'll get through this difficult time, and you'll feel differently about all of life. I promise."

His mom glanced at Sue Beth, and a familiar look of hurt flashed through his mom's eyes. These women had been by one another's sides all his life. What was going on with his mom and Sue Beth? They wouldn't tell him even when he asked.

Luella drew a breath. "Let's focus on the other aspect of why we're here—our businesses."

His mom had opened her furniture store, Blue Sails Casual Living, almost twenty years ago, and it'd always meant a lot to her, but this past year, with his dad gone, the store had become her heartbeat. The other Glynn Girls rented space inside his mom's store, and they'd wanted to move to a bigger, better location for many years.

The front door to the office swung open. "Ladies." Walter Prescott, a former schoolmate of his mamas', although a few grades ahead, strode inside carrying his briefcase. He had on a suit, which Gavin would never understand. Why would a lawyer on a hot island in South Georgia need to wear a suit?

"I apologize for keeping you waiting." Walter went straight for his office. "Let's go." The five of them stood and followed him. He spotted Gavin. "You're looking more fit every time I see you."

"Thanks." Gavin was no more fit today than he was five years ago, but apparently the image of him being overweight was the one ingrained in people's minds.

Walter moved behind his desk. "Sit. Let's get started. Again, I'm sorry to be so late, but an urgent call came in on my home office line as I was leaving my house."

Everyone but Luella sat.

It didn't surprise Gavin when Luella, a historian and writer, picked up an old-looking book from a shelf and gently flipped through its pages. "It must've been a long conversation."

"It was." Walter opened his laptop and pressed the space bar. "But let's talk about why you're here." He set the laptop to the side and looked at each of them briefly.

There was silence for a moment, and Gavin let it hang, giving his mom the right-of-way. All eyes moved to her.

She cleared her throat. "We have two topics: Sapphira's estate, which I'll let you discuss with Gavin, and moving Blue Sails Casual Living from its current location to a new one."

"Sure, we can discuss both. Do you have the lease?"

She passed it to the lawyer. He took a minute to read over it. "What exactly is the issue with the lease, Julep?"

"I'm under lease for five more years, but we want to move locations. The owners of Home Décor are retiring, and they're closing the store come fall. That location is ideal for Blue Sails. Our foot traffic and profits would increase a lot."

"That is a prime location," Walter agreed.

His mom flopped the folder against her lap. "We tried to contact the property management company about it, and they own both locations. But they haven't returned our calls. That makes no sense."

Walter nodded, but he didn't offer any explanation.

Sue Beth stood and went to his desk. "Come on, Walt." She walked two fingers across the desk toward him and stopped halfway. "You've given us legal advice since Julep borrowed money and closed on the lease for the store all those years ago, and you represent the property management group too. Rumor has it they're selling to another property management company. If that's true, we need a head start, an edge of some kind, because half of the businesses in town will want that location, and God knows if anyone needs it, we do."

Walter peered past Sue Beth and looked at Gavin's mom. "Julep, are you in financial straits?"

She nodded. "I'm sure you heard about the personal injury lawsuit. Well, I've mortgaged my house for all its worth, and since the store is in my name and I rent parts of it to the girls, I pulled every bit of the equity from Blue Sails. The money could only be borrowed through a balloon note, and *all* the money is due July twenty-first."

Sue Beth stepped back from the desk.

Walter's shoulders drooped. A minute later he rubbed his chin. "Okay. What I'm going to tell you will be common knowledge in a week when a letter is sent to all tenants. We went to closing yesterday, and there's a new property management group taking over. It's Seaside Properties, out of New York. They purchased the entire strip of Pier Village shops, which includes your place as well as a few stores not in the village, including Tidal Creek Grill and the Lighthouse Inn."

"What about Home Décor? Was it purchased by Seaside Properties too?" Luella asked.

He raised both hands. "I can't discuss that particular piece of property."

"Why?" Sue Beth put her hands on her hips.

"I can't discuss that either."

"But it's a reasonable thing to assume that Seaside Properties also purchased Home Décor, right?" Dell asked.

Gavin felt a little bad for ganging up on Walter, but his mamas needed this win.

"It's reasonable." Walter leaned back in his chair. "But ownership of the building aside, if it becomes available to rent, it'll only be on the market for a New York minute."

"Of that we're sure, which is why we're here, following leads on little more than rumors and hunches." His mom pointed at the lease on Walter's desk. "Since there are new owners involved, are we still bound to our current lease?"

"Seaside Properties could release you from that contract in order to accept a contract on another store of theirs. But if you go through the process of getting a new lease, your financials will have to be disclosed to them, and I can't imagine why they would agree to let you move to a more expensive, prime location when you have so much debt on your current store."

Sue Beth grinned. "You leave the whys of it up to us. We'll convince them . . . if you can tell us when they'll arrive."

"But there's a leasing process, and—"

"We realize that," his mom said. "Is it safe to assume someone—owner or manager—will come to the island soon?"

"There are two owners and a property manager, and all three of them will come here to finalize various aspects of the transaction. Their plane arrives around nine in the morning next Wednesday, and they'll come to this office for a pretty long meeting. I expect we'll be done around noon. I've arranged for Georgia Sea Grill to cater a meal afterward."

"Oh no, no, no." Sue Beth returned to the lawyer's desk. "We need you to cancel the catering and send the men to Neptune Park. We'll have a spread of food, the likes of which they've never seen, set up on one of the picnic tables under a live oak."

Walter angled his body, once again peering around Sue Beth. "Is this the plan, Julep? To win their favor through the Glynn Girls' Southern hospitality and good food?"

Gavin had the feeling that his mom should be the one edging in close to Walter, not Sue Beth.

His mom nodded. "It'll give us the edge Sue Beth mentioned, a way to introduce ourselves, chat, and leave a good impression before any other potential tenants realize Home Décor is up for rent."

"Okay, I'll walk with them to your table and make introductions." He turned to Gavin. "You have a question about Sapphira's estate?"

"Everything we've done to get squared financially hinges on the balloon payment Mom mentioned, and in case the date didn't click when she said it, that's due two weeks after Sapphira's estate is legally mine."

"It'll sell fast." Walter snapped his fingers. "But most buyers can't offer a contract one week and be ready to close the next, so you'll need a cash-only buyer."

"I agree, but it's a little more complicated than that. I need every penny I can squeeze out of the sale, and I can make the most profit by taking the home apart and selling historic, reclaimed pieces—the shiplap, hardwood floors, wainscot, light fixtures. Then I can remove what's left of the house and divide the lot into two lots."

"Yes, that would greatly increase the bottom line." Walter drummed his fingers on his desk.

"I need to start—"

"Don't." Walter raised his hand. "Sapphira gave her granddaughter until July sixth of this year to claim her inheritance. I'm sure it's frustrating to continue giving her time to return when no one has seen or heard from her in twenty-five years. Did you know that Sapphira hired two law firms prior to mine to find Siobhan, and none of us has had the slightest lead?"

His mamas' faces tensed, but they nodded. They'd known Siobhan and cared about her, but only Sapphira had refused to give up hope that she'd return. Gavin could only remember snippets of her, or maybe he only remembered what Saffy had told him.

"Nonetheless"—Walter sat up straight—"I can't change what's in her will. You'll come to my office on July sixth, sign papers, and Sapphira's home will become legally yours. But not a day before then."

Gavin's hopes sank.

"But"—Walter interlaced his fingers—"you didn't inform me of your plans, and I never ride past anything on that side of the island . . ."

Luella smiled. "And the only people who have any legal right to try to stop Gavin are in this room."

"What are y'all saying?" Sue Beth looked from one face to another.

Gavin stood. "That we need to shut up, get out, and do whatever we need to do without bringing it to his attention." He gestured toward the office door. "Glynn Girls, after you."

5

Tara tried to lift her hand. Why was her body heavy as a stone? High-pitched beeps continued to echo.

"Tara?" Hadley spoke softly. "We're here, honey. We're here. Elliott and me. You're in the hospital. You sustained a severe head injury, but you came through surgery like a champ. The doctors relieved the buildup of blood inside your skull, and your vitals are excellent. But you need to come back to us now. Please just open your eyes."

It felt so familiar . . . trying to wake, trying to move toward Hadley's voice. She longed to ask about Sean and Darryl, but her jaws seemed wired shut. Panic surged through her, and a mother's desire consumed her. *Where are the boys? I have to find them. They need me.*

Laughter stirred her memories. She knew those laughs, had spent her days lavishing in them and trying to coax them out of her boys. The beeps faded away, as did Hadley's voice. Tara's body felt light again, and the creek she stood in became clear, cool water. Everything seemed to glow in the most brilliant golden hues she'd ever seen. She willed herself to move, and without lifting a foot she rose out of the creek and floated past through the thick forest and across the hiking trails until she was at the foot of a mountain with its sheer rock face jutting skyward into the glowing amber depths of the sky.

Sean was there, looking up at the face of the mountain. Gigantic trees and flowering bushes with radiant blooms surrounded them. She followed Sean's gaze and spotted Darryl climbing. They were laughing and cracking jokes. Where were Darryl's harness and ropes?

"Boys?"

Sean turned. He grinned, but there was sympathy in his eyes. "There you are. We were told you were coming." He walked to her. "I'm sorry."

"For what?"

"I'm sorry for you, for the struggle it will be."

"We've talked about this." Why were the colors around them—the leaves, the golden sky, and the mountainside—so brilliant? Why was the air so very light, as if the purest of pure? Even the gray slab rock shimmered with a bazillion tiny specks of colors beyond all imagination. "You don't have to be sorry, Sean. I love my life. Since you and Darryl entered my life, it's the best life I would ever want. The only one, really. All I ever wanted was family, and you boys gave that to me. You and Darryl mean everything."

Sean reached for her and put his hands on her shoulders. "You've told me that time and again, but now that I can see your heart, I know it's true." He cradled her face in his hands, something he'd never done before. "It'll be hard, T-Mom." He kissed her forehead. "It'll be hard—beyond what you'll be able to bear for a while. Cling to these moments. It'll help. Fight."

"Fight?"

"No battle is a guaranteed win on Earth. Not all things are yet under His feet. Fight. And take comfort that it's glorious here for us."

"Where are we?"

Sean's mouth moved, and his face had a sweet expression, but she couldn't make out his words.

Darryl broke into laughter, and she looked at the side of the mountain. "Look, T-Mom, no biners, no ropes." He laughed and let go.

"Darryl! No!"

But he didn't fall. He hovered there for a moment, pushed away from the face of the rock with his feet, and sailed down to her.

"What are you doing?" Tara grabbed his arm and turned him around. "Are you okay?"

"You didn't tell her?"

Sean studied her. "I did, but she can't seem to grasp it."

Darryl towered over her, looking concerned. "But there's so much to say and so little time."

"What do you mean?" Tara asked. "What are you talking about?"

"We were given a special dispensation."

"What?"

The light behind the mountain grew stronger, but it had no golden glow. It was whiter than white, like lightning, but steady and constant. Hadn't she seen that light before? Voices accompanied the light, singing harmony so beautiful it defied words. She didn't know the song, but it was magnificent.

Sean's face glowed with joy. "You have to go now, T-Mom. You survived. We graduated. The final graduation of all times, and for ourselves, we would have it no other way. But you must go, and remember, fight, T-Mom. Fight hard."

"Go where? And fight who?" Confusion clouded her mind. She was sure what was happening should make sense by now, but try as she might, it all seemed just outside her comprehension.

"Back. We almost had this conversation yesterday, but fear grabbed your thoughts and stole you away. Now you need to go back. Hold on to the truth beyond the pain. We're safe from all harm, all sickness and disease."

She didn't want to go, but she could feel herself being tugged away. "No! Wait! I need you! I've always needed you!"

Darryl reached out for her hand, their palms barely touching as she was being pulled elsewhere. "There's work to do and prayers, but people here love humor and pranks as much as you do." Darryl laughed. "It's fun, so much fun."

"What people?"

The light grew too bright, and she could no longer see anything but white light. Voices surrounded her, cheering her on, singing to her words of victory.

"You're the best," Sean said.

"The very best," Darryl agreed.

Their voices joined in the chorus of words she couldn't understand. The light dimmed, and she knew she was being separated from her boys. *Go to St. Simons Island.* Why had those words come into her mind?

"Wait! Boys! I need you. Please don't leave me. I need you!"

Darkness grew thick. Strange sensations ran through her as light and love turned to heaviness and pain. The weight of her body grew greater by the moment.

"Tara?" Gentle fingers brushed against her forehead. "It's time to wake up. Come back to us now."

She pried her eyes open. "My boys. Where are my boys?"

Hadley and Elliott were on one side of her bed, touching her arm and stroking her head. "Sweetie, we're sorry."

And she knew.

They were gone. Something dark and heavy fell over her. Pushed against her. Pulled her down. She rolled in it, black tar clinging to her heart and mind. Its fumes were suffocating.

Grief.

Too heavy to bear. Tar, with its putrid, suffocating smell, gathered stones and debris at every turn of thought and hurtful memory, and all of it clung to her.

"No. Please." She blinked, trying to focus. "I need them. Please."

Hadley's and Elliott's tears quietly fell onto the sheets as they gently held her wrist or shoulder.

"We're here for you, sweetie," Elliott said. "We'll get through this."

But Tara didn't have it in her to survive. Not this. She squeezed her fists, tears running down her temples and into her hairline. A few moments later her palm tingled. Was there something in her hand?

She lifted her hand so she could see it, and she opened it.

The rock. Darryl's rock was in her hand.

She clenched her fist, holding it tight. Was it real? Was she dreaming again?

"Hadley. Elliott."

Their faces were over her, forcing an encouraging smile through their tears.

Tara opened her hand again. "Do you see it?"

Elliott leaned in. "Yeah." She looked at Hadley. "A rock?"

It was real! Tara closed her hand and clutched it to her heart. "Darryl gave it to me. He pressed it into my hand before I was pulled away."

Hadley leaned in, looking at the rock. "I . . . guess a friend of yours must've brought it to you."

"Darryl gave it to me right before I woke."

"Honey." Elliott stroked her forehead.

Tara's brain couldn't hold a thought. She closed her eyes. A jolt shot through her, and she woke and looked around the room. "My boys. Where are my boys?"

"Tara, they're gone."

Gone?

The word was too heavy to bear. She closed her eyes, and the idea of going to St. Simons Island whispered again. Inside her mountain of grief, a bit of hope took root.

⟹

Tara stood in the front yard, staring at the half-demolished cabin with a blue tarp stretched over the gaping hole in the roof. The remnants of the huge hemlock tree, cut down by the tree service earlier today, were spread across the property. The cabin that held so many memories—memories of more love than Tara had dared to hope for while growing up in foster care—was as broken and as useless as she was.

The boys' voices echoed in her mind, calling to her, teasing her.

Why couldn't God have taken her too?

Her head throbbed, and the earth beneath her feet felt like sand on a watery shore. The storm had hit six days ago. She'd awakened in the hospital four days ago. They'd buried her brothers yesterday. And every minute since she had awakened, she'd struggled to believe the tragedy had actually taken place. She hated sleeping because waking made it all new again. Each time as she began to wake, her mind and heart had to relearn the truth, and the shock started all over again.

Elliott and Hadley were with her, just as they had been with her through every step since she woke. Their husbands, Trent and Monroe, were both in the medical field, and they'd had to return to work today. Tara couldn't have asked for the men to be more supportive or kind than they'd been, but today it was just the women and a baby. Hadley wore an Ergobaby carrier, and her three-month-old son, Shepard, was very content inside it.

It felt as though the funeral were still in progress. A sea of people had attended the graveside service, and the wake was packed. The news had spread across the state, news of her brothers' young, promising lives lost, and news recounting the story of how the three of them had stuck together as an unconventional family. Maybe the news had traveled farther than North Carolina. Tara didn't know and didn't care. But it'd been an honor to behold a sea of people at the graveside service. There were so many friends from Sylva that the wake couldn't be held at someone's home. The small church she and the boys attended couldn't hold that many people either, so it was held in the largest fellowship hall in Sylva. But something was wrong, weird wrong, as if she were imagining that they were gone.

"Are they really gone?" Her raw throat ached, and her voice came out no louder than a whisper. The reality felt impossible, beyond the ability of her mind and heart to accept it. What seemed far more real was that Sean and Darryl would walk up from the pond or return from a hike and assure her they were alive. They'd hug her and let her know that the misunderstanding was due to her head injury, that the lingering effects of the brain trauma were distorting the truth, and they were just fine.

She reached into her jeans pocket and felt Darryl's rock. How had that been in her hand when she woke? She wouldn't ask Hadley or Elliott again, because they would try to convince her that someone had put it in her hand. Her need to hold on to the hope that this rock was a gift from God—that she'd actually seen and talked to her brothers—was too strong to accept any other explanation. Nothing could protect her from the on-going shock and grief, but the dreamlike vision kept her sane from one moment to the next.

Elliott slid her arm around Tara's shoulders and squeezed, but she didn't answer Tara's question.

"If you hope to salvage things from the elements, we need to start going through the cabin, T." Hadley held a large plastic bin with folded cardboard boxes and a box of black garbage bags.

Tara nodded.

They went up the steps and crossed the threshold. Memories of the day of the storm about knocked Tara off her feet. She willed herself to do what she'd come for. She tried not to pay attention to the broken windows or mutilated furniture and appliances. The three of them went into her small bedroom, and while her friends began sorting ruined from salvageable items, she saw a hundred tiny moments play out in front of her. The boys had been so young. They'd come to her room needing something, especially Darryl at five years old, until she finally felt like a mom.

She meandered into Darryl's room. Sean slept in the loft, and the stairs had been too badly damaged to use them, but half of his things were on this level. The room had water damage, and small branches of the tree had scattered items around. She picked up every picture she could find and held it close.

She wanted to help Hadley and Elliott, but all she could do was stand and field questions as the three of them went through her brothers' personal items. Tears obscured her vision and made her throat tight and painful. When she couldn't take one more minute of packing up Sean's and Darryl's lives—the life they'd shared—she went outside and stood in the yard, staring at the cabin. How could this be happening?

Shafts of sunlight came through the trees. The thick aroma of the fresh-cut hemlock tree filled the air, as did the songs of birds. Life was filled with mind twisters—amazing one minute, crashing in with unbearable pain the next.

But it was the power of one particular feeling that she couldn't seem to tame. She was sure if she reached out just so—like a child standing on a porch and reaching through the rails to feel the pitter-patter of rain falling from the sky—that her brothers would grab her hands and say, *We're here, Tara! We never left. The tree falling has made your mind play a horrid trick on you.*

"Tara,"—Elliott squeezed her shoulder—"it's getting late."

Tara blinked, and the daydreams of her brothers being alive were smothered by reality. The morning sun was gone, and the huge circle sat high in the sky. The baby was awake on a blanket in the yard. Last time Tara took note of him, he was asleep in a car seat next to Hadley as she sorted items. She could hardly recall how lunch tasted, but she remembered Hadley insisting she take a few bites.

Her friends had lives they needed to get back to. Hadley had two more children at home that her husband and in-laws were tending to while Hadley tried to do the impossible—give Tara the strength to cope. Elliott was seven months pregnant with her first child and worked full-time as a nurse practitioner. They had homes filled with love and needs and people waiting for them to return. She remembered those days as if she, as Sean had joked, were a desperate old mom who needed her kids.

"Yeah," Tara whispered. The roof was demolished, and there was no staying here, not that she could cope with sleeping here just yet. She clutched the rock in her hand. "I need to get my suitcase."

"It's here." Elliott held up a suitcase and pointed at Hadley's SUV, which was filled with boxes of things important to Tara.

"Thank you." Tara could barely whisper. How did anyone survive times like this without loved ones?

"I think that's it, T." Hadley passed her a picture that'd been hanging on the wall in the kitchen.

Tara squeezed the broken frame, and then they all headed to the car.

She couldn't live like this—lost, stuck in limbo, dependent on her friends to take care of her as if she were a child.

St. Simons Island. The thought drifted into her brain like fog rising from the valley. The trip had meant so much to Sean and Darryl. They'd saved their hard-earned money to buy her a ticket, and the plane would leave Asheville airport in five hours.

Hadley and Elliott were in the front seats talking quietly. The baby had fussed when Hadley moved him into his car seat, but he'd settled down after a few minutes.

"Guys?"

Hadley turned down the blasting AC. "Yeah?"

"I . . . I need to get away for a while."

"You're welcome to stay with me indefinitely." Elliott rubbed her protruding belly. "It'd be wonderful having extra hands when the baby is born in August. I . . . I think it'll be a bit healing to hold new life."

"Yeah, I look forward to that, but first I need to go to St. Simons. Sean and Darryl were so excited at the prospect."

"That's not a bad idea," Hadley said. "I volunteered to help at nature camp for my older two children starting tomorrow, but baby Shepard and I could get away for four or five days sometime toward the end of next month."

"I can buy a plane ticket easy enough. I have my clothes. Just drop me off at the airport."

"What? No." Hadley removed her sunglasses, staring at Tara from the rearview mirror.

Elliott was doing her best to turn and face Tara in the back seat, despite her expanded abdomen. "Tara, honey, you need time to heal from the head injury."

"We saw the doctor this morning. She says I'm healing fine."

"But we didn't ask about traveling, and you're clearly still addled. If you could see yourself through our eyes, you'd be concerned too."

"So I'm confused. Half of the population in the US travels in that state of mind all the time."

"This is different, Tara."

"You two quit high school and took off with no money and no support system. I didn't like your plan, but I helped because I trusted that you knew what was best for you. And today you have masters' degrees and families."

"It's just not a good idea." Hadley squeezed the steering wheel until her knuckles were white. "If the grief and brain trauma weren't enough stacked against you, you're on powerful medication that can also mess with your mind."

"I'm fine. I have my debit and credit cards, a cell phone, and luggage. Even on this medication I'm far better off than you two were. I can do this. I'll purchase another plane ticket."

"Actually you wouldn't have to buy a ticket." Elliott shrugged.

"You didn't cancel my reservation?"

"It was on my to-do list, but I forgot about it until just now."

"See,"—Tara looked out her window—"it's settled."

"No, it's not." Hadley slowed to stop at a red light. "We can't let you do this. You don't even sound like yourself, and your ability to know where you are and what's going on changes from one hour to the next."

"I need to do this. It was important to Sean and Darryl, and we spent two years planning it. I don't mean to sound ungrateful for what you've done for me, but I have the right to do this. Head injury or not, I'm a competent adult, and you're not my legal guardians."

Hadley's shoulders slumped. "I guess we could get to her quickly if need be. It's a six-hour drive."

Elliott looked over her shoulder again, meeting Tara's eyes. "You'll call us every single day so we can hear your voice?"

"And text." Without taking her eyes off the road, Hadley tapped on her phone, which was sitting on the car's center console.

How was it possible for this conversation to sound so normal when Tara felt detached from her body?

Her friends drove in silence, clearly uncomfortable with the plan. But Tara needed this, and they'd have to get over their hang-ups. Legally they couldn't stop her.

Hadley let out a big sigh as she pulled onto the freeway that led toward the airport. "Pull up your ticket on your phone and check in. We'll be there in thirty minutes."

⟹

Tara's ears rang, and her head swam with dizziness, but her heart felt just as shattered as it had before boarding the first plane. After a two-hour layover in the Atlanta airport, she was finally walking down the Jetway to board the plane for the second leg of the flight. She hadn't planned to drive, because none of them—Sean, Darryl, or her—wanted two vehicles to deal with on the island. Tears filled her eyes. They'd looked forward to riding in the same car for the road trip back home after the vacation. She moved to her window seat and stared out. The cloudless sky was a dusky blue as the day drew to a close. She longed for the boys to be there as she arrived, just as they'd planned.

She dug through her purse, unzipped the safe pocket, and clutched Darryl's rock. Holding it securely, she closed her eyes, and soon she could hear his voice. A flight attendant talked of safety, and Tara wanted to be respectful and listen, but the boys called to her, and she relaxed into a world where her grief didn't follow.

Sean stood outside the driver's door of his car. "You're sure we should go?" He pointed at Tara's head. "That was a lot to go through."

She touched the stitches starting near her temple at the hairline and going back toward the crown. "I'm fine." The cabin had a blue tarp stretched across the roof and nailed in place. They'd have to hire a contractor to rebuild the rafters and replace the roof. "We survived, thanks to your answering the phone and listening to me."

"Uh, yeah." Darryl went to the trunk, toting his suitcase. "We're all fine. Some of us more than others."

Sean hugged her. "We'll see you next week. Text us when your plane lands, and we'll pick you up at the airport."

His arms felt warm, and it seemed as if she'd been aching to hug him.

"Enough gushy stuff," Darryl fussed while taking his turn hugging her. "We'll meet you at the airport in a week . . . unless me and the bro are having so much fun we forget what day it is."

"Me and the bro." Sean rolled his eyes. "He was named valedictorian?" Sean winked. "Text us. We'll come get you."

They got into their car and waved, gravel crunching under their tires as the vehicle crept down the long driveway.

The plane jolted, and Tara woke. Her head throbbed. Was it time to take another Vicodin? It was dark out the window, but clearly they'd just landed. Sean would be ecstatic if they found some of her family roots while here, but that wouldn't happen. Still, he'd temper his disappointment quickly enough, and they'd have a great week.

The flight attendant's voice came through the speaker, okaying passengers to turn on their phones. "Welcome to Brunswick, Georgia, and the Golden Isles." The woman finished her spiel, and everyone near Tara started moving around and getting their belongings.

Tara turned off Airplane mode and texted both brothers at the same time. She received an instant response from Darryl.

I'm on the island having fun. Catch me if you can. If you can't, I'll come find you soon.☺

She waited her turn to move into the aisle, and she fell in line behind the file of people. Despite her pounding head, she was excited to be here, thrilled to share this time with her brothers. She texted them both again and received the same instant response.

Hmm. Seemed like Darryl had set up the message to autoreply.

A woman behind her said, "Are they picking us up?"

Tara glanced back. The woman appeared to be in her seventies.

A man behind her, who looked to be about the woman's age, smiled and responded, "I'm sure they will. I just haven't heard back yet."

Tara smiled and held up her phone. "We may have to hitchhike."

The woman laughed. "Maybe so. I volunteer for you to catch a driver's eye, and we'll sneak into the vehicle behind you. St. Simons Island bound?"

"Yes."

"It's not far," the man said. "Only fifteen miles, including crossing the causeway. We could walk it except my wife packed everything, including the kitchen sink, I think."

The woman laughed. "I did not pack the sink."

The man chuckled.

Tara put effort into looking and sounding normal, but the strange feeling wouldn't let up. She felt disconnected from her body. But the doctor had said to expect to feel disoriented. Maybe that's all it was—she was disoriented. Traveling made a person feel that way too, not to mention opioids, so maybe that's why she felt far worse than just disjointed and weird.

Once they reached the doorway of the plane, there wasn't a Jetway—only steps that were steep and narrow. She slung the strap of her purse around her neck, wearing it cross-body style, grasped the round metal handrails on each side of her, and slowly went down the steps. As soon as she stepped on the tarmac, she turned around, making sure the older woman had her footing. She then followed the crowd. While waiting on her bag to arrive at the luggage carousel, she called Sean again. When he didn't pick up, she left a voice mail, and then she called Darryl, leaving him a voice message too.

Where were they? She got her bag and left the airport. Beyond the airport drop-off and pickup area, all she could see in the darkness were flat roads, flat horizon—everything flat.

Interesting.

But she saw no signs of her brothers.

A car pulled up to the curb, and a man and woman about her age got out. They welcomed the older gentleman and lady she'd spoken to earlier and put their suitcases in the trunk. The older man spoke to the young couple, and then he turned and approached her. "Did you reach your party?"

"No. It's my younger brothers. I guess . . ." She wasn't sure what had happened. They'd teased about forgetting her, but had they really done so? ". . . they forgot."

Every word seemed enveloped in thick fog, and her thoughts were like rocks skipping across the water. Surely some sleep and finding her brothers would make her feel better.

"Young people can be like that. Our children dropped us off at a museum one time, and we had to take a taxi back." He chuckled. "When they realize what they've done, you need to use this incident to gain sympathy for decades to come."

She wanted to agree with him, but something seemed so out of place.

"Where are you going?" His wife leaned over to ask.

Tara had to pause to remember the name of the hotel. "The Lighthouse Inn."

"Ah, on Mallery Street. I know right where it is. We'll pass by it on our way to our rental house. Come." He looked at her suitcase. "The hardest part will be finding room for your lone small suitcase in the trunk with our fifteen hundred."

"Thank you." Her heart ached with relief. Once she was at their hotel, she and her brothers would find each other, and their week of fun would begin.

6

L uella hastened along the St. Simons Island fishing pier. The pungent scents of salt water and fish assaulted her nose as the sea breeze whipped around her, carrying the sounds of children's voices as they laughed and played. Oh, how she'd love to take her time, but she had only a few minutes before her friend's class was over, and Sue Beth needed her help carrying the heavy easels back to her car. Dell and Julep were using the shop's hand trucks.

Lucky that her black dress flats were comfortable.

She breathed in the aroma around her. It wasn't a bad smell, at least not to her. Her daddy used to bring her to this pier to fish starting when she was just a tiny thing. That was closing in on fifty years ago.

One of the pier regulars was fixing some bait on his fishing pole. Luella grinned. She needed to keep moving, but she couldn't help but take a moment. "Mornin', Roger. Coming to my tour tonight? I'm changing the route."

Changing the locations she went to allowed her to share the history surrounding more sites. Besides, locals were more prone to take the tour again if it had new places and information.

The middle-aged man snorted. "Good to see you, Luella, but I think I'll pass. You know, I couldn't sleep after hearin' your stories last week. I did write you a good Welp though."

His teenage son, Frank, shook his head, rolling his eyes, but he was smiling. He cast his own line, and the lure plopped in the choppy water. "Dad, that website is called Yelp."

"Nope. It's Welp. I'm never sleeping again thanks to Luella Ward's ghost tour."

Luella chuckled as she waved goodbye. A gust of wind from behind blew her silver and black ringlets into her face. She swooped her hair back and tucked it behind her ear. Unlike her friends she was proud of going gray and refused to color her hair. It seemed to help her business as a local historian and author. Or maybe that was just in her head.

At the east end of the pier, a group of five adult art students had their easels set up facing the striking white-and-black lighthouse sitting on the shore above gray rocks and sprawling live oaks. Numerous clothespins secured each person's paper to a fixed panel on the easel, a necessity against the nearly constant wind. Luella glanced at the paintings as she approached.

Sue Beth's cheery drawl cut through the breeze and the caws of the nearby crows as she gave instructions. "Thank you so much for painting with me today. Feel free to hang out as long as you want, but I need to take the easels in about five minutes. Be sure to take your creation with you."

Sue Beth noticed Luella and then grinned, giving her a small wave.

The art students started to pack up their paints and pictures. Luella reached into the canvas bag hanging over her shoulder, pulled out a bottle of water, and handed it to her friend. Sue Beth thanked her, opened the drink, and tilted her head back to take a sip. The pink streaks in her blond hair were a shining example of her unique style and free spirit, which she'd had for the forty-one years Luella had known her.

Forty-one years. How was *that* possible?

They'd met at Epworth By The Sea, a church summer camp on the island, when they were eleven: Luella, Sue Beth, Julep, and Dell. The four girls had made a pact to be lifelong friends—the Glynn Girls. And they had kept that pact and added another member: their former art teacher, Sapphira O'Keefe. Well, basically they kept it. In the past year and a half, things had been touchy between Julep and Sue Beth. Luella was doing what she could to help smooth out that relationship.

She studied Sue Beth. Whatever this animosity was between her and Julep, it *had* to be only a speed bump. After all, fights were normal even among friendships like theirs, right? Surely the two would agree that what the four of them had was worth a little work.

Sue Beth used a handkerchief to dab sweat off her upper lip, careful not to swipe her lip gloss. "Are my Glynn Girls ready to impress at this picnic? I made my famous peach cobbler and gave it to Dell before my class began."

"Of course we're ready. Last I saw Julep she was minutes away from pulling her fried chicken out of a sizzling deep fryer. It'll be the tastiest, fanciest picnic our guests from New York have ever had."

"For our shop's sake it better be. We *need* that corner storefront if we want to emerge as the premier home goods store in all of Glynn County."

Twenty years ago their current location was a solid one. The Glynn Girls pulled together to help Julep open Blue Sails Casual Living, and each of them had built a successful business inside that space, helping one another as needed. But lots of changes had happened on the island since then. Not the least of which was St. Simons's population—and their competition. It was Julep who took out a starter loan and signed the original lease, but the businesses that took place inside the store were bread and butter for all of them.

Julep's skill in balancing their expenses and income had allowed the store to have unique pieces and keep an edge over the rest of the saturated market. If they could get the corner storefront, their possibilities seemed endless. Sue Beth would be able to spread out. Right now she subleased and taught art classes in the upstairs loft and sold her original paintings in the store. But in the new building with a completely separate loft entrance, she'd have the room to hire additional art instructors and host even more people. Dell rented a small studio in the loft too for her photography, and she specialized in portraits. With her eye for home decoration, room staging, and arranging, she was brilliant at staging the store. She'd turn that corner store into something special, no question. What Luella did day to day wouldn't change too much: writing in the store between waiting on customers. But the increased foot traffic would give her a greater chance to sell her books on the island's history, as well as her widely published travel guides to other cities.

Sue Beth and Luella helped the students remove their paintings so they could pack up the wooden easels and haul them to Sue Beth's car.

"Seems like"—Luella shifted her easels to get a better grip—"a successful class." They weren't so much heavy for her as awkward.

"Yep, it's a good little group. I never get quite the class turnout that Sapphira could."

"Miss Sapphira was something special." The thought of their former art-teacher-turned-friend made Luella smile. They were still mourning her loss in surprising ways each day. "But your art classes will pick up as more tourists arrive for the summer."

"Yeah. Hope so." Sue Beth was puffing as she carried three easels.

"Besides"—Luella set her easels down against the pier, giving Sue Beth a moment to catch her breath—"if you had more students, we'd be carrying even more!"

They laughed.

Sue Beth exhaled and lifted her easels again. She seemed to be struggling a little. Maybe Luella should push harder for Sue Beth and Julep to join Dell and her in their twice-weekly yoga classes or perhaps come with her on her daily brisk walks in the still-cool mornings. But no amount of working out would help the fact that summers on the island were hot, especially this time of day.

They finally made it to the parking lot and approached Sue Beth's green Jeep.

"Phew." Luella laid her easels on the ground next to the Jeep and wiped her forehead with the back of her hand. "Where are your boys when we need them?"

"I know, right?" Sue Beth chuckled, putting each easel in the back of her SUV before closing the tailgate and dusting her hands off. "They grew up on me. And then to top it off, all three got married and didn't even ask my permission to move off the island. How rude."

Luella chuckled. "The nerve. But I never hear complaints from you when the grandchildren visit."

"I should have borrowed Gavin from Julep to give us a hand. But she would *not* be happy with me if I did that. Do I look okay? No stray paint?" Sue Beth held her hands out and turned around for inspection.

Luella looked Sue Beth up and down and then adjusted Sue Beth's collar to be even on both sides. "No paint that I can see. You look great." Luella glanced down at her own go-to "nice clothes," consisting of black slacks and a tan button-up shirt. "I hope I don't look too out-of-date."

"Nonsense, you're adorable." Sue Beth smiled and then frowned. "I forgot to put on a watch. But I bet we're late."

"Punctuality doesn't seem to be our strong suit."

"But it is Julep's and Dell's. Let's go before we're in trouble."

They hurried across Neptune Park.

Oh, how Luella loved this area. How many times as a child had she run along this same sidewalk from the parking lot, along the seaside near the rocks, then on to the picnic area and playgrounds? She'd loved coming here at high tide to watch the Atlantic Ocean splash against the rocks. At low tide she'd be on the sand, setting up a picnic. Nowadays low tide provided just enough sand to take a little stroll on the beach. She sighed. Erosion had changed so much of Georgia's Golden Isles. The fact that they were one of the fastest-changing landmasses in the world with a unique history and population was what led Luella to study and write about the island.

They approached the picnic area and found Julep in the shade under the many arms of the giant live oak at the center of the park.

"Took you both long enough." Julep had her arms crossed. "We could've used a hand." When the sea breeze gusted, she uncrossed her arms and smoothed her shoulder-grazing dark brown hair.

Gavin passed them going the other way, nodding hello. He was carrying a cooler with boxes stacked on top, probably to remove from sight the empty containers used to transport the food.

"Psh. All of you need to stop and take a good look." Dell surveyed the immaculate picnic table. She held her hands out, framing it as though it were the subject of one of her photos. "Even if Luella and Sue Beth were here to give their opinions, do you think this spread could look any better? You don't mess with perfection. And this picnic looks like something straight out of HGTV, y'all."

A lovely blue-and-white, pastoral-patterned quilt covered the concrete picnic table. Two two-tiered white porcelain serving trays were in the center of the table. One held fried chicken on the bottom tier and fresh biscuits on the top tier. The second had slices of watermelon on the bottom tray with fresh strawberries on the top. A large glass bowl of ice was also in the center of the table, and a second glass bowl sat inside it full of potato salad. A blown-glass pitcher of iced tea was shedding beads of water courtesy of the humidity. Each place setting had antique china, a glass filled with ice, and shiny silverware on cloth napkins.

Dell lifted the digital SLR camera from around her neck and snapped a few shots. "Beautiful job, girls."

"There they are!" Sue Beth pointed at three men walking toward them. Walter had on a full suit. The other two, probably midforties, were wearing button-up shirts and dress pants. "Didn't Walter say there would be three men flying in today?"

"Yeah," Dell said. "Someone's missing. But we'll convince these two, and they'll convince the third guy."

"All right, Sue Beth." Julep stepped forward to stand next to her. "You're the cute one. Pull yourself together and go flirt."

Not this again. Did anyone think it was funny when Sue Beth flirted or when Julep encouraged her or made jokes about it? The thinking was stereotypical—every Southern woman flirted to get what she wanted.

Sue Beth put a hand on the center of her chest as if to steady her heart, her eyes wide open. "Excuse me? I'm *married.*"

"Never stopped you before," Julep whispered, barely moving her lips.

Luella shot Julep a look. That remark was uncalled for. Why had Julep taken so many potshots at Sue Beth lately? "We all know this is a professional meeting, right? Flirting shouldn't factor into it."

The men approached the table, and Walter nodded at them. "Good afternoon, ladies. What a beautiful spread. I'd like you to meet the owners of Seaside Properties. This is Stan. And this is Rick."

"Oh, hi!" Sue Beth spoke first, and then the Glynn Girls echoed the greeting.

Walter introduced the men to each of them.

"How are y'all liking our island so far?" Sue Beth moved her hand, inviting the men to observe the gorgeous view of the seaside and the draping branches of the live oak above their heads.

Rick swatted a bug on his forearm. "It's . . . rather hot."

Really? Luella hadn't seen or felt any bugs today, and the sea breeze had been wonderful and cooling.

Stan smiled as he looked around. "It's absolutely beautiful. And flat." He turned to Rick. "Maybe we should invest in bicycle rentals. The shade and breeze make it feel like the perfect temp to me."

"Maybe."

Sue Beth smiled. "Where is home for you? Since the property management group is based in New York City, is that where you're from?"

Rick pulled a small bottle of hand sanitizer from his pocket, squeezed a dollop on his hands, and rubbed them together. "It is."

Dell gestured at the table. "Oh, then you are in for a treat of Southern cooking. Come sit. I'll fix plates. Walter, please join us."

After the men sat, Dell, Sue Beth, and Julep each prepared a plate for the men, making pleasant conversation while doing so. Luella poured Dell's famous sweet tea into their glasses.

Once the men had their plates, the women joined them and made small talk while eating. Although Walter had nearly polished off his food, Stan and Rick still had almost full plates. Luella glanced at Dell. Should they keep pushing food on these businessmen? But Dell was already spooning helpings of peach cobbler on dessert plates. She passed them to Julep, who set them at each place on the table. Luella nudged her foot against Julep's leg and nodded toward the men. It was as good a time as any to broach the subject of the corner shop.

Julep seemed a bit nervous. Her smile trembled. "We are so glad to be a part of your investment, and we believe that your group has a good vision for the future of the island. As you may know, our store has been a staple of St. Simons for nearly twenty years, and we've been growing out of our current building for quite some time. We've been eyeing the corner shop between Mallery and Oglethorpe. The owners have been wanting to retire for some time, and when they do, we'd like to move from our current place to the other one, *and* y'all own that property too . . ."

Stan wiped his mouth with a corner of his cloth napkin. "Now that sounds like a strong plan, right, Rick?"

Rick nodded. "It does. But, ladies, as good as your chicken and potato salad are, you are barking up the wrong tree. The property manager makes all those decisions. You'll have to take that up with him when he gets here. His name is Charles McKenzie. We just buy and leave."

"Pardon?" Julep blinked, and the plate in her hand tilted forward, as if she forgot she was holding it. The dessert slid off the plate and plunked to the ground. Her cheeks were growing brighter pink by the second. She leveled the plate, and Dell plopped another scoop of peach cobbler on it without missing a beat. "This visit is your only time to be on the island?"

"Sure. We can't spend physical time at all our investments." Rick turned down a corner of his mouth. "Which is too bad. But Charles McKenzie will be hands-on. He was supposed to fly in with us but had to cancel at the last minute. He'll live here on the island for now. Anything you need from Seaside Properties will go through him."

"Great." Luella smiled and tried to make her tone positive. "When can we meet Charles?"

"Oh, he should be here tomorrow."

An awkward silence descended, and the men shook their heads, declining the cobbler. The two men had barely made a dent in the copious amounts of food they'd been given, and yet they were full?

Stan stood. "Meeting all of you has been fantastic, but we're on a tight schedule. This was quite the picnic."

"Quite." Rick folded his napkin and stood. "We were expecting just snacks of some kind."

"Thank you, ladies." Stan shook hands with each of them, and the men traded a few goodbye civilities.

Luella looked at the untouched bounty on the table. All the work they'd put into this meal and for what?

As the men walked off, all four women were left sitting there, staring at the abundance of home-cooked food left untouched.

Gavin walked up and nodded his head in the direction of the men. "How'd it go?"

Julep flopped down on the concrete picnic table bench and leaned her forehead against her palm. "Take a guess, Son."

"Gavin, you must be hungry. *Someone* needs to enjoy this masterpiece!" Dell's voice cracked a little. She lifted the fried chicken platter.

7

It was soft beneath her . . . a bed. Tara tried to open her eyes, but an intense, head-splitting pain drew a groan from her. Finally she could pry one eye open.

Darkness. She moved her head to look around. This room . . . this bed . . . the feather pillow smelling of lavender—they weren't hers. Where was she? What day was it?

She sat up slowly. The glowing green of a digital clock aggravated the excruciating pain in her head. She forced herself to push through and read the time: 1:21 p.m.

Another look around the room. *Is this . . . a hotel?*

With some effort she shoved back the layers of fluffy bedding. The sheets and comforter were heavy, as if weighted. She swung her feet off the side of the bed and stretched them until they touched the scratchy carpet. Pressing a palm against a temple seemed to help. Well, maybe a tiny amount. Her fingers touched . . . stitches?

Oh yeah, the roof fell in and she hit her head. No wonder she had a headache.

Tara stumbled across the floor and into a small adjoining bathroom. She rummaged around the dark room's countertop until she found her zippered travel bag. Apparently she'd remembered to pack it. After several moments of digging, she found the Vicodin. The doctor had warned her that she might have severe headaches for a while. She unscrewed the cap, swallowed one pill along with as much water as she could force down, staggered back to the bed, and eased down on top of the duvet, closing her eyes.

She stirred, peering at the clock. Twenty minutes had passed. Thank heavens her headache had subsided enough so she could think a little. Wherever she was, the room was dark and cool, and the white noise of the air conditioner soothed her head.

She stood and opened the light-blocking curtains, immediately wincing at the blinding sunlight. She closed them again and struggled to place herself in the strange surroundings. This had to be the St. Simons hotel room that Sean helped her book. Where were her brothers now?

Oh. Of course. They wouldn't be asleep this time of day.

A small desk with a charging station was in the corner of the room, and her white iPhone was plugged in. Had she done that, or had someone else? She walked over and picked up the device. Where had all these texts come from?

She unlocked the phone and started opening them.

Hadley: Love you, Tara. Haven't heard from you in a while. Please call me when you get this message.

Elliott: Can you give us a check-in?

Lynn: We're praying for you. Call soon.

The list of texts continued. Tara touched the stitches again. Why was everyone back home so worried about her? She rubbed her temple. Where could her brothers be? Ice cream on the pier? Or maybe they'd rented bikes?

She went back into her phone's texts and scrolled down until she found Darryl's name. The last text he sent read:

I'm on the island having fun. Catch me if you can. If you can't, I'll come find you soon.☺

Well, that didn't tell her a lot. Her brothers and their pranks! *Where* on the island? Oh well. She typed back a reply.

I'll come meet you. What are you up to?

The same message immediately bounced back from Darryl. He must have set up an autoreply and didn't have his phone where he could reach it. After a minute with no additional response, she copied the message and sent a duplicate to Sean. Surely one of them had a phone with them.

She scrolled back to Hadley's text, asking for a call. She might as well do that to ease her friends' minds.

Hadley answered. "Tara?"

"Hey, Hads. I got your message. I'm here on St. Simons. I'm okay, other than a wicked headache. But I took some medicine."

"I'm so glad to hear from you. Another few hours of no calls or texts, and Elliott or I would be driving your way."

"Sorry." When had she seen Hadley and Elliott last? She had some vague memories of her friends in the hospital with her. Or was that part of a vivid dream, one of many she seemed to be having ever since the storm?

Hadley cleared her throat. "You know, as it turns out, I could actually get away this week. I think only God could order my life where I can take off spur of the moment. It wouldn't be any trouble. My girls are at camp all week, and a friend of mine could volunteer at the camp instead of me. I'd stay out of your way, I promise. But I would be nearby just in case."

Why were they fussing over her so much? It was a huge imposition for Hadley or Elliott to drive all this way. They needed to stay home and tend to their families. Besides, Sean and Darryl could help her if it came to that. "No, that's okay. I'm fine, I promise. I was just sleeping in. It's only my first day. Lots of people get jet lag, no head wound required."

"Tara, honey . . . it's Thursday. You've been gone two days."

Thursday? How could it be Thursday? "R-Right."

Suddenly the dark of the hotel room closed in on her. She needed to go out and find Sean and Darryl. Then everything would be okay. "Sorry. You know, I'm just dealing with a lot."

"Vicodin by itself is enough to completely disorient you, but the doctor was pretty adamant that you need to continue taking it for the next few weeks. He believes the research that indicates the less pain people experience after surgery, the faster they'll heal."

"Okay. Not a problem." How long would her brain function in a fog like this? It was weird and disorienting. "But I don't need anyone coming down. I'm okay. I think I'll go eat something and find some strong coffee."

"Food would be a good idea." Why did Hadley sound so hesitant?

Tara rubbed her forehead. "Did someone get the roof repairs started? I'll need a roof on my house soon."

Hadley sighed. "It makes me feel a little better to hear you ask about it. Yes, we have the process started, and we'll figure out the insurance when you return."

"Great. I'm going to see if this hotel can extend my stay for at least another week. Might as well, with the roof and all."

"If that's what you need."

"It seems like the best possible thing for me now. Besides the immediate need of coffee."

"Okay. And, Tara . . ."

"Yes?"

"I'm here for you, however and whatever you need. Elliott is too. We love you. You know that, right?"

"Sure. Thank you." Tara opened the curtain and looked out the window. The trees were covered in Spanish moss. Hadley was really over the top about this injury. Had she scared Hadley and Elliott that badly in the hospital?

They said their goodbyes, and Tara ended the call. A box of granola bars and a liter-size bottle of water sat on her dresser, some of which she must have eaten and drunk the previous day while she rested. She opened a bar and took a few bites while she got the shower going.

In no time she was dressed in the new white eyelet midi dress that Sean had purchased for her. She slipped her small leather purse across her shoulder. Thank goodness the headache was much better, although not completely gone.

She stepped out of the room and pulled the door closed to lock and then frowned. Sean's and Darryl's suitcases weren't in the hotel room. At least she hadn't seen them. Maybe they were tucked in a closet. Or maybe they left them in the car. She'd ask them about it when she found them.

She walked through the halls, into the hotel lobby, and out the front door into the brilliant sunlight and cringed at the shock of pain it brought. She got a pair of sunglasses out of her purse and chuckled when they fogged up after going from the air-conditioned hotel to the hot, humid air of South Georgia. She pulled out her cell and took a photo of herself with fogged-up sunglasses and then sent it to Hadley and Elliot. They were sure to appreciate it, and maybe it would put them a little more at ease about her being here.

Tara snapped picture after picture on her phone as she walked down the village street. She loved cute, small towns, and this one was heavy on the charm, which explained why it was also heavy on the crowds.

After calling her brothers' cell phones again and getting no answer, she grabbed a burger and fries from the vintage-looking café near the pier. When she finished her food and walked outside to the seaside park, she noticed the lighthouse.

Something fell into place.

Sean had talked about climbing the stairs of the lighthouse. Maybe that's where they were, waiting for her. She could imagine Sean taking lots of photos from the tower, using his nice camera.

As soon as I find them, everything will make sense.

8

L uella checked the time on her watch. Despite it being an antique, it kept the time well . . . after several repairs. It was almost nine, and her ghost tour would start in just a few minutes.

She loved the island at night. The strong fish smell of the pier lessened in the evenings, so the air just smelled like the sea. She turned on her battery-powered lantern, and it emitted a soft, golden glow. Later, when the group walked under the live oaks during the tour, it would be eerie and dark. They'd need her lantern to find their footing. Just as important, it added to the ambiance she was going for. She fluffed the big skirt of her maroon Civil War–era replica dress and felt her hair to make sure every strand was pinned up as it should be.

Thankfully it wasn't so hot at night as it was during the day with the sun blazing. The nighttime breeze was intense enough to cool the early-summer air *almost* to light-jacket weather. Rain was in the forecast for later in the evening, but from the radar she had just looked up, the tour should be fine. She'd met a few patrons already and chatted with some of them. There was nothing like sharing the specialness of the island with eager listeners.

"Hey, Lu, got a minute? I just finished cleaning and straightening the shop." Julep's somewhat gravelly voice made Luella look up. Julep had smoked for many years but gave it up cold turkey when her late husband, Mitch, was diagnosed with lung cancer a few weeks before his accident.

"I have about one literal minute before my tour begins." Luella grinned at her friend. "Just joking since you'd asked that way. I have around ten. What's up?"

Julep let out a sigh. "I feel that it may be time to ask Sue Beth to move her art classes out of the store. I have so much pressure on me now, and every time I see her, it makes my blood boil until I feel like a kettle about to screech."

Luella nodded. "The two of you have had a hard go of it recently. What happened now?"

"Well, I had some really important clients coming to the store. You probably remember the Marshalls, the family who will be renting some of our antique china and many other decorations for a fall wedding at the Historical Society building. Sue Beth was late to her own art class. Again. So all her students were waiting around in the store since she had the key to the loft, where the class would be held."

Wasn't this something that could wait until later? "I don't really see why—"

"It was a class where they paint each other in their unmentionables. Can you believe that?"

"Oh my. So when they were in the store, they were . . ." Surely adult women wouldn't allow themselves to be in such a state in public.

"Well, they were all wearing housecoats. But trust me, anyone walking in felt uncomfortable. Despite the robes being terry cloth, I think it was apparent they didn't have clothes, for day or night, under those housecoats. Why would anyone think it's okay to be in an upscale furniture store with only a housecoat over their underwear?"

Luella nodded. She didn't want to be in the middle of this disagreement. She needed to stay neutral. "But if I'm remembering right, Sue Beth holds those classes with only women, all of them close to our age, and the classes focus on body positivity and appreciating the forms that the Lord created. She calls what they paint 'tasteful bikinis.'"

"She gets to act so foolish when *I'm* the one who has to maintain the store and keep our customers and reputation." Julep's voice was a growl.

"But getting that corner store unit would fix the issue of Sue Beth's classes, right? The loft would have its own separate entrance and the students—and Sue Beth—wouldn't have to come into the shop every day."

"Yeah, but she would still be *right there*. Right above me."

Luella opened and then closed her mouth. Sometimes Julep just needed to vent before getting back to herself. Although it'd been eighteen months since Mitch died, her friend was still deeply grieving his passing. Sue Beth was the easiest target for Julep's frustrations, usually because Sue Beth didn't think through how her actions would affect others. But . . .

"Julep, what's really going on between you and Sue Beth? Things have been weird for a while. It feels like there's something I don't know."

Julep glanced around at the gathering tour crowd and leaned in closer. "There is something, and I'm tired of keeping quiet about it. We had a get-together the day Mitch was diagnosed. Do you remember that?"

Luella nodded, her heart beating faster. "The gathering was already planned, and you guys didn't cancel it."

"That's right. I was in a panic, and Gavin was helping me research and verify what the doctor had said. Sue Beth and Mitch were talking outside. I walked out and saw the two of them. She was hugging him in a way that you *don't* hug your best friend's spouse."

Luella blinked. Was Julep implying . . . "You think she was throwing herself at Mitch?"

"No." Julep made a disgusted face. "Not that. But she was stealing the moment *I* should have had with him. It's what she does. Steals moments that don't belong to her."

Sue Beth was known for being a flirt, although Luella wasn't at all sure Sue Beth realized how her behavior came across. Still, whenever the Glynn Girls ran into people from Sue Beth's middle and high school days, they told stories of her being popular and flirting with all the boys. But her personality aside, when a couple had a ticking clock, it was a betrayal for a friend to steal time from them.

A crowd of people had started to gather around Luella and her lantern.

It wasn't the time to speak about anything sensitive with her walking-tour group waiting. She leaned close to Julep. "Let's talk about this over a cup of coffee tomorrow morning. Now come take a walk with us. I know you've heard the stories before, but maybe walking will help clear your head."

Julep nodded, looking a bit relieved to do something more than stew in her frustration and hurt.

Luella released her hand. "Good." She turned to raise her lantern. "Gather 'round, everyone." She projected her voice to get the attention of the whole group. A quick count told her there were twenty people. She studied each face for a second, deciding who she'd ask questions of on the tour. She smiled at them. "Are you ready to meet the ghosts of St. Simons Island?"

She hit all her favorite points and stories. They walked below the Lighthouse Inn and down a dirt road. It was hard keeping her mind off the revelation Julep had shared, but she tried to focus on the tour. Every few minutes Luella stopped the group and told them a story about the island's history and inhabitants. But her favorite stories she saved for the end.

Luella held up the lantern and gestured for her tour group to stop. She had stories to share before they got to the lighthouse. Each path and every step they took on this island was steeped in history, sometimes beautiful and sometimes ugly.

The group gathered around her, and she studied their faces. "How many of you have heard of St. Simons's most famous ghost, Mary de Wanda?"

Two people in the group raised their hands, and there was a new face in the group. It wasn't unusual for people to start tagging along during her tour, and she really didn't mind, as it helped spread word of mouth. The addition was a man of medium build, about her age or maybe a little younger, with gray-blond hair cut very close to his scalp. He was dressed nicely, which was a little unusual for someone walking around the island. He had his arms crossed as he was listening, frowning.

Interesting.

Luella focused again on the story she was going to tell. She held up her lantern and looked out over the beach, which was now at low tide. The clouds had parted enough that moonlight shined a wavy path on the water. It was a prime night for people to make good use of their imaginations. She turned back toward the group. "This is one of my favorite stories and one that involves some of my own ancestors, the Demere family. It's really quite romantic but also sad.

"In 1824 Mary was a teenage ward of *the* Raymond Demere. You've probably noticed Demere Road, which is named after the family. They were wealthy planters, and young Mary acted as their house servant. But she was very beautiful, and Raymond's teenage son fell in love with her. They met in secret to plan their marriage. One morning the son told his father that he planned to wed Mary. Not wanting his son to bind himself to a girl of lower social caliber, the father got into a heated argument with the son, which ended with the son rowing a boat away from the river landing, heading to the mainland for a few days to cool down.

"Unfortunately, bad weather started rolling in. The wind began blowing, causing the waves to get higher and higher. Turns out, a hurricane was headed to St. Simons. Full-blown hurricanes are pretty rare for our area. Mary could hardly contain herself, and she searched and searched for the young man all day through the storm, holding her lantern in the blinding wind and rain."

Luella held up her battery-powered lantern for effect. "When the hurricane finally subsided, she saw it: the young man's capsized boat. In her unbearable grief Mary flung herself into the rolling waves. Her love for that young man was so intense she was willing to join him in his early watery grave."

The group was silent. Luella let her words hang in the air before continuing.

"Since that day lots of people on the island have claimed to see Mary, with her flowing long hair and white dress, holding her lantern high. She gets her name from the Geechee people who live on St. Simons and the surrounding Golden Isles. They call her Mary de Wanda. She wanders endlessly, looking for her lost love. We even have written accounts of air traffic controllers seeing her walking on the tarmac. And many respectable people, both residents and visitors, have seen her. I've heard tales of people seeing a woman in white walking on this very beach, but by the time the viewer reaches the bottom of the stairs to the sand, she's gone."

Luella smiled at the wide eyes and murmurs from the group. "I'll let you take a few minutes to walk around the area, and then let's gather on the lawn in front of the lighthouse. But we can't take too long, because I think I feel some rain coming on."

The group dispersed, chattering away.

Someone tapped Luella on the shoulder, and when she turned, she saw it was the well-dressed man.

"Excuse me. I'd like to have some words with you regarding your little tourist shakedown."

What? She blinked.

"You just led a group of people into the garage of my hotel and told them about a crew of"—he used his fingers to make quotation marks in the air—"*spirits* who run up and down the stairs. And you told these potential guests to beware of staying on the third floor."

Who *was* this guy? "Pardon?"

"Don't even bother denying it."

"I'm . . . not. It's part of my tour and has been for years. No one on the island has ever minded."

"Well, I'm managing the Lighthouse Inn now, and I don't believe in ghosts. Moreover, I find your slander of this fine hotel offensive."

"Slander? Just . . . just who do you think you are?" Complaints on Yelp were one thing, but for someone to confront her like this in the middle of the tour was just rude. Couldn't he wait until after the tour?

"My name is Charles."

"Now listen here, *Chuck*." Her heart was pounding, but as much as she wanted to turn and run, she couldn't abandon her group. She pointed a finger at his imposing chest. "I am a historian. This isn't some cutesy little scam to take tourists' money. This is our island's unique history, and it includes folklore that dates back to the sixteenth century. I have slandered no one. If you don't want me to take my groups by your hotel, that's fine. But you are not in charge of what history I include in my tours."

He raised a palm. "Ghosts? Really? You think that anyone takes this seriously? And did you just call me *chump*?"

"If the shoe fits." An inner voice was screaming caution, saying *no, no, no*. She couldn't make enemies. She and Blue Sails Casual Living needed friendship and cooperation from each business on the island. They needed each hotel's continued recommendation for visitors to come to their shop.

But how could she just let this Charles . . . this . . . this . . .

Oh no.

Charles. Could this be the Charles McKenzie the property managers said was coming?

Before she could pull her own metaphorical foot out of her mouth and try to smooth things over, someone screamed. Luella spun and saw it was a woman on her tour.

Luella ran to her and put a hand on her shoulder. "Are you okay? What's wrong?"

The woman pointed toward the top of the lighthouse. Luella followed her line of sight up to the top of the tall structure. A woman with long blond hair and a flowing white dress stood behind the five-foot metal railing.

What in the world?

The lighthouse and its museum had closed for the day long ago. What was someone doing at the top?

"It's Mary!" A man yelled, and several others started murmuring. A few gasped every time the figure moved.

"Mary de Wanda!"

Luella looked over to Julep, whose eyes were wide. Julep pointed upward at the lighthouse. "Got a good explanation, Lu?"

The figure certainly *looked* like Mary de Wanda. But that was absurd, right? The people in the group were snapping picture after picture with their phones.

Julep pulled out her own phone. "I'll call Gavin. He can get someone to open the museum. A visitor must have gotten trapped up there. Somehow. Right?"

"I suppose." Luella looked over to Charles. His jaw was slack, and he was staring upward. Good. In light of his accusations, the best thing that could happen was her tour seeing a real ghost.

Not, of course, that Luella believed in such a thing.

9

Tara looked down from the lighthouse balcony. She grasped the cold, wet metal rail to steady herself. No stars shone in the cloudy sky, but she could see a group of people on the grass below the lighthouse, looking at her and pointing. Had the lighthouse museum closed without her realizing it?

"It's Mary!" A man shouted from the ground, and others did the same thing.

"Mary de Wanda!"

A light rain fell on Tara's face and shoulders. She had to be right about the museum closing. Walking up the steep, narrow stairs had made her head spin. She'd even gone back down . . . but what happened next? Like a figure appearing through a haze, a memory sparked. At the bottom of the stairs, she'd sat down behind a propped-open door, out of the way of other visitors, to close her eyes and . . . and what? She frowned.

She must have fallen asleep. Had the medication made her that drowsy?

The next thing she recalled was opening her eyes, fighting disorientation, but a desire to climb to the top of the lighthouse and search for her brothers again had overpowered her.

She looked around. So if the museum was closed, all the doors must be locked. How was she going to get out? What if the people yelling at her called the police? Would she be arrested for trespassing? Or worse, sent to a hospital for evaluation? She was putting on a good front for Hadley and Elliott, pretending to think and feel far more normal than she actually was.

If she was sent for an evaluation, she might be declared unfit to be on her own, she'd have to go home, and she'd never find her brothers on the island. Their hard-earned vacation would be over before it'd begun—

No. She couldn't let that happen.

She ran back down the spiral stairs, around and around, heart pounding. She couldn't just go out the front door, even if it was open. Not with all those people on the lawn. She'd have to explain why she was in the lighthouse, and she couldn't face doing that. Was there a back exit somewhere? Wait a minute. There. At the bottom of the stairs, where the lighthouse connected with the keeper's house, there was a door. She hurried to it and frowned. An emergency exit. But she had no choice. She cracked the door open, cringing, but no alarm sounded. Thank heavens for that. She peered through the door she'd just opened and saw bushes and a brick path that led somewhere. Based on what she had seen from the top of the lighthouse, this door was on the opposite side of the building from the crowd.

She went through it and pushed the door closed behind her. It clicked. Had it locked? She glanced around and saw a family walking toward a parking lot with towels over their heads to shield them from the rain. She leaped over a railing and ducked behind a bush. Years of living in foster care group homes had taught her how to lose people and fade into the background.

Oh, why did she wear white today? Just the color to ensure she could be seen at night. Her long blond hair didn't help either.

She rubbed her temples. If she could think straight. But, no, it was as though she were under murky water. Her thoughts flowed every which way, carrying away anything coherent.

But she knew one thing: if she had any hope of losing the group on the lawn out front, she needed to move.

The rain and dim lighting helped. With any luck she was far enough from the crowd that they wouldn't be able to see her. She pushed herself out of the bush and ran toward the parking lot, moving to the opposite side of the line of parked cars.

Who was this Mary de Wanda they were yelling about? Would Tara be in any less trouble for trespassing if she were that Mary person?

As she hurried toward her hotel, a memory surfaced, playing across her mind like some old reel-to-reel film . . .

> Darryl lying on their worn couch. His feet propped up. A St. Simons Island travel guide in his hands. A huge live oak with Spanish moss was on the book's cover.
>
> "T-Mom, listen to this." Darryl wiggled the book. "We may see a real ghost. Get ready to be scared. The legend of"—Darryl lowered his voice—"Mary de Wanda. She wanders around the island. And . . . well, that's all she does. Ooooo."
>
> "Doesn't sound very scary to me." Tara threw a pillow at him. "You still believe in ghosts at seventeen?"
>
> Darryl chucked the pillow right back at her. "As much as I do the Easter Bunny. Yet somehow my Easter basket gets filled with candy every year."

Tara smiled at the memory. They always had such fun together. But if they had fun, why was this profound sadness clawing at her?

She stopped. The hotel was just ahead. Would the boys be there by now? If so, she would've heard from them. She checked her phone. Nothing from either of them. Should she go to her room and go to bed? She stabbed her fingers through her hair. Her mind got more muddled when she slept. Besides, good memories came to her when she walked around. The light rain wasn't unpleasant. It helped her feel less sleepy.

I'm already wet. Might as well go for a walk on the beach. She turned and made her way down two darkened streets and a set of wooden steps. She slipped off her shoes and walked onto the sand. Was she some modern version of Mary, wandering around the island, trying to find her sanity?

Gavin drove his pickup to the parking lot adjacent to the lighthouse.

Bryan released his passenger seat belt, looking unsure of himself. Gavin remembered his first day of shadowing someone. It was a bit daunting. "Lieutenant, you sure we shouldn't call the police? I mean an intruder could be armed."

Gavin glanced at him. He'd looked jittery throughout the five-minute ride from the fire station. "Nah. I'm not even sure there's a reason for us to be here, except Mom called and asked me to come." He turned off the truck and removed the keys from the ignition.

His mom said she, Luella, and a group of about twenty people saw a ghost—or trespasser—at the top of the lighthouse. Checking out the area was the only way to ease everyone's minds.

Since it was a slow night at the fire station, he'd agreed to come. First, he called the Historical Society's security company. According to the woman he spoke with, to their knowledge no alarms had been triggered.

Gavin clipped his dispatch radio to his blue EMT uniform in case a real emergency occurred while he was dealing with these shenanigans.

The state tried to preserve as much of St. Simons Island's natural habitat as possible for the sea turtles that laid their eggs in the sand at night. Hence, the island had very few lights, and even those were dim. This created a dark island, which helped people's imaginations during Luella's ghost tours. Odds were good that Luella had simply worked her ghost tour into some kind of group delusion.

He exited the truck, and Bryan was soon at his heels. They walked toward the lighthouse, the fragrance of rain on asphalt mingling with the salty smell of the ocean.

"Mercy, Gavin, what took you so long?" His mom held an umbrella, and her scowl made the taut lines in her face stand out even in the dim light.

He drew a breath. *Lord, give me patience.* "I called the security company for the lighthouse. They said no one triggered an alarm, and they have no reason to believe there has been a break-in."

A few people huddled under umbrellas behind Gavin, murmuring as he spoke with his mom. Ah. The ghost tour attendees.

Gavin cleared his throat, eyeing them. "This doesn't mean there's a ghost in the lighthouse."

"Actually, Mary hasn't ever been spotted in the lighthouse before." Luella twirled a parasol-style umbrella that was balanced on her shoulder. "The lighthouse ghost is a man."

What? Gavin repressed any hint of a sigh. "Glad we cleared that up. I'll walk around the lighthouse and try the doors." That should satisfy everyone.

As Gavin walked across the grass, the ghost group, Bryan, Luella, and his mom followed him. Fine. Whatever. He stepped onto the front porch of the keeper's house, and everyone else did too. He pulled at the door.

Locked.

He knocked on it.

Silence.

Gavin turned to his mom. "Happy?"

She narrowed her eyes. "We would've seen if anyone came out the front door."

Oh, for— "Just wait here."

Gavin snaked around the crowd and jogged to the back of the lighthouse. The emergency exit door was locked too. He ran to the door of the Historical Society building and peered through the window.

Locked.

He ran back to the porch, shaking rain out of his hair as he climbed the steps. "I looked all around the building, and I don't see anything out of the ordinary. Can we chalk this up to a weird, rainy night?"

Luella stared toward the ocean. "Mary is almost always spotted on roads near the beach or walking on the sand. People have also seen her at the airport."

"Seriously, Luella?" He hoped he sounded respectful and not dismissive, but good grief.

Bryan shifted, wiping rain off his arms. "One time I thought I saw her on the beach here by the pier. But I was only twelve."

Some members of the ghost tour nodded, while others whispered to people close by.

"So like, you saw her last year, Bryan?" Gavin turned to his mom and Luella. "Fine. We'll look for your ghost on the beach. Come on, Bryan."

"Lieutenant." Someone's voice, probably Jimmy's, came through the radio. "Find anything at the lighthouse?"

Gavin pushed the button to reply. "Negative. Just going to take a quick look on the beach per request, and then we'll come back to the station."

Speaking into the radio clipped to Gavin's front pocket, Bryan said, "Miss Luella thinks we'll have better luck on the beach if it's Mary de Wanda they saw." Gavin released the button and turned the radio away from Bryan.

"Mary de Wanda? Like the ghost?" Laughter cackled through the radio. "That's why they called y'all?"

Great. Just what his crew needed—more fodder for their pranks. Gavin shot Bryan a glare, but the young man didn't appear to notice.

They reached the bottom of the boardwalk stairs and stepped onto the sand. It was low tide, so there was a small strip of sand next to the prominent rocks. In a few hours when the tide came in, those stairs would lead straight into the rolling surf. Even though they were in the middle of summer tourist season, the beach was empty because of the dark and the rain.

Gavin walked a few steps along the rocks and looked down the beach toward the pier. "I think we're done here."

Bryan's shoulders drooped. "Okay."

"I thought you didn't want us to find an actual trespasser?"

"I didn't say that. And seeing Mary is totally different."

Gavin shook his head, grateful Bryan was too distracted to notice the gesture. "Let's head back. We're gonna get enough grief as it is."

Bryan walked ahead of him and up the stairs. As Gavin was about to step onto the first wooden tread, something caught his attention in the direction away from the pier. He stopped and looked harder. The rain and the mist coming off the ocean didn't help, but . . .

It was a figure in a white dress.

"Er, hold on, kid. I'm going to jog down the beach, and I'll be right back."

Gavin ran across the wet sand toward the figure. Of course it wasn't a ghost, because that would be ridiculous. But if a woman was out here on a night like this, she could be lost. And if she didn't know about the extreme tidal differences of St. Simons, she could end up stepping in an oyster bed, as he had as a teen.

"Excuse me, miss?" Gavin waved at the figure.

The woman turned. She was in her twenties or thirties. She fit Mary's description: flowing white dress. She was also barefoot, and her long hair was plastered to her neck and back from the rain. He was still at least a thirty-second jog from her.

She needs you. Help her.

He'd felt this kind of intuition before but never this strong.

He cupped his hand and called to her. "I'm an EMT. You weren't by any chance at the lighthouse earlier?"

She turned and bolted.

"Wait! I promise you aren't in trouble!"

He blinked, trying to keep sight of her, but she faded into the darkness and rain. He stopped, staring. *What just happened?* Chills ran over his body. Did he just see Mary de Wanda? No. No way. In fact, he felt as though he'd seen a friend in trouble. But why would she feel like a friend?

Whatever the answer, if the men at the station learned that he saw a lone woman wearing a white dress on the beach and that when he called to her, she disappeared, he would be harassed for life.

10

Luella straightened on the tall stool in front of the wood-and-glass counter as Sue Beth walked around her, examining her. The usual smells of the store—a combination of fresh magnolias, old books, and aged wood—tingled in her nostrils as she drew a deep breath. She longed to reach for the hot coffee sitting in front of her in the ceramic travel mug, but she didn't dare. Not even coffee was worth extending Sue Beth's *beautifying*.

Blue Sails often bustled during this time of year, but right now the only sounds Luella heard in the shop were the occasional scribble of Julep's pen and the ticking of the large antique clock by the old-timey cash register. Customers would arrive as soon as they opened, or so she hoped.

Sue Beth stopped behind Luella and clipped a barrette on the back of Luella's head a bit too tight, pinning the curls that often fell in her face. Sue Beth strolled around to look at her from the front. Luella would've refused this makeover as completely unnecessary, but she was trying to indulge Sue Beth, who had really been catching it from Julep of late. But seriously, who needed makeup and a new hairstyle to have a conversation as one business-person to another? Would Charles be more likely to accept Luella's apology if she had rosy cheeks and glimmering lips? But Sue Beth needed a win, and Luella could deal with this for her sake.

Maybe.

Luella held her breath. Would she pass muster?

Her friend pursed her lips and then twisted them to the side. "Let me get my makeup kit. It's in the loft."

Luella let out a breath, deflated. "This is silly. And appearance completely aside, someone else needs to go talk to him."

"Nuh-uh. You made the mess; you gotta clean it up." Sue Beth flipped her hand over, gesturing at Julep, who was leaning over a financial ledger and making notations. Her pen was topped with a silk flower she'd attached to prevent customers from walking off with it. "Of the four of us, I thought the person who'd offend this man would be prickly-pear Julep, not our pleasant-as-punch Luella." Sue Beth grinned at Julep.

Julep glanced at Sue Beth out of the corner of her eye before her gaze turned back to the ledger. Probably didn't want to dignify that comment with a response.

"Be right back." Sue Beth ran upstairs.

If only there had been time for her to talk to Julep privately about the bombshell she revealed last night before the tour. Although Luella didn't understand much about what had happened, other than the brief events Julep had described, she knew Julep felt betrayed by Sue Beth's comforting Mitch. It was such a horrible blow for Julep when they learned his days were numbered, and for another woman—a good friend, no less—to take Julep's place as his confidant, even for an afternoon, was unforgivable to Julep. To make matters worse, Mitch up and died mere weeks later.

But after Luella offended Charles and the commotion at the lighthouse, well, Luella and the girls needed to focus on fixing that mess.

Last night the Glynn Girls had met after the ghost tour to discuss a game plan. Dell would make a pie, which Luella would then walk over to the Lighthouse Inn, where Charles was staying since he was now managing it. Sue Beth would help prep Luella with the right words to say *and* help her achieve the right "look," whatever that meant.

Sue Beth scampered down the stairs. "Here we go." She set the bright flowered bag on the counter. "Why, exactly, is Charles in such a dither?"

"Well, it seems he's easy to offend." Luella took a sip of her coffee.

"Although, for all his ranting about not believing in ghosts, he sure beat a hasty retreat after we spotted Mary at the top of the lighthouse."

Sue Beth shivered. "That whole thing last night gives me the heebie-jeebies." She set several round makeup containers on the counter.

Luella shrugged. There had to be a logical explanation for what they saw last night. She just didn't know what it was yet. "It's peculiar. And stranger still that Gavin saw a similar woman on the beach afterward. I don't quite know what to make of it myself."

A familiar knock sounded at the front door. Dell liked to knock in the rhythm of one of their former high school's cheers, similar to "shave and a haircut" but more complex.

Finally. Luella scooted off the stool. "I think I'll skip the makeup, Sue Beth." She smoothed the skirt of her dress. "Your kelly-green sundress is a fashion upgrade from my normal wardrobe. Surely it's good enough for *Chuck.*"

"Can't have you showing up to apologize in one of those prehistoric getups you wear for your tours." Sue Beth sniffed.

"Antebellum," Luella corrected over her shoulder as she hurried across the store to unlock the door. Dell had a key, but the lock was a pain to jiggle open. It was both amusing and not surprising that Julep was the sole person who could unlock the thing in any dignified manner.

"Ta-da!" Dell held up the pie as Luella opened the door.

Luella smiled. "Thank you so much for making the pie. Any chance you want to deliver it?"

Dell stepped inside and put the pie in Luella's hands. The glass dish was cold from the refrigerator and had a clear, high-dome cover protecting copious amounts of whipped cream.

"No way, sugar." Dell held up her hands, fingers splayed. "You stepped in it; you clean the shoe."

Luella sighed. "Great. Sue Beth said something similar."

"Well, best get it over with then." Dell shooed her toward the open door.

"Ugh, fine." Luella was almost out the door that Dell held for her. She turned back toward those in the shop. "I'll report back afterward."

"Remember what we talked about." Sue Beth winked. "Use charm, Luella. Lots of charm."

Julep looked up from the book on the counter. "Don't listen to that advice. Just be yourself. I saw him last night, and he's kind of cute. Maybe you can even get a date. For once."

"Ohhhh." Sue Beth waggled her eyebrows. "Wouldn't that be fun?" She waved at Luella, who returned the gesture to all three women and left.

Luella went down the sidewalk, shaking her head. "I get dates . . ." But Julep was sort of right about Charles's looks. Still, a man could only be considered cute if he wasn't being an utter pain.

If there was one thing Chuck excelled at, it was being an utter pain.

She hurried to the inn and opened the sliding-glass front door. This inn was just a few hundred yards from the lighthouse. Had any of the tenants seen the woman at the top of the historical structure last night? As much as she wanted to know, she didn't dare ask and bring up ghosts again at Chuck's hotel.

She approached the front desk. "Is Mr. McKenzie working today?"

Clarissa, the college-age redhead working the front desk for the summer, flashed white teeth in a big smile. Luella had met her a few times when taking tour brochures to hotels around the island. "Why, yes. He's in his office. Want me to get him?"

No. "Yes, please."

Clarissa scratched her head. "I suppose I should have asked if you have an appointment, Luella."

"No appointment. Mr. McKenzie and I, uh, met last night."

"Oh, that's right!"

How did she know that already?

Clarissa reached behind the counter and held up a pack of Luella's tour brochures. "Mr. McKenzie came storming in last night and told me to throw these out. But it seemed wasteful, so I just stowed them back here for you."

Figured. Luella would have reached out to take the brochures if she wasn't holding the pie with both hands. "Er, yes. That's part of why I want to talk to him."

"May I help you?" A familiar low voice came from somewhere out of Luella's line of sight.

Speak of the devil. She looked to find Charles walking through an of-fice door behind the hotel counter. He approached the front desk.

Luella flashed a smile that she hoped was as cute as Sue Beth's. "Ears burning?"

He scrunched his brows. "What?"

"It's an idiom that derived from the supersti— You know what? Never mind." Mr. I-Don't-Believe-in-Ghosts wouldn't want to hear it. "May we chat for a few minutes? I won't keep you long."

"Sure." He opened the door that led behind the counter and held it open for her. "We can talk in my office. This way."

Luella followed him into the small office. The shelves and walls of the square room were bare. Several unopened boxes were stacked in a corner. A laptop sat on the large oak desk.

Charles gestured for her to sit in a leather office chair in the center of the room, and he took the chair behind the desk, staring at her and waiting for her to speak.

Was he trying to make this as awkward and uncomfortable as possible? She set the pie on the desk and smoothed Sue Beth's dress over her knees. Then she looked up to catch his eyes. They were a rather nice combination of green and blue, eyes that she would enjoy studying . . .

On anyone else.

Luella cleared her throat. "I wanted to come in person and apologize. I was rude to you last night, and I don't want you to think that's how I am. I brought you this pie." She picked it up and leaned forward to scoot the cold pastry in front of him.

Charles tilted his head to the side. Maybe he was considering why she had put it in front of him. He straightened. "Apology accepted for the tone of our altercation. Although I was partially at fault as well. I had just arrived on the island yesterday, was suffering a bad headache, and the first thing I encountered was two different guests who wanted a full refund because they had heard something about the rooms being haunted."

"That had to be frustrating." This was the first she'd heard of her tours decreasing business on St. Simons. Normally people were curious to stay in the locations she mentioned. "It's the stairs actually."

"What?"

"The stairs are haunted, not the rooms."

His lips thinned. "I see. You know that your apology and"—he picked up the pie dish, looked underneath it, and then set it back down—"whatever this pastry is don't change the fact that I must insist you not include my hotel in your program."

Luella nodded. "This island has enough rich history to cover, so I can do that." *At least until you are gone.*

Charles released a deep breath. "Well, good. Glad that matter is settled. What kind of pie is this by the way?" He held it up. The filling was obscured by whipped cream, and the bottom was a graham-cracker crust.

Well, snap beans. Luella should have asked Dell what the pie was. "It's an icebox pie." Maybe that would be a sufficient answer.

He blinked several times. "Should I know what flavor that term refers to?"

The jig was up. She rubbed the back of her neck. "I . . . don't know what flavor it is. I didn't make it."

He tilted the dish to the side. "It doesn't look store-bought."

"Dell made it."

He arched an eyebrow. "So you're apologizing with someone else's pie?"

Her face went hot. "Well, Chuck, not all of us fit a man's view of how a Southern woman should spend her time."

"Oh, I can see that." Was he messing with her? She couldn't decipher his expression.

Luella stood. "Okay, then." She took two steps toward the door of the office.

"Luella, is it?"

What now? "Yes." She turned to look at him.

He smiled. "I didn't mean that as an insult." He ran a finger around the edge of the pie dish. "It's kind of endearing, really, bringing me a homemade pie made in a home other than your own. So, for this picnic that Stan and Rick have been telling me about—which I assume you were a part of—did you fix any of the food?"

Luella found that his face looked handsome when it wasn't scowling, but she still didn't care for this string of questioning. She gave him her best stare down. "I took a cooler of ice and sweet tea. And, yes, before you ask, I do know how to boil water to make tea, thank you very much."

He broke into a chuckle.

"Glad I could bring you some entertainment along with your pie." In spite of herself she found herself laughing too.

Charles stood. "Look, I'd like to reach a compromise with you. I have some hotel business to attend to today, but would you like to grab a cup of coffee tomorrow morning—assuming they have that on St. Simons Island in this heat—and talk about this shop location you and your friends want?"

Really, she should stop while she was ahead and on amicable terms with the man. But the other Glynn Girls would be none too pleased if she declined an opportunity to talk about the store.

She smiled at him. "We do indeed have coffee on St. Simons. Year-round even. Let me ask my friends what time would work best to meet with you."

Charles rubbed the back of his neck and stared at the pie. "Ah, well . . . I was thinking more of just the two of us, if that's okay with you. I consider myself an observant person, and I noticed you don't wear a wedding ring. Sorry if that's too forward."

Oh. She looked at his left hand as he dropped it from his neck to his side. No ring there either. She stared at him. Was he implying what she thought? "Like a date?"

"That's what I had in mind, but you seem skeptical."

Skeptical didn't begin to cover it, and before today she'd always known when a man was going to ask her out. "You caught me without my biscuit buttered."

Confusion flittered through his eyes.

"I mean you caught me flat-footed."

"Ah." He grinned. "Since your biscuit isn't buttered, how about we keep things simple and have breakfast one morning? I imagine you know a good place to go."

"Sure." Sharing a meal would give her a solid opportunity to explain how important it was for the Glynn Girls to rent the Home Décor space. "It couldn't hurt to get to know each other a bit."

"That's what I was thinking." He smiled. "Are you free Tuesday, say eight o'clock?"

She nodded, her heart pounding. What was she doing accepting a date with Chuck?

"Good." A serious thought seemed to come to him. "Be sure to bring that biscuit."

Luella grinned. Sue Beth, Dell, and Julep would be thrilled.

11

Gavin turned over on his side, making the metal frame of the twin-size, sleeping-quarters bed creak and shake. He had almost drifted back to sleep when something pulled him awake. Had his phone buzzed? His mom didn't text him on his overnight shifts at the fire station. So who was texting at this miserable hour?

He leaned over the side of the bed and felt around on the floor for the device. No luck. If anyone needed him, they could just call the station.

He flipped onto his back and closed his eyes.

Lights flickered through his eyelids. He groaned and forced his eyes open. Shimmering in the air above his bed was a glowing image shaking back and forth. Was that . . . a dark-haired woman in a white dress?

He sat up just in time to see it fade away. Was he dreaming?

Something scraped against the wall, and then he heard a muffled snicker.

Oh . . . you have to be kidding m—

The lights flickered on and off.

"Ahh!" Three grown men wearing white sheets rushed in the room shrieking. Gavin jumped a little out of pure reflex.

They started whooping in laughter, falling over, and slapping one another on the back.

Gavin shook his head. "Glynn County's proud 'Guardians of the Rock' yukking it up."

Jimmy pulled the sheet off his head, laughing so hard he had tears in his eyes.

Gavin tossed his own sheet off and kicked his feet over the side of the bed. He stood and walked over to flip on the light switch.

Wow. He must have been sleeping hard earlier in the night, because someone had managed to string up a semi-translucent fabric screen near the foot of his bed. A projector hooked to a MacBook sat on top of a stack of books on the floor.

Gavin walked over to touch the screen. With the lights on, it was easy to see, but in the dark it had looked like a ghost. "You know, I'm not even mad. This is a legit setup. Where'd you knuckleheads get this idea?"

Jimmy wiped the inner corners of his eyes. "YouTube."

"You say you aren't mad now, but let's see how you feel after the video of you goes viral." Dan tapped the small video camera in his left hand. "This thing films in the dark."

Great. More ways for people to laugh at him. "Well isn't that *special.*"

"You sound like your mama—all grouchy." Jimmy grinned.

"Maybe because it's around four in the morning, and I could be sleeping."

"How'd we do?" Dan shook the screen, making the ghost woman move back and forth. "This look like your Mary?"

Gavin walked over to the bed and sat on the edge. He started to slide on his shoes. "Not even close. Wrong hair. Besides. I didn't see a ghost. I saw a real woman."

"A woman who *disappeared.*" Jimmy wiggled his fingers.

Gavin stood, stretching his arms behind him. "A woman who left the area when I called out to her. I'm not sure what Luella and her tour saw at the lighthouse, but when I saw that woman on the beach, I had a sense that she needed help. Not that she was trying to find her ghostly betrothed."

Dan closed the video camera. "You never know. Sometimes our hunches lead us to people who need us."

Something scraped on the opposite side of the wall, near the bed. Gavin looked over at it.

Dan cupped his hands around his mouth and yelled, "Bryan! You can stop with the scratching. It's over."

A few moments later the young man ran in. "Aw man, I missed it?"

The waves lapped at the shoreline mere feet from where Tara sat on a towel. She watched families play as the tide continued to steal the strip of sand between the water and the large rocks that protected the earthen embankment from erosion. Sunlight danced across the top of the water, and people fished from the nearby pier. Despite the searing heat and thick, humid air, she took a deep breath and dug her toes into warm, cushy sand.

It'd been a long day, a confusing day. She woke this morning to find a bill under her hotel door, thanking her for her stay. When she went down and talked to the management about staying longer, she was told the place was booked. She had to check out. The desk clerk was nice, even made some calls and inquiries for another place Tara could stay, but in the end Tara settled her bill and left her luggage there. She'd called a dozen places too, looking for a room, and had no luck. Her legs ached from a long day of walking, looking for her brothers and stepping into every hotel she could find. It seemed if she called a hotel, it might be easy for them to say they were booked, but she'd thought if she went to the desk, they might find something. They hadn't.

It was nearing five now.

The bottom of her to-go cup was an inch deep in the sand beside her. She'd bought a large iced coffee with her brunch at a nearby restaurant and toted it with her the rest of the day. There were dozens of great places to eat within easy walking distance. Those things were nice, but nothing quite added up. The calendar on her phone said she'd landed here six days ago. Something had to be wrong with the app.

She wrote a text to each brother:

WHERE ARE YOU?

Darryl's phone immediately pinged with the same annoying message about catching up with her soon.

How long from now was *soon*?

She pushed those thoughts aside and tried to enjoy the moment. On the upside of how bizarre she felt, she'd been sleeping a lot, so she was sure she'd sleep well wherever she chose to curl up for the evening. She'd talked to Hadley or Elliott for a few minutes each day, because they both insisted on hearing her voice regularly. Yesterday Hadley had kept her longer than Tara's preferred supershort calls. Sundays were slower paced, and Hadley had insisted on a bit more time with her. These days Tara liked texting rather than talking. It was easier to hide her confusion and mounting fears in a text. When she'd texted Hadley about resting so much, her friend responded that was the best thing she could do right now.

What Tara hadn't texted Hadley was that she'd yet to connect with her brothers and that she no longer had a room to stay in. As a child, when things got crazy like this—like when her mom disappeared for weeks at a time or when social services moved her in with complete strangers—she simply hunkered down, remaining quiet and not drawing any attention to herself until life began to make sense again. She could do this. Sean and Darryl had no idea how vulnerable and half crazy she felt right now, and she wouldn't tell them.

She opened her wallet phone case. One place said they might have confirmation later today of a weeklong cancellation by a guest who didn't think he could make it to St. Simons Island. She was hoping to receive a call or text from them, but her phone indicated she hadn't. If worse came to worst, she could sleep on a park bench tonight, and if she did, when she saw Sean and Darryl, they'd hear about it for life.

The round bottle of Vicodin bulged in her capris pocket. Had she waited long enough to take another pill? Her head didn't hurt, but it really took the edge off her worry, and sometimes she felt like one of those seagulls in flight. She didn't think it was quite time to take another, though.

She set the phone beside her and picked up her coffee, reminding herself to relax. And hoping time didn't jump again. Sometimes she checked the clock or date on the calendar, and it said one thing, and an hour later it showed that a day had passed. Maybe it wasn't that she was losing her mind. Maybe it was the app. But she knew the drill. Keep her head down, tell no one anything, and wait out the madness.

Besides, there were some niceties of this vacation and a pleasant solitude while waiting for her brothers to arrive. But her chest carried a dull ache that hadn't completely gone away since that man chased her down the beach four days ago. It'd felt like a dream—an ominous being in a fireman's uniform chasing her through the darkness as rain blurred her vision. He'd appeared out of nowhere, a man with broad shoulders and a powerful stride trying to get at her. Had the incident really happened?

A panicked shriek pulled Tara from the depth of her lostness. It was like trying to wake from anesthesia. Warmth splashed up the back of Tara's legs. Was she sitting in water? She looked down, and her heart raced. The tide was touching the rocks, and the strip of beach to walk on was under water. She blinked, trying to focus, and a terrified scream shattered every lost, swirling thought.

Was Tara dreaming?

"Mama!" A child screamed.

Tara blinked, desperately trying to see beyond the world that had held her captive of late.

"Daddy!" A little girl, maybe four, was calf deep in water as she clawed at the rocks, trying to hang on. "Somebody! Help me!"

Move!

The deep voice demanding she *move* startled Tara, and she jumped to her feet. Water was inches over Tara's ankles now. How had it come in so quickly? She sloshed as fast as she could, holding out her arms. If the girl lost her balance, she'd hit her head on a sharp rock. "Come, sweetie." Tara reached for the girl. "I'll get you to your mama and daddy."

The little girl looked terrified, but she didn't hesitate. She slung her arms around Tara's neck and held tight. The feel of a tiny body clinging tight was familiar, and Tara ached for bygone days as if something had stolen that time. Tara hurried to the wooden steps, grabbed the rail, and pulled herself out of the sinking sand.

The girl was a featherweight, so once Tara was standing on something solid, she easily scampered up the wooden steps with the child in her arms. A woman facing away from the ocean and toward the climbing trees was yelling, "Isabella!" But the girl in Tara's arms was as limp and unresponsive as a noodle. Were they together, or was the woman looking for a different child?

"Ma'am," Tara yelled as loud as she could while running down the boardwalk.

The woman turned, her face red and panic-stricken. "Isabella!" She had a stroller in front of her, and she wasted no time turning it around and running toward Tara. "I thought I heard her screaming. Is she okay?"

Isabella lifted her head. "Mama!" She reached for her mom and fell against her, sobbing. "Where were you? I couldn't find you."

The woman held her. "I'm sorry, baby. I'm so sorry." She looked at Tara. "Thank you. My husband?"

Tara looked behind her. "I didn't see anyone else." Tara hurried back down the wooden walkway to the edge of the steps. The ocean water had risen and was above the third step now. She didn't see anyone, and when she turned back toward land to tell the woman that, the mother was not there.

For a moment Tara wondered if any part of what had just happened was real. Then she saw the woman marching down the sidewalk as she held the little girl and pushed the stroller. "Where were you?" She stopped in front of a man carrying two large foam cups. She released the stroller and with the flat of her hand hit his chest. "She could've died."

The couple moved their argument down the sidewalk, but their raw emotion felt familiar and consuming. Tara's heart raced with panic as if she were the one faced with losing someone.

A few minutes later the woman returned and hugged Tara. She spoke kindly while introducing herself as Gwen and her husband, Craig. Tara nodded, trying to smile and look normal, but she felt detached and weird. If they noticed it, they didn't call her out on it. The woman's words were muffled, but the sentiment was clear—she was grateful not to lose a life more precious than her own. It made Tara grateful for her brothers. They were all she had, and their lives were more precious than her own. As the man and woman thanked her a dozen times, Tara reached into her pocket to check her phone.

Oh no!

She ran to the far end of the boardwalk. The waters churned, banging against the jutting rocks. Her towel was floating out to sea, but there was no sign of her phone.

"Did you lose something?" Craig was right behind her, peering at the water.

Tara saw no reason to make him feel worse about the incident. "Evidently a towel." She pointed. "And my shoes." At least she'd put Darryl's rock in her suitcase this morning rather than carry it with her.

"We're packed up to head home, and we have towels and a half-dozen pairs of sandals and tennis shoes in our car. Your feet look about my wife's size."

"Something for my feet would help." The pavement was seriously hot, and sometimes the grass had prickly things.

"Sure. Come this way." They walked toward the parking lot.

Did he say they'd checked out of a hotel? "I've been staying at the Lighthouse Inn, and I was hoping to find a new place to stay." She reached into her other pocket and felt a few bills. That's all she had now. The rest of her cash, along with her credit cards and phone, was in her wallet phone case.

"Have you checked into private home rentals along the marsh?" he asked.

She shook her head, her mind spinning about how to replace her credit cards. She'd have to call Hadley or Elliott. They'd have answers. Except . . . she couldn't recall either of their numbers.

She tried to focus. "How do you get there?"

He gave her detailed directions, and Tara tried to take mental notes, but holding a thought had become so very difficult. Life felt like a dream she couldn't wake from, or maybe it felt as if she'd somehow stepped through a portal into a land of scattered, broken thoughts and lost time.

Gwen was in the parking lot, standing outside a vehicle with its doors open. "Everything okay?"

"Yeah. She lost her shoes in the tide."

"Oh. Let us buy you a new pair." Gwen reached for her purse.

Tara shifted from one foot to the other, unable to stand on the hot pavement.

Gwen passed her daughter to Craig. "But let's deal with those burning feet right now." Gwen opened the back of the van and tossed a towel onto the pavement.

Tara hopped onto it.

Gwen pulled a few pairs of athletic shoes from the back of her vehicle. "I have several sizes, ranging from six and a half to seven and a half."

Something caught Tara's eye, and she looked to her right. The man who had chased her down the beach four days ago was standing nearby. At least when she checked her wonky calendar on her phone earlier today, that's how long ago it appeared to be. He was next to a truck, maybe twenty feet away, talking to another guy. Ready or not, she needed to get out of here. "Any size, really. Maybe a seven."

"These. And"—Gwen reached into the vehicle—"socks."

He'd worn a uniform the night he'd chased her but not now. A fireman's uniform? Maybe. The fireman guy looked her way, and he seemed instantly fixated on her. Did he recognize her? If so, would he call her Mary like the others had when they saw her at the lighthouse? Hopefully he had no idea she was the one in the locked lighthouse or on the beach that night. Today she had on big sunglasses, a tank top, and capri pants, and her head was covered by a silky floral scarf. The head covering helped to protect her sutures from sand and sun. She had an inch-wide strip from her temple back that had been shaved, and ocean air tended to flip her hair in every direction, revealing her injury, so she'd covered it.

She needed to find her house and stay there, hidden, quiet, and out of this man's way. Her house? Yeah . . . it had to be around here somewhere, didn't it?

"Wait!" A man called.

Was it fireman guy calling to her or Craig? She didn't stop to find out.

12

G avin knew the locals, and the woman in the floral scarf wasn't one, yet something about her felt familiar, maybe nostalgic, which was really weird. He tried to shake the feeling, but his heart picked up its pace as if he were on his daily run, and his eyes stayed glued to her as she disappeared around a corner.

As a firefighter EMT he saw unspeakable tragedies regularly, so it didn't make sense that he was experiencing an adrenaline rush for no apparent reason. Was it possible he knew her without realizing it? Maybe someone he'd gone to middle or high school with for a few years before she moved away?

He walked over to the man who'd yelled for her to wait. "Everything okay?"

"Yeah." The man looked down at what seemed to be a pair of socks in his wife's hands. "I mean . . ." His brows furrowed, and he glanced at the last spot where the girl had been seen. "Yeah." He shut the hatch to his vehicle.

Gavin closed his eyes for a moment, centering himself. Taking control was second nature to him, and within a few seconds he had his attention back on the samples of antique walnut shiplap in the bed of his truck. He walked back to Roy Ashe, the potential buyer. "I'll have ten thousand square feet of shiplap by nightfall tomorrow." He had been busy for days meticulously gutting Sapphira's house, even sleeping there.

"That's great. It's really tough to find this much antique walnut shiplap, but twenty dollars a square foot? That'll cost two hundred thousand dollars. I'll pay sixteen. Not a penny more."

Gavin needed the cash in hand, but he wasn't bargaining with this builder of fine homes. The man would raise the price by six dollars per square foot for his wealthy clients, and Gavin's gut said he was a bit shady, possibly the kind of developer who shorted his workers regularly.

Gavin closed the tailgate to his truck. "I need to get back to work."

"But . . . we're negotiating."

"I don't think we're getting anywhere." As much as Gavin needed the cash, he wasn't budging. He'd waited nearly two years to dismantle Sapphira's homestead. He knew its value, and he needed every penny of it. "The price is two hundred thousand. Firm."

"Do you have any antique sinks, tubs, lighting fixtures, door knobs— that sort of thing?"

"Tubs and lighting fixtures have been removed. Sinks, doors, and door-knobs are still in place. I'll have eight-inch wide walnut door casings, wain-scot, and similar items soon, but right now I'm still dismantling shiplap."

"Could I take a look at the place?"

Gavin had run an ad in the paper and online. This man was the first to respond. From the start Gavin felt uneasy about him. That's why he'd set up their meeting at the parking lot of Pier Village to show him a sample. He was a builder, and he lived two hours from here. Gavin had nearly a hundred and fifty thousand dollars of reclaimed building materials under a tarp in the carport.

"Not today." Gavin needed to move the goods to a secure place, perhaps back inside the home, but that wouldn't happen between when this man saw it sitting on the driveway and when Gavin fell asleep for the night. "Maybe in a day or two." Gavin tapped the side of his truck. "You can decide and text me about the shiplap, but if someone else is willing to purchase it, I'll sell it."

"I'll take it." The man pulled out his checkbook. "All of it. Will ten thousand dollars hold it until I have my guy get a truck here to pick it up?"

"Sure will. But he needs to bring a cashier's check for a hundred and ninety thousand dollars, and I need it in hand *before* he loads the shiplap."

"Not a problem." He held out the check. "Text me the address, and he'll be there tomorrow night at nine. When you're ready, I'd like to be the first one to see all the rest of it. Okay?"

Gavin nodded and put the check in his billfold.

The voices of tourists faded, and soon Tara focused on her feet as she tried to find her running stride. She had on running shoes. Where did she get them? When did she put them on? If she had on running shoes, why did she still have on her everyday clothes? Her head hurt with each jarring step. She tuned out the questions and focused on running, trying to smooth out the jolts.

Shade trees brought some relief from the heat. Sidewalks disappeared, and the man's directions jumbled in her head, the turns and names of streets becoming too wobbly and gray to remember.

Sweat ran down every part of her, and the sand from the ocean had chafed more skin than not. She stopped and closed her eyes, trying to sense what she needed to do. The heat of the day was waning, and birds were starting to sing their evening song. A weird sensation came over her. Her heart felt like the needle on a compass. She turned in various directions until the hidden compass pulled her onward. She opened her eyes and began walking. The sun hung low in the sky across the open marsh. A dock jutted out from what appeared to be someone's backyard, and its wooden walkway went out into the marsh. She was walking toward the dock when she spotted to her right a blue tarp on the roof of a house she couldn't see.

Home!

Tears welled. She crossed the road and jogged down a short street until she was in the front yard of the house with a blue tarp. It was cute: white clapboard and brick with red trim.

But the only thing that looked familiar was the tarp. Had the workers changed the outside of her home? There was an old-fashioned streetlamp in the front yard, a fenced backyard, and . . . Tara ran to the driveway side.

Oh, how wonderful. There was an outdoor shower, enclosed for privacy. She moved to it, opened the swinging door, and turned on the water. She doubted it was connected to a hot water source, but she stepped in anyway and began peeling out of her clothes. There were soap and shampoo dispensers. She removed her scarf and rinsed the sand, sweat, and grit out of her hair and off her body. Then she lathered up her clothes and rinsed them. The tepid water felt delightful. She turned off the water and wrung out her clothes as best she could. She had no way of drying off, but at least she felt clean again before she put her clothes back on.

She didn't know why her shoes were sopping wet. She'd taken them off while showering, hadn't she? But they squished with water as she walked around the house, looking for signs of life. She put the wet scarf around her shoulders. It seemed a good idea, for the sake of her sutures, to let her hair and the scarf dry before she put it on her head again. Once inside the fenced yard, she saw no fencing along the back of the yard, but there was an orange electric cord running from the house and into a garden.

Oh, a garden. It looked like a nice one, and she was hungry, but she continued walking around the side of the house. One entire exterior wall was glass, and it had five different doors. If this was her house, she had no doubts that Sean and Darryl had left at least one unlocked, maybe all of them. She tried a knob. It was locked, so she continued down the line. The handle of the very last door turned, and she opened it. "Hello?" She stepped inside. "Sean? Darryl?" Part of the roof was missing, and the blue tarp felt familiar. "Hello?"

The house echoed with the sound of her voice, but it seemed she heard Sean answer softly, *You're home.*

Tears welled. She'd felt so very lost for days, and now she was home. Although ... her circumstances didn't really add up. Nonetheless she walked through the rooms. Someone had gutted the place. Why? Numerous walls were missing, and only studs were still in place. Light fixtures were gone, and loose wires hung in their stead. Why would anyone tear apart her house?

She meandered to a set of spiral stairs and climbed them. The loft had a large bed, a full bathroom, and lots of water damage from the hole in the roof. At least the workers had increased the size of Sean's loft. He'd like that. Even so, the walls were stripped bare. She went back downstairs.

Her stomach rumbled. She pulled the wet dollar bills from her pants. Three ones. That wasn't enough to buy dinner. She went into the kitchen. There was a row of five tomatoes on the counter along with a loaf of bread. Just in case this wasn't her house, she put the three ones on the counter and smoothed them.

After locating a cutting board, she sliced a tomato. She found mayo and deli cheese in the fridge, so she added that to her sandwich and plopped it on a plate. While eating she meandered again through the house. One antique door was locked. On a stripped wall with a lone nail, she spotted a skeletal key. She tried it, but it didn't budge. After setting her plate on the floor, she tried again. With a bit of jiggling and a shove of her hip against the door, it finally opened.

She remained in the doorway. Faint chills ran down her arms. The walls were intact. Moreover, they were covered with framed and unframed pictures and paintings.

Giggles and laughter filled the room. Love was everywhere—drops of sunlight falling like rain.

The room had two easels, art supplies, and lots of pictures. It had layers of dust, as though it were a shrine. Where was she? Why did this house feel like home while looking completely unfamiliar? Dusk had settled in, making it a little hard to see. A photograph lay on a paint-stained counter, and she picked it up.

It was of the St. Simons lighthouse, and it was similar to the one Tara had from her childhood. An older woman and a little girl were side by side, looking at each other. The girl was grinning, and the woman's eyes held love. The girl had blond hair, and something else about her seemed a bit familiar. Tara flipped the picture and viewed the back.

Sapphira and her precious Siobhan, 1991

Loneliness wrapped around Tara anew, and she was envious of the girl whose name she didn't know how to pronounce. What must it have been like to be loved by someone while growing up? She put the picture back where she'd found it.

She hadn't been loved as a child, not by any relative. But she had Sean and Darryl now, and that was enough. They were a family that knew how to be there for one another, how to be a safety net, except she currently couldn't find them.

Her imagination beckoned her to forget reality and enjoy the moment. In her mind's eye she saw the woman showing the little girl how to make certain paint strokes and how to mix colors. The girl giggled. "Like this, Nana?" She swooped a glop of paint across the canvas.

"You're a natural." Nana smiled, but it soon faded. She took the little girl's hand and crouched beside her. "Our time is running out."

"I don't want to go. Please don't make me."

Tears trailed down the woman's face, but she smiled. "You'll be fine. I promise."

"I want to stay with you."

"I want that too, my sweet Siobhan. I want you here with me."

Was that how *Siobhan* was pronounced—*Shivaun*?

The older woman held the girl's chin. "You're amazing, Siobhan. You remember that. I've prayed for you, and you'll be fine. I'm sure of it. But remember wherever you go, whatever happens, this is *your* house and your home. Yours. Do you understand me?"

The girl nodded.

"What's the address, Siobhan?"

The little girl repeated it.

"That's right." The woman kissed her face a dozen times, and Tara could feel it on her skin. "You always remember that. I can't keep your mama from taking you. I tried. I hired a lawyer, and we did our best. Still, I have no legal right to hinder her plans, but I'll always be here. This home will always be here for you."

The voices faded, and when Tara opened her eyes, her cheeks were wet from the emotion the dreamlike scene had stirred in her.

Voices broke through her thoughts. Were these real, or were they her imagination playing games with her like Nana's and Siobhan's voices?

Women laughed, and Tara knew they were real.

"I just need to set this inside, and we'll be on our way."

Inside?

Tara left the art room, tiptoeing until she was able to peek around a hallway wall so she could see the glass doors.

The lone unlocked door was open now, and four women were hovering just outside it. "It breaks my heart to tear down Sapphira's house. She spent more than twenty years holding on to this place, neither moving nor renting it, all in hopes that Siobhan would return."

Siobhan? Why would Tara have imagined saying that name right?

"Oh, honey," a woman said, "we know all that, but you keep saying it as often as you need to."

"Look," one of the women gasped, and Tara thought she'd been spotted.

"There's a purple hydrangea blooming amid the pink ones."

"Is that on the same bush?" one asked.

"Yeah. Look."

The women stepped away from the door, and Tara used their distraction to scurry through the living room and kitchen and out the side door, which put her on the driveway. She looked for somewhere to go for cover until they were gone. If the house was sitting empty, she could come back and sleep in it once the women were gone, right? She scanned the nearby properties.

The garden.

She hurried across the backyard, slipped between rows of corn, and crouched. Her heart pounded, and as the minutes passed, she sat in the dirt, waiting. Sugar snap peas dangled from the vine in large clusters. She pulled the damp scarf off her neck and tied the ends of it to create a cloth carrier, and as she picked the sugar snaps, she put them in the scarf. She ate one and found it succulent and tender. They would make a nice breakfast.

After picking about four cups of sugar snaps, she was overwhelmed with tiredness and sank to a comfortable sitting position.

Who was she? What was she doing stowing away in someone's garden? She'd been through a lot in life, but she couldn't recall ever feeling this disconnected. Sleepiness took over, and she rested her head on her hands. Mosquitoes bit and other things too, but she was too sleepy to care.

Metal banged, and Tara bolted upright. Blackness was everywhere. Where was she, and why was she covered in dirt? She got up, still holding a scarf full of sugar snaps. A light shone from somewhere, illuminating a path, so she followed it.

Moments later a woman screamed, a bloodcurdling howl, and then she clutched her chest. "What are you . . ."

The woman looked behind her, and Tara saw a small house she'd not noticed before. "Thief!" The woman pointed. "Luella. Dell. Sue Beth! Someone's stealing our crop!"

Three women came barreling out of the building. "Julep! Are you okay?" someone asked.

One woman banged something metal against a pot. Another had a flashlight, but she dropped it, and the last . . . had a gun!

Tara released the scarf and took off running.

13

Luella's stomach rumbled as a waiter passed her and Charles's table at Café Frederica. The man balanced a heaping tray of food and headed toward a larger group. Oh, what divine smells! She savored the fragrance of the salty-tangy hollandaise sauce that came on the café's eggs Benedict, which she'd ordered. The mouthwatering smell of breakfast—the savory scent of cooked bacon mingling with orange juice, eggs, and fresh-roasted coffee—filled the dining room.

Charles spilled some sugar while pouring it into his coffee. He almost dropped his spoon while putting it into his mug to stir the coffee. Was he nervous?

"So what's the farthest from the island you've ever traveled?" He set the spoon on a napkin. "I've met a few people here who say they haven't left Glynn County. But I don't think that's you."

"Very true." Luella drummed her fingers against the laminated table-cloth. "Hmm, I think the farthest I've been was Prague, when I was in college. It was a study-abroad program." Flashes of the long-ago trip popped up in her mind—the six-hundred-year-old, multicolor, multiplated astronomical clock and strands of opera music sung by voices that were nothing less than angelic. The trip had changed her perspective on life and her goals. That was the beginning of her longing to travel and understand history. "You?"

"Actually, until I was employed by Seaside Properties, I'd hardly ventured outside the Northeast. My dad owned a hotel in upstate New York. I worked there while growing up and helped when I could after college. When Dad retired, I took over, and I never really needed to travel for work, and I had responsibilities that kept me close to home. About the time my life had some real freedom, Seaside Properties offered to buy the hotel. I helped broker a deal my dad would accept, and then my dad agreed to sell it. The company hired me to manage properties for them. Since then I've traveled some, managing a property for about a year, just until I get things running smoothly. Then someone takes over for me, and I go elsewhere. It's allowed me to finally see a few new places, and I love it."

"So basically you waltz in, straighten out any issues caused by the buyout, and leave?"

He nodded. "Pretty much."

Had he been single his whole life? Few were. Her own choice to willingly forgo marriage and family life in order to travel and write didn't work for most people. It would be nice to hear a bit about his story. "Any children?"

"Two, and good ones. A son and daughter. Do you have kids?"

"No. Never married, never had children." She didn't want to elaborate, but why? Maybe her reasoning would sound pathetic to him. "Where have you traveled to recently?"

He leaned back, smiling and looking relaxed. "I've spent a lot of time in DC helping to reopen a hotel that had been through extensive remodeling. I visited the Smithsonian so many times while I was there that I think even blindfolded I could lead anyone through the museum by this point."

"Lots of history there, of course. But I'm afraid the most time I've spent at the Smithsonian is a day."

Their waiter came back and set two steaming plates on their table. After thanking her, Charles bent his head to bless his food. Luella did as well.

The food tasted every bit as good as she'd anticipated.

Charles swallowed a bite of his blueberry-stuffed French toast. "This is tasty. Thanks for the recommendation."

"St. Simons doesn't have a huge variety of restaurant choices if you're used to a big city. Still, we've had lots of growth and new businesses pop up in recent years." Both a boon and a hassle for Blue Sails. Luella hated the fact that competition had been eating into the store's profits.

He speared a blueberry with his fork and gestured to her. "But your shop has been a St. Simons Island landmark, yes?"

"We've been in business a long time, but I don't know if you'd call it a landmark. And it's really Julep's shop. She foots the bills and does the lion's share of the work. The rest of us pay her a little rent and lend a hand when time allows."

"The relationship between you and your friends is like nothing I've run into before." He chuckled. "I've heard several interesting and conflicting things about you Glynn Girls from other locals."

Was this her opportunity to talk about the property? "And you were left wanting to know more?" She used her knife to cut another bite of the eggs, ham, and English muffin.

He shrugged, but he was smiling. "My interest is piqued, yeah."

She set her utensils down, leaned forward, and held up a finger. "I'd be happy to tell you some of the Glynn Girls' most humorous and prized secrets. But we'd need to go on a second date somewhere more private."

"More private?" His green eyes held an emotion she couldn't define.

"Yeah. In return I'd like you to seriously listen to me explain why it's so important to let us girls have that prime spot for the store." What could she say to help him warm up to the idea? "If you'll let us rent that store, I'll even throw in telling my tour groups that your hotel is most definitely *not* haunted. Nope. Just a quiet old building. Stay there and you'll sleep like a baby."

Charles studied her. "Is this some sort of a barter system you use, Miss Ward? Trading dates for favors?"

Realization of what she'd said hit hard and fast. She sat straight up.

"Wait." She splayed her hands toward him, making the table shake. "I-I didn't mean . . ."

He held her gaze. "As tempting as that offer is, a pretty face and interesting conversation can't sway a business decision."

"Oh . . . that sounded so horrible, didn't it?" She was too embarrassed to think. "I'm not like *that*. I mean, I go on dates, but . . ." She trailed off as she realized he was chuckling through closed lips. "You're messing with me!"

"Guilty. Sorry. But add this conversation to the picnic and you Glynn Girls trying to butter up Stan and Rick . . . Well, I had to harass you a little."

Luella laughed. "That picnic plan wasn't my idea. I went along with it because we're getting a little desperate. It's a long, convoluted story that includes Julep losing her husband and debts piling up. Julep needs several things: a shop on a corner so Blue Sails isn't hidden in a row of stores and more space so the sales floor can be expanded and more space for us girls. Blue Sails could sell more furniture if we carried a larger selection. I'm sorry if I'm being bold, but I can't stomach you giving the best location on St. Simons Island to someone less deserving than Julep."

His smile fell a little. "I admire your loyalty and tenacity, but—"

"If you would just hear me out, I know it would make a difference." Luella could feel the door of opportunity closing.

"Luella, I've heard enough. You're an intelligent, educated woman. You must know it's never a good idea to allow someone's personal struggles to sway a business decision. They are separate matters, and they need to stay that way. It would do more harm than good if you share too much about the store's financials, so let's just stick to other topics."

She wanted to hit the table, but she kept herself in control. Oh, she just had to help him understand! But he was right. She was pouring out emotions about her personal connection to the store owner, and he needed business information. "St. Simons goes through small businesses like an ice cream truck goes through Popsicles in the summertime. But Blue Sails has been profitable and stable from the start. Julep is savvy when it comes to home furnishings and making a steady income. When her husband, Mitch, died, it threw her for a loop and caused a few financial issues. But all we need is a better location to make up for the extra she owes."

Charles took a sip of his coffee. "I'm sorry losing her husband has been so hard on her."

"Yeah, it's been hard. Both Julep and Mitch had been lifelong smokers, although Julep quit the day Mitch was diagnosed with end-stage lung cancer."

He nodded. "My mom was a smoker. It gave her emphysema."

Luella fidgeted with her cup. "I'm sorry to hear that. Mitch didn't know he was sick until it was too late. The doctors gave him only a few months to live. I've been close to Julep most of our lives, but I'd never seen her struggle with anything like she did the news that she would lose Mitch. They'd been in love since they were teens."

"I'm sure watching his health decline was a nightmare." His voice was soft.

"It would've been, but he didn't die of cancer. At some point along the line, he decided to give people on the island the best New Year's fireworks display they'd ever seen."

Charles cringed a little as if he knew what was coming.

Luella sighed. "But something went wrong. We're not sure what. Mitch was in a small, uninsured boat just off a private marina with all the fireworks." Luella closed her eyes, taking a moment to regroup. "The boat exploded, taking out some of the marina."

"How long ago?"

"Eighteen months, and the event—both the fireworks going off and Mitch's death—were so over-the-top that the whole county hasn't stopped talking about either of them. If Mitch had been thinking clearly, he would've known better than to set off fireworks without the proper authorization, but I believe his recent diagnosis had him too addled to think. Anyway, the damage was far more than Mitch's life insurance covered. Julep's mortgaged her house and pulled equity out of the shop."

Charles studied her, both brows raised, and she realized that without meaning to she'd ventured back into emotional territory and shared too much that had nothing to do with good business sense.

She leaned in. "Okay, so she now owes rent and an equity payment each month, but Julep's business isn't a gamble. She's turned a profit for twenty years."

"I'm sure she has."

Luella waited for him to elaborate, but he said nothing else. They finished their breakfasts in silence. Should she prompt him to say anything more?

The waiter dropped off the bill as he walked by. Luella reached for the black check holder. "I'll pay for it. I'm the one monopolizing the conversation."

"No, no. I invited you." Charles scooped it up before Luella could grab it, stuck a credit card in the slot, and handed it back to the waiter when he passed by on the opposite side of the table.

Luella had been on enough dates to know when one was dead in the water. They'd started out clicking so well. What had happened?

He drew a deep breath and let it out slowly. "Some of this is my fault, but I wish you hadn't shared with me the financial aspect of Julep's dilemma. I *can't* give you that vacancy you want."

"What?" A few diners nearby looked up from their meals. She flashed them a mind-your-own-business look. "Why?"

He rubbed his temples. "You just told me about the debt involved, and the only purpose of getting a larger store with more overhead is so she can purchase more goods from the wholesalers, which will be even more debt. If your business goes into bankruptcy, we're tied up in the court system, unable to make you move out right away and unable to collect rent owed—or most of it anyway. As it stands, we have several other surefire applicants."

What had she done?

The server returned to the table and handed him the finished check. Charles nodded at him and filled out the tip and signed the receipt. "Part of the mistake was mine. I didn't mean to ask questions that would cause you to share the store's debt, and I shouldn't have invited you, knowing you were part of the group attached to this bid."

They picked up their belongings and left the restaurant.

How could she have messed up this situation even more? What was she going to say to the girls? "Charles, please just tell me you'll give our proposal a fair look. Don't take what I said over a friendly breakfast as a reason not to do so."

He nodded. "I intend to. But you've raised some red flags."

Yep. Like she stuck her foot in her mouth again. The way she did every time she got near Chuck.

14

A welcome breeze came through the open windows of the back bedroom as Gavin gently pried a walnut board away from the stud, using a hammer and small crowbar. Once he'd created a small space between the shiplap and stud, he slid the crowbar into his tool belt and grabbed the thin, but sturdy, pry bar. He eased it between the two pieces of wood and tapped the hammer against it. Splitting the shiplap would ruin it, and he needed every square inch to meet his quota.

He tried to stay focused and keep his hands steady, but he longed to nap for a bit. The king-size mattress upstairs was a moldy mess from the storm that took off the roof last spring, but the twin-size mattress on the floor in the living room called to him. That's where he'd slept of late, but it would probably be midnight before he gave in to the desire. His two twenty-four-hour shifts had allowed for little sleep this week. It seemed as though every time the EMTs and firemen returned to the station to sleep, another call came in, which was fairly typical during tourist season. What wasn't usual was his working every free second on dismantling a house. When the work wasn't so painstaking, he'd ask his buddies to help him.

"Knock, knock." His mom's voice echoed through the empty house.

"In the back bedroom."

His mom stopped in the doorway. "Hey." She had a lunch tote in hand, hopefully with lots of food for him.

"Hi." He angled the pry bar slightly and tapped it more. Once he created enough space between the stud and shiplap, he'd slide a pair of metal shears between them and cut the nail. He'd discovered that was the best way to free the shiplap from the stud without splitting it. "Did you find what you were looking for last night?"

"Was I looking for something?" His mom's brows furrowed.

"I think so. When you came by to drop off dinner—which was quite tasty, so thank you—you or one of the girls went into Sapphira's painting room."

Before Sapphira passed, she'd been very clear that the painting room was to be left untouched for as long as possible, giving Siobhan to the last minute to come home and claim everything inside that room. Of course Saffy had no idea they would dismantle her beautiful home and sell it off bit by bit. She had, however, expected them to move into it or sell it. But removing the home was the only way they could divide the property in half and sell each part to a builder.

"None of us girls went in there, Gavin. We were inside this house for less than sixty seconds before driving to Brunswick to shop for a new lantern for tomorrow night's annual celebration on the marsh."

Gavin withheld a sigh. His mamas and their annual reciting of the poem in period clothing seemed really out there to him, but he held his tongue.

"That aside"—his mom fluttered her hands—"it reminds me of why I'm here. You need to watch your reclaimed goods closer. Get them off the driveway."

"A man is coming in about three hours, and we'll load all the shiplap onto his truck, so no need to worry about that."

"Good, because there was a thief hiding out in our garden last night. We scared her off."

"Oh, good gravy, Mom. No one likes vegetables enough to hide out in a hot garden and steal them. You sure it wasn't a bunny?" He put the pry bar and hammer in his tool belt and slid the metal shears in place.

"Yeah, yeah. I know. You think I'm full of nonsense all the time. But I know what I saw, and after you chased a vanishing woman down the beach last week, I'd hoped you'd have a bit more respect for what people see. There is no proof you saw anyone, but you did."

"True." He squeezed the shears, trying to put enough pressure to cut the nail without adding stress to the antique walnut plank. "But your creature was a little bitty scared rabbit who happened to startle you." He grimaced, hoping all pressure was being applied to the right spot.

She pulled a piece of material out of her purse. "You think a bunny was wearing this?"

Gavin's heart lurched, and he clenched the nail cutters. The nail popped. He studied the plank, and thankfully his sudden movement hadn't caused it to split.

It looked like the scarf the woman was wearing yesterday, the one who'd grabbed his attention and then disappeared. What was it about her that intrigued him? He was a nose-to-the-grindstone kind of guy, and any female close to his age was nothing but trouble. He'd learned that by the ripe age of twelve. He'd been overweight, and the girls at school and church had made him a target, taking out their angst and insecurity on him.

"Mom, there were three wrinkled and damp dollar bills on the counter last night."

"Were they my tip?"

He studied her. Like an unsuspecting wave crashing in, he suddenly realized what was going on. The woman who'd disappeared on the beach. A woman with a similar build beside his truck yesterday. The opened door to Sapphira's room. The scarf. The missing food. The three dollars. The wet pavement and footprints near the outdoor shower.

He closed the gap between them. "So you're in cahoots with the firemen on this one, huh?" He took the scarf from her and shoved it into his shorts pocket. "I'll keep this. Someone will want it, and I'm not giving it back without a payoff of some type. But I'm proud of you, Mom."

She seemed confused. "I'm in cahoots with no one . . . except the girls in trying to get a better shop and you concerning Sapphira's house so the debtors don't take our home. Okay, fine, I'm in cahoots plenty, but not with the firemen. You think the guys put that woman up to hiding in our garden?"

"It's sounding that way."

She set the lunch tote on the floor. "Two of your favorite sandwiches."

"Thanks."

"We set a trap in the garden, and it's attached to an air horn, so if you hear it go off, call the police."

"So they can arrest a terrified bunny? Or maybe it'll be the woman the firemen hired to pull a prank."

"Gavin, I'm serious. It was a real woman, not a rabbit, and even if your pals hired her, which I seriously doubt, she had no right to steal our food. That garden is our contribution to the needy—from selling the food and donating the money, to giving fresh produce, to canning it—and we work hard for the yield."

"Ah, now I get it. You're going gangbusters to keep anyone from taking produce because you intend to win the annual competition of whose garden has the largest harvest for the needy."

She huffed. "Maybe." She angled her head. "We did the gardening work, and we get to use its produce however *we* choose, not some thieving misfit who is hungry because she smoked too much pot."

Whatever else he thought of his mom's little speech, he was convinced she wasn't in on the prank his firehouse buddies were pulling. "Fine. If I hear an air horn, I'll rush over there and set the intruder straight." He chuckled. "So where are you off to all gussied up in gardening clothes?"

She appeared to be freshly showered, hair done, and makeup on, but she had on her clean but stained and slightly worn work clothes.

"The Keenagers are collecting produce, washing it, and divvying it up into pecks to sell at the farmer's market early tomorrow morning. All proceeds go to the needy."

"I thought the whole idea of the Keenager group was to have fun—keen old-timers reliving their youth."

"It's not the whole idea, no. Even the church teens work to give back to the community."

"As long as it's not to a hungry thief, right?"

His mom rolled her eyes. "What if she's out to destroy our garden just because she can? But we've fixed that. Thieves take because they can, but she'll be in for a huge surprise if she comes back."

Gavin paused. "What did you—"

"Julep?" Dell rushed inside. "There you are." She grabbed her hand. "We're late." She waved at Gavin. "Hey, handsome. I'd love to chat, but bye." She threw him a kiss without so much as a pause.

Gavin set his tools aside and ate a few bites of a sandwich before returning to his work. Dusk fell, and his muscles ached, but there wasn't time to take a break. He'd promised Roy Ashe ten thousand square feet of shiplap by nightfall, and it would take every minute to make that happen.

Dusk eased into the room, stealing his light. He attached three clamp work lights to various studs and angled them at the wall he was dismantling.

A blasting horn pierced the air, and someone screamed.

Seriously?

"Not funny, guys," he mumbled. "I've got too much work to do." While slipping the hammer and pry bar into his tool belt, he went through the house. Soon he was crossing the backyard. The air horn finally shut off. He pulled out his tactical flashlight and swept its beam across the thick foliage of the garden. He saw what appeared to be white skin or maybe clothing. "Get caught, did ya?" He grabbed his phone from his pocket and dialed Lieutenant Jimmy.

"Hey, Gavin." The man sounded pleased to hear from him. "What's up?"

"I don't have time for this." He plowed through the rows of corn.

"Okay." Jimmy laughed. "You need a hand with something?"

Gavin stepped out of the cornfield and paused the light on a woman in the middle of the sugar peas, fighting to get free of barbwire. "My mamas, the four of them, set a trap for your hired help. I imagine, since they used barbwire, that she may need medical assistance. I like a prank as well as the next person, but this needs to stop."

The woman tried to back away from him, and she yelped in pain. Gavin shined the light in her face, and that one glimpse changed his tone. She had terror on her face, and if she was acting, she needed to be in Hollywood, not on this island.

"So is she real this time, man?" Jimmy asked.

Gavin realized he still had the phone to his ear. "I'll need to call you later." He ended the call and put the cell in his pocket. He shoved the flashlight vertically in his tool belt so it gave light without being intrusive. "It's okay, ma'am. I'm here to help."

She shook her head and tried to move away from him. "They called the police. The woman holding the gun said they would."

A gun? Did the Glynn Girls pull a gun on this woman? Well, whatever was going on, she definitely wasn't a rabbit, and he was beginning to think she wasn't hired to pull a prank either. He saw a shiny liquid running down the woman's arm, and he'd seen that same thing under the light of the moon too many times not to recognize it. She was bleeding.

"My name is Gavin, and I'm an EMT. I want to help you, okay?"

"You chased me down the beach . . . in a uniform."

"Ah, that was you. I didn't mean to scare you. I was in my fireman's uniform." There was no way he could get close to her with metal cutters until she trusted him. "I told you my name. It's Gavin. What's your name?"

Her breathing was short and shallow, and he wanted to free her before she passed out. If she went limp right now, she'd be punctured with a dozen barbs. What were his mom and the girls thinking to do this?

"Mary."

Okay, so maybe this was part of an acting skit. Was that real blood and real barbs or not? He ran a finger across a nearby piece of wire. Yep, it was real. But he'd bet money that wasn't her name. It would be too big a coincidence, even for such a common name.

"Okay. I'm going to step closer, and I want you to remain in place. Can you do that?"

She gave a slight nod.

"Look." He held up the metal cutters. "Five to seven snips with this, and you'll be free. Okay?"

Again she nodded.

"Good. Very good." He moved in closer, half expecting floodlights to come on and his buddies to start applauding and laughing, calling him gullible. But on the chance she could be for real, he continued onward. "Are you hungry? Is that why you're here?"

"I lost my phone, cash, and credit cards at the beach yesterday when the tide came in."

"I'm sorry to hear it. The tides catch a lot of people off guard." He removed the flashlight from his belt and lowered the beam. "I just need to look in your eyes and check your pulse before we cut you free from the barbwire. Okay?"

"Why?"

"I need to know if I should call for an ambulance."

"No!" She jerked one way and then another, trying to get free. "I'm not crazy. I . . . I'm waiting for my brothers."

Why would she use the word *crazy*? Had the word been used against her, or was her thinking so addled she felt that way?

"That's good about your brothers. Very good." He kept his voice on soothe mode. "I'll help you find them, but they would want you to get medical help if need be."

"I don't need it."

"Then let's prove that together. Okay?"

She scowled at him. "Fine."

"Good decision. You're doing well. Just take a few deep breaths." Usually he'd call people by name when he was helping them through an ordeal. It was soothing and reassuring to them, but he didn't believe Mary was her name. He stepped close enough to touch her. "I'm going to use the flashlight and look in your eyes." He did as he'd said and realized her pupils were large, as if she was on a narcotic, and one pupil was more dilated than the other, which often meant a concussion. But each pupil responded to the light. He caught a glimpse of what seemed to be a suture. He turned the light to it. "You've recently been hurt, haven't you?"

She nodded. "Surgery."

Her hair had been shaved an inch wide, and the cut and sutures were clearly done by a surgeon. "Yes, I can see that. What medication are you taking?"

"Vico . . . something."

"Vicodin. It's powerful." It could disorient and confuse her as well as make her overwhelmingly sleepy, dizzy, and have poor judgment. "Is it helping with the pain?"

She nodded. "You don't need to call for help."

He was sure she needed to be seen, but it wasn't an emergency situation. "I agree."

She relaxed at his words, and her knees almost buckled.

He cupped his hand under her elbow and steadied her. Whatever else was going on, she was terrified of an authority uncovering her secrets. "It's just us." He flashed the light at her feet. "You balanced."

"Yeah."

He studied her. She was about his age and absolutely beautiful.

Her eyes were brimming with tears. "Where are the mountains?"

An ache for her made his heart shiver. "The mountains are at home, I imagine. And my guess is someone is missing you. But we'll figure all of that out. I promise." He passed her the flashlight. "I'm going to get my metal cutters out of my tool belt. Are we good?"

"Yeah."

"You hold the light on the spots while I cut, okay?"

"Thank you," she whispered.

A surreal feeling seemed to float from the far reaches of the planet and settle around him, as though for a moment he'd connected with the real woman hiding underneath the odd behavior and confusion.

"Not a problem." He snipped here and there, cutting out sections of barbwire and tossing them to the side. How did the Glynn Girls intend to get back into the garden with this much barbwire everywhere? And how much damage had they done to their plants in the process? "Do you remember how you got to St. Simons Island?"

"By plane."

"Do you know when you arrived?"

"Last week, maybe Tuesday."

"And today is Tuesday again, so seven days ago."

"Yeah, my phone said about that before it drowned."

"Your phone told you when you arrived?"

"I keep losing track of time, and the calendar had notes of when my plane arrived, and it highlights each new day."

"It's good that you're clearheaded enough to know you were losing time and how to center yourself. That says good things about you."

She wiped her forehead, looking a bit agitated, but she didn't say anything.

"Problem?"

"I don't need you to assure me I'm worthy of breathing air. Okay?"

Somehow standing under the silvery moon while inside a garden felt like déjà vu, but that made no sense.

"Okay." He cut another section of barbwire. "Your head injury— Did that happen before or after you arrived?"

"Before."

Things were already making a little sense, but he wouldn't ask for her name again. It would make him sound as if he didn't trust her, which he didn't, but sounding that way put people on the defensive, and an EMT's goal was to calm victims and win their trust.

"Okay, just a few more snips. I'm on your side. You know that. So could you do me a favor and come inside? I need to tend to the cuts and scrapes." He also needed to get enough information to reach out to her family. "My mom has a good first aid kit." He gestured toward his house.

The young woman's eyes grew large, and she backed away as far as the remaining barb would allow. "One of the women who live here is your mom?"

Disappointment with his mom twisted inside him. He needed to talk to her about this, about how to treat people even in the face of fear. "No one's home right now. It'll be just you and me, but when Mom realizes what she's done, she'll be so very sorry. I'm a pretty good cook. I could fix you a plate of food, maybe some French toast, bacon, and a nice glass of cold milk. Do you like milk?"

She nodded.

"Good." He removed the last barbwire.

She glanced at the house and then behind her, and he feared she would bolt.

"It's safe. I promise. I won't let anyone threaten, chase, or yell at you."

She aimed the flashlight at his face. He clenched his eyes shut before trying to open them, hoping to look as nonthreatening as he knew how.

He gestured for them to start walking toward the house. "How did you get hurt?"

"I got them out. I called and ran and ran, and I got them out before the tree fell."

He was sure that made sense inside her head, but he wasn't able to put too much together from it. "A limb of a falling tree injured your head?"

She nodded.

He reached inside his pocket and pulled out the keys to his mom's house. He unlocked the door, flipped on the light inside the kitchen, and waited on the young woman to go inside first.

"Who did you get out?" He went to the medicine cabinet and got the first aid kit.

"My brothers." She nodded her head, reminding him of a bobblehead doll. She looked as if she was caught in a conversation inside herself. "I did. I got them out. They're all I have." Her eyes filled with tears. "Everything. All of it. There is nothing else. And I . . . I got them out."

He'd seen a lot in his years as an EMT. Knowing people and trauma as he did now, he wasn't sure she had gotten them out.

"You can sit right here." He pulled out a tall barstool.

She sat. "I was out for an early-morning run while they slept, and a storm came out of nowhere." Her eyes reflected confusion. "I reached them. I did. I reached them." She kept mumbling that same phrase while Gavin cleaned out the cuts on her arms, dabbed ointment on them, and covered them with Band-Aids.

Several car doors slammed.

The young woman stood, fear radiating from her eyes.

"It's okay. You're safe. They'll apologize to you, every one of them." Gavin motioned for her to sit, but she backed farther away.

She pointed at his face. "No." She glanced toward the garage door and then glanced at the side door, evidently plotting her escape. "Thank you." She touched her arm near one of her puncture wounds. "I . . . I owe you."

"You're confused and hungry. We can help."

"We did it." His mom's voice was clear, coming from the driveway and heading their way. "We won again."

The young woman bolted out the side door. Gavin followed her.

She turned and held up her hand. "No!"

He stopped, although he wasn't sure why. Maybe because he thought a second encounter with the Glynn Girls would be more traumatizing than her spending another night on her own in the balmy night air. She disappeared into the darkness.

"Gavin?" His mom came out of the house. "What are you doing here?"

"You caught someone in your trap, and I had to cut her loose, literally. Really showed her who's the boss, Mom, and even inflicted more pain on an already injured woman."

Mom looked toward the area where the girl had disappeared. "I'm sorry, but she was stealing."

"She was hungry." He went back inside.

"Then why not knock on the door and tell us that?" Sue Beth asked.

"Yeah." Mom followed behind him.

"More injuries?" Dell asked.

"She's recently had a head injury and surgery. I saw the sutures." He put the first-aid items back into the kit. "Someone somewhere is missing her. I'll make a few calls and see what I can find out." He closed the kit. "If you see her again, try being less fearful and mean."

"We're not scared." Mom scowled and put her hands on her hips. "And we're never, ever mean."

"You used barbwire to booby-trap someone who was hungry, someone who left what seems to be her last three dollars on the counter at Sapphira's to pay for the tomato, cheese, and two slices of bread she ate."

"If she's so innocent, why did she run?"

"Uh, last time you saw her, you ran at her and yelled at her. Did one of you actually brandish a gun?"

"Not a real gun," Dell said. "It was that wooden one your dad made for you and painted black when you were little. I guess in the dark it looked real."

"That aside, it's illegal to set a booby trap. Maybe you should call the police on yourselves."

"Illegal?" Sue Beth gasped. "Then what Luella said earlier tonight was true."

He looked at Luella. She held up her hands. "When your mom screamed for help, I ran outside banging pots and yelling to scare off whoever had frightened her, but I wasn't a part of setting the trap. We came back here to disassemble it."

"She's right," Mom said. "When Luella told us it was illegal to set a trap, we left what we were doing and came here. Still, there should be some way to keep no-count people out of our garden."

"No account?" Gavin could hardly believe his ears. Had she not heard him describe the young woman as traumatized and injured? His mom had struggled emotionally since his dad died, but in this moment he hardly recognized her. This wasn't a matter of her gut saying a particular someone may not be trustworthy. This was her judging everyone who was in a bad situation as less worthy than herself. "Mom, are you proud of me being a fireman?"

"Very much so, but what's your point?"

"If firemen thought the way you just expressed, we'd need proof of someone's worthiness before being willing to put our lives on the line. It's wise to be cautious, Mom, but you crossed over into thinking you're better than someone in need."

"It sounds like she'll return. If not here, then to Sapphira's place," Luella said. "We'll get some fresh produce and put it in baskets for her. Maybe clothing too?"

He nodded. "She seems to have only what's on her back."

"Oh, the poor thing." Dell dug through her purse and pulled out her phone. "What size is she? I'll buy her a couple of shirts and shorts and underwear."

"That's just asking for trouble," Sue Beth said.

Dell rolled her eyes slightly. "Gavin, any idea what size?"

"No, but I'd guess she's about five feet, five inches, a hundred and fifteen pounds."

Dell typed the info into her phone. "We'll go out immediately and get some things for her. Right, girls?"

"Yeah," Julep said.

"I'm in too, I guess." Sue Beth nodded. "Seems like I've been too busy sounding like my grandma did about her garden."

Luella glanced at the clock. "The only clothing store I know of that's still open is the boutique on Market Street, and it closes in thirty minutes. We better move it." She held open the door, and the four of them hurried back to the car.

Gavin needed to get back to work. Before he left his mom's house, a loud beeping sound echoed in the quiet. It dawned on him that it was a work truck of some type backing up. Hadn't he heard that same sound about thirty minutes ago? He'd been so focused on the woman that he hadn't realized he'd heard it until now. The buyer! Oh no, no, no. He stormed out of the house and across the backyard of his mom's house to Sapphira's property.

The dim light of the carport reflected against the flat blue tarp where shiplap used to be. He lifted the tarp. All the shiplap was gone. He went to the mailbox to see if the man had left the check there. He hadn't. Gavin hurried inside, half hoping to find a check but expecting to find the wood was gone.

He was relieved to discover the stacks of shiplap inside the house were still there. He pulled his phone out of his pocket and called the buyer. He got a voice mail.

"Mr. Ashe, this is Gavin Burnside. The shiplap has been picked up. We need to discuss payment ASAP." But Gavin knew that tracking the man down and actually getting paid wasn't likely. He wouldn't give up easily. There had to be people in the neighborhood with surveillance cameras.

He looked up, staring at the water-stained ceiling. "I needed this sale."

"I . . . I got them out. I did." The whispery voice echoed through the room.

Gavin eased across the floor, searching for "Mary." He spotted her sitting on his mattress, holding her knees and rocking back and forth.

"I called. I reached them. I got them out in time." She looked up at him. "I did."

Great. Just what he wanted, absolutely no place to rest while he stayed here all night to keep watch over what was left of the shiplap. He sighed. "Yeah, I heard that same thing." He motioned at the mattress. "Go on. Lie down. You need sleep."

She raked her fingers through her hair, pulling it away from her face. "Why are you in my house?"

"What?"

Her eyelids opened slowly, looking heavy. "We've met." She gestured at his tool belt. "You're here to fix my roof, aren't you?"

"Uh, maybe." What was he supposed to say? "But why I'm here aside, one of us needs to sleep. I volunteer you."

She drew a breath, shaking her head as if trying to ward off the sleepiness. A moment later her eyes searched his. "We need to talk about your work. You're taking too much of my house apart. I don't understand."

"I'm sure you don't. It might make more sense in the morning." But only if her thinking cleared, and he doubted that one night's sleep would make *that* much difference.

"I didn't let that man take any shiplap from inside. He tried. Wanted the wood. I said no. You had no right to sell any shiplap."

"You saw the man?"

"Yeah. Brusk, mean man." She rubbed her arm near where the barbwire had cut her.

Gavin's mind raced with hope that she could help. "Could you pick him out of a lineup?"

She stood quickly, stumbling before she grabbed Gavin's shirt. "No police." She balled her fists around his shirt and tugged. "Please, Gavin. Please."

He needed to file a report, but he could keep her out of it. "I need to file a report."

"No." Her voice was husky. "I . . . I can't make heads or tails of anything. But they'll take me somewhere, and I'll never find my brothers."

He hesitated, and her eyes darted from one door to another, and as much as he just wanted to be left alone, he didn't want her to run off, not like this. "They could help locate your brothers."

"No. You don't understand. If the authorities find out, they'll take them from me. I'm just eighteen."

What? He knew she'd passed eighteen about a decade ago. Still, if she was this confused, it made no sense to include anything about her being able to identify the man in the police report. He'd go to the station to file the report and leave her out of the report altogether.

He led her back to the mattress on the floor. "No police. I agree. Now get some rest."

She sat on the mattress, her brows knitting slightly. "What did you do with my bed?"

He forced a smile, but he was more than ready to end all conversations. "Let's stop talking now. You need rest." And he needed time to think and gather his wits and pray about the stolen shiplap before he exploded with frustrations.

"You don't want to answer my question about the bed?"

"Like I said, you need rest. Just do us both a favor and lie down and close your eyes."

"You just want me to stop talking."

She was astute, even when too confused to know where she was. He didn't answer, and she lay down. A moment later her eyes were closed and her breathing was even.

What a royal mess. He needed a way to get his shiplap back or be paid for it. He needed more time to meet his financial obligations. What he didn't need was a stranger thwarting what needed to be done while thinking this was her house.

15

Luella lifted the multiple layers of her dress and stepped off the old wooden dock and into a small rowboat. It was a good thing their period clothing had smaller hoops rather than the full-size ones, or the four of them would never fit into this rowboat. The salty breeze swirled around her, stirring her skirts. The air was warm and humid but not uncomfortable. Overall it should make for a nice solstice celebration of friendship—if her friends could manage to get along.

"Eek!" Sue Beth squawked as she nearly fell into the marsh. Dell, who stood on the dock, grabbed her arm and steadied her.

"Thank you." Sue Beth breathed a sigh and shook the heavy skirts of her dress. "I'm not used to these costumes like you, Luella."

"Not used to it?" Julep rolled her eyes. "We've only been doing this for what, *fifty* years?"

Sue Beth huffed. "Well, excuse me." She moved toward a seat in the rowboat. "And your math's wonky, Ms. Accountant. We've been friends for forty-one years, we've recited this poem for thirty, and we've only incorporated the period costumes for the past five or so. And wearing a nineteenth-century dress once a year hardly makes me an expert at walking in it."

Julep started to get into the rowboat. "That's right. I forget that you prefer strutting around in unmentionables."

"Unmentionables? Were you raised in the eighteen hundreds?"

Dell stepped forward, getting between the two. "Come on, girls. This is supposed to be a peaceful time to reflect on our many years of friendship. I mean look around us." Dell gestured at the sky glowing with the pink and golden embers of early sunset. It's as perfect as Mr. Lanier described. Not raining like last year." She stepped into the boat.

Luella offered an arm to steady her as the vessel rocked.

Julep followed, and Luella fought a frown. The tension between Julep and Sue Beth was getting to a boiling point. Maybe they should all consider seeing a therapist together to talk out the issues. Wouldn't that be a sight? The counselor would be hard pressed to get a word in edgewise.

Julep sat down on a seat and grabbed a paddle. Luella manned the other side. Surely reciting their favorite poem would help their moods. They paddled down the meandering river, deeper into the marsh. On the shore across one lane of the highway was the famed Lover's Oak, where years and years ago Sidney Lanier was inspired to write the poem "The Marshes of Glynn."

Since there were no public docks in Brunswick near Sidney Lanier Park on the marsh, it was kind of Tidal Creek Grill to let them use their dock year after year to do this.

"This is good enough," Julep muttered, pulling her paddle into the boat. Flecks of sweet-tea-colored marsh water spattered the hem of her dress.

Apparently this was where they'd stop tonight to recite the poem. Luella tried to catch Julep's eyes, but it wasn't working. Maybe the next few minutes would shift the mood for everyone. Luella opened the bag she'd brought and passed out the four battery-powered lanterns. Dell turned each one on, clicking the flame into existence before passing it to one of the women.

Millions of insects chirped in the marsh around them. Sue Beth held the tattered old poetry book, the one Luella had found many years ago in an out-of-the-way place off the island.

Luella held up her lantern in the deepening shadows. She knew the poem by heart. She might as well begin.

Glooms of the live-oaks, beautiful-braided and woven
With intricate shades of the vines that myriad-cloven

Clamber the forks of the multiform boughs,—
Emerald twilights,—
Virginal shy lights

She continued through the verse. Her voice, carrying Lanier's words, enveloped the small boat, and she could almost see the words flowing into the natural world they described. The marsh symphony played by katydids and crickets served as the perfect accompaniment.

Each woman took a verse, as they did every year. But tonight felt different. The poem and the marsh were beautiful, as always. But it seemed they were just going through the motions. What was happening to her group of friends? As she looked at their faces in the flickering lantern light, a strong feeling rose in her chest: *This could be the last year we do this.*

Julep started the third verse but faltered as the buzz of a motorboat interrupted the flow of poetry. All four women looked from the horizon toward the noise.

No. Not him.

Charles McKenzie, riding in the small fishing boat that Luella recognized as belonging to the restaurant manager. Maybe she should try to hide behind the other three women. He hadn't actually met any of the other Glynn Girls. She could lie low, and maybe he would just move along. She slunk down behind Dell, who was wearing the most voluminous dress.

The motor on his boat slowed to a mere putter as he drew closer. What must he be thinking about their odd getups?

"Ladies,"—he cleared his throat—"I'm truly sorry I have to ask, but what is going on here?"

Sue Beth stood and held up her candle-powered lantern. "We're reciting an important poem. Today is the summer solstice."

Luella couldn't see Chuck, but she could see Sue Beth. Her friend flashed her bring-the-charm smile.

"Uh-huh." Chuck didn't sound charmed. "I noticed you cast your boat off from a private dock belonging to the restaurant."

"We did, but we have permission. Just ask Bill. He's known us for more than two decades." Sue Beth's voice remained upbeat.

"Unfortunately Bill isn't working tonight."

"We have a right to use a boat on the water," Dell said.

"You do. That's true. The only thing I can request is that you not use the restaurant dock. I'm a manager with the company that recently acquired the Tidal Creek Grill. We're working on improving the dining experience, and this . . . spectacle is currently taking away from an important event at the restaurant this evening."

"Oh, we're *so* sorry!" Dell's accent dripped off each syllable. "We're not trying to cause anyone any trouble."

"Uh . . ." Charles seemed to hesitate. "Luella?"

Fiddlesticks. She'd been spotted. She sat up straight and waved at him. "Hi there, Chuck."

A look of understanding washed over his face. He had put together who they were. Fantastic.

The corner of his lip twitched as though it wanted to curve into a smile. "I guess I really shouldn't be surprised to find you mixed up in this." His left eyebrow lifted too. Was he amused?

Luella stood, and the boat rocked under her. Sue Beth gave a small *eep* before sitting back down a little too hard. Luella held her chin up. She wouldn't let him thwart her or embarrass her again. "As a historian I appreciate period costumes and reading classic poetry, like Sidney Lanier's 'The Marshes of Glynn.'"

He studied her for a moment. "I was at the restaurant as you rowed away, and I overheard a customer ask if you were crazy and if you were part of the restaurant's entertainment. There needs to be separation between your, uh, uniqueness and the restaurant. I have to go. Finish your poem.

Enjoy your evening, but this will be your last time to use the restaurant's dock for this kind of evening." He gave her the trace of a smile. "I hate to be difficult like this."

But you're so skilled at it, Chuck.

"Thanks, sugar." Dell waved, still seated in the boat. "We'll be done soon."

Sue Beth, who apparently had recovered from any embarrassment about her near fall, smiled, held up her hand, and wiggled her fingers goodbye.

Julep said nothing, nor did she look at Charles as he motored off toward the restaurant.

Luella sat down beside Dell. The boat was silent for a full minute, with only the evening insects piping up with their input. Luella looked at her friends, dressed in their period costumes, each face downcast. "Are we as crazy as it looks from his point of view?" Her voice rang out on the flat tidal creek.

"I'd never thought so before, but . . ." Sue Beth shrugged.

"But we made a huge feast to bribe the wrong people, and they weren't even hungry," Luella finished for her friend. "I went out with a man"—she gestured her thumb backward toward Charles—"and accidentally proposed trading a date for a favor. And we caught a poor girl in a trap, for Pete's sake!"

She would've stopped the plot for the garden trap if she'd known about it. How involved had Dell and Sue Beth been in its creation? Regardless, all four of them were culpable for how their group had acted recently. Were they as out of touch with people who crossed their paths as it seemed of late?

Julep scowled. "I don't want to hear any more about the garden trap. I've already gotten an earful about that from Gavin." She turned off her lantern and picked up a paddle. "I think I'm done."

Luella used the other paddle, and they made their way back to the dock in silence. The sweet sound of the katydids seemed wrong now.

Their boat drifted to a stop, bumping against the dock. Luella pulled the small vessel up to the dock so everyone could disembark.

Sue Beth gave Dell a hand up. "I can't believe we won't be able to use our spot on the marsh anymore."

With everyone else out of the boat, Luella grabbed the bag containing the lanterns and stepped onto the dock. "Well, with any luck by next year a certain visiting property manager will be gone, and we can go back to doing things as usual."

"No, that's okay." Julep held up a hand. "This yearly celebration of friendship used to mean more to me. I'm ready to stop."

Luella, Dell, and Sue Beth watched as Julep walked away.

"Who's surprised to hear that out of Sourpuss?" Sue Beth scowled. "Take care, girls. See you at the store tomorrow. We have Luella's book signing to prepare for." Sue Beth waved as she left too.

Dell nudged Luella with an elbow. "So . . . you went on a date with Charles?"

Ugh. "Regrettably."

"Care to elaborate?"

Luella shifted the weight of the bag to the other arm. "I'd rather not. Somehow when I'm around Chuck, I act as though I have only one oar in the water."

Dell nodded and rubbed her chin with her thumb. "It is *terribly* interesting to see you get all flustered over a man. Hmm." She snapped her fingers. "I think it'll finally happen after all these years. I call dibs on matron of honor."

Married? They couldn't stand each other. "Dell Calhoun, I've half a mind to shove you into this beautiful marsh we've been describing. You could get to know all the fish, terrapins, and herons right up close."

Dell just cackled, walking toward the shore.

16

Gavin checked his iPhone screen yet again. No texts. No missed calls. He clutched the phone, his hand trembling. He fought the urge to fling the device against the bare wall. All that would do is incur more expenses he couldn't afford. He slid the phone into his pocket.

After Mary fell asleep, the Glynn Girls stopped by with a few pieces of clothing—whatever they could find in her size before the store booted them out because it was closing time. He didn't want to leave Mary or his shiplap, so he got his mamas to stay at the house while he went to the station to file a report on the stolen shiplap. But he'd heard nothing from the police.

A dust-buster vacuum whirred inside Sapphira's art room. Mary had kept herself busy today cleaning and fixing meals. For lunch she'd fixed BLTs and homemade tomato soup from the groceries and garden vegetables he'd brought in.

He'd taken his breakfast and retreated up the spiral staircase to eat and work. It was nearly impossible to look her in the eye while he continued to take apart the house. But he hadn't gotten off so easily for lunch. She'd put place settings on the island and the soup already in a bowl. He'd taken a seat and tried to make small talk about the weather and the vegetables from the garden. That was her favorite topic—fresh produce fed the soul. Whenever he asked questions that might give him a lead on where to look for her family, she told him her private life was none of his business.

Oh, how he wished that were true.

But whether they stuck to small talk or he tried to get answers, the air around them seemed to vibrate with awkwardness. Despite her self-control and her kindness to prepare food for him, she was clearly frustrated that he kept taking *her* house apart. As out of place as it seemed, he felt guilty about taking *his* house apart. Well, this old house was as good as his.

Now it was nearing dinnertime, and he knew no more on any topic—the whereabouts of his shiplap or who this woman was—than he'd known last night. He could take her to the police station, and they would provide a safe place for her somewhere until she remembered who she was or someone turned in a missing person's report.

So why couldn't he do that?

With a pry bar in one hand and a hammer in the other, he gently pulled another strip of shiplap away from the wall.

His phone buzzed. He hoped it was a neighbor calling or the buyer making arrangements for payment. He suspected that was wishful thinking. He eased the tools from the board and jammed them into his tool belt. He'd gone door-to-door asking if anyone saw a man removing shiplap from his garage. Not only had no one seen anything, but also when they checked their security footage that included some of the shared road, none of it showed the face or license plate of the man who'd taken the shiplap.

He pulled the phone out of his pocket. Jimmy. He slid a finger across the screen. "Hello?"

"Hey, man."

Maybe, just maybe, his buddies at the station had been able to pull some strings and get a bit of information about the mystery woman.

"What's up?" Did he sound calm? He felt like Saffy's house looked—stripped bare and broken, with only thin tarp where the roof should be.

"I've made a number of calls to various authorities about your Mary. No one has filed a missing person's report that matches her age and ethnicity. There's been no report of someone with head injuries leaving a hospital without being in someone's care."

"No one?"

"Strange, isn't it? Sorry for the bad news. I waited to call you until the evening because I really thought I'd find some information about her."

Couldn't just one thing go right? "Thanks for taking time to do that. Someone's gotta be missing her. She keeps talking about her two brothers. You'd think they'd be panicked and have filed a missing person's report. I ran searches as best I could online, even looked up 'missing persons' for every state, but I came up with nothing. The result might change if I had some sort of personal information to go on."

"Maybe you could gently push her to talk to you more, and then we'd have more to work with."

Because that went so well. "Yeah. Thanks again." He ended the call, walked down the short hall, and knocked on the door to Sapphira's studio.

The whirring sound stopped, and she opened the door.

"Just checking on you. How are you doing?"

Her brown eyes bore into his. "I'd be much better if you'd put my house back together. Of course that's hard to do without the wood."

Gavin nodded. "If it helps any, I'm trying to get the shiplap back."

"Yeah, so you can sell it."

How could she be so clearheaded about the things he didn't want her to understand and so confused about the things that would get her out of his house and into caring hands?

She set the hand vacuum on a nearby shelf. "How is the roof repair going?"

Gavin didn't answer. He hated lying, but what was he supposed to say?

She narrowed her eyes and pointed one finger at his chest. "Wait, did you take anything else apart?"

Guilt skittered across his skin as he glanced behind him at the new pile of shiplap he'd gleaned throughout the afternoon of waiting on calls.

She moved past him. "Ugh, seriously?" She flung a hand up. "You have to be the worst roofer ever. Who hired you? It sure as blue blazes wasn't me.

And my brothers wouldn't even know where to start looking for a good re-pairman." She paused. "On the other hand, since you aren't good, maybe they *did* hire you." She looked forlornly at the shiplap. "Are you as bad at being an EMT as you are at roofing?" She knelt beside the wood. "What have you done?" She gazed up at him, her eyes swimming in tears. "It's our home."

An ache made his heart drop.

She closed her eyes and drew a breath. When she opened them, her tears were gone. "I worked so hard to keep us together, living inside this old cabin that my brothers' grandmother's dad built."

Would she share a last name? Although he had to admit that was a strange way to word things—her brothers' grandmother's dad? "So your great-grandfather, right?"

"Not mine, no." She ran her fingers across the wood.

Her brothers' great-grandfather wasn't her great-grandfather? That meant they had to be stepbrothers or maybe half brothers or adopted. Per-haps if he asked the right question, she would give him something to go on. "Maybe your brothers did hire me. What are their names again?"

"I just don't think they did. They leave those kinds of things to me." She seemed to be counting each plank. "Did Hadley hire you?"

Finally a name. "Yeah, that's who hired me." He looked at his screen, pretending to search for her in his contacts. "What was her last name again?" He hoped his guess was correct that Hadley was a woman.

Concern and compassion radiated in Mary's eyes. "Do you have mem-ory issues? That could explain a lot."

He should've taken a drama class in school, but, no, he'd played the saxophone in marching band for four years, and what good was that now? Absolutely none. "Memory issues are causing me a lot of trouble at the mo-ment." Not *his* memory issues, but that wasn't the point. "So what is Had-ley's last name?"

"Hadley Granger Birch."

He opened Facebook on his phone and started typing her name. He couldn't believe it when only one name showed up in the queue. Was there only one Hadley Granger Birch on Facebook, or did others have their pages hidden? Or maybe she wasn't on Facebook. He tapped on her name. Once he was on her page, he clicked on Message.

> This is Gavin Burnside. I'm an EMT with Glynn County, Georgia, St. Simons Island. I have a young woman with me who gave me your name, but she seems to be having a few memory issues.
> If you may know her, please contact me.

He filled in his phone number and hit Send. He'd barely tucked his phone into his tool belt when it vibrated.

No way was this call from that Hadley person. If it was, she probably had the Facebook message app on her phone and notifications turned on. He removed the cell and looked at the screen. The number didn't have a name, so it wasn't from someone in his contacts. If this was Hadley, he needed to slip outside so he could speak freely. He started toward the door.

"Wait." The young woman stood. "We need to talk."

"Okay." He held up one finger. "But I need to take this call first."

"But I—"

Gavin stepped outside and swiped his finger across the screen. "Hello?" He closed the door behind him.

"This is Hadley Birch. Is Tara with you?"

"Probably. She's a petite, athletic-built woman, mid- to late-twenties. Dark blond hair. Brown eyes."

"Yes! That's our Tara! Tara Abbott."

The relief in her voice almost matched his. He knew someone somewhere had to be missing Mar—no, Tara.

"She doesn't know her name?" Alarm had replaced the relief in her voice.

"It's probable that she knows it, but she hasn't shared any names of people in her life other than saying yours a few minutes ago."

"I'm so glad you reached out."

This woman sounded sincere and trustworthy, but Gavin wanted to verify a few things before he went any further. "When was the last time you spoke to her?"

"We talked on Sunday, and we texted Monday morning. But we've been unable to reach her since then. I called the Lighthouse Inn, but they said she'd checked out Monday morning. Where is her cell phone?"

Gavin was completely satisfied with her answers. If he wanted to go one step further later on, he could call the Lighthouse Inn and verify Tara had stayed there that week, but that wasn't necessary. "I think she lost it in Monday's high tide."

"Can you please stay with her until we can get there?"

I can't get rid of her. "She thinks the house I'm deconstructing is hers, so staying with her won't be a problem."

"Why would she think that?"

"Something about the tarp on the roof, I think."

"Oh, because her roof had a tarp over it."

"And her brothers. Where are they?"

"What?" Hadley sounded horrified.

Gavin's worst fears for the woman jackhammered his nerves. "She's waiting on them to arrive. She said they should've been here days ago."

"Oh, dear Father, no." Hadley broke into sobs. "I never should've let her board that plane alone. What was I thinking? I'm sure it's apparent to you that she recently sustained a traumatic head injury and had surgery. She insisted she needed time there, the place she was supposed to meet Sean and Darryl."

"Ma'am, it's okay. Everything will be fine." His training took over, but he didn't feel particularly calm. "Take a deep breath. Is someone there with you?"

"Yeah. My husband. Can you hang on?" All noise stopped. Hadley must have muted her phone. He peered through the glass doors and saw Tara. The name fit her somehow. If he remembered correctly from Saffy's Irish folk stories, it was an old name that had a lot of meanings—tower, star, and the ruins of the Halls in Ireland.

Tara moved into the kitchen and opened the fridge. She was probably starting dinner, hoping against hope that her brothers would arrive and she'd have plenty of food for them.

"You there?" Hadley's voice was gravelly, as if she'd been crying, but she seemed calmer.

"Yeah."

"Gavin, I'm going to tell you what's going on, but I don't think you should tell Tara just yet. She needs to be seen by a doctor first. Would you be willing to take her to one while we travel there?"

"Yeah, but the truth of the matter is that this wispy blonde would rather enter a tobacco-spittin' contest than go anywhere with me."

"I'll handle that part in a few minutes. Tell me about her symptoms."

Gavin explained what he'd seen and his evaluation.

"All of that sounds good. I would still like a doctor to look at her before we dump reality on her, but it doesn't sound like she needs to be taken to the ER. Do you have a physician who would be willing to see her? I'd really prefer her to be seen by someone you trust rather than by someone unknown."

"Yeah. I've been going to my doctor for two decades. I trust him, and I'm sure he'll see her. He owes me a few favors." One of the perks of living on a small island all his life is he knew everyone and they knew him.

"Good. Did something happen that set her back?"

"Not that I know of." Gavin thought of the barbwire incident, but she was already struggling by that time, wasn't she?

"She's closest to Elliott and me, and we're both coming. I know our husbands will want to see her too, but it'll take a little time to clear our work schedules. We may not be able to leave until midmorning or noon tomorrow, but she needs to be surrounded by family . . . or as close as it gets for her."

As close as it gets?

"I'm not sure where we'll stay. I know it's the island's busy season—"

"I'll find a place for you." Gavin had so many questions, but now wasn't the time. "Worst-case scenario you'll sleep on air mattresses at my mom's house."

"That'll work just fine. Thank you."

"And her brothers?" He was sure Hadley was too upset and too focused on Tara's well-being to realize she hadn't clarified about the brothers. He hadn't wanted to ask before she calmed a bit, but now, before the call ended, he needed to know.

Hadley poured out the heart-wrenching details.

Gavin was used to seeing horror stories play out in front of him, but his eyes moistened at hearing the trauma of Tara's life. Even penniless, confused, and stubborn, she was obviously the kind who would give up her life as a teen to raise two half brothers.

He cleared his throat. "She's in good hands until you arrive." If he had to lose a day or two of work until Tara could be safely passed off to loved ones, that was no problem with him. But the bank might take exception to his doing anything other than getting the money he owed them. "I'll take the phone to Tara now, and you can talk to her."

"Thanks. I'll make sure she'll get in a car with you tomorrow to go to the doctor's."

Gavin dreaded what tomorrow would bring.

17

The paper on the exam table crinkled with every move Tara made. Waves of nausea hit, and her head throbbed with the most peculiar feeling. The small room inside the doctor's office smelled weird. Dizziness had caused Tara to lie back on the table several minutes ago, and now she stared at the ceiling tiles with their imperfections and small stains.

"You doing okay?" Gavin was in a chair near her, apparently doing as Hadley asked and sticking to her like gum on a shoe. Did Hadley not trust her to hear what the doctor said to her? Did Hadley think she was that addled?

"I'm fine. Thanks." She tried to keep her voice gentle as she lied to him once again.

Last night Hadley had apologized for being so far away, although she didn't say where she was. She did say that she and Elliott and their families were on their way. Had they been on a trip together? She also said that, until they arrived, Tara needed to cooperate with Gavin. That made little sense, but Tara could add it to her long list of what simply didn't add up of late.

Gavin woke her at six thirty to get ready. Who needed an hour to be ready for the day? Certainly not someone who'd worked full-time while parenting two boys.

Anyway, he'd interrupted her sleep because it was time to fulfill her promise to Hadley and go with him to the doctor's office. They'd arrived first thing, seen the doctor, gone down the hall for blood work and a chest x-ray, and been sent elsewhere for a CT. Apparently the doctor ordered everything stat. What on earth had Gavin told him to get that kind of response?

Now it was three in the afternoon, and they were waiting to see the doctor for test results. Tara was dizzy and nauseated, maybe because Gavin had taken control of her Vicodin. Apparently she'd been consuming a few too many each day. She hadn't had one since last night at bedtime, and odd as it seemed, once in a while she caught a glimpse of something that made sense.

"What time are Hadley and Elliott arriving?" She wanted them to help her find Sean and Darryl.

"They got stuck in a long traffic delay, but they expect to be here by five."

There was something in how he said that info. "I've asked that already, haven't I?"

He offered a lopsided smile. "Not a problem."

There was a tap on the door, and Dr. Baudean walked in carrying a large manila envelope and a folder he was reading. He was a thin, gray-haired man.

He looked up from the chart. "How are you feeling, Tara?"

She sat up, her head spinning. "A little dizzy and nauseated."

"I'm sure." He smiled and took a seat on the stool. "Your CT looks good. Very indicative that your head injury is continuing to heal, although memory issues may linger for months yet. But I think I may have found two sources adding to your exhaustion, dizziness, and confusion. You've been taking too many Vicodin pills, and I've already talked to Gavin about that. I won't snatch the pills away, but the sooner you can substitute Advil for Vicodin, the better. It'll help clear up your thinking. Your blood work indicated you had an infection. The x-ray confirmed you have pneumonia."

"But I've not had a cold or the flu or a cough."

"Sometimes being under anesthesia and the following days of bed rest can lead to pneumonia. One of the side effects of Vicodin is it suppresses coughs. And pneumonia causes confusion in a certain percentage of people. Some of my patients say it's like having dementia. Yours is also compounded by the Vicodin and a serious head trauma." He closed the patient file and tapped it on his knee. "Here's the good news. A round of steroids and strong antibiotics should clear up any confusion that's being caused by the infection. You'll get a shot of both before leaving here to give you a boost, and then you'll take two medications daily and breathing treatments for ten days. The rest of the cognitive issues from the brain injury should ease with time."

"Should?" That was a horrible thing to say to her.

"Taking good care of yourself will help." He smiled. "I have other patients waiting. Gavin will step out, and the nurse will be in shortly to give you the shots. You need to be seen again in two weeks."

Tara nodded, and within thirty minutes she was in the truck with Gavin on the way back to her house. She stared out the window, watching endless flat land or open waters pass by. When she was in the house, it was easy to forget there weren't mountains around her because there were huge, sprawling trees in the yard.

"Where are Sean and Darryl? I . . . I don't understand."

"I know you don't." A faint, sad-looking smile crossed his lips. "Hadley and Elliott will be here later today."

He pulled into the driveway and turned off his truck.

Why had the roof guy taken her to the doctor? Even with Hadley and Elliott out of town, she had other friends. He was a stranger.

She studied the house. "Are you the roof repairman?"

He stared at the dashboard.

"Hello?" Tara whispered.

The young man looked at her, and she no longer saw a difficult, unskilled roofer.

"No." His voice was barely audible.

She studied the home, once again taking in how different it looked. Maybe the man hadn't made that many changes to it. Maybe . . . "Is this my house?"

He hesitated before slowly shaking his head.

Embarrassment burned as tears fell. "I feel caught in a dream world, and I can't hold on to anything that makes sense of what's happening."

He drew a slow breath. "I know."

That was it? That's all he had to say to her?

Something wasn't right, and it was more than just her memory issues or the confusion associated with pneumonia.

Her gut said that whatever was going on, it was deeply, unchangeably wrong.

Sunlight filtered through the front glass window of Blue Sails. The decorative Spanish moss hanging from the ceiling undulated in the air conditioner–produced breeze.

Sitting in an antique chair at the table, Luella closed her pen and handed a customer a signed copy of her latest release, *Lights in the Spanish Moss: Ghost Stories of St. Simons.*

The woman she had just met, Christy, flashed a smile. "I'm just *so* tickled to learn that you also write the Demere's Culture Guides. I have copies of Atlanta, St. Augustine, and Savannah."

This new book had Luella's real name, Luella Ward, on it. The other guides she had written were under the pen name of L. Demere. She'd liked how *Demere* looked on the cover, and she had liked the anonymity of only her closest friends knowing who the real author of her travel guides was. When she began them twenty years ago, she didn't do book signings, so no one was the wiser that she was a woman.

She returned the woman's smile. "I'm glad you enjoy them! I love traveling, but St. Simons has my heart. I hope you enjoy this book too. Maybe come join my tour tomorrow night?"

"That sounds fun." The woman waved as she exited the store, carrying her new book.

It was hard to stay focused on the day-to-day stuff, like the ghost tours, but what else could she do? The money she made today would go directly into the struggling shop. She wished she could do more for Julep and Gavin. It seemed all she'd done recently was bungle things with Chuck.

Julep tapped Luella's shoulder. "We need to have a Glynn Girls meeting. Can you take a break?" From the strain in her voice, something was bothering her.

Luella nodded. "Sure." She reached under the table and pulled out the cardboard Back Soon sign and set it on the center of the pile of books.

She followed Julep into a large room behind the counter and register that served as the shop's storage and meeting room. The rest of her friends were already there.

Various unopened boxes were scattered throughout the room. Papers and packing material cluttered the floor. There were no decorations. A cold sense of irony struck Luella as she walked in. There was a stark difference between the immaculately staged front of the shop and this inner hideaway. Was that what she and her friends had become? A showy facade but nothing settled in their hearts?

She shook off the thought and tried to focus.

Julep looked around at each person standing in the room. "So, as we discussed earlier, Gavin went to the doctor with Tara. Her friends are still en route." They had found out the identity of Mary, also known as the garden thief, that morning. Gavin had shared a news article with them about the accident in Sylva, North Carolina, where the young woman's brothers died.

Sue Beth put a hand on her chest. "Bless her heart. I've been praying for her all morning."

Julep crossed her arms. "Well, she needs more than our prayers. Gavin's been ill as a hornet with me since the whole garden debacle, especially in light of what we learned about her. And with all he's doing, I need him not to be mad at me."

Luella touched Julep's elbow. "You're worried about what Gavin thinks of you?" Shouldn't she be worried about the young woman herself?

Julep didn't answer the question. "We all know she's basically homeless for the time being. All she's got are the clothes on her back, plus the paltry things we were able to grab here in town before the shops closed. She lost her phone and wallet and doesn't have her suitcase. She seems to trust Gavin, and he's doing his best to get her set up. But let's be honest. The man lives on a twin mattress at Sapphira's, has used the same generic soap for men since he was eighteen, and wears khaki shorts or a uniform almost every day. He's not going to be able to help her feel *human* the way we girls can."

Dell tapped a finger on her dimpled chin. "I think helping Tara is a great idea. Let's go to my niece's boutique. Won't take us ten minutes to get there. She gives excellent family discounts, and we could buy summer clothes that haven't sold yet."

Sue Beth put a hand up. "Oooh, and one of my art students is a soap maker. She gave me a basket of homemade lotions and soaps that smell *divine,* and I have several that are unopened."

Julep nodded. "Good plan."

"Glad you like it." Dell pulled her keys out of her purse. "And then we'll go by the convenience store and get anything else we can think of that would make her feel more comfortable."

"But I also need to do something to let Gavin know I get it about the garden."

"As luck would have it, today is one of the farmers' market days," Luella said.

"Oh, I like the way you think"—Julep shook a finger at her—"because we plucked ours clean two days ago. And Tara clearly likes vegetables. I'll purchase a bunch of fresh fruit and vegetables that would fill any hankerin'."

Luella's heart warmed at Julep's generous plan, but was her intention in the right place? "I'll go with you."

Julep angled her head in the direction of the storefront. "Don't you need to man your signing booth?"

"Let's close up shop early. It's slow anyway, and I can always sign here on other days. I'll put a note on the door for customers."

Julep clapped her hands together. "Then we have a plan: Dell and Sue Beth will go to the boutique, and Luella and I will obtain some fresh nourishment."

Two hours later all four were on the porch of Sapphira's house, their arms bulging with bags. Julep knocked.

Gavin answered the door, and his eyes widened. "What on earth are you four doing? What's all this?"

"Use your eyes, Son. We're bringing Tara a few gifts."

Gavin put a hand on the doorframe. "A few?"

Julep leaned in toward Gavin. "I'm hoping"—she lowered her voice—"this will make it up to you for my actions in the garden."

Dell leaned her head forward next to Julep's. "Can we speak with her—if she'll see us?"

Gavin looked over his shoulder. "Um, I suppose so." He moved out of the way, and they squeezed through the door along with all their gifts.

Tara, who was sitting on a barstool sipping a glass of water, had a look on her face that said to Luella she might want to bolt out the back door again, but she stayed where she was. A nebulizer breathing machine was on the counter beside her, and it appeared that she'd already had at least one treatment. Why would she need that?

Gavin held a hand out. "Tara, meet the Glynn Girls. Ladies, this is Tara."

"We are *so sorry* about the garden incident. It was an awful idea. I don't know what we were thinking." Sue Beth was speaking loud and drawing each word out as if Tara were a small child or had an impaired ability to understand English.

"I forgive you." Although Tara addressed the Glynn Girls directly, she had a far-off look in her eyes, as though she was preoccupied with other thoughts. Luella imagined she must feel a great deal of confusion. If it wouldn't completely overwhelm her, Luella would've liked to give her a hug.

Julep set her bags of produce on the kitchen counter attached to the bar where Tara sat. "We brought you a few items that might come in handy, as well as some fresh produce."

As Tara studied the produce, her brows furrowed.

"Please accept it. Not for me, but for my son." Julep nodded toward Gavin. "He had to clean you up after my harebrained trap idea, and I think it would mean a lot to him for you to feel better."

Tara looked at Gavin and back at Julep. "Um, okay."

Sue Beth set her three bags next to Tara's stool. "Girls, where are our manners? We never properly introduced ourselves."

The next few minutes were spent with Sue Beth monopolizing the introductions, followed by Tara opening bag after bag of clothes and soaps, with an increasing amount of hesitancy.

Should they have done this? Helping out someone in need was a good thing, but Julep's intentions still felt misguided. And as usual, the rest of the Glynn Girls were going along with it.

A car's tires crunched the gravel-and-shell driveway.

Tara stood. "Hadley." Her voice was no more than a whisper.

This must be the friend from North Carolina.

Tara went to the front door and into the yard. Luella and the rest watched from the open door.

A young, curly-haired woman, approximately Tara's age, exited the passenger side of the car before the vehicle had even come to a complete stop. She ran across the yard and pulled Tara into her arms.

18

Tara fidgeted as she waited for the Glynn Girls and Gavin to meet Elliott and Hadley, plus their families. This necessary politeness was taking entirely too long.

"Goodness." Julep wiped her brow. "Let's get out of this heat." She motioned toward the front door. "Y'all must be in need of a refreshing beverage and perhaps a restroom."

Elliott put her hand on her protruding stomach and nodded. "I'd appreciate a bathroom."

Dell opened the door, smiling at everyone as they went inside.

Tara wanted to scream, "Where are Sean and Darryl?" Instead she fell behind the others and went inside. How long did it take four adults with a baby and two children to get situated so a real conversation could take place?

The old house, its studs where shiplap used to be, echoed with idle chat.

Goodness! Tara was sure she'd explode soon. Hadley had promised her on the phone last night that they'd talk about where Sean and Darryl were just as soon as she and Elliott arrived. Tara's news was disheartening—brain injury, pneumonia, and this wasn't her house. Her skin still burned with embarrassment that this home didn't belong to her, but the only thing that really mattered was the whereabouts of her brothers. Her pulse raced. Why was no one simply telling her?

Fear seemed to break free inside her and spread like rushing waters from a dam. Why were her friends acting as if everything was peachy keen?

"Hello?" Tara's sarcastic tone couldn't have been missed by anyone, and the room fell silent. "What is wrong with you?" She looked from Hadley to Elliott. "You know I'm desperate to find Sean and Darryl, and you stand there pretending this is a wonderful gathering of new and old friends."

Hadley pursed her lips, looking apologetic as she nodded. "You're right, and I'm sorry." She passed her three-month-old to her husband and whispered something. He gathered their two girls and went out the front door with all three little ones.

Elliott waddled toward Tara, hand held out, sadness etched on her face. Tara backed away. "What?"

Gavin motioned to his mom. "Let's give them time to talk."

"Stop!" Tara hissed. "Someone tell me where Sean and Darryl are!" She looked from one person to another, and what she saw terrified her.

Hadley moved in. "Tara, sweetie."

Alarms rang loud and clear, warning Tara of the lies to come. "No! They're fine. I got them out!" Tara fisted her hands. "I got them out!"

Hadley and Elliott stayed close, as if ready to grab her whether she fainted or made a run for it. Tara jerked air into her lungs. "Where are they? What's happened?"

Hadley put her arm around Tara. "What do you remember, T?"

Tara told the events of the morning the storm hit: That she was out for a run. That she saw the storm coming and called her brothers to tell them to get out of the loft. How she ran home as fast as she could.

"Tara, you tried to call them. Every part of who you are since before you were born strove to reach them by phone or by racing there in time. Something in you seemed to know they were in grave danger, and no one could've tried any harder, honey. No one."

Tara's head spun and her legs trembled. "I got them out," she whispered.

Hadley held her tight. "As you ran into the cabin, the tree that fell and hit you . . . killed them."

It couldn't be true. It just couldn't. Thoughts and memories swirled, a confusing jumble of brokenness amid half-normal behavior. Green grass under her feet. Hadley and Elliott beside her. A sea of sad faces. Two freshly dug graves with a coffin hovering over each.

A scream like a wounded animal pierced the air, and Tara realized it was coming from her. She sank to her knees, and Hadley and Elliott never let her go. Hadley brushed Tara's hair. "We'll get through this. I promise, we will."

But Tara felt cold, and her vision turned a reddish brown.

"Step back." That was Gavin's voice, and she felt his hands on her back and her body being stretched out on the floor. Her feet were lifted. Trent said something and hurried from the room. He was a doctor. Where was he going?

"Tara," Gavin said, "breathe deep. Come on, deep breaths. That's it."

She could feel herself returning.

"Now clench your fists. You can do it. Clench them and breathe deep."

Trent returned, and a horrible aroma entered her nostrils.

She opened her eyes. Trent flashed a light in her eyes and checked her pulse. Gavin was above her too, his blue eyes boring into her. *He'd known.* Everyone in this room had known the truth—the pretenders who'd kept their mouths shut and her friends who'd rushed here to set her straight. Humiliation joined forces with the overwhelming grief. How was her life now void of Sean and Darryl? Was Gavin relieved that she finally got it so he could go back to his life unimpeded? Were Hadley and Elliott already weary of dealing with her?

"Just remain still, Tara," Trent said.

She could feel the weight of the loss settling inside her body, and she didn't have the power to sit up or stand. Eyes bore down on her, and she turned her head. The live oak she could see through the window, with its weeping Spanish moss, seemed to cry with her.

Voices murmured, probably about her, but Tara no longer had it in her to listen or care. Trent and Gavin rose and backed away. Hadley and Elliott knelt on each side of her and grasped a hand, saying words of hope that sounded foreign and impossible.

Those in the room talked among themselves. Tara's dizziness eased even as the finality of her loss continued to gain strength and beat against her. She tried to sit up, and her friends helped her.

Julep held out a glass of water. "Sip on this."

Tara had no strength to decline anything, so she took the water and sipped it. Her cheeks were wet. Her mind muddled. Her body weak.

"This isn't my area of expertise," Trent said. "I do research on children with apraxia. But pneumonia is serious business for anyone, but especially someone who's under this kind of emotional stress."

"There's one more thing," Gavin said. "I counted the pills in her prescription bottle, did the math from the date it was filled to see how many she was supposed to take, and she's been taking two to three times the amount prescribed."

"We're lucky she's still alive," Trent said.

Hadley brushed hair from the side of Tara's head, looking at the incision. "I want to get her home and take care of her."

"But home isn't a warm or inviting place anymore," Elliott said. "We want her there because it feels right to us, but to her it's a nightmare on steroids. I think rushing her into a new environment could be a mistake."

"My home is just right there." Julep pointed through a window toward the garden.

Tara longed to refuse, to say she was fine, and to stand, ready to at least head north and find a hotel for the night. But while her thoughts and emotions raged, her body seemed captured in a straitjacket, and she couldn't find the strength to voice anything.

"A few days of bed rest would go a long way, I think," Elliott said. "Then she'll be decently ready to take her own steps toward going home."

"It'll be tight quarters with all of us," Julep said, "but you're welcome to stay as long as you like."

Hadley and Elliott helped Tara stand. They slowly walked across the yard, humidity bearing down. It was still daylight when Tara was given her meds and tucked into bed. When the door closed and Tara was alone, she cried herself to sleep.

19

G avin pried another cabinet from the kitchen wall. He was making progress, both in removing goods and selling them, but not concerning the stolen shiplap. He'd done all he could, but there was simply no proof who took it. The whole money issue was on his mind, but mostly what held his thoughts captive was Tara.

Because of her memory and health issues, maybe he'd caught only a glimpse or two of the real Tara, similar to the first time he saw her that night on the beach. It was dark and rainy, but he saw her. And she was unforgettable.

At breakfast time Hadley had walked over with a plate of food, and he'd asked how Tara was. *"Much better,"* she'd said. *"Our evidence is that she's grumpier than a trapped bear at the end of winter."*

Of course she was, but that was a good sign.

He heard a noise and glanced out the window toward his mom's house. Tara. She was dressed and rushing from the house. She went to a lawn chair and plunked down. This was his first real glimpse of her in five days. He wasn't at his mama's very much, but when he was, he saw Elliott and Hadley going in and out of her room, taking food and medicine. He could hear muffled voices when they talked to her or read to her, trying to nurse her mind and soul back to health.

Elliott flew out the back door, her hands under her round belly, holding it as she went to Tara, voice raised. Tara looked up at her, responding. He couldn't hear the words, but the movements said they were in a heated argument. That's what trapped bears did—growled and jerked about.

Should he intervene? Right now no one was home except Tara and El-liott. Hadley's and Elliott's husbands had flown home yesterday to get back to work, leaving their wives the vehicle. Hadley had taken her girls to a water park, and his mamas were at their shop, working. They should be free within the hour, and all of them were coming to his mom's house to cook a meal for everyone. He wasn't sure why other than they were enjoying being good hosts, but he was glad to see an improvement in his mom's attitude.

Tara stood, said something, and then walked off, heading for the road. A minute later Gavin's cell phone rang, and Elliott's name was on the screen. He accepted the call. "Hey."

"She ran off, and I'm too pregnant to keep up."

"I see her cutting through Sapphira's driveway going toward the road. I imagine she's ready for a little space to herself."

"Yeah, she says we're smothering her."

She'd been sharing a bedroom with Hadley's family, all five of them. She and Elliott were sharing a room now that the husbands were gone. But with Elliott and her husband in the medical field, they'd taken the most stringent, cautious path to healing—mandatory bed rest.

"But we're arguing." Elliott drew a deep breath. "It started last night when we told her we have to go back home in two days—all of us. We can't stay any longer. She accepted that, but then we told her she has to go with us."

Gavin was sure the notion of going home was agonizing to Tara, but Hadley and Elliott had missed a lot of work since the incident. Odd as it seemed, he would miss her, but everyone had to be realistic. "She's better. I know she is, but her emotions are bound to surpass her ability to reason just yet, and you can't change what needs to be done because of her reaction." He went out the front door and watched as she walked toward Gould's Inlet.

"Thanks, Gavin. That helps. Maybe she does need a little time without Hadley or me breathing down her neck. But she left her new phone here."

"If she's not back in thirty minutes, text me. I'll come get her phone and take it to her. It'll be easy to find her in broad daylight." He was watching her as she got to the end of the road where it connected with sand that led to Gould's Inlet. She ducked under tall shrubs on the back dunes and would probably follow the footpath until she came out the other side of shrubs and beach grass onto the sands of the beach.

"Thank you."

Tara sat on a large piece of driftwood. If Hadley and Elliott needed to return to North Carolina, they should go without insisting she leave with them. She focused on her surroundings. Maybe that would calm her.

There was nothing but sand between her and the edge of the ocean, but that distance was the length of a football field. The ocean gently rolled onto the beach. Sunlight sparkled on the unceasing tiny ripples. Beyond the inlet the vastness of the water stretched way beyond her ability to see where it led or where it ended.

Several families and pets played on the beach and in the water.

What should be an endearing thing to watch now ripped her apart.

What did Tara have? Memories. And each one broke her heart anew.

Everyone she knew had family. She could hardly look at Elliott and Hadley without crying. Their lives were filled with love and happiness and expanding families.

What had she done so wrong in life that she was once again left without family? What had any of them done so right that their lives were filled to abundance?

Her heart thudded with pain that never let up. Sean and Darryl were gone, now and forever. How would she survive? Emptiness had taken root, and it was growing with each passing day, painfully so, forcing her heart to make room for it just as Elliott's womb made room for her growing child.

"God?" she whispered again, and with every mumble of His name, she felt more betrayed and less comforted. How could He let this happen? Why would He ask her to raise her brothers and then snatch them away like this? She lifted her chin, staring into the heavens. "It's too much. I'm broken. Is that what You wanted?" She looked at the horizon. "Was I an experiment of some kind? Let's see what this one lonely girl can take throughout life and still be able to breathe?"

She continued to pour out her pain in silence, apparently to the One who'd caused it. When a shadow fell across her, she turned to see why.

Gavin . . . with a bottle of water, a woman's straw hat, and her silk scarf in his hands.

He sat on the log and held out the bottle of water. She didn't want anything from him, but rather than tell him what she thought, she took the bottle.

"Thanks." She opened it and guzzled more than half of it.

He held out the hat and scarf.

She took them. "I keep wishing I could go back to not knowing."

He stared at the water. "It's an unbearable thing, and I'm sorry."

Words came easily for him. Sounding sincere and thoughtful seemed second nature. She should be grateful for all he'd done, but she didn't care that he'd provided food and a safe haven in his home or that he'd held the secret until Hadley arrived. Did the pain inside her have her numb to every other emotion? "Why are you here?"

"Elliott's concerned."

"We're fighting."

He nodded.

She took a sip of water. "I'm not wrong."

"You may be. I'm not sure you're well enough to tell yet, and you're not either."

Maybe he was right. "Could you go away now?"

He put his hands on his knees, looking as though he was going to spring to his feet, but he didn't get up. "I can. Don't forget that the Glynn Girls are fixing a big meal tonight for you, Hadley, Elliott, and the kids. It'll be ready in less than an hour."

"It's a goodbye dinner, but I . . . I can't go back to North Carolina. I'll go crazy if I have to see all the places where Sean, Darryl, and I went together. The three musketeers—that's what Darryl called us." She chuckled, but fresh tears broke free. "They were so full of life and love and goodness and kindness. Why did they have to die?"

Gavin sighed. "I'm sorry."

"Yeah, sure," she mumbled. He wanted her out of his house and life, but that was no reason to be snide. The need to apologize hung thick between them. While fighting with herself, she wove the scarf through the holes at the crown of the straw hat and tied it. But she still didn't have it in her to say she was sorry.

She rose. "Look, I'm in no shape to be civil to anyone, so I'm going for a walk . . . alone. And I'm not coming to the dinner."

He stood. "I assured Elliott I would find you, and I have. If you insist on time alone, do it in a way you can be reached." He held out her phone.

"I need time without people or a phone."

"Can't have both. Not yet."

"If I take that, I'll feel tethered to my past. Something in me starts waiting to hear from Sean and Darryl." She didn't take it. "I'm doing well, and I promise I can handle a night on my own."

"A night?" His eyes held disbelief.

"I need to walk, think, try to sort through things. I can't breathe with Hadley and Elliott hovering."

"This conversation is circular, Tara. Bottom line, it's too soon for you to be wandering around by yourself for hours without a phone. And a night is entirely out of the question."

"Did my staying at your place and eating your food brand me as your property or something?"

He studied her, and his eyes reflected sincerity. "That's not what's going on here, and I think you know it."

"Look, you've been generous and kind. I know you have, although my emotions seem incapable of feeling gratitude. Still, my mind grasps it, so thank you. But I'm leaving now. That's the end of it." She started to leave. "Don't follow me."

He sighed and nodded.

She put on the hat and walked off, no clue where she was going, but the longing to disappear into nothingness was overwhelming. She could feel his eyes on her. Where could she go to disappear from the few who knew her?

20

L uella pulled the last of the meat off the cooked chicken as Julep stirred the roux for the chicken potpie. Dell had her hands in biscuit dough, because piecrust just wasn't nearly as good on top as buttermilk biscuits. Sue Beth was cutting fresh, steamy corn off the cob.

Elliott was the only one at Julep's so far. Hadley and the children hadn't yet returned from the water park, and Gavin had gone to find Tara. Surely everyone would be here by the time supper was ready. It wasn't Tara's last evening. Tomorrow night was, but not all of them could get together tomorrow night.

Luella spread the meat into a large baking dish and washed her hands. The tension in the house tonight wasn't much better than last night. Tara didn't want to return home just yet, and apparently she and Elliott had argued about it again today.

Clearly Tara had grit, lots of it. How else had she pulled herself together at eighteen and raised two amazing young men? But that hardheaded determination was misguided right now as she balked at her friends.

Luella meandered onto the back porch. With her palms against the porch railing, she leaned in and admired the immaculate yard that Julep kept. Birds chirped and swooped down to the bird feeder. The house was on a raised foundation to prevent flooding during a storm, and it made for a really nice view of Julep's and Sapphira's backyards. This land where Julep's house sat was once Sapphira's property, but she gave the small lot to Julep and Mitch to build a home on before Gavin was born.

The porch door burst open and banged against the side of the wooden house, making Luella jump.

"Gavin just called me." Julep waved her cell in the air. "I'm sketchy on details, but Tara took off, insisting Gavin stay behind. He followed her at a distance, and last he saw her, she was getting on his old bike, the one from Sapphira's shed. We're going to tail her discreetly." Julep hurried down the porch steps. "Elliott will wait here in case she returns."

"You think the four of us can be discreet about anything?" Luella followed Julep with Sue Beth and Dell right behind them.

"Well, we're going to try." Julep strode into the shed. "He doesn't want her on her own just yet. I think he's afraid she'll relapse and forget where she is. We should be able to catch up to her on our bikes."

Luella winced, thinking of the bikes, but she followed Julep anyway. Last summer in an attempt to help Sue Beth and Julep start exercising, the four had decided to bike together once a week. They each purchased a bicycle to be stored in Julep's shed since her neighborhood was a good area for cycling. Part of their mistake was they bought old, heavy bikes, like they had during childhood, and none of them had a gearshift. If they'd purchased new, lightweight bikes, biking would have been easier.

Every ride was disastrous.

The first time they'd gone out it'd been ninety degrees. Dell fainted. The second time Sue Beth rode into a parked car and then got mad at Julep for laughing at her. And every time they rode together, they argued about which route to take.

"Are you sure that's the best plan?" Luella gestured toward her car. "Maybe we should drive."

"No." Julep pulled the shed door open. "We'd end up spooking her when she noticed a car following her around. Besides, what if she goes down some of the footpaths in the area? How would we follow her in a car?" She jerked the wheel of her bike from its floor rack. "Now let's go. We've no time to lose."

They grabbed their bikes, hopped on, and took off down the driveway.

"Which way?" Luella looked for signs of Tara.

"Gavin said west . . . I think."

"One block west takes us straight into the marsh." Dell ground out the words.

"Yuck!" Sue Beth wiped one hand and then the other down her slacks while trying to get her balance. "They're a little dusty, but we can still rule the road." Her bike wobbled. "Maybe."

They peddled out of the driveway.

"Just exactly when did we ever rule the road?" Dell asked. "Sue Beth tried. She sideswiped a car like she owned the road."

"Please be careful, and don't snuggle up to any cars, moving or parked." Luella chuckled.

Sue Beth nodded and giggled.

Julep stopped abruptly at the *T* in the road, looking in each direction. "She won't. She just mistook the car for a man and snuggled right up."

Sue Beth pointed a finger at Julep, and again her bike wobbled as though she might lose control of it altogether. "That's just mean, Julep Burnside."

This tedious bickering again? "Ladies, please. Shall we make a decision and go?" Luella didn't know which way they should go, but there were acres of marshland straight ahead, so going due west was out. If Tara had gone south, they might never spot her. There were several long roads she could've taken, including one that led to the causeway and off the island. She was young and athletic and had a more modern bike, so a long ride was a real possibility. But if she'd gone north, they had a good chance of spotting her. The north end of the road was a dead end.

"Let's turn right and go around the block. Maybe she's still on this end of the island."

They started pedaling again, riding around the block and circling back to Sapphira's house.

"Did anyone see any hint of her?" Dell asked.

"No," Julep grumbled.

From the corner of her eye, Luella saw movement. Someone walking.
Sapphira?

That was nonsense. Luella turned, focusing on the movement. Goose bumps ran up and down her body. Tara was pushing a bike across the green lawn and toward the road, about three hundred feet from them.

"Look!" Luella nodded toward her.

Clearly Tara had gone down the dead end and was now coming back this way. She appeared to be studying Sapphira's house. Was she thinking about going inside it again?

Tara didn't turn around, so she hadn't spotted them . . . yet. She walked to the asphalt road, hopped on her bike, and began pedaling again. Once on the road that paralleled the marsh, she took off much faster than Luella expected.

"Let's move." Julep kicked her pedals into motion.

Luella trailed behind Sue Beth and Dell. Even now, something about seeing Tara walking through Sapphira's yard caused fresh goose bumps, despite the balmy heat of the late afternoon. She pedaled harder to catch up.

"Oh . . . a . . . firefly . . ." Dell's words seemed to disappear in the breeze.

What? Was it possible? Luella pedaled up beside her. "Did you say she looks like Sapphira? Because I was thinking the same thing."

Sue Beth turned around to look at Luella over her shoulder. "Who does? Tara?"

Dell giggled. "Um, I said 'I think I ate a firefly.' But whatever floats your boat, Lu."

Luella shook her head, but the image wouldn't clear. "There was something about the way she looked coming around the corner of the house."

Dell looked back toward Sapphira's house, and her bike wobbled. "Could it be because it is Sapphira's house and you often saw her working and moving around in the yard?"

Julep's hair whipped in the wind as she turned her head. "Could y'all keep it down? We're trying to tail her quietly."

They all focused on riding for several minutes, and then Dell stood up on her pedals, seemingly trying to pedal harder. "She's really booking it." Her voice stayed low.

"We're"—Julep was leaning over the handlebars, almost panting—"going to lose sight of her."

Tara turned down another street, and they all struggled to catch up. Stupid antique bikes. They weighed about as much as Luella did, and it felt like the brake was on the whole time one was pedaling.

"Doesn't she have pneumonia? How in the world is she in so much better shape than we are?" Sue Beth's words sounded far away.

Luella glanced behind her. Sue Beth was too far back. The rest of the girls would have to stop and wait for her if she lagged any farther behind. "Did you hear her, Julep?"

Julep groaned in response. "I'm sure the whole island heard her whine."

Tara made another turn, and by the time they were around the corner, they didn't get even a glimpse of which direction she'd gone. They rode through the Mallery Park neighborhood, looking down other roads she might have taken. Nothing.

Julep circled her bike back around, and Dell and Luella followed. Were they going to convene to make a plan?

Julep skidded to a stop in the grass next to Sue Beth. She jammed a finger in Sue Beth's face. "It's your fault we lost her!"

"*My* fault?" Sue Beth panted. "What's your problem, Julep? Other than the permanent burr in your britches the last year and a half."

"You're so slow we ended up losing her. I guess we needed to get someone's husband involved to motivate you to book it!" Julep rapid-fired each word.

Sue Beth flushed red and stepped off her bike, letting it fall. "That's it! I've had enough of your contempt! I've half a mind to slap you silly."

Julep got off her bike and threw it on the ground. "Try it, Sue Beth. Make my day, and just try it."

Luella and Dell exchanged a look of panic before jumping off their bikes.

Luella stepped between the two, holding her hands up as though she were calming a wild horse. "Whoa, whoa. No bloodshed here, please. This island has seen enough war in the past. No need to add to that now."

Sue Beth pointed at Julep. "How *dare* you? You constantly imply that I was up to no good with Mitch. Why?"

Julep raised a hand as if she was going to go around Luella and hit Sue Beth, but she lowered it. "The way you flirt certainly isn't noble, Sue Beth. He was *my* husband! And I know you."

Dell joined Luella in standing between the two, ready to block a blow or two if need be.

Sue Beth clenched her fists, peering around Dell and Luella. "Do you, now? My husband and I don't even like each other most days, but I know he wouldn't try anything with one of my friends—or any other woman. Mitch was in love with you his whole life!"

"And you just couldn't stand it, could you?" Julep tiptoed and leaned one way and then the other, looking around the peacemakers. "You were desperate to steal any crumbs of that love you could."

"I've had a reputation for being a flirt since we met. Although I don't see that in my behavior, clearly others do. But never once"—she held up her index finger, shaking it at Julep—"had it bothered you until Mitch died. Why?"

"Because my minutes on this earth with him were ticking off so loudly each one was like a cannon going off! And you, one of my own Glynn Girls, stole time from me so you could enjoy your moment in the sun. You wanted his attention solely on you, and you took it!"

"Are you off your rocker? I don't know what you're talking about!"

"We had a gathering at our house the day we received his diagnosis, remember?"

"Yeah."

"I didn't want Mitch to be away from my side for a second, but Gavin and I got distracted for just a few minutes. When I started searching for Mitch, I saw you, my good old friend Sue Beth, all cuddled up with my husband! You were stealing my time with him. That's what you do—flirt and steal moments with men who aren't yours!"

Sue Beth rolled her eyes. "Give me a break!" She punched the air, gesturing in the direction of Julep's home. "He was talking to me about dying, and he wanted me to promise I'd never leave your side. Which, by the way, is the only reason I'm still here after the way you've treated me since he died!"

Dell caught Luella's eyes as they held their ground between the quarreling pair. "You're awfully quiet, Lu."

"Yeah, I'm wondering if I need to borrow a garden hose from one of those houses and fill this dirt crater with water. Maybe we could sell tickets. Two Glynn Girls fighting it out in the mud. Could get rid of Gavin's debt that way."

Julep and Sue Beth glared daggers at her, but if she could direct some of their anger onto herself and away from each other, then her quip had served its purpose.

Julep dropped her gaze to the ground and then muttered a curse word and sat in the grass.

Luella watched as remorse worked its way past the anger. Julep didn't actually think Sue Beth was trying to steal Mitch. She was just angry. Angry that the love of her life was gone. Angry that Sue Beth had dared to soak in a few private moments that could've been hers. It hadn't helped anything that they'd kept their plans to have the gathering while Julep was panicked and raw from the news of Mitch's diagnosis.

"Sue Beth, I'm sorry." The words were only a little louder than the sound of a car slowly going down a long gravel driveway.

Sue Beth pulled back as though she'd actually been slapped. She blinked several times. "What?"

Julep looked up. "I think you heard me. I'm sorry."

Sue Beth dropped to the grass next to Julep, folding her legs under her. "I forgive you, Julep."

Julep leaned on Sue Beth's shoulder and wept. Sue Beth wrapped her arm around her, and Dell and Luella sat on her other side, placing their hands on her back.

Julep pulled back, wiping her eyes. "I'm seeing everything wrong, aren't I? I've been lost since the day I found out Mitch had cancer." She put her hands on her chest. "Look at what I've become."

Sue Beth shook her head. "What *we've* become. We were so connected that when you lost a part of you, we all lost a part of ourselves."

Dell nodded.

"That's right," Luella added. It was unfair for Julep to take on everything as her fault.

Julep looked from person to person. "If you girls did anything wrong, it's because you followed me into it. I became bitter, and I dragged my friends with me."

Maybe that had a little truth in it, but Julep didn't choose to lose Mitch. She had spent most of her life being kind and loving, and loss had just knocked her off course. Luella put a hand on Julep's knee, hoping to bring a little comfort.

Julep smiled, but the corners of her mouth just barely lifted. "I had no idea that I'd lost myself to the point I'd be cruel. I wanted to handle losing Mitch in a way that would make Gavin proud of me, and he's so disappointed. I don't want to be this person anymore. Or ever, ever again. I want to make a difference with my life."

Luella rubbed Julep's blue-jeaned knee. "We can start with Tara. And then look for anyone else we can help."

Dell put a hand on Luella's and Julep's shoulders and bowed her head. Sue Beth put her hands on Julep and Dell, and Luella closed the circle, putting her hands on Dell and Sue Beth. They bowed their heads and closed their eyes.

Julep began. "Lord, we are coming to You, humbled and desperate for Your grace. Forgive me. I accepted Your gifts with open arms, knowing they were part of this temporal world, but I've not coped well with the loss. And if it's Your will, help us find Tara. We want to show her love."

Silence fell on the group. Luella sent up her own silent prayers. For forgiveness for not stepping up to heal this rift earlier. For safety and mercy over Tara, wherever she was on the island. For guidance in navigating this new beginning.

With a shared "Amen," they each retrieved and dusted off their bikes.

"Sue Beth, you can go first." Julep's voice was gentle now.

Sue Beth smirked. "So I can hit a car?"

Everyone chuckled as any remaining tension evaporated like the rain in June after the sun comes out.

"Okay, fine." Julep's voice sounded years younger. "We'll ride as a group. With any luck we can spot her. Or even better, she'll make her way back to the house, and we'll meet her there."

They were off, joking about old memories, warning each other of potholes, and remembering their girlhood on the island.

They circled through the Village shops, waving at their building as they passed Blue Sails, and then rode into Neptune Park. The picnic area was coming into view, and beyond that was the lighthouse.

Luella pointed at the white tower rising over the live oaks. "It closes soon, but she could've bought a ticket to enter it. Do you think she might have climbed the lighthouse again?" Maybe she liked the feeling of looking down over the live oaks of Neptune Park and green grass that stretched to the beach and ocean.

"It's possible." Dell sounded hopeful. "We at least know she couldn't bike up the spiral stairs of the lighthouse, so if she's in the lighthouse, we'd see the bike she borrowed from Gavin on the ground nearby."

Sue Beth skidded to a stop, hopped off the bike, and laid it down left of the sidewalk. "Girls, look!" She pointed and went running over to the picnic area under the largest sprawling live oak.

Tumbling across the ground was a straw hat with a familiar scarf tied to it. The one Tara had been wearing.

"Aha!" Sue Beth grabbed it and lifted it above her head with both hands like a prize.

Luella muffled a laugh at the bystanders who were eyeing Sue Beth as if she were crazy. If Sue Beth noticed them, she didn't say. That was a trait Luella had always admired about her. She didn't mind looking silly if it could help a friend.

Julep nodded. "Good eye, Sue Beth. This means she *did* pass through here. Let's try the lighthouse."

They got back on the bikes and continued on the sidewalk. When they got to the lighthouse area, they disembarked on the soft green grass.

Julep stopped in front of the white gazebo near the lighthouse and, in a voice so quiet that Luella almost didn't hear her, said, "We found her."

They all came closer to take a look.

Tara was asleep on one of the benches with Gavin's bike on the floor of the gazebo.

21

The darkness had begun to lift, but it wasn't yet sunrise. Gavin stopped removing antique doorknobs and took in Sapphira's house. It looked like a day-old, gutted fish left on the pier by mistake. This had been Sapphira's home, and she'd loved this old house. She'd spent Gavin's lifetime praying Siobhan would find her way back to it. His only recollection of Siobhan seemed to be from a few old photos and the stories he'd been told over the years by Sapphira and his mamas.

The mangled house made him uneasy. What had he done? He'd dreamed of taking it apart and selling it bit by bit so he could get his mom out of debt. Now the house was a mess, and he had a small profit to show for it.

Still, his plan had been practical. Tara's love of this old home, as well as his guilt, were misplaced. Her sentiments had dredged up nostalgic emotions for him, but he had a job to do.

He sighed. He had no idea how he should feel about Tara, but he couldn't stop thinking about her. Last night Hadley had texted him a sincere thank-you, saying that his mamas had found Tara, and she was safe. She'd also sent the clip of Darryl's valedictory speech. Gavin must've watched it two dozen times, maybe four dozen. It was insightful, and Tara had been entirely too cute sitting there with a lap full of flowers as her brother embarrassed her. He imagined that the home the three of them shared had overflowed with love and energy and hope.

Oh, stop already. You sound like the poetry your mamas like to read.

But he seemed incapable of changing his thoughts to something else.

Anything. It wasn't that he was interested—not like that. She was vulnerable and hurting, and he wanted to check on her, as he would anyone he'd spent that much time around.

He grabbed his phone and texted his mom, asking how things were going. If she was asleep, the Do Not Disturb feature on her phone would silence the incoming text.

His phone rang with a call from Mom. "Hey. How's Tara?"

"Asleep for now," she whispered. "But I need you to go by the coffee shop. Bring six coffees with cream and sugar and seven sausage-and-egg biscuits. Can you do that?"

"Sure." He picked up the truck keys from the counter and went outside. "I'm assuming you're at home."

"No!" she snapped. But she didn't say anything else, and he waited.

His mom sounded irritable again. She'd had insomnia off and on since his dad died, and when it was at its worst, she snapped and growled her way through the day. But this cynical, ill-tempered woman wasn't who she'd been when he was growing up. She'd been kind and giving and laughed a lot.

"Mom?"

"Yeah. I'm here. Sorry, Gavin. I . . . I'm trying to do better, to be better. Apparently it'll take more than just deciding to change. Guess the upside is that you're a patient son."

He couldn't find his tongue. *Wow, just . . . wow.* What had caused her to see the issue? "Not a problem, Mom. It's a rough time for you."

"Thanks, sweetheart. I'm not at home, or I'd make my own coffee."

He started his truck. "I'll be at the café in five. I just need to know where you are."

"The gazebo near the lighthouse."

"At dawn? Why?"

"You'll know as soon as you get here. See you in a few."

Birds chirped loudly, waking Tara. She tried to open her eyes. Her head was on a pillow, and a blanket was over her, but what was the hard surface under her? Where was sh—

Oh. Oh no . . . Fresh grief pressed in, ripping at her heart. Gut-wrenching memories of waking in the hospital and burying her brothers flooded her. She sat up, wiping tears. It felt as if she were learning the news for the first time. No wonder that when she fell asleep on that plane and dreamed of her brothers being alive, she woke up believing it.

A noise caught her attention, and she looked up. She was inside a gazebo. A foggy memory floated through her mind. She came here last night, but last night this place was a typical empty gazebo with benches. Now there was a beanbag chair, two air mattresses, and a lawn chair, each with blankets and pillows.

"Hi, sweetie."

Tara started at the woman's sudden appearance and blinked. Oh, it was Julep.

She sat on the bench next to Tara and circled her arm around Tara's shoulders and squeezed. "Waking is the hardest. It's as though sleep shifts the weight off you and waking returns it tenfold. I can't really understand or imagine what you're going through, but I lost my husband eighteen months ago. We'd been married thirty-two years and in love for even longer."

Why was Julep sharing things that Tara had no strength to carry? Tara looked away and was startled again. Dell, Sue Beth, and Luella were there too.

Julep patted her shoulder. "A recap: we found you last night and wanted to be sure you were safe. So one of us stayed by your side while the others got some creature comforts. Hadley and Elliott came to check on you at separate times during the night, but Hadley's three aren't sleeping well, and all of them were up most of the night. Since I've not heard from them in the last hour, I imagine they're catching a bit of sleep. And we are here for you."

Julep looked from her friends to Tara and back again. Was she nervous?

Dell took a step toward them. "Other than maybe a glimpse or two of Julep, you haven't seen us since your friends arrived, and I know what Julep said sounds strange. And we know we've been awful to you, and no amount of gifts can make up for it. But we're here for you, hoping you'll let us help."

Why would Tara want their help? And why did she feel so apathetic toward others? She couldn't explain it, but then she shouldn't have to. "I just want to be left alone."

"And that's fine in due time," Luella said. "Right now isn't that time. Take a few minutes to think about it. You've needed someone by your side since you landed here."

Memories of arguing with Elliott before storming off hit hard. Maybe Tara should be horribly embarrassed by how she'd behaved yesterday, but her broken heart seemed to eclipse everything else.

Dell crouched near her. "Since it's our understanding that you don't intend to return to North Carolina just yet, why not let us be your soft place to land? Just for a few weeks. You'll need a place to live, and we can provide that, free of charge."

Despite their appearance of sincerity, Tara couldn't get past the desire to be on her own. "That's kind . . . and sort of creepy."

"You need accommodations and a safety net, basically a whole situation." Julep held out her arms and then gestured to her three friends. "*We* are that situation."

Were they serious? They could be mean when the mood hit, and she had the puncture wounds to prove it! Julep had graciously given Tara and her friends a place to stay and fix meals. Apparently their current mood was kind and gracious. What would tomorrow's mood be, especially once Tara's friends were gone?

A broad-shouldered young man came around the corner of the museum. She didn't need to blink twice to know who it was. Maybe Hadley and Elliott thought he was valiant, but all he'd proved to Tara was that he was good at pretending. He could look her in the eye, probably wanting to be free of her, and act like he'd been hired to repair the roof of her damaged home.

She'd acted like a fool, and he let her, knowing the truth the whole time. Why couldn't he go away and leave her to stew in her embarrassment? Regardless of the head injury and delusions about her brothers, she shouldn't have been so stupid to believe his house was hers.

Still . . .

She closed her eyes. What she wouldn't give to go back to not knowing.

Gavin slowed as he entered the gazebo. "Hi." He had a tray of coffee and a bag of what had to be food in his hand. He held out the tray of coffee to Tara.

She backed away. "No, I'm good."

The women took the coffee and bag from him.

"Thanks, Gavin." Julep took a sip of the coffee. "We were telling Tara that she could stay with us, any of us really, and each one of us wants to house her."

A breeze caused wisps of Tara's hair to cross her face. She raked her hands through it and tucked what she could behind her ears. "I appreciate the offer . . . or at least I'm trying to, but please go back to your lives."

"But, honey," Sue Beth said, "you need us." All four women nodded and moved in a little closer.

"Look"—Tara glanced at each woman—"you want to help. I get that. But you can't make my loss more tolerable, and I sure as blue blazes don't need strangers breathing down my neck, thinking they know what's best for me. I forgive you for the way you treated me. Now please stop being my shadow. Despite how it seems, I can take care of myself." She just wanted to find a hole—somewhere out of sight—and crawl into it until some of the pain eased. She had a little money set aside and no bills to speak of, so she'd be okay while licking her wounds.

She went down the few steps of the gazebo and started across the lawn. The sound of footfalls caused her to turn around. Gavin was right behind her. "What's your deal? Go tend to your mamas. Go back to your life. You have your house back, and—" A fresh thought worked its way free. "Oh, that's right. You need me."

"Need you?" His brow creased.

"I'm your connection to the shiplap thief."

"Uh, no, you're not." His demeanor hinted of a man she'd yet to meet—one less patient and less agreeable. "I'll handle that on my own. But unless you've changed your mind about not going back to North Carolina with your friends, you should take my mamas up on their offer."

"So that's why you want me to stay—to be chivalrous or at least pretend to be, right?" He wanted her help. She was sure of it, but he didn't have it in him to be honest about it.

He pursed his lips and sighed. "I did a lot of pretending, and I'd be angry too if I were you."

"I'm glad you approve."

"Okay." He splayed his hands, barely opening them, as if gently surrendering. "I'm the target of your anger. I get it. And my mamas are too. But the bottom line is Hadley and Elliott are not going to leave you in St. Simons on your own. And for good reason. It has not gone well for you, believe it or not. You are essentially homeless without money or resources. Maybe you have friends in a different state that you can spend time with. I don't know. But if you choose to stay in St. Simons Island, you'll have to prove to your friends that you have someone to look after you."

She barely held back a scream. "I'm perfectly fine looking after myself!"

"Oh, sweetie." Julep started toward her with her arms held out.

Gavin held up one hand to his mom, and she stopped cold. "No, Tara, you're not. You will be. Maybe as early as a couple of weeks from now. But not yet."

Who did this man think he was? "Do you tell everyone around you how they will handle things?"

"If the situation calls for it, yep. Case in point, what do you need to do this morning to care for your health?"

What? She tried to piece together what he meant, but it was too much of a riddle. "That's not the point."

"It is *precisely* the point. And the answer is that you need to take the medicine the doctor prescribed. That will include two pills, to be taken after you've eaten, and a breathing treatment."

"I would've remembered that. I just woke up and haven't even had my first cup of coffee before you started in on me."

"I offered you coffee." His faint smile wavered a bit.

"Fine." Tara removed the shawl from her shoulders. "I'll go back with Hadley and Elliott." How was she going to cope living in a place that came with a dozen memories per minute? She shoved the wrap against Gavin's stomach. "Happy?"

"No. If you want to stay, then do so. Just agree to the terms."

"Your terms."

He rubbed one temple. "Hadley and Elliott are beating themselves up for letting you come here on your own."

"Then let *them* say so. This argument is between them and me. You're not part of it."

"*I'm* saying so." His soft-spoken voice held confidence and authority, but his demeanor had no hint of threatening behavior.

"You just took it upon yourself to fight the battle for Hadley and Elliott."

He said nothing. Apparently the conversation was over. Maybe if she solved his shiplap situation, he would see that she was clearheaded enough to be on her own. She'd overheard Gavin leaving voice messages for the buyer-turned-thief. He had the man's number, and even though Gavin didn't believe she'd seen the man face-to-face, she'd easily convince the buyer of the truth.

"Do you still have my phone?"

"I have it." Sue Beth held up a purse the size of a bowling bag. "It's in here somewhere."

"Find it, because I can identify the shiplap thief. I'll tell the buyer Gavin had the original deal with." Tara held out her palm toward Sue Beth.

"What?" Gavin glanced at his mamas. "No. I want you to stay out of it. These men are shady."

"Just let me do this one thing. Your shady guy will never know who I am."

"No."

"You don't want me to prove I can think clearly enough to be on my own. Is that it?"

"This conversation is over. I've said what I needed to."

Sue Beth stepped forward, holding out a phone. "I found it."

Tara tapped on the photo app and showed a picture of her wounds from a week ago, zooming in on the bruises. "This is what that guy did to my arm."

Julep leaned in, studying the phone in Tara's hand. "You took photos of your injuries?"

"Hadley did, wanting to take note of my injuries while they were fresh so we could talk about everything once I was feeling clearheaded. And we did, although I'm not sure why she used my phone to take the pictures in-

stead of hers. But it's proving to be convenient, so let's put it to good use."
She looked to Gavin. "Your shiplap guy's number?"

He shook his head. "Nope."

"I'm not putting myself in harm's way if that's your concern."

"Just let it go. Your head wasn't in a good place that night. You can't
pretend it was."

She couldn't argue against the fog of confusion she'd been submerged
in when that man came into Gavin's home. Even now, her grief and the
unreality of her world jumbled her thoughts, but to get everyone to leave her
alone, she had to sound like an intelligent, grounded woman.

Dell waved her phone in the air. "I got it. Took me a few to find the
name of the company in a text Gavin sent."

Gavin looked at Dell. "What are you doing? Trying to prove you'll be
her buddies? That you're the ones to stay with because you know how to
help her do whatever she wants, regardless of how unwise or unsafe the
plan is?"

"Gavin." Dell thrust her phone forward. "We need that money to go
toward the balloon payment. All of us are in the same fight to make that
balloon payment, and if she can help, we—"

"No. The guy is sleazy. I don't want him thinking Tara could testify
against him, and I don't want him having any of your phone numbers."

"But if we gave her the buyer's contact info and she anonymously sent a
photo of the bruises," Sue Beth said.

His eyes narrowed as he looked at each mom. "Stop this." His voice was
hardly more than a whisper. "Now."

Dell lowered her phone. "Sorry, Tara. I . . . I can't."

Sue Beth's smile held an apology. "Sorry," she whispered.

Apparently God had spoken.

Tara rubbed the bruise the thief had caused when he shoved her down
before storming out of the house. "This whole thing reminds me of a bad

movie where the men know exactly what needs to be done and the women are too stupid to figure out anything useful."

"This is no movie, Tara."

"And I'm not a useless oaf. During my worst days when I completely believed my dream that my brothers were alive, I still managed to rescue a girl trapped by the incoming tide, and I stopped that man from stealing any of the shiplap in the house."

Fresh hurt roiled through her. Her thoughts and opinions used to matter. Is this what it would be like now because of her head trauma? People would assume she was too addled to know what she *knew* to be true? Her eyes filled with tears.

"Honey, you okay?" Sue Beth asked.

Tara wiped her tears. *No.* And she wouldn't be for a really long time, maybe not ever. But it was time to gather her belongings and get off this island. Her thoughts shifted to her suitcase and Darryl's rock. Since relearning the truth of her brothers' deaths, she'd been missing Darryl's rock but had forgotten where it was until now. Apparently no one else had given one thought to the fact that she might have come to the island with a suitcase. "I need my suitcase from the hotel." She went to the bike she'd taken from Gavin's shed.

"You're sure no one's picked it up for you yet?"

She nodded her head. "Apparently, no one's thought about it, including me. It's at the Lighthouse Inn, not far from here."

"You can't carry a suitcase on that bike," Julep said. "Sue Beth will go with you to my house." Julep hurried down the gazebo steps. "Luella's car is still parked at the store from when we carpooled yesterday. She'll go by the hotel and get the suitcase. We'll meet you at my house in just a bit."

Tara nodded. Sue Beth grinned as she tiptoed across the dewy grass, apparently trying to avoid getting her bare feet wet.

Tara didn't wait. She got on the bike. It was time to go see Hadley and Elliott and make plans to head back to North Carolina.

22

W hy?" His mom stood at the foot of the gazebo, her hands on her hips. "Why are you determined to run her off?"

Gavin remained in place, watching Tara go down the sidewalk on the bike. "You're not thinking about this situation for what it is. You're romanticizing it."

"That's not fair." His mom waved her index finger at him. "First we're selfish where she's concerned, and then when we reach out, we're doing it for the wrong reasons?"

"Yeah." Dell shrugged. "I'm confused too. We were trying to help her. Isn't that what you wanted, for us to see her value and be kind?"

"I was hoping for something between random cruelty and taking her on as a long-term project. She doesn't need to be patronized this way."

"That's a horrid thing to say about her." His mom shook her head. "She's a bit headstrong, but she's a lovely and genuine woman."

"I'm aware." Too aware.

He wasn't one to use his phone for anything except what was needed. He didn't play games on it or go to social media sites. But he'd spent all his downtime during the night, when he should've been catching some z's, reading the Facebook pages for Sean, Darryl, and Tara. His heart ached for her loss—for the world's loss—because it was clear that Sean and Darryl believed in making a positive difference in their corner of this planet.

Gavin watched as Tara turned a corner, moving beyond his line of sight. "She's locked inside grief and shock. That's the world she'll remember, and it's about all she's actually seeing right now. We're a fog—a misty, muddled dream that only sort of exists. If you're thinking she's capable of building any kind of relationship, especially one where you'll receive gratitude and recognition, you need to think again."

"That's your problem?" The lines on his mom's face twisted and bunched. "You think we're too shallow to see this thing through unless we get some kind of reward back?"

"He may have a couple of points," Luella said. "One, she's at the beginning of a very long journey. She could continue to improve, or she could regress several times along the way. Do we really have what it would have taken if she'd chosen to stay?"

"I don't know." His mom slapped her hands against her thighs. "We barely got a chance to try before it ended."

"There's no *trying* on something like this, Mom. It's full commitment, or don't go to the altar. You do understand the stress of the coming weeks, right? The reality of our finances? We could lose the house. Where would she stay then? If we lose the house, we lose the business too. How up for helping anyone will the Glynn Girls be if that happens?"

"I don't know, but our house isn't the only place she could've stayed."

He knew the living situation for the other Glynn Girls. "Luella's place is tiny."

"Well, yeah." Luella wagged her finger, a smile on her lips. "But for the sake of my ego, could you at least clarify that I'm thrifty so I can travel for months at a time every year without thinking about a mortgage?"

Gavin gestured at Dell. "Her place is Grand Central Station with her adult kids and grandkids coming in and out as though they lived there. Dell doesn't have room for a miniature pup when her family is there. That leaves Sue Beth's home."

"Not a good place for Tara." Dell shook her head. "Sue Beth's husband is a curmudgeon."

"Dell," Luella scolded.

"Well, he is. And everybody standing here knows it."

Luella bobbled her head, apparently conceding to Dell's point. "Gavin's right about the memory thing too. Years ago when my aunt was in her thirties, she lost her husband to cancer. After he passed, I made time each day to talk with her on the phone. I baked for her and cleaned her house and poured so much effort into helping her get through that time. Years later that time came up in a conversation, and I realized she had no recollection of all I'd done. None."

"That's ridiculous. When Mitch died, I wasn't like that." His mom studied him. "Was I?"

"Yeah, you were," Dell said. "It wasn't complete lack of recall, but at first you could hardly remember Gavin's name, let alone when you'd eaten or who'd come to visit or why you had a can opener in your hand."

Gavin nodded. "The pantry would be empty, and we'd make a list together. You'd go to the grocery store, list in hand, and come home with nothing but sardines."

His mom blinked. "We don't eat sardines."

"Trust me, I know." Gavin shuddered and winked at her. "The difference between you and Tara is you knew for years that Dad's health was declining. He was a heavy smoker who hated fruits, vegetables, and exercise. You'd told me a dozen times over the last decade that each of you understood you could be left here without the other at some point. Because of the cancer diagnosis, you had a few weeks to say goodbye." That hadn't been enough, but to be in Tara's shoes was unimaginable to him.

"*We* had that. You're included, but I see what you're saying. Truth is, I should've had at least six more months than I got, but I guess nothing actually prepares a person." His mom shrugged.

"There's still-not-prepared-enough, and there's totally-blown-apart-by-the-shock-of-it. For all intents and purposes, Tara has lost two children. It never felt possible to her that she could lose her brothers, these boys that she was working every day to give a good life to so they could embark on adulthood as unscarred and full of hope and promise as humanly possible."

His mom's brows furrowed. "How do you know what she was like as their guardian?"

"Darryl's Facebook page. He was quite open about who she was to him. Sean was more discreet, but he describes a woman on a mission for his best interests."

His mom sat on the steps of the gazebo and motioned for him to sit beside her. Dell held out a cup of coffee to him, and Luella opened one of the wrappers to a sausage and egg biscuit. It was their apology. He took the coffee and biscuit. That was his acceptance of their apology.

His mom leaned her head on his shoulder. "Most days I'm in denial that we might really lose the house."

"And I hope we don't, Mom, but, yeah, the possibility turned into more of a probability the day the man stole the shiplap." He wouldn't remind them that it was their harebrained booby trap that caused him to miss the buyer's arrival.

"But Tara said she saw the man."

"And on that same night, she wanted to know what I was doing in *her* house. You know—the large beach home that she mistook for a cabin in the mountains of North Carolina. You have to let go of what Tara says she remembers about that night."

His mom squeezed his arm. "Yeah, okay. I trust you. And I get that she's inside a world exploding with grief far beyond what I've gone through. But whether we have a house or no house, I think we were up to the challenge of helping her. Is that it? We throw in the towel after one night of looking after her?"

Luella shrugged. "I think it has to be."

"Mom, she decided to go back with Hadley and Elliott. Let it be. They're her family. They know her and love her the most."

"Well, to be fair"—Dell grabbed a blanket off the floor and folded it— "she only agreed to go back because you were doing all you could to push her in that direction."

He couldn't argue with her on that.

His mom turned to Luella. "My house is full of guests, and I should go home now. You're going to the hotel to get her suitcase, right?"

Dell elbowed Luella. "Yeah, you're going to the hotel now, right?"

Luella moaned. "Apparently so." She ran her fingers through her wind-tossed curls and tugged at her wrinkled shirt. "This current slept-outdoors look should confirm Chuck's opinion that I'm a true-blue weirdo."

The women were into girl talk now, and Gavin tuned it out, his thoughts centering on Tara. He'd done what needed to be done. That's who he was by nature—figure out what needed to be done, and do it.

So why did he feel that he'd just said a forever goodbye to a close friend—one who fell just short of detesting him?

23

Luella walked into the Lighthouse Inn. The coolness of air-conditioning hit her sweaty body, and chills ran down her arms. How hot would it be by noon?

Clarissa was manning the front desk again. Perhaps she could answer Luella's questions. That would be one way to avoid embarrassing herself in front of Chuck again. So why was she walking toward his office?

Luella, stop!

Still, she crossed the lobby, her body feeling more in control than her brain. Maybe it was too early for him to be in. *Heavens to Betsy, woman! Make up your mind. Do you or do you not want to see him?*

She paused outside his closed office door. Her T-shirt clung to her from the sticky salt air and bike ride here. Since the Lighthouse Inn was closer than her car, it'd made sense to bike here, get the suitcase, and then walk both to her car that sat a block away. But maybe she should've thought this through a little better. She brushed her hands down the wrinkles, which did absolutely nothing to help the appearance of the shirt.

The door had a shiny new plate on it.

Charles McKenzie, Senior Property Manager

"Thank goodness he cleared that one up," she muttered. Didn't every resident on the island know that within days of his plane landing?

Why did this man discombobulate her? Maybe she and the girls were a little nuttier than she'd realized before meeting him, but she loved her life and her friends just as they were. She'd dated her fair share of men over the decades, and caring what they thought had barely registered with any of them. Why were this man's reactions on her radar?

Come on, Luella. Pull it together. You're too old to be confused over a man. She drew a deep breath and knocked.

"Come in."

Chuck sounded cheery. Maybe that would work in her favor. She wiped sweat off her face, put on her best smile, and opened the door.

He glanced, jolted, and almost dropped the book he was putting on the shelf. "Ms. Ward."

"Mr. McKenzie." She closed the door behind her. *Why? Why did I do that?* "Do you have a moment?"

He nodded, smiling. "I do. I'm just adding some finishing touches to my office." He set the book on the shelf. "What brings you here?" The skin around his eyes crinkled, the sign of a man who smiled often.

Here's hoping he'll ignore the embarrassing run-in at the marsh.

She ambled to the chair facing his desk and sat. "I'm here as a favor to a former guest of yours. Her name is Tara Abbott."

He walked to the front of the desk and leaned against it. "You know Tara?"

Why had he moved in so close? She hadn't showered or brushed her teeth or hair. Sitting behind his desk was the least he could do in her present state, wasn't it?

Keep things light. "Is that a trick question?"

"No." He chuckled. "Obviously you know her, and I don't typically remember the guests' names, but she left her luggage with us. Is she still on the island?"

"Yes, and I'm here for her suitcase." At this rate of exchanging info, she could be out of here before she stuck her foot in her mouth or did something stupid. Again.

"I couldn't hand it over to you without getting her ID and a signature via fax or text, but—"

"Wait." Fire seemed to engulf Luella's heart. "Let me get this straight. I came to you with Tara's name and the information that she left her suitcase here, which clearly matches your knowledge of the situation. And yet despite that and despite knowing me, you can't release her suitcase without her ID and signature? I knew you were a stickler about rules, and that trait is probably part of the reason you're managing what feels like half of this island, but heavens to Betsy, Charles."

He studied her. "You're right."

"Really?" Luella regretted that response. "I mean, yes, I am, but I didn't expect you to think so." His reactions and responses continually caught her off guard. When it wasn't annoying or offending, she found it quite refreshing.

He smiled. "Unfortunately, your point doesn't actually matter." He moved back to the seat behind his desk and typed on the keyboard. "We don't have it. We held on to it for a week, but then I shipped it to the address she listed when making the reservation." He seemed to be studying info, maybe a shipping receipt. "Should I call UPS and get the package sent back here? It was picked up at ten in the morning two days ago."

Not the news Luella wanted to give Tara. She'd leave the island before the suitcase could return. "I suppose not. But thanks for the info."

His eyes held concern. "It seems odd she didn't come back or send someone sooner. Is she okay?"

How much should she share with him about Tara? While mulling that over she noted again that he really was a very nice-looking man. Always pulled together and clean. She ran her fingers through her hair, trying to focus. Why was she so hung up on how she looked . . . and smelled? "She's . . . struggling a bit."

"Struggling?"

Had Chuck met Tara? Maybe not since he didn't seem to know how confused she was. "You didn't meet her, did you?"

"Not that I recall."

Should she share that Tara was the woman on the top of the lighthouse after it'd closed on the night they met? Would that clarify anything for him?

Charles moved the mouse, clicked on something, and then focused on Luella. "My team said she asked to stay for additional nights, but we were booked. They tried to find her another hotel but couldn't. You know how peak season is. I was told she left, saying she'd return for her suitcase by the end of the day. Is there a problem?"

Were his concerns centered on how well his team dealt with the situation? "I'm sure your staff was as helpful as they could be. She's just a bit confused right now."

"Ah." He nodded and paused. "Did she see you and your friends chanting on the water?"

Luella almost laughed but stopped herself, refusing to do as much as smile. He'd timed his quip with expertise, catching her completely off guard. She narrowed her eyes at him. "No, that would be you. Remember?"

He chuckled. "Ah, yes, I seem to recall that." His smile was lopsided now. "You're an interesting woman, Luella."

What? "I think the description you're looking for is 'nuttier than a fruitcake.'"

"Does anyone eat fruitcakes often enough to know if they have nuts?"

"It's a Southern saying."

"You have a lot of those."

"We do. It saves us from having to think up things on our own."

He chuckled. "I hadn't thought of that."

"Of course not. You gotta be Southern-smart to figure that out." She leaned back in the chair. "Reading would help." She suppressed a smile and turned her head, taking a quick inventory of his bookshelves. Clearly he was a reader. The spines from a familiar series of books took up half of a shelf. What? Was that an almost full set of her Demere Cultural Guides? She hoped she looked nonchalant as she got up and walked closer.

I'll swanee . . .

"Would you like a cup of coffee?"

He had *her* books? Not one or two, but the entire series, and based on the bindings, he'd read them more than once . . . or someone had. Maybe he picked them up at a garage sale and hadn't even opened them.

"Ms. Ward?"

She blinked and refocused her attention.

He stood at the coffee maker on the far side of his office, holding the carafe. When had he gotten up and crossed the room?

"Uh, yeah . . . I mean, no. But thanks."

He set the carafe on the warmer and went back to his desk.

She gestured toward the books. "Have you read all the books in your case?"

"Definitely. But I own far too many books to keep them all, so the ones on my shelves are my favorites. Why?"

He had to know who she was. Had to. This was a setup—him putting her books on his shelves, the ones she wrote as L. Demere.

"Do you like books, Luella?" He picked up a stack of books and moved toward the shelf.

"Uh, yeah, you could say that. This is a joke, right?"

"A joke?" He paused, books in hand. "Did I miss something?"

She studied him. The man seemed truly clueless. "I just thought . . . Never mind. I seem to be wrong more than right of late."

"Happens to everybody at times."

If he didn't know who she was, then the fact that her books were counted among his favorites was staggering. He intrigued her in a way few men had in her lifetime. Had she ruined all chances of their becoming friends? Adding a man near her own age to her list of enjoyable people to spend time with could introduce some much-needed zest to her off time. A book lover was always game for spending hours in a used bookstore.

"Yeah, I suppose it does." Should she let him know who she was or let him keep his illusion that L. Demere was a refined, knowledgeable writer? "You know, I'm not as weird as I've seemed in some of our encounters."

Why did she say that? It was like highlighting in his mind every weird thing she'd done since they met. It only made her look worse and made things more awkward between them. "Anyway, I should go." She headed for the door. "I'll let Tara know about her suitcase. Thanks."

"Luella?"

His voice seemed to hold several sentiments, including gentleness and encouragement, and she was powerless to leave even if she wanted to.

She turned.

He smiled, looking into her eyes before he turned to shelve another book. "I don't think for a moment that I know who you are because of a few unusual encounters."

He what? Her heart pounded, delight suddenly fighting to leap out and praise his open-mindedness. But she refrained by the skin of her teeth. "People tend to make up their minds pretty quickly about one another."

"I learned my lesson on that one." He seemed unwilling to look at her and kept his attention on the books as he shelved them. "I thought I knew my wife, but after ten years of marriage and two young children, I realized I'd never known her, not even close. She looked as if she had everything together, looked as if she believed in loyalty and regard for others, but that was a lie."

Luella fought to find her voice. His vulnerability floored her, and she could sense the pain he'd gone through. That's why he'd refused to assume who she was. "I'm sorry."

He dropped his hand from the shelf. "It's long over, and none of that has bothered me for more than a decade. But it was a hard lesson, and I'll never forget it." His words hung in the air for a moment, and then he glanced at her, the left corner of his mouth curling in a lopsided grin. "I've found I'm warming to the quirks of you and your friends. Maybe I could join you for the reading of Sidney Lanier's poem next year if I'm still on the island. Unless the poem reading is an invite-only event."

What a strange conversation. "I thought we weren't allowed near Tidal Creek Grill?"

"Oh, you're certainly taking that show somewhere else. But I'd still like to come."

Close your mouth, Luella, and go. But she walked over to the bookcase and traced the spines of the Demere Culture Guides with her index finger. She probably had a silly grin on her face. Julep always said she was terrible at poker. "You know, L. Demere is doing a book signing at *our* store this Friday."

"You're kidding."

What do you know? He actually looked interested. "I'm not. There's a special updated twentieth-anniversary edition of the *St. Simons Island Culture Guide* coming out. Did you know L. Demere's first book was written about St. Simons?"

"I didn't. I need to get it." He grinned. "You're telling me one of my favorite travel writers is coming *here*?"

She raised her shoulders and hands in her best attempt at a nonchalant shrug. It was all too much fun to string him along. "Maybe I should have told you about the book signing earlier. If I had, maybe you'd have been more open to giving us a bigger, nicer shop." Time to come clean. She couldn't wait to see the look on his face when he found out he had been reading her books.

The phone rang, making her jump.

He flashed her a smile. "Excuse me." He picked up the receiver, and after a few seconds he sounded miffed. "What?" He listened and then gave a list of short answers. "I said no. You do nothing until I get there." He hung up. "I'm so sorry, but I need to go." He gathered his briefcase and few belongings as he spoke. "I'd love to talk more, but it will need to be at the book signing."

She held up a finger. "Okay, but I just need to tell you something real quick—"

"It'll have to wait." He walked to the office door and pulled it open.

"But—"

"Sincerest apologies, Luella." He gave her a nod. "We'll talk later."

Well. At least he took his business seriously. Very seriously. She'd never felt that kind of intensity about her work. "Okay."

"I trust you know your way out."

"Yeah, I'm fine. Go."

"Thanks." He rushed off, leaving her standing in his office door.

Oh well. At least I tried.

24

T ara sat in a recliner, staring out a window.

Voices echoed inside Julep's home—Hadley's girls playing, the Glynn Girls talking as they prepared supper, and her friends discussing the best way to load the luggage on top of the SUV.

Had all conversations before now been ninety-five percent twaddle and she just hadn't realized it?

The house had too much of it. She'd returned here from the gazebo yesterday morning and slept here last night. But the solitude of the bike ride and sleeping in the gazebo night before last had been more soothing to her soul than being in a busy home. Hadley wanted to head out around the kids' bedtime so they would sleep the whole way home.

Her thoughts returned to Sean and Darryl. She longed to be with them, to hug them and laugh with them and scold them and help prepare for the next phase of their lives. There was always a new, next chapter, and they'd worked together to be ready for it. How had it all ended without warning? What was she supposed to do with her days? The bustle of her own family was gone, just completely over.

"Tara?" Hadley put her hand on Tara's knee.

Tara blinked, trying to hear her.

"It's time to eat."

Tara peered beyond Hadley to see her friend's two young daughters— May and Isla—staring at her. How many times had Hadley called to Tara? Beyond them was Julep's dining room with the Glynn Girls and Tara's friends and their families.

"Yeah, sure." She followed Hadley into the dining room and sat.

The mealtime prayer and following conversations around the table barely registered. If the truth of her brothers being dead had set her free, she'd been freed inside a dark, windowless room. Why hadn't God taken her too?

Luella touched Tara's leg, and Tara tried to see beyond the darkness of the windowless room. Luella nodded at Hadley.

Tara turned, realizing Hadley was asking her something.

"It was May's idea for us to bring your laptop. When we bought you a new cell phone, we used the last phone backup you'd made to your laptop to set up your new phone."

"Thanks." She smiled at seven-year-old May. But what did Tara need a cell phone for? To be more painfully aware that Sean and Darryl weren't calling or texting? And to be constantly reminded they would never call or text again? "That was very smart of you, May."

May grinned. "Mom says that your phone now has all the texts you've ever sent or received on it."

Tara nodded. "I am grateful not to have lost those."

"Auntie T,"—May shoved a bite of steak into her mouth—"what's wrong with your voice?"

Hadley smiled at May. "Let's talk about it later. Okay, sweetie?"

"There's something different?" Tara asked.

"It's just temporary." Elliott wiped her mouth with a napkin. "It's not well researched, but people who are in the throes of grief often have a different speaking voice than before the incident."

May angled her head. "That's it! All the joy is missing from your voice." May's little face contorted. "You used to laugh all the time."

"I guess so." Tara forced a smile. "But that's okay, May. It's human to go through really sad times, and it's okay to sound and look different from that point onward." She winked. "It would be far sadder if I was the same person after Sean and Darryl died as I was before, right?"

May propped her elbows on the table. "I hadn't thought of that."

Elliott cleared her throat. "When you feel like getting on Facebook, you should look at your home page. There's been an outpouring of love and condolences."

"I will. I don't know when, but I will."

"You sure you want to keep waiting?" Hadley asked. "It seems like that could be cathartic."

"If I thought that, I would hop on Facebook and read every comment. If I wanted to go home to grieve, I would've said so. Apparently my way of grieving doesn't meet with your approval."

"I didn't mean . . ." Hadley drew a slow breath. "It was a suggestion, T."

"Yeah, and is going back to North Carolina a suggestion too?"

Hadley pursed her lips. "Lynn from the grocery store set up a Go-FundMe page for you, and it's also filled with an outpouring of love in messages and donations. Someone anonymously donated five thousand dollars, and we guessed it was your boss from the outfitter store."

Tara hadn't thought of her two jobs one time in the last . . . "How long have I been here?"

"Sixteen days." Elliott put her hand in Tara's.

"Odd." It felt as though it'd been a lifetime in some ways, as though nothing had ever existed outside of her need to find her brothers. Her arms ached with a hunger to hug Sean and Darryl.

"Lynn said they would hold your position at the store for as long as you need, and George Webb from the outfitter store said the same thing."

"You had two jobs?" Sue Beth asked.

Tara nodded. "One paid the bills, and the other offered great discounts and funded our love of outdoor adventure. Plus the outfitter store allowed Sean and Darryl to work in their bike-repair shop starting at a young age."

She liked her coworkers at both places. They had become friends, and Lynn and Webb, which is what most people called him, almost seemed like relatives. Lynn was the age of the Glynn Girls, so she was a bit like a mom, and Webb was old enough to be her dad but was extremely fit. They occasionally came to dinner with their spouses. Sean and Darryl had worked for Webb in the summers and on weekends.

Her brothers.

She missed their smiles and laughter so much she could hardly breathe, and thoughts of the day she agreed to raise them returned to her again. "My rock!" She looked at Luella. "Did you get my suitcase?"

"Oh." Luella fidgeted with the condensation on her glass. "I went by the hotel, and since you hadn't returned to the hotel, the manager thought you couldn't find another hotel and must've gone home. He shipped it to the address registered with the hotel."

Tara longed to hold the rock, but that desire made no sense.

"Well, that's not so bad." Elliott squeezed Tara's fingers. "I'll take you to the cabin to grab your suitcase tomorrow evening."

"Okay." She stood. "Thanks." Did she look as disoriented as she felt? "I need to go for a walk."

"Sure, sweetie." Hadley held up a bottle of pills. "Take your medicine first, and take your phone with you. We're leaving in about two hours."

Tara downed the pill with a few swallows of water. She thought it odd that they would travel at night, because the kids might be wide-awake once they got home in the middle of the night. But that wasn't Tara's responsibility. Actually, she didn't have any responsibilities anymore. Even work had served only one purpose—to take care of Sean and Darryl.

She went out the door, down the stairs, and to the narrow asphalt road. The screen door creaked, and she knew someone was keeping an eye on her. Ignoring it, she walked to the road that ran parallel to the marsh and went right. When a long pier came into sight, she went to it. The air vibrated with sounds of creatures she didn't recognize. She breathed deep, smelling the marsh and the nearby wildflowers. The sun edged toward the horizon, and the sky held a multitude of shades of blue and orange.

"God, I don't want to be here on this planet." She wiped her tears. "Please, I can't take any more. Help me."

Unsure what she was asking, Tara dropped the prayer. Did it matter what she wanted or needed?

25

L uella and the Glynn Girls quietly followed Tara, probably a hundred yards behind her. The young woman deserved to grieve in peace, but Luella couldn't let Tara get out of sight. Julep, Dell, and Sue Beth said they felt the same way. But the other Glynn Girls hadn't seen what Luella had—the moment when Tara looked like Sapphira.

Perhaps it happened because Sapphira had been a rare woman with many rare qualities, and in that moment Tara had seemed to have them too. Or maybe it was just the overwhelming sadness Tara bore. Sapphira had carried a similar burden for more than two decades. Luella didn't know why, but Tara felt like a part of her now—as if she somehow belonged to her.

Tara walked to the far end of the pier where the narrow planks opened to a gazebo over the marsh. She seemed to gravitate to gazebos, whether on this side of the island or near the lighthouse. She seemed so lost, and Luella ached as though she suffered the loss with her. Julep took Luella's hand. Oh. The girls were going to pray. She joined them in praying, eyes open, as they watched the soft summertime dusk take over the marsh. It was like being inside a dream.

The longer they held hands, quietly praying, the stronger Luella's desire grew to walk to the pavilion and say something that might stir the young woman's heart with hope. But what could she possibly say?

"Come on." Luella tugged on Julep's hand before releasing it. They walked the long stretch of creaking boards. Tara turned and glanced at them, her face wet with tears. Luella moved to one side of her, and Julep came up on the other side.

Luella leaned in, catching Julep's eyes. "'Glooms of the live-oaks, beautiful-braided and woven . . .'"

A chorus of Glynn Girl voices finished that first line.

Yes. This was right. Reciting the poem for Tara in unity, in love, in hopes of lifting some of the grief off this young woman, and so they continued reciting the poem, and Luella's heart stirred.

"... And my spirit is grown to a lordly great compass within,
That the length and the breadth and the sweep of the Marshes
    of Glynn
Will work me no fear like the fear they have wrought me of yore
When length was fatigue, and when breadth was but bitterness
    sore, . . .

"... To the edge of the wood I am drawn, I am drawn,
Where the gray beach glimmering runs, as a belt of the dawn,
For a mete and a mark
To the forest-dark:—
So:
Affable live-oak, leaning low . . .
Bending your beauty aside, with a step I stand
On the firm-packed sand,
Free . . ."

Yes, Lord. Let Tara be free . . .

"Ye marshes, how candid and simple and nothing-withholding
    and free
Ye publish yourselves to the sky and offer yourselves to the sea!
Tolerant plains, that suffer the sea and the rains and the sun,
Ye spread and span like the catholic man who hath mightily won

God out of knowledge and good out of infinite pain
And sight out of blindness and purity out of a stain.

"As the marsh-hen secretly builds on the watery sod,
Behold I will build me a nest on the greatness of God:
I will fly in the greatness of God as the marsh-hen flies
In the freedom that fills all the space 'twixt the marsh and the
      skies:
By so many roots as the marsh-grass sends in the sod
I will heartily lay me a-hold on the greatness of God."

Such powerful words! Words to encourage and heal. The Glynn Girls' voices rose as if each one sensed the same thing. Their passionate voices spoke every syllable of the poem until coming to its end.

On the length and the breadth of the marvellous marshes of Glynn.

They stood in silence, listening to a summer's eve on the marsh—birds singing and insects chirping.

Tara shifted and clutched Julep's arm. "Do you hear the whisper?" Tara's skin was covered in goose bumps.

The women glanced at each other, shrugging their shoulders ever so slightly.

Tara's eyes were wide. "I can't leave here yet. I can't."

"What did you hear?"

"A whisper. It sounded like Sean saying *stay.* I know it might not be real. It could be a symptom of my head or heart trauma. But . . ."

"It's okay, Tara." Julep put her arm around Tara. "This land is filled with unusual things, long shadows, and odd noises."

Tara backed away from the four women. "I . . . I need to stay here. On St. Simons. Please."

"We would welcome you, sugar"—Sue Beth put her hands on Tara's shoulders—"but it's not our decision."

The Glynn Girls nodded.

"Gavin is as patient as the day is long," Dell said. "And he's never stood his ground with us the way he did the other day. We gotta respect that."

Tara peered beyond them, gazing across the marsh again. "But you'd let me stay with you if he agreed?" A few moments later she looked at Luella. How could she refuse? She nodded, and when Tara looked at the other Glynn Girls, each of them nodded too. "Then he'll have to approve it. Where is he?"

"He's at work. We're not supposed to go to the fire station unless someone at the station extends an invite."

"There are no exceptions?"

Julep shrugged. "I'm a bit unsure." She tilted her head. "But as I think about it now, it seems that with Gavin being single and having no children, he's never interrupted by family coming to see him." Julep narrowed her eyes. "It's time we change that."

Tara's lips tugged into a smile. "Am I family?"

"Most definitely." Luella grinned.

"It's the station I've passed half a dozen times over the last week, right?"

"Yeah, that's it," Dell said.

Tara walked away, and her step seemed to have a little lilt to it.

The Glynn Girls followed, and Luella had a feeling they'd all be on bikes again soon.

Real soon.

26

G avin chopped carrots with a vengeance before dropping them into a simmering skillet of onions and mushrooms. He and the men had been out on a call since midafternoon, and it was past eight. Everyone was hungry, and four men were making dinner while the others tended to the equipment.

His mind returned to the debt threatening to ruin his credit and take the home his parents had built together. He had continued taking Sapphira's house apart, and next week surveyors were lined up to survey the property and break it into two lots. But unless a miracle happened, despite selling off parts of Sapphira's home to the highest bidder and breaking the land into two lots, he'd still be short by at least two hundred thousand dollars, maybe three. Hopefully not four.

"Lieutenant!" Bryan ran inside, a grin a mile wide on his face. "She's here."

"Yeah?" Gavin wiped his hands on the towel-turned-apron draping from the waist of his blue pants. "Your mom arrived early? We could set an extra pl—"

"Not what I meant."

Gavin plunked celery onto the cutting board and slid a knife across it. Several men flocked to the kitchen window, and murmurs rumbled. Seconds later ghostly sounds filled the air, the same ones the men had played off and on since his encounter with Mary at the beach.

"This again?" Gavin asked.

The men elbowed each other and chuckled.

"Lieutenant." Bryan leaned in. "It's *her*. I'm sure of it."

Something in the boy's eyes said he wasn't teasing.

Jimmy waved his hands slowly through the air, making spooky noises. "It's Maaaarrrryyyy."

"Here?" Gavin set the knife down. "At the station?"

"On the driveway near the road." Bryan's eyes were wide. "Should I ask her in?"

Gavin went to the window, and the men made room for him. The sun had set, and the night sky had a hazy purple glow. He skimmed the landscape.

Tara . . .

Her feet were on the ground, straddling the bike he rode as a teen. She had on the white dress, and a breeze tousled her blond hair. The sight was unforgettable.

"No." Gavin turned. "I'll go to her."

Jimmy clasped his shoulder. "Did you hire someone to prove to us Mary existed?"

The men chortled.

"Look." Derrick pointed. "Your mamas are at the corner near the stop sign, watching her."

The men broke into laughter.

"Do you think they've become ghost chasers?" someone asked.

Gavin held up one hand. "Someone man the stir-fry on the stove. I'll go see what's up, but let this one be, okay, guys? Turn off the haunted sounds, and act like men with good sense for just a few minutes. Is that too much to ask?" He strode out the front door and walked toward her, his heart pounding like crazy. What was with that?

The Glynn Girls were staying a couple hundred feet back. Did Tara know they were there?

"Hey." He smiled. "Out for a last evening ride?"

Her focus seemed glued to the open bays of the fire station. "I . . . need to stay here . . . on the island."

She needed to? He glanced at his mamas. "I don't think—"

Tara looked him directly in the eyes, and even in the growing darkness he could see tears glistening. "Please."

Beyond her grief he could feel her displeasure at having to be here, her dislike of him. He was a thorn in her flesh. Why couldn't she see that it was in her best interest to leave with Hadley and Elliott? His mamas' hearts were in the right place, no doubt. But they were often scattered and forgetful and absolute mischief magnets.

As he thought about her request, he turned a bit, positioning himself so he could see his mamas, the firehouse, and Tara simultaneously. The recording of the "ghost sounds" grew louder, and the raggedy ghost figure they'd dangled over Gavin's bed now hung out the window, dancing in the wind. Gavin moved again, going to the other side of her, causing her to turn toward the road and away from the station. Would that keep her from becoming aware of the nonsense? "Listen, Tara, I really do think it would be better for you to go back. Give yourself some time to heal physically. Then you could return here in a few months."

The music grew louder, and the waving of the Mary ghost intensified. If he wasn't trying to distract Tara's attention, he'd turn and issue an order—a loud one.

The Glynn Girls rode past Gavin and Tara on bicycles.

"Pardon us." His mom's voice was polite, but her face said she was about to have a conniption.

Tara didn't seem to notice.

Luella and Dell rode into an open bay. His mom and Sue Beth dumped their bikes outside the bay. A moment later he saw Luella pointing a finger at Jimmy, and it took a lot to make Luella lose her cool. Ten seconds later all ghost noises stopped, and soon after, the ghost figure was pulled inside. The bay closed, and he imagined his coworkers were being chewed out by the Glynn Girls.

Hell had no fury like four mama hens . . .

She stared at the sidewalk. "It's peak season, and you don't like that I won't be able to find a place other than staying with one of your mamas."

"That's not the issue." How could he explain that her willingness to live with strangers in order to stay on an island she had no connections to was indicative of her condition? Or explain that his mamas were scattered and busy? In her condition it wasn't a safe or healthy way to live. She needed someone looking after her emotional and physical health, and she wasn't choosing the people who could give her the best care.

"Tara, the best situation for healing and recovery is at home with your friends."

She put her fist against her chest. "I don't know why I felt such a need to come to St. Simons after the funeral, but whatever the reason, I'm not finished here. I know that much. Maybe I only need a week or two, but now's not the right time for me to leave."

Part of him—the illogical, emotional part—wanted her to stay. He inhaled. "Okay." What else could he say? *It's a free country, but you can't stay on my island because* . . . Because what? He had no real reason that would work in her mind, only his.

"Good." A hint of a smile lifted her lips. "I have to go back and tell Hadley and Elliott as gently and positively as I can that I'm staying, and even so they'll need to talk to you and the Glynn Girls."

"Okay, but any of us can reassure them only a certain amount."

"My promises to them and your word on it to them will be enough."

What was Gavin agreeing to? And why?

He stifled a sigh. "You've got your phone with you, right?"

She nodded.

"I need to see it for a minute."

"You're going to track me?"

"I'll only use that function if no one knows where you are and you aren't answering texts or calls."

Her face mirrored disgust with him and maybe hurt. He understood both sentiments. It was an unfair position to be in. She'd gone from being an independent woman, a successful leader of a home, to yielding to a stranger she neither liked nor worked for. There were few things people liked less than having their freedoms curtailed.

"Come on." She gestured to the bikes near the bay. So she had seen them pass. Had she also been aware of the ghost nonsense and teasing? "Seriously? With the Glynn Girls on watch, I'll do well to be allowed to shower alone."

Gavin sighed. "I get it. Still . . ." He held out his hand. The Glynn Girls worked long hours most days.

She reached into her bra, pulled out the phone, and slapped it against his palm. He went into Settings and allowed her phone to share locations with his so he could ping her phone easily and know right where she was . . . or at least where her phone was. If she chose to be difficult, he couldn't do a lot about it.

"You done?" Her voice had an edge to it.

"Almost." He needed to go into the App Store and download the Find My Friends phone app. He sent a ping from his phone to hers, and then he sent a text from her phone to his and responded to it. Both worked. "All done." He passed her the phone. "As I said, I'll only use the Find My Friends feature if all other ways have failed."

"Then why do I suddenly feel like I'm a child?"

He imagined it was because she felt powerless, but she was in no state of mind to recognize that it wouldn't always be this way.

⁓

Tara hugged and kissed May and Isla as she buckled each girl into her car seat. The streetlamp and overhead car lights cast a golden glow on the baby's and the children's faces. They didn't look sleepy, but Tara imagined once the lights were off and the car was in motion, they'd be asleep in short order. "I'll send a picture of somewhere on the island each day to your mom's phone, so you ask her about it."

"Are you going to do selfies, Aunt T?" May asked.

Tara couldn't imagine pasting on a smile and posing long enough to do a selfie. "I think I should stick to nature, and when you look at the picture, you try to figure out where on the island I was when I took it."

May smiled and wrapped her little arms around Tara's neck. "I'm glad you're better."

"Me too." She winked at Isla and waved one more time before closing the door.

Hadley, Elliott, and the Glynn Girls were on the driveway. Tara had asked the Glynn Girls to stand on the driveway with her to reinforce to Hadley and Elliott that she would be well watched this time. Her sister-friends needed all the encouragement they could get in order to drive away without her.

Hadley tackled her with a hug. "I'm praying you find what you're looking for."

"Thanks. But either way I'll be fine this time, Hads."

Hadley sniffled. "Yeah," she sighed. "You will." A minute later Hadley released her. "We love you, T."

"I know. Who else but sisters, blood related or chosen, would use vacation days to nurse me back to health? And maybe one day I'll be emotionally strong enough to make it up to you."

"Just get strong for us, okay?" Hadley took Tara by the shoulders. "You do it for you and all God wants for you in this life, not because you owe us anything."

Tara nodded. "Thanks."

Elliott embraced Tara, holding her so tight she could hardly breathe. "I don't understand your need to stay, but you'll explain it to me when you get it figured out, right?"

"I will." Tara held her. Finally she let go. She stood in the driveway, waving until the vehicle was out of sight.

Julep, Luella, Dell, and Sue Beth moved in close to Tara, waving too. It could be a heartwarming snapshot, except she was void of any warmth.

Would this be her life from now on, going through the motions of love for others' sakes while feeling only sadness and a desire to be left alone?

27

On the sidewalk in front of Blue Sails, Luella smoothed an advertisement against an A-frame poster stand. She looked over it again. Good. Everything listed was correct. The book cover of the new edition of her St. Simons Island guide was splayed across the poster, along with the signing info: "L. Demere HERE at Blue Sails Casual Living starting at 10 a.m. today. Come get the inside scoop about St. Simons Island! Refreshments provided."

Hopefully it would draw in people walking by as they enjoyed their time on the island. Dell had made lemonade, sweet tea, and cookies, which would be worth it even for nonreaders. The street was certainly busy enough that they should get some walk-ins. Luella had also advertised by placing posters around the island, on her Facebook page and website, in local libraries, and everywhere else she and the Glynn Girls could think of. Like the last signing, all profits would go toward Gavin and Julep's debt. If only that could be enough. Still, she was glad to help.

She checked her antique watch—only twenty minutes until start time. Would Charles really come? She'd not seen him since she went to the hotel a couple of days ago, but she'd texted with him, telling him that Tara was staying on the island. He responded, saying he'd send for Tara's luggage, and when it arrived, he'd have an employee drop it off at Blue Sails. It just didn't feel right to reveal who she was in a text.

Apparently work had kept him busy since he received the call that interrupted them on Wednesday, and she didn't doubt it would be that way through high season. Running Seaside Properties was a full-time job, and managing the Lighthouse Inn on top of that was just insanity. Still, she hoped he'd show up, because she wanted to see his face when he realized *she* was the travel writer he had so enjoyed.

"Good day, Ms. Ward." Chuck's deep voice startled her.

Wish granted, I suppose. Her face grew warm, but she turned around to face him, offering a smile. "Mr. McKenzie." This formal greeting seemed to be their thing.

He shifted a briefcase from one hand to the other. "I know I'm a little early. Is L. Demere here yet?"

Luella hoped Charles's good sense of humor could navigate them through the next few minutes. "Yes, she most definitely is."

He tilted his head, examining her. Was he onto her already? "Ah, she's a woman. I wasn't sure. Her bio on the books leaves it ambiguous."

"Her publisher said that sometimes helps sales. That was especially true for nonfiction and travel writers two decades ago. Once she built an audience with her pen name, it made little business sense to reveal it."

"Interesting."

"Um, come on in." Luella opened the door to Blue Sails and held it. Although the store wasn't open yet, she had left the door unlocked so she could return after she set up the sign. After Charles walked in, she locked the door. Not, of course, because she didn't want to be interrupted while setting the record straight. It just wasn't time to open yet.

Or so she told herself.

He looked around the shop. "You girls really have this place looking good. Do you mind being called 'girls'? I usually avoid that word when talking to women. Men don't like being called 'boys,' so I aim to treat both genders equally, but since you're called the Glynn—"

"It's fine." She held up her hand. "No explanation needed. And the credit for the appearance of the store goes to Dell, not me. But I'm sure you aren't surprised to find that out."

"I'm not in the least bit surprised at that."

Dell had set up a large, round table covered with a lavender cloth on which sat an oversize glass pitcher of freshly squeezed lemonade and ice, with lemon slices inside for garnish. Clear plastic cups for the lemonade and piles of book-shaped sugar cookies awaited customers. Dell's creations looked as nice as if a bakery had made them.

Luella walked around the table she and Dell had set up for signing books, drumming her fingers. She took a seat in the tall, upholstered antique chair. She felt his eyes on her but didn't look up from her books. She picked up a copy of the St. Simons guide, opened it to the first page, and signed it *L. Demere.*

"Wait a minute." He laughed, a booming sound that she was sure the other girls could hear from the kitchen and the upstairs art studios. "You're *serious?*" He beamed at her, face red as he laughed.

She held out her hand to him. "Hi. I'm Luella Demere Ward, also known as—"

"L. Demere." He picked up a book and read the back-cover copy, which included a bio worded to hide her gender while instilling a sense of confidence in her knowledge. "Okay, okay." He shook his head. "You got me. You win. *Now* I'm surprised."

She rather liked his caught-off-guard laugh. She took the book from him, still grinning as she waved the pen. "It's Chuck, right?"

"I think I prefer Mr. McKenzie."

"Chuck it is." She signed "To Chuck" with a flourish, closed the book, and handed it to him.

"How much do I owe you?"

"Actually, I changed my mind." She snatched the book back. "We don't need your money on principle."

"But you're willing to change your mind if I let you rent the new shop, eh?"

He was sharp and a good sport. How could she keep their game going? She tapped the book against her palm. "I think that's fair. And since we have an agreement, here's your book." She handed it to him. "I'm just teasing of course. Please take this copy as a gift. And I feel a bit guilty that I didn't clarify before now. I was going to tell you, but we got interrupted."

"Sure you were." But he was smiling. "I have something else I was hoping L. Demere would sign." He opened his briefcase and pulled out a worn paperback.

"Well, I swanee. That's one of my first guides!" She accepted the book.

"What's a swanee?"

She sat up straighter and fanned herself with her hand like a true Southern woman. "Dear sir." She batted her eyes and deepened her accent. "You would not have a real lady say the word *swear,* would you?" She lowered her hand and smiled. "At least that's what my grandmother told me that word meant. Please don't ask me to share what the words *dadgum* and *dagnabbit* replace, or I shall have to faint."

He grinned, shaking his head.

She returned her attention to the book in hand. "This is crazy." She eased her fingers over the front cover before turning it over. "Kitty Hawk, North Carolina, birthplace of flight." This took her back to her start as a travel author. At the time she hadn't been sure if she could make a living this way, but traveling and writing stirred her heart more than anything else ever had. "My friends married young, and I needed roommates in order to travel and write at will. When not on the road, I spent years sharing a tiny apartment with three or four people at a time." She chuckled. "I was much easier to get along with back then, but it was hard work keeping the peace with most of those roommates. Still, I considered it a small price to pay."

"I have to agree." He leaned over to tap the cover of the book in her hands. "After reading your guide, I took my kids there. It was an amazing trip. No stress, because the guide covered everything in an easy-to-follow format. We made wonderful memories that we reminisce about to this day. That was the beginning of my buying every travel guide by L. Demere."

She was the cause of some of his favorite memories? "I . . . I'm speechless."

"I'd like to bottle that and use it at will."

She laughed. "I bet you would."

He touched the cover again. "I feel a bit silly asking now that I know the author is you, but would you sign it?"

"I'd be honored." This time she wrote "To Charles and family," along with one of her favorite quotes about the dunes that made Kitty Hawk famous. She returned his book, and he held it in one hand.

He shook his head, smiling. "I have to say, Luella, I'm completely captivated. I have been since the first time I saw you."

She couldn't think of a time in her life when a man described himself as being captivated by her. And it was happening *now*? Wasn't she old enough to be beyond all this? "You mean from the first time I made a fool of myself in front of you?"

"A well-traveled, intelligent woman doing *ghost tours* of all things. But I find myself thinking of you wherever I go on St. Simons, and it makes me smile every time. I . . . hope I'm not sounding like a fool."

Her heart raced. "No!" *Whoa. Dial it back, Luella.* "No, you're not. I'm just surprised." She looked down at the pile of unsigned books on her desk for a moment before meeting his eyes. The strength of her attraction to him shocked her.

"Maybe you could see fit for us to go on a real date."

"I . . . I'd like that."

"You sure?" His brows knit. "Your words and the look in your eyes don't seem to be saying the same thing."

He had the annoying habit of seeing the truth. It was just plain unnerving. She fidgeted with a new book. "I . . . I know we could be really great friends. But I'm not looking to marry. I've never longed for marriage or kids, and I can't see that changing now."

He studied her. "Do you always discuss your aversion to marriage before the second date?"

"No, but we have a spark." What was she saying? "Or at least I feel it . . ." Her face was on fire now. "But it doesn't change anything."

Another lopsided smile crossed his lips. "Since you told me you've never been married, I've wondered how that was possible. A woman like you had to have plenty of chances."

"Do you date much?"

"Me?" He laughed. "I had coffee once with this really cute author. Oh, wait. You were there."

She chuckled. "That can't be it."

"Pretty much, yeah. The way my marriage ended did a number on me. I was done trusting women. When my wife sent word through the lawyer that she wanted to see the kids only one weekend every two months and I could have sole custody, I poured myself into work and raising happy, well-adjusted kids."

Wow, that had to be so much easier said than done. "I'm sure you've been quite successful at both, but it seems to me you've been missing out on the good parts of dating. Some dates are duds, for sure, but others have led to meaningful friendships. The dating might not go anywhere, but the friendships can be important."

The smile was gone from his face, and his eyes bore into hers. "I'm beginning to feel jealous of men I've never met."

She grinned. "But no hanky-panky. The good Lord wouldn't approve."

Charles continued to study her. "I suppose He wouldn't."

The soft sound of a throat clearing made them both look. Dell stood next to the beverage table. "So sorry to interrupt, but I think your adoring public is awaiting, L. Demere." She pointed at the window. There were five or six people in a line outside the store.

Luella's cheeks warmed. She was being so silly. Was Charles okay with her desire to date but never marry?

"Have a good book signing, Luella." He gathered his things and went toward the door. "See you tonight?"

Her skin flushed. "Definitely."

Dell raised a brow, looking smug with a told-you-so smile on her face.

"Oh, hush your mouth." Luella gestured toward the door. "And unlock the door."

Charles glanced back, brows creased. Then understanding apparently dawned on him. He nodded at Dell. "Whatever you said, I think I fully agree."

Dell giggled. "Good for you, Chuck."

28

Sitting in a beach chair with her heels dug in the sand, Tara stared out at the sandbar and sea. Darryl's rock warmed her hand, and she rubbed her thumb over it again and again. Since her suitcase had arrived on the island two days ago, she'd kept the rock with her at all times, and somehow this small, lifeless thing—no bigger than a stack of five half-dollar coins—helped her feel an ounce closer to the life she once had.

A blanket lay next to her, keeping her Bible and the study guide she'd been going through with her home group relatively sand-free. She couldn't concentrate for even a full minute at a time. Her mind zipped and clanged like a wobbly pinball machine.

It seemed that every religious saying she'd ever heard was being said to her on Facebook: God took Sean and Darryl because He needed them. God is testing you. God caused this to happen for a reason.

What did those things even mean? That God killed her brothers? That He did this so she could become a better person? That God is so impatient, unkind, and weak that He had to take her brothers immediately?

Anger churned. But whom was she angry with? God? Or the twisted, empty sayings that tormented her? Or herself for being unable to hold on to hope and love and trust?

Most people who wrote to her on Facebook were trying to encourage her and help her. But what was said usually just confused her and added to her grief. Coworkers, church friends, her home group, Sean's and Darryl's schoolmates, and strangers by the thousands all had an opinion about why this happened. Their desire to comfort her was undeniable. But too many of their posts were actually hurtful. The more confusion that entered, the less she felt capable of surviving. Her anger and grief seemed to grow stronger each day. If she could stop those emotions from growing, maybe she could stop feeling as though she were free-falling into the abyss. That wouldn't be much, but it would be a start, wouldn't it?

"Tara?" Gavin's calm voice was undeniable. Why did it grate on her nerves?

She turned, trying to see around the broad brim of her hat.

He stood some five feet away, a large brown bag in his hand. "Sorry. You didn't answer the last five texts, and since I had to leave the house to look for you, Mom sent food."

Clearly she was also capable of feeling extremely annoyed. Did he have to talk to her as if she were a child? But even in her ongoing ire and stupor, she knew he'd been kind and gracious when he didn't have to be. He owed her nothing.

"Thanks." She nodded and turned her focus back to the openness of the sandbars and ocean. That was about all she was good for these days—sitting and staring. The island made that easy, whether she was at the dock over the marsh or here in Gould's Inlet or on the beach near the lighthouse. These spots were where she came to breathe, as breathing didn't seem to come naturally anymore.

But maybe she was expecting too much. Sean and Darryl had left this life for the next one four weeks ago. Had she awakened in the hospital with this rock in her hand? Or had she dreamed all of that, including waking and asking Hadley and Elliott about the rock? If she'd asked them then, she didn't dare ask again. Tara needed to believe that Sean and Darryl had been allowed to visit with her, that she'd actually seen them in the next life, happy and having fun.

"It's nice here."

She jolted at the sound of Gavin's voice, having completely forgotten about him. He'd taken a seat on the blanket next to her beach chair, and he'd put the bag of food between them.

She swallowed the desire to ask him to leave. What difference did it make if he was here or not? Evidently she could tune him out. He picked up her Bible and gently ran his palm across the old leather cover.

The verse that stood out the most came to her again. She hadn't memorized it verbatim, but the words she did recall came to her over and over: *Be gracious to me, O LORD, for I am in distress; my eye is wasted from grief; my soul and my body also. My life is spent with sorrow, and my years are now with heavy sighing; my strength fails, and my bones waste away.*

Would God help her? Or would she waste away like the psalmist? She had loved her brothers so very much, but now her love for them had nowhere to go, no outlet. She was caught in a logjam and didn't know how to unjam it. Maybe she needed to see someone, a professional, because it was evident that her emotions were too heavy to carry on her own.

"You doing decently okay?" Gavin set the Bible back in its place.

She bit her tongue, refusing to ask if he had a different tone he could use. "Well enough to know I owe you a lot of gratitude."

His expression didn't change at all as he stared toward the ocean. "You're welcome. Anything you need, just let me know."

He seemed to be going out of his way to be kind, or maybe this was just who he was, still . . . "Could you stop talking to me like this?"

His blue eyes opened wide. "What? I didn't realize . . ."

"That it's annoying?" The evening wind picked up, and she tugged her hat tighter on her head. "I know your business voice now and the beleaguered son voice you use with the Glynn Girls at times. I'd prefer something neutral. But really anything that's not EMT-to-trapped-child voice would be appreciated."

He stretched his arms out behind him and planted his palms on the blanket. "You should eat something."

She wasn't hungry, but her trembling fingers and throbbing head assured her she needed to eat. Still, she couldn't imagine opening the bag and eating. The smell would turn her stomach.

Gavin stayed in place, looking out at the ocean. He'd done nothing but be kind since she landed in his life, and as the minutes ticked by, some hint of remorse worked its way past everything else.

She sighed. "I'm sorry."

He didn't turn to look at her. "It's okay, Tara. You're way past being able to cope. And I do have a tendency to sound condescending without meaning to."

"One might think your uninvited guest wouldn't nitpick."

"But one would be wrong, right?" He smiled. "I don't mind."

"Anyone would mind. I would if the tables were turned, so why not you?"

He shrugged. "I get it. I'm impressed you're able to get out of bed and dress. You're up and on that bike every morning."

"Only because I want to get out of your mom's house as soon as possible."

"Yeah, somehow I resemble that statement." His soft laughter indicated he had a sense of humor about the trials life brought.

"See"—she pointed at him—"that's an acceptable tone. Real. Honest. *Not* patronizing."

He had a room at Julep's, but he'd been staying at Sapphira's. Was he staying elsewhere because Tara was living at his mom's place or because he wanted to keep thieves from stealing anything else? His mom had told her that before his dad died eighteen months ago, Gavin had lived in his own house in the next town across the causeway.

He picked a piece of beach grass off the sand and fidgeted with it. "I'll work on the tone."

"Thank you," she sighed as if he were driving her nuts.

A subdued smile crossed his lips as he stared out into the vastness. They sat there in silence as dusk settled and the voices of families faded. He reached into the bag, opened a bottle of water, and passed it to her.

She took it, and once the water touched her lips, she could hardly stop drinking. "Do the people you've rescued who've lost loved ones ever recover?"

"I think so. I'm not on that end of things much, but we get letters, and sometimes people come by the station years later, bringing food and thank-you notes. It's a long haul. I know that."

She liked his honesty.

He tore the grass into two pieces. "Those who do best seem to be the ones who find a cause and do it in honor of the ones they've lost."

"A cause?"

"Yeah, you know, a worthy thing to honor the one who died. I went to school with a girl who was a few grades ahead of me, and she died in a car wreck on her way to school during her senior year. She'd been a track runner with a college scholarship due to her skill. About six months after she passed, her parents organized an annual 5K run. People paid a fee to enter, and local businesses donated money too. Her parents created a nonprofit, and they use every penny of that money for a college scholarship program."

Something stirred inside her, as though a tiny shaft of light had entered the endless caverns. "That's an interesting thought."

"But the scholarship is only a tiny piece of the difference it's made in people's lives. I'm one example. Everything about my life has been altered because of that one thing."

"Yours?"

"My dad and mom and I all had—or have—addictive personalities. For Dad and Mom it was smoking. For me it was sugar. I was a normal size toddler, but by first grade I was overweight. By middle school I was obese, only a few pounds away from being morbidly obese."

She pinched his biceps. "You're muscle and bone." After she'd taken the liberty, she realized it wasn't appropriate, but he didn't seem to think anything of it.

"Now. Not then."

"And one girl's death motivated you?"

"No, but it was a piece of it. Jenny had been one of the few girls in my life who was nice to me, and—"

"I doubt that's an issue for you anymore, present company excluded." She hadn't known how starved she was for some type of normal conversation.

He grinned, nodding his head. "Single women being nice to me?" He chuckled. "True."

"Looking back at the last few weeks, I'm guessing you are between girlfriends."

"*Between* would be the wrong word, but, yeah, no girlfriend." He pulled a plastic container out of the bag. "Am I telling you this story or not?"

"You are."

He opened the container and got out a fried chicken wing. "So a year after she died, her parents had the first 5K run organized in her honor. I'd wanted to be in that race from the moment I heard about it, but I could hardly walk around a block, let alone run it." He broke off the drumette and held it out to her. "If you want to hear more, you'll eat."

She rolled her eyes and huffed, but she took it and bit off a hunk. "Go on."

A barely-there smile crossed his lips. "I'll wait."

She finished the drumette, and her hands trembled a little less. He offered her more, but she shook her head. He pulled out another plastic storage container from the bag, and when he opened it, she saw an array of fresh fruit.

He ate a grape. "From the moment I heard what her parents were planning, months before the 5K, I began walking a little farther every day. That first race I walked every inch of it and finished hours after everyone else.

The Glynn Girls and Jenny's mom were there clapping for me. It was embarrassing . . . and wonderful. Jenny's mom was so proud of me, and she made me promise I'd do it again the next year. I took it as a challenge to be in better shape, hoping not to be last by several hours. And here I am, physically chasing off my addiction every single day of life." He held the container toward her.

She'd eaten all she could tolerate for now, and she shooed it away with her hand.

He picked out another grape. "After I lost a decent amount of weight, I wanted to make a difference in other people's lives, so I became a volunteer at Boys and Girls Club of America. It's an after-school program, and typically I'm there working with kids two afternoons a week. We do a lot of physical things: running, sailing, and various sports."

"I like running . . . or used to, hiking, and rock climbing. I could rattle off two dozen things of who I once was. But all I'm capable of doing now is asking God a thousand times an hour *why?* I'm not sure I'll ever be me again if I can't get an answer. Why leave me here? Why take them? Why did I let them sleep in the loft? Why didn't I think to have that stupid tree removed? Why didn't God cause Sean or Darryl to hear the cell phone ringing?" She broke into sobs.

Gavin passed her several paper towels from the bag, and then he rubbed her back, offering no answers to her questions. She must've wept hard for ten minutes before she could gain control. She wiped her face, took a deep breath, and then she drank the rest of her water.

Gavin removed his hand. "God is love, and anything we think He did outside of how love would behave, we're mistaken. He didn't take them, Tara."

"The LORD gave, and the LORD has taken away."

"The context of that verse is different than that sound bite, but let's assume it means exactly that. For every verse like that, there is another one that presents a different perspective, saying He gives and He protects. The clearest thing we know about God is Jesus, and He came to give life abundantly. He came to show us the way, and Jesus refused to rain down fire—or trees—on anyone. The other thing I know to be true is that if God considers it a sin for you to do something, there is no way to justify Him doing that same thing. Do you think the God who does all He can to get you to walk in love and forgiveness and kindness would murder your brothers?"

"Murder, no, but He had to allow it. How else could it happen?"

"That's the tough question, isn't it? I wish I knew what to tell you. I know our world is a fallen place."

"You should read my Facebook feed or private messages. Clearly half of everyone who's leaving a message has some sort of 'this is why' answer."

"Too many people think they can figure out the God equation."

"I'm in no mood to guess what that is. Care to clarify?"

"When the Word addresses a topic, it gives us partial understanding, but people's brains are quick to kick into gear, coming up with an equation so they can solve it. They may not be able to do earthly math or science, but they're convinced they've figured out all of God's equations."

"I'm being told a lot of things, but a clear favorite is that all things work together for good to those that love God. So what are they saying? That Sean's and Darryl's deaths will work out for my good more than if they'd lived? Are they confident God meant for that verse to be taken literally in every circumstance?"

"People want to be comforting, and in their minds that's an encouraging, hopeful thought."

"But it's not. It's equal to saying God did this, but—wink, wink, smile—He's got a plan for something better that He wouldn't have given you without this loss. What?" She thrust out her hands and screamed. "What?" She sat back. "It's so wrong to preach that to me right now that I don't even know where to begin."

"If it helps, it's not intended to increase your grief. People want to encourage, and they're trying to sum up God and the universe in simplistic terms that are helpful."

"And you? What do you believe?"

"I shared the most important part when I said who Jesus is, but I believe God is love and we should walk in love. Oh, and when it comes to explaining the God equation to a hurting soul, never miss a good chance to shut up."

She laughed, and it echoed across the hot, humid inlet. "Not that you have an opinion or anything."

He chuckled, holding his index finger and thumb an inch apart. "Uh, maybe just a little."

She tapped the sides of the empty water bottle. They sat in silence until his phone rang. He ended the call and sent a text. She had no doubts that he was telling the Glynn Girls he'd connected with her. He just sat there with her, saying nothing else, and it seemed as if she could breathe again.

"Why would God ask me to drop my life at eighteen and pick up theirs if He knew all my years of trying to fill them with love and hope and every type of learning and healthy foods and such wasn't going to matter anyway? Their lives ended before they really began."

"It matters what condition a person lived and died in. Every crumb of love matters, and I'd dare say you gave a feast."

She could recall a thousand times she needed to be more patient, more understanding, more aware that life could end, and she couldn't will her way out of it. "I was also picky and demanding and—"

"And they died knowing you loved them, knowing you believed in them, knowing you wanted the best for them. They died with happiness, hope, and thankfulness in their hearts. Love did that, and you were love's vessel."

Love's vessel.

She'd never thought of anyone like that, but she liked it. "Then they were a vessel to me too."

"No doubt."

"You believe in love a lot."

"I do. It's the most real thing we come in contact with every day. I see it all the time. If love would not do anything cruel, Tara, God would not do it. God is love. It doesn't have to be syrupy or sentimental, but it's kind and patient. It protects and preserves, and it doesn't fail."

"My love didn't protect or preserve, and it clearly failed."

"No. Your love protected and preserved for as long as it was in your hands to do so. I saw the clip of Darryl's valedictorian speech, and it's clear that your love did not fail. The moment they went from this life to the next, God's love met them without the necessary aid of a human vessel."

Could she at some point, maybe months from now, become a vessel of love again? The world was hurting, and it made sense why people did their best to come up with a God equation, whether it was fully right or not. But if people got the one big thing right—love—everything else was unimportant by comparison.

No wonder grief overwhelmed her. She was a shattered vessel, and her love had poured out onto the sand. But she didn't have to stay that way forever. Love was a living, growing, renewing thing. God was a potter, and she was here on earth, able to be a vessel again . . . someday.

29

Morning dew covered Gavin's work boots as he walked the front part of Sapphira's property with the land surveyor. Gavin swatted at a mosquito. "Like I said when we talked last month, my goal is to divide the one large lot into two lots, giving each an equal amount of road frontage if possible."

"That won't be a problem. I called the planning-and-zoning department, and the good news is this property doesn't have to abide by the new ordinances. It's grandfathered in to the original zoning rights, and because it's being passed to you through an inheritance, the original zoning laws pertain." Tommy pulled a folded plat out of his jeans back pocket and opened it. "I studied this, and there's a landlocked triangular piece of property at the back of the lot, to the side of the garden. It sits a little oddly, but I think that section is almost a fourth of an acre. Is your goal to make money or share the lots between relatives?"

Gavin's hopes picked up. "Make money."

"Then if you sold the piece closest to Fourteenth Street, call it Lot A, with a driveway easement to the triangular piece of property, you could divide this into thirds instead of halves. But the problem with that is you'd need to give ingress/egress easement through Lot A, and that would reduce its value, because it would mean less land, *and* the new owners would have to share the driveway with neighbors. Still, even with losing some of the profit from Lot A, having a third lot would be a bit more profitable."

Gavin studied the plat.

Tommy folded it to show a smaller segment of the land. "The ideal solution would be if the fourth of an acre lot could tie its ingress/egress easement to the existing driveway that abuts the land that faces Thirteenth Street." He pointed to it on the plat. "But people don't easily sell rights to use part of their driveways."

"My mom owns the property that abuts the triangular piece of land."

"Then you may be all set." He circled an area with his finger. "This is your mom's land?"

"Yeah."

"Would she be willing to grant ingress/egress easement rights to her driveway?"

"I'm pretty sure. Yeah."

"You check into that. It'll take six to seven hours to survey this before I begin the office work on it. We should talk again before the crew and I leave for the day. If she's willing, I can handle all of that with a quitclaim deed and her signature. Then I'll record it at the courthouse."

Gavin held out his hand. "Thank you."

"It's your land. I'm just doing my job."

"Yeah, but a third piece of property? I never considered that was possible."

"It's hardly worth it unless you can attach easement rights to your mom's driveway."

Surely Gavin could do that. He pulled out his phone and ran a Google search for what a small lot in this area would bring. He stared at the info until his lungs demanded he take a breath. If they could get an easement and therefore create a third lot, he might come within fifty to a hundred thousand dollars of paying back everything he owed. He could take out a new loan for that amount and pay off the entire balloon payment on his mom's house and business equity and not have any remaining debt. He'd assumed all this time that best-case scenario was he'd have a certain amount of debt left over but it would be manageable.

He loved his mom, but he really didn't want to live with her while helping her make payments that were so high they'd have to live frugally for decades.

A tinny sound of voices, laughter, and music caught his attention. Was that coming from Sapphira's backyard? He went that way, opened the wooden gate attached to the hollow brick fencing, and saw the source of the noise. Tara was in an old Adirondack chair, under the shade of a live oak near the garden area where Sapphira's property and his mom's property met. A brass fire pit was sitting near her chair.

Tara was engrossed in whatever was on the screen of her phone, but it sounded like footage of her and her brothers doing something. They hadn't talked since their time on the beach two days ago. She was usually away from the house, on her bike, possibly avoiding the Glynn Girls and him. But he needed to let her know about the surveyors. They were unloading and setting up equipment now. It wouldn't be long before they came around the corner, likely startling her.

He strode toward her, memories flooding him. As a kid, he'd spent many a summer evening in this yard catching fireflies, running through the sprinkler, and poking the fire just to watch the sparks fly skyward. Sapphira hadn't been a blood relative, but, nonetheless, she'd been his Saffy for as far back as he could remember, regardless of whether he called her Saffy or Sapphira.

"You need a fire and the fixings for s'mores."

Tara looked up. "Start a fire now? It's before eight and already nearing ninety." She pressed something on her phone, and the noise stopped.

"Yeah, you're right. Best to wait until dark,"—he glanced at his wrist as if he had a watch—"which is only about twelve hours from now." He sat.

"Don't you have demolition work you need to be doing?"

Usually when he came within ten feet of her, she either left or invited him to do so. Still, he had a feeling if they'd met under better circumstances, they would've hit it off. Or maybe he just wanted to believe she would feel for him a little of what he felt for her *if* the circumstances were different.

He brushed dirt off the arms of the chair. "I do, but I needed to let you know that three men are surveying the property today. You'll see them within the hour, I think. I wanted to give you a heads-up. I'm kind of excited. I got some good news."

"And you're here because you need to tell someone and no one else will listen?"

He suppressed the grin her words stirred. "Exactly. You're it."

"That explains a lot about your pretending to be a roofer so I'd hang around."

His heart warmed at her newfound ability to voice humorous sarcasm, but he couldn't laugh about anything to do with that time. Not yet. It felt disrespectful of all she was going through.

"Yoo-hoo." His mom waved from the back porch of her house. "We're bringing coffee and food. Don't go anywhere, either of you."

Gavin looked to Tara. How would she feel about that plan? He certainly had enough work to do that he could leave and let the womenfolk gab.

"What are you looking at me for?" She raised her brows. "Oh, I get it." Her eyes held a bit of amusement. "Fine. I'll let you stay in your yard long enough to eat food your mom fixed. I'm nice that way."

He laughed and waved at his mom. "Okay."

"So why are they all off on a weekday morning?"

"The shop doesn't open until ten, and some days they have work to do there hours before it opens, and other days they leave here seven minutes before opening time and arrive three minutes early. But a heads-up about tomorrow. They're taking off the whole day to pack up Sapphira's art room."

"The Glynn Girls are growing on me. I was just curious why they were home. So what's your good news, Gavin?"

Was she doing as well as it seemed? He hoped so. Oh, how he'd prayed for her. She would grieve hard for years to come and to a painfully deep degree for the rest of her life, but hopefully it no longer had total control of her as it did during the first weeks. Being well enough to go through the motions of life while grieving was a necessary step in the right direction.

"My news is that I just learned I should be able to get three lots out of Sapphira's property instead of two."

"That *is* good news. Congratulations." Tara looked at Sapphira's house. "I still find it sad you're tearing down that beautiful old home."

"Yeah, me too." He interlaced his fingers. "But long story short, the Burnsides owe a lot of money."

"With the third piece of property, will the finances still be short?"

"Depends on numerous things, but I'm guessing a little bit, yeah." He figured probably fifty to a hundred thousand dollars short. But if that was all they still owed when everything was said and done, he could take out a new loan for that amount, and then he could once again afford a place of his own and help his mom make the monthly payment. When Tara first arrived, he'd been overly concerned about everything working out, but since then he'd been reminded that his troubles were just money. That's it.

She fidgeted with the casing on her phone. "You could let me rattle that developer's cage and see what comes of it."

"I appreciate it, but I can't."

"Because of my brain injury? If so, I'm better and clearer with each passing day. I even know not to do stupid things like claim a man's house."

He smiled. "I'm glad to hear it. I am, but—"

"Your loss." She shrugged. "Literally."

Goodness. Whether chasing her down a dark beach, looking into lost eyes, or seeing her now—she was fascinating.

His mamas were loud as they came out of the house and crossed the yard.

"Coffee?" Sue Beth held out a tray of mugs to Tara and then to him. They each took one.

Tara leaned in toward him. "You're being ridiculously stubborn, Gavin."

His mom held out a tray with two plates, each with a bowl of grits and a bacon biscuit to the side. "I heard that." His mom frowned, a hint of humor in her eyes. "Come on, Gavin, try to use the sense God gave you." She turned to face Tara. "Don't worry about him, sweetie. If he had an idea, it'd die of loneliness."

Luella set a tray on a small table beside a chair. "Why, he could throw himself on the ground and miss." She winked at him.

"He could what?" Tara laughed.

"Oh, she's lying like a dog." Dell reached in and pinched Gavin's cheek. "Some might say if his brains were leather, he wouldn't have enough to saddle a june bug, but I know better."

The women were on a roll, clearly trying to entertain Tara at Gavin's expense. He didn't mind. But he needed to act as if he did, so he pursed his lips and shook his head. "And they say all of this without having a clue what's at stake."

Tara ate several bites of grits, taking in more food in this one sitting than he'd seen her eat since he met her. She set the plate on a nearby coffee table.

"Oh." His mom blinked as she swallowed a mouthful of food. "I guess we did, didn't we?" She made a shooing motion, as if that piece of info was unimportant. "But I have no doubt that Tara's right and Gavin's wrong."

Gavin swallowed a bite of food. "Thanks, Mom."

"Oh, honey, anytime, just anytime at all."

"Regardless of what he's done wrong, we can set it right through any means necessary," Sue Beth chortled. "All y'all know that's true."

Gavin shook his head and leaned toward Tara. "You do realize what you've started."

"I'm beginning to, yeah." She sipped her coffee, looking rather smug about the whole thing. "But how was I supposed to know your mom's hearing was that good?"

"Well, whether you meant for your words to be heard or not, the real point is, Are you enjoying our banter about it?" Dell gave a high five to the air.

"Yeah," Gavin mocked. "Because if it opened up a line of insults for me and you enjoyed it, you probably just stumbled on the first step to becoming a Glynn Girl."

"Julep!" Dell said. "Tell me he did not just say that."

"Ohhh, son, you're making us madder than a wet hen, and one of us is likely to cream your corn," Sue Beth said.

They laid on the Southern sayings, and their accents grew thicker with each passing minute.

Tara leaned toward him. "Maybe having four mamas is a tad taxing."

"Only Sunday through Saturday." Gavin took a sip of his coffee.

"Gavin!" All four of them yelled at him, gasping as though he'd broken a commandment in front of the preacher.

"Ladies." Tara spoke softly, and the group settled down. "Who has the phone number of the man who sent someone to pay for and get the shiplap but stole it instead?"

"I do." Sue Beth raised her hand. "But, honey, we talked about this."

Tara's eyes met his, and he saw clarity and strength, and standing against her suddenly seemed wrong.

"Great," he mumbled. "Just what I needed." He raked his hands through his hair. "For all five of you to push me around." But he was amused. "Okay. Contact him. But you don't give your name or any personal information."

"You mean like your house address?" Sue Beth asked. "The place he's already robbed."

The women chuckled.

"Hey." Tara held up one hand. "Come on, now. Be nice . . . at least until I get my way."

His mamas chortled.

Gavin suppressed a grin and mocked a sigh before getting serious.

"Watch what info you share, Tara. And you send the picture to my phone. That way he won't get your phone number. Your complaint to him won't look as legit that way, but I'm not willing to do it any other way."

His phone pinged with the image Tara had sent. Gavin saved the picture and attached it to a text to the man. Then he passed his phone to Tara. "It's all yours."

She smiled, typed a message, and sent it and the image to Roy Ashe. Gavin couldn't make out all the words, but he knew she briefly explained what had happened that night. Then she waited.

The six of them ate and chatted.

"Tomorrow's the big day." His mom's smile was sad.

"Because you're packing up Sapphira's art room?" Tara asked.

"It's the day I go to the lawyer's, and the house I'm taking apart officially becomes mine."

Tara's eyes grew wide. "You've been demolishing and selling parts of a home that doesn't belong to any of you?"

"It's mine. No doubt. But I started the work before the legalities were complete because the money I owe is due soon. I have a work crew coming tomorrow afternoon, and we'll remove all the brick as carefully as possible." Gavin hoped this news didn't bother Tara.

Dell tossed her coffee onto the grass. "Out of respect for Sapphira, we've kept her painting room intact until the day the house is officially Gavin's. Starting midmorning tomorrow we'll go over each item, deciding to pack it up to sell or to keep."

"That's going to be a lot of work," Julep said.

"I could help . . . if you'd like a hand," Tara offered.

Her response was better than Gavin had hoped.

"That's very sweet," Luella said. "And we'd love your help. Gavin has a schedule to keep, and a bit of youth is just what we need to get the job done. He's banking that the house will be ready for demolition day after tomorrow. The debris will be hauled off, the survey complete, and the lots put up for sale by this weekend."

"That's crazy." Tara's brows knit. "Who could get all that done that quickly?"

"Gavin." His mamas' voices rang in unison, and then they laughed.

Luella winked at him. "He's been working on more than the demolition. Every aspect has been worked out in detail—like an Amish barn raising, only in reverse. He has crews for the big stuff, a lawyer for the estate issues, a surveyor for the land, and four women to pack up an art room."

"Five," Tara added.

The women cheered quietly, and Gavin couldn't have been more pleased.

"The balloon payment is in two weeks," his mom said. "So we're praying that within a week he can sell what will then be two properties to a cash buyer."

Gavin wouldn't mention to the group at large about the possibility of the land being divided into three parcels. He needed to talk to his mom in private about that so the others didn't influence her decision. Maybe she'd hate the idea of sharing her driveway with neighbors.

"Bidding wars are very likely to happen during that week." Luella set her plate on a table, looking disinterested in food. "There's no land left to sell on this side of the island."

"But how do you go to closing on two pieces of property in a week in order to meet your balloon payment?" Tara asked.

"A couple of possibilities." Gavin held up two fingers. "The buyer has available cash, or the contract is solid, and the bank will accept that and give me a grace period—as long as it's under contract with real money behind it."

"Wow, that's a lot riding on everything working out with precision."

"Gavin can pull it off." His mom sounded like . . . his mom.

Tara ate a few bites of her bacon biscuit and then checked his phone.

"Ah, he's read the message. Now it's time to call." She placed the call and put it on speakerphone.

"What are you trying to pull, Gavin? I'll have my lawyers—"

"Mr. Ashe," Tara said.

"Who is this?" Roy snapped.

"The girl in the picture. Did your shiplap guy tell you I was in the house that night? And that he caused those bruises? That he shoved me to the floor before getting into his truck and fleeing with the shiplap from the carport?"

"Like I told Gavin, if someone stole that shiplap, I'm sorry. But it wasn't me."

"True. The man wasn't you. But I can identify him. Then you'll have paper and electronic trails where you moved money in order to buy the wood and then moved it back once you had the wood without having to pay for it. My guess is, once I turn over that picture to the police, a real investigation will begin, and it won't take them long to locate the home where you had the shiplap installed."

"Wait. Who is this?"

"The girl your employee used brute force on. That's all you need to know. Ask him. I'll tell you something else too. After I encountered your guy, Gavin had to take me to be seen by a doctor. A CT scan revealed a traumatic brain injury."

"What?" The man mumbled something. "I knew nothing about . . . I need to call you back."

The call ended.

Gavin wasn't sure what had just happened. "What are you doing?"

"Banking that fear will do its job. I did have a CT scan the next morning after that guy pushed me around, and it showed a head injury. I didn't lie. Mr. Ashe is calling the guy now to find out what took place. When he realizes his guy played rough, fear will do the rest, and you'll get your money."

Realization swooped through Gavin. "That guy assaulted you."

"He was rough while trying to get past me, not bad enough to injure me more than a few bruises. But I wasn't going to let him steal from *my* house." Tara's wry smile worked its way through Gavin. She was stronger than he'd given her credit for.

Guilt trickled into his consciousness. "Tara, I'm sorry. I was so focused on the shiplap and your need for me not to call the police that I didn't do due diligence to ask and listen. I just wanted you to go to sleep and let me think."

"*I* hardly knew what to believe about what I saw or thought to be true during that time. But feeling threatened—like when you chased me down the beach in your uniform, and that man twisted my arm and shoved me hard, and I smacked the floor? Those things are clear."

Her strength and graciousness reached into his chest and plucked out his heart. It now belonged to her more than to him. "Still, I could've listened as if it mattered, even if it'd only happened inside your mind."

Her lips pursed and she frowned. "That'd be weird. You were a stranger being kind to an intruder. All limits of what you should've done had been reached." She brushed hair from her face and tucked it behind her ear. "But back to the subject at hand. When Roy questions his man who stole the lumber rather than pay for it, and Roy hears in the man's voice that something happened that night, his fear of just how much proof we have and how badly this could play out for him will do the work for us. But you talk to him from now on. I'm out."

Gavin's phone rang, and the name Roy Ashe was on the screen. "Gavin speaking."

"I won't discuss this over the phone. I'll meet you on St. Simons Island Pier tomorrow. Will two p.m. work?"

"Yeah."

"I'm not saying I was involved in what happened."

"Of course not."

Men like Roy never admitted to wrongdoing, even when the proof was overwhelming and a guilty verdict was returned. But Gavin believed the man who came to get the shiplap had intended to pay for it. He was an opportunistic thief, and he'd taken the goods wherever Roy told him to, probably ensuring a good-size bonus, while making both of them guilty.

"But I'll pay you," Roy said, "in exchange for you signing a nondisclosure agreement."

A knot twisted in Gavin's gut. If debt didn't own him right now, and if Tara's testimony would hold up in court, Gavin would press charges based on principle. But debt did own him. Moreover, if the incident went to court, a lawyer would destroy Tara's testimony in a matter of minutes. She'd been very confused at the time of the incident, and it wouldn't take long for any lawyer to prove she'd had a recent head trauma and thought the house was hers.

The knot in his stomach tightened. "You didn't return my calls or texts the night of the incident, and I turned in a police report."

"Yeah, I know. They've been here and questioned me. But none of that matters if you don't press charges and you contact them to say it was a misunderstanding. Tell them you were gone during the time you were supposed to be there to sell us the shiplap. The man took the shiplap, and you've been paid."

"So you want me to lie to the police to cover your backside?"

"Actually, everything I just said is true."

"Except you had no intention of paying for the shiplap until right now."

The line was silent for more than a minute. "I'll add twenty percent to the price, and you and that girl sign a nondisclosure."

"No. She's left out of this."

"Then your signature is worth nothing. She could turn around and sue my company after I pay you."

"She won't." Gavin was sure of that. Her retelling events or identifying anyone during that time would never stand up in court. "But you'll have to take my word for it."

"Fine," Roy snapped.

"And you'll still give me the twenty percent increase." But that forty thousand dollars above the agreed-upon price would become Tara's, not Gavin's.

"At the pier tomorrow afternoon at two."

The line went dead, but Gavin's heart soared. How was it possible he'd get paid for the shiplap after all?

Tara smiled, and he had his answer—one vulnerable, mixed-up woman who knew what she was capable of when no one else, including him, had a clue.

30

The quiet voices inside Sapphira's painting room faded as Luella scanned the different paints, clay sculptures, and art papers. Even though Sapphira had been gone close to two years, the room still looked as if she would walk in at any moment and give an art lesson. Luella had loved her high school art classes with Sapphira. At one time or another, at one location or another, all the Glynn Girls had taken art classes from her. That's where the bond with Sapphira began, and it had lasted until Sapphira died without warning at seventy-three. She'd been in this very room, painting and probably praying that Siobhan would find her way back, when she had a heart attack. She'd called 911, saying that she needed help, that she'd started feeling sick and dizzy twenty minutes earlier. Gavin was at the station, but by the time the EMTs arrived four minutes later, she was gone.

Luella closed her eyes. Sapphira's infectious laugh and her fervent prayers for Siobhan echoed in Luella's memories. Oh, how she missed their fifth Glynn Girl. Maybe that was why she saw Tara as Sapphira the other day. Tara could make a perfect fifth Glynn Girl. It seemed right somehow that she was here with them now, ready to help pack up this room.

"I can't believe it's time to take this room apart." Sue Beth had tears in her eyes.

Dell wrapped an arm around Sue Beth's shoulders and squeezed. "We knew it was coming. And we'll save everything that's precious to us."

"So . . . the whole thing?" Sue Beth waved an arm in a circle.

With scissors in hand Tara put one hand on a huge roll of Bubble Wrap and the other hand on the glassine. "It all has to be moved out of here, so let's get this done before Gavin rips the hardwood floors out from under us, leaving us with nothing but that stinky, yucky subflooring." She looked at all the supplies. "Not that I know anything about packing up artwork."

"We'll teach you"—Luella sighed—"if we can make ourselves get started."

"Home stretch, girls." Julep clapped her hands and pushed up her sleeves. "I'll miss Sapphira's house too, especially this room, but I'm so grateful we can give all this to Gavin to put an end to my financial mess."

Gentle morning sunlight spilled across the dark hardwood floors as Dell passed out pairs of nitrile gloves.

Dell lifted the first canvas oil painting from the stack leaning against the wall. Julep talked to Tara, giving detailed instructions for properly packing artwork: place a thin layer of foam on the floor and cover it with glassine, put the painting face down on that and tape it in place, and then add layers of Bubble Wrap with the smooth side facing the painting. More tape and wrap until the packing is six inches thick. The works that weren't on canvas could be rolled and slid into hard cardboard tubes.

Before long they had a system and were making good progress. Occasionally one of the girls would tell Tara a story connected to a painting even though she didn't seem very interested. She simply nodded and kept moving.

Luella paused to watch Tara work, observing how she packed the precious artwork with meticulous care. Tara had some color to her face today, and she had the strength to do more than just carry the weight of grief.

Even so, it'd only been a month since her brothers died and only two weeks since she relearned their fate. That was no time at all to deal with the depth of Tara's loss. But some people had an inner drive to feel normal, and Tara seemed to be one of them. Luella had seen that in Julep after Mitch died. The first few weeks she had been gung ho about donating the bulk of

Mitch's things and eager to participate in any church charity events she could. But then at times the heavy load of grief would catch up to her, and she'd crumble.

Tara had a lot of times of crumbling ahead of her before she'd be able to climb this mountain of grief. Wait! Tara mentioned she was a rock climber. Maybe that metaphor would make sense to her.

Not that this was a good time to share it.

"Luella." Julep waved her hand close to Luella's face. "Are you going to pull your weight here?"

Dell winked at her. "She's probably daydreaming about her new gentleman friend."

"Ooh, you need to spill *all* about your most recent date." Sue Beth sidled over and elbowed her.

Luella made a zipper motion over her lips. "Sorry. I'm not penning a tell-all about my personal life."

Dell giggled. "That's because it's only recently that she's *had* a personal life."

Luella shot a glare at Dell, who shaped her hands into a halo over her head.

Truth be told, things were amazing between Charles and her. So much so that she didn't want to trivialize it by blabbing to everyone. She pulled out a piece of paper from the stack she was working on. Maybe getting back to work would provide a distraction.

Tara held up a painting of the lighthouse. "This reminds me of a painting I have . . . only mine has ocean water."

"Yeah, the world has a lot of lighthouses."

"True." Tara put the painting facedown on the glassine.

"Oh, girls! Doesn't this bring back memories?" Luella lifted the pencil-and-watercolor sketch of the colorful snow-cone stand that used to be on the corner of Magnolia and Mallery. The red-and-white kiosk had an old-fashioned ice shaver that the owner, Mr. Pat, had found in a New Orleans pawnshop. He'd long since retired, but the memory of the refreshing treat served in little yellow paper cups was as strong as ever.

Tara scooted closer and touched the painting with her gloved hands, her fingers barely brushing the thick watercolor paper. "How odd."

Julep gave a short laugh. "Yeah, I suppose an old-timey stand like that wouldn't be common in North Carolina. Don't make us feel our age even more than we already do when hanging around young folks like you."

Tara smiled, shaking her head. "No, I've seen little stands like this in small towns. What's odd is that this looks like one I've dreamed about time and again." She pointed at the sign next to the snow-cone stand in Sapphira's picture. "Even down to this advertisement with a long orange drip running down it, as if real juice stained the ad."

"So like a déjà vu?" Sue Beth wiggled her fingers.

Tara angled her head, studying the art. "I'm not sure that's the right term." She looked off to the side, a cloud coming over her face.

Dell's brows wrinkled as she regarded Tara. "What happened in your dream, honey?"

Tara made a face. "Never mind. It's not *that* interesting. And like most dreams, it doesn't make much sense." She gestured. "Let's roll it up and move on."

"Aw, I need a five-minute break." Sue Beth sat on the floor and leaned against a set of shelves. "Tell us the dream."

Julep and Dell sat too, but Luella held the artwork, watching Tara's face as she studied the piece.

Tara closed her eyes. "In the dream I was a child . . . maybe five, I think. I was stuck in a hot room and terrified. There was a little boy with me who was a couple of years younger. The room kept getting hotter, and I knew I had to take care of the boy. I was yelling, yanking, and pulling on doors, but I finally managed to roll down a window."

Julep drummed her fingers on her knee. "Roll it down? From inside a room?"

Tara shrugged. "It's a dream. What can I say? Anyway, I helped the boy climb out, but he was all red and sweating. So I started asking people for change until I had enough, and I bought him a snow cone, a red one. And the stand looked *just* like this one. Weird, right?"

It couldn't be . . .

The paper slipped from Luella's hands and floated to the floor. At that same moment something in the closet hit with a horrendous thud. Chills ran up Luella's arms, but she ignored them and checked to see what had fallen. She found a large set of tempera paints on the floor that Sapphira had never opened.

She'd been saving them for Siobhan to return.

What on earth . . .

Luella returned the paints to the shelf, going over Tara's dream in her mind. It had a lot of similarities to an event that had happened to Siobhan and Gavin about twenty-five years ago, only the "room" was an older clunker of a car.

She glanced at the other Glynn Girls, all of whom were staring at Tara and looking as stunned as Luella felt. Was *this* a dream? Some sort of upside-down world from which Luella would wake?

"Th . . . that's quite a dream." Luella tried to smile. "Thanks for sharing it."

The others chimed in, muttering much the same.

Tara smiled. "Anytime you need to while away the hours listening to recurring dreams, I'm your girl."

Julep stood and dusted off her jeans. "Whew, I think I need a break from this packing. How about some sandwiches? I'm famished." Everyone nodded.

Tara raised an eyebrow. "We ate less than two hours ago." She looked at her wristwatch. "It's only 10:30."

Julep fidgeted with her hands. "Tara, maybe you'd like to go check on Gavin. We'll fix lunch."

"He's at the lawyer's office, and then he has the meeting with Roy Ashe at the pier."

"Oh, yeah." Julep glanced at each Glynn Girl as if asking for help.

Tara picked the artwork off the floor and passed it back to Luella. "But if you guys are going to break for lunch, I think I'll go for a bike ride before it gets too warm."

The Glynn Girls all spoke at the same time:

"Good idea." Sue Beth nodded.

"Nice plan." Dell gave a thumbs-up.

"Yeah." Luella smiled at her.

"Okay . . ." Tara removed her gloves, studying them. She opened her mouth as if to say something more but just shrugged. "See you in half an hour or so." Then she walked out of the room.

Luella remained at the door of the painting room until she heard Tara leave the house, and then she inched the art room door closed and joined her friends in the center of the room.

The Glynn Girls stared at one another, speechless.

Luella's mind spun. It *couldn't* be. Impossible. Siobhan and Tara, one and the same? This was like a twist in one of her ghost stories. But what else could possibly explain Tara knowing about the snow-cone incident?

Julep took a deep breath, looking at the ceiling, let it out slowly, and then finally broke the stunned silence. "Okay. We need to go over the facts. Surely there's a logical explanation. People dream things all the time. How many tens of thousands of people do you think have dreamed of a snow-cone cart and begging for money to buy a cone?" She pushed her sleeves back again. "But whatever is going on, we need to figure it out and plan our next steps."

Sue Beth raised a hand. "What *exactly* do we remember about the snow-cone incident? Are we *sure* the stories are the same? It's not like Gavin's the only kid to get a cherry slushy after getting overheated. And Siobhan couldn't have been the only little girl to help another kid out of a car."

"Right!" Despite Dell's declaration her voice wavered. "I mean Tara being Siobhan would be crazy. Wouldn't it?"

Luella set the picture on a bookshelf. "I think the most telling part was that she saved the boy from a hot room by *rolling down* a window to escape. Good thing the car didn't have automated windows 'cause Cassidy had locked the car and taken the keys."

"Yeah." Sue Beth snatched the hair clip from her head and pinned up her hair again. "Clearly Tara has no idea she was in a car. I'm a little foggy on the details, perhaps because it happened twenty-five years ago. Can someone refresh my memory about whose car the kids escaped from?"

"I can." Julep nodded. "I'd just had my third miscarriage—the last one before Mitch and I gave up on giving Gavin a sibling. I needed to get to the hospital because the pain was so bad. I thought maybe it was an ectopic pregnancy." Julep's face creased. "Mitch was on a jobsite. As a carpenter he was often an hour or two away from home. He headed home as soon as I reached him. Luella and Sapphira were out of state. Sue Beth, you were laid up sick with the flu, which is probably why the details didn't stick with you. Dell dropped everything to take me to the hospital, but we had to find someone to stay with Gavin. I could see Siobhan in this very backyard playing. I called Cassidy, and she was willing to keep him. I . . . I thought Gavin would be fine until Mitch could get back in town."

Luella brushed her hand down Julep's arm. "It was a reasonable thing to think."

Julep stared out the window. "While Dell rushed to my house to pick me up, Cassidy walked over to my home. I gave her cash and the keys to my old car so she could buy lunch and dinner for Gavin, Siobhan, and herself. Sometime after Dell drove me to the hospital, Cassidy took both kids with her in my car to find a fix. Apparently she decided to leave them locked in the car. I still can't believe I was that stupid to leave Gavin with her. Even with as much pain as I was in, I should've known better."

Dell sighed. "It wasn't your fault. Or mine. We didn't know at the time how hooked Cassidy was. None of us did. Not even Sapphira. Gavin was a restless, active preschooler—not someone you could pen up in a waiting room—and you didn't want him to see you in unbearable pain."

"I remember the reasoning, Dell!" Julep looked down and drew a breath. "But I was his mother." Her tone was softer now. "And I should've known I was putting him in danger."

Dell patted Julep's arm. "We were panicked, and you did what you thought was best for him. It's all any parent can do."

How long had it been since they had mentioned Cassidy's name? Years. She was only a few years younger than the Glynn Girls. In some ways she seemed troubled early on. She wasn't like her free-spirited, artistic mom or her confident, businessman dad or anything in between. By middle school she was unhappy, anxious, and miserably uncomfortable inside her own skin. All of that seemed to grow by leaps and bounds when she was seventeen and her dad died. Luella swallowed a lump. A little more than a year later Cassidy gave birth to Siobhan, and she never named the baby's father. Around the time Siobhan was born, Cassidy started experimenting with drugs, probably looking for an escape from her anxiety and self-loathing. In the blink of an eye, she was hooked, despite all the love Sapphira tried to give her.

Where was Cassidy now? Luella had thought about her and little Siobhan many nights during her prayers. Cassidy had let her mother name the baby as a thank-you for letting them live in her home and for being a free babysitter. But Cassidy never liked the name Siobhan. Had she changed her daughter's name to Tara and then abandoned her? That made little sense. Then again, Cassidy's life made little sense for someone who had been loved deeply by her parents.

Julep continued to stare out the window. "Mitch drove me home from the hospital that afternoon. But when we arrived, there was no one at our place or Sapphira's. Mitch and I drove all around the island. We were panicked. Then I saw my boy sitting under a tree with red all over his shirt. I thought the worst"—she gave a shaky laugh—"until I realized it was just cherry snow cone. And there was Siobhan, sitting with him in the shade of the live oak, holding his hand and talking to him about the seagulls. She'd gotten them out of the car and bought a snow cone to cool Gavin down. She was a smart girl and resourceful. We took them to the pediatrician to be checked, and they were fine, but only because of Siobhan."

Luella wiped beads of sweat from her face. Rehashing this situation somehow made it feel even hotter than it should. "So that's where Tara's story converges with our memories. It wasn't long after that when Cassidy left town with Siobhan. Poor Sapphira. What a heartbreak that was, and she had to carry it for the rest of her life."

A thought struck Luella. "Do you realize this weekend will be the first time in twenty-five years there won't be any lawyer's office running an ad in a paper that says, 'Desperate grandmother looking for Siobhan O'Keefe, born in Glynn County, Georgia, St. Simons Island, on April 1, 1987'? And offering a reward for any leads. According to Sapphira's instructions, now that the house is in Gavin's hands, her lawyers will stop paying for the ads."

Sue Beth pointed to a painting of the ocean. "We girls could've gone on a cruise several times for what Sapphira, or her estate, paid lawyers for placing those ads in various newspapers, changing the state or cities she put them in, always hopeful someone would reach out."

Julep wiped sweat from her forehead. "Tara's the right age." Her voice was little more than a whisper. "Maybe there was a reason she was drawn to this house . . ."

"Let's not get ahead of ourselves." Sue Beth pulled out her cell phone and waggled it. "We should call Hadley. She could put this whole thing to rest by telling us that Tara was born and raised somewhere in North Carolina."

Luella shook her head. "She was in foster care. It's possible she could be Siobhan."

Julep grabbed her own phone from a nearby shelf. "We won't know until we ask." Standing in the center of the group, she touched her screen and put the call on speakerphone.

"Hello, Julep." Hadley's voice sounded upbeat.

"Good morning. You're on speaker with all of us."

"Hi, all. Is Tara with you? Is she okay?"

Dell leaned in. "She's currently on a bike ride. She's been helping us with a cleaning project this morning."

Julep cleared her throat. "Listen, we have an odd question, and we thought it best not to ask Tara directly. At least, not yet."

"Not a problem. What is it?"

"Where was Tara born?"

Hadley was silent for a moment. "I'm glad you called me instead of asking her. That's an emotional question for her because she doesn't know. Her mom abandoned her before safe haven laws existed, so her mom left no clues that could lead people to finding her. If Tara is remembering correctly, her mom was in some major trouble at the time and didn't want to go to jail. Drugs were involved. Possibly other things too. Tara's birth certificate is a generated one, created by the state of North Carolina, and the info on it is based on their best guess of where she was born. She knew her birth date, and she remembered she was from Georgia, but she thought the town was called Ocean, and there is no Ocean, Georgia."

Ocean, Georgia . . . Luella's breath caught. Ocean Road was two hundred feet from here, and at a nearby intersection the street name changed to Ocean Boulevard. Residents couldn't enter or leave Fourteenth Street without traveling on a road named Ocean. So maybe the name Ocean had stuck in Siobhan's mind when her own name hadn't.

She leaned in. "What *is* her birthday?"

"April 1, 1987."

Luella's heart about stopped. Julep pressed a hand against the wall, jerking air into her lungs.

Siobhan's birthday.

"Wait, is this about the ad in the paper?" Hadley continued. "Are you picking up where Sean and Darryl left off? They planned the trip to St.

Simons because they believed Tara had a family connection there somehow. Sean and Darryl meant for it to be a surprise adventure for her."

Luella's head spun. After decades of Sapphira's searching for Siobhan, had her lost granddaughter returned home without knowing it? If so, the repercussions of this were staggering. Luella willed her voice to be steady. "Did Tara know her mom's name?"

"It may not be her real name. Tara said they moved a lot, and her mom changed their names just as often. It was a confusing childhood, to say the least, but her half brothers had the same mom, and they knew her as Cassidy Banks."

"Cassidy." Julep sank to her knees.

Luella took the phone from Julep. "Thanks, Hadley. We're sorry for this strange call. There's a lot of info that we're processing. We'd appreciate if you didn't mention this conversation to Tara just yet. We'll get back to you soon. We're proud of Tara's progress. She's got some steel somewhere underneath all her pain." And if she was actually Siobhan, she'd need it. "Listen, we need to get back to work. Thanks for taking the time to talk with us."

"I'm proud of her too. Don't worry. I won't say anything about us talking, but don't hesitate to call if you need me. Thanks for looking after Tara."

"Bye, Hadley."

Silence hung in the room like a heavy blanket. What were they going to do?

"Hello?" Gavin called out. "Finally the house is mine free and clear."

Luella turned to find Gavin beaming as he came into the room. He waved a folder of papers in his hand. "All that's left to do is meet Roy at the pier and get a nice, fat check for the shiplap, but I've got some time before meeting him." His brows furrowed. "No whoops or hollers or hugs?" His eyes narrowed. "What's wrong?"

"Son,"—Julep went to him and cradled his face—"we need to talk."

31

Gavin's heart raced as if he were finishing a sprint or charging into a burning building. He clenched his fists to keep his hands from shaking. This couldn't be true. He longed for fresh air, but his feet were glued in place. Sapphira's studio was spacious, but the walls seemed to be closing in.

Tara was Siobhan?

"Luella, how accurate is this information?" Gavin trusted her investigative process. From her years of research for her writing, she knew when information was or wasn't adding up.

"I fully trust it. No DNA test required. Tara's not trying to make any puzzle pieces fit, and yet a lot of pieces do fit, Gavin." She put a hand on his elbow, and her eyes caught his as she peered up at him. "Siobhan's and Tara's birthdays match. Their mother's name is Cassidy. Tara has had a recurring dream that is almost identical to an event that happened here. When she was a child, she said she was from 'Ocean, Georgia.'"

"Wait." Sue Beth picked a bug off her shirt and released it. "There may be another way to know. Remember, Siobhan had a completely white patch of hair on the back of her head, some type of genetic anomaly."

"Does Tara have it?" Julep asked.

Each person shrugged and shook her head.

"Would Siobhan still have it?" Julep asked.

Luella nodded. "The likelihood is high, because it's like having a dark birthmark. It was about a fourth of an inch wide and probably wouldn't go away. But I don't need any other proof to know she is Siobhan."

Gavin forced air into his lungs. Tara had told him it was her house. And it was. She was the rightful owner of Sapphira's inheritance. How was this even possible? "And you discovered all of this because she recognized a *painting*?"

His mom held it up to him. "She was awed that this snow-cone stand matched one in a recurring dream of hers. We questioned her, and most of the events in her dream are what took place more than twenty years ago when Cassidy left the two of you in a locked vehicle with the windows rolled up."

They had to be wrong. "I remember hearing that Siobhan saved my life but only that somehow the two of us got stuck in a car in summertime, and she got me out. When I asked why we were in a car by ourselves, I didn't get much of an answer."

His mom's face distorted as if she was embarrassed. "I . . . I didn't want you to know the whole story." As she told him the details, her fingers trembled, and she rubbed her forehead. "I should've known better than to leave you in Cassidy's care. Siobhan—Tara—got you out in time. Even at five she had more sense than her mom."

"I need air." He strode to the living room and went out the first of five glass double doors that ran along the back of the house. He breathed in deeply the humid air that was saturated with the fragrance of nearby honeysuckle. He closed his eyes.

Tara saved my life? The news was crazy.

He'd always had the memory of the tang of a cold cherry snow cone and it being held out to him by a friend he loved. And surely at the time he'd felt a strong bond toward his hero friend for getting him out of that car and being so kind, but he didn't remember that part.

He moved to a lawn chair and put his head in his hands. He could feel his mamas hovering near him, no doubt not knowing what to say.

"For heaven's sakes, Son, say something."

He lifted his head, taking in Sapphira's home and yard, both given such meticulous care in hopes Siobhan would return one day. Despite the fact that the property legally belonged to him as of today, it was Tara's.

What would he do? He would be ruined financially! *Mom will lose her house, maybe her business.* But what was left of the place, as well as all monies earned from his taking it apart and selling it off to the highest bidders, belonged to Tara.

Gavin drew a heavy breath. "We have to give everything back to her that we can. The land, the money—all of it."

Mom crumpled into a nearby chair. "But we maintained it, and you're the executor of the will. You have power of attorney in all matters. Can't you keep any money for that?"

If only he could. "We maintained it out of the escrow account Sapphira set up, and I've already received compensation for being the executor. We used it to pay debts." Gavin looked heavenward. "How much can one person take?" Tara had been through so much. How could they spring this on her too?

"Wait a minute." Dell patted his shoulder. "Come on, Gavin. It'll be okay." She gestured at his mom. "You two have each other, and"—she made a circle motion—"and us. You and Julep can get a small house somewhere. Your credit won't be ruined forever. You're young and strong. This is just a setback."

She'd misunderstood. "Tara." The word came out as a whisper.

"Oh." Dell grimaced. "I hadn't thought . . . You're right. This is sure to alter her world too and not in a good way."

"Will it?" Sue Beth shook her head. "Why? She's inheriting valuable land with a home . . ." She looked at the shell of a house. "Well, the land is valuable. She doesn't need a house anyway."

"Shh." Julep put her index finger over her lips. "Stop talking and think about the whole twisted, ill-timed mess, Sue Beth. Even if it's ultimately good news, it's a lot to deal with."

Gavin's stomach felt as if he'd been tossed on a ship riding rough waves. Sapphira had spent Tara's lifetime trying to find her, and she'd grown up in foster care anyway. Her brothers had wanted to give her the gift of finding her roots, but they died a week before they could do it.

What would all of this do to Tara?

He studied the house. "I've gutted it." He could hardly breathe. "I was so sure it wouldn't hurt anything to start taking the house apart before the date in the will. I . . . I betrayed Saffy's trust." How had he gone from being ecstatic over finances to being a broken soul—in one morning?

A phone buzzed, and his mom pulled hers from her shorts pocket. "It's Tara." She flashed a desperate look at Gavin, swiped a finger across the screen, and pressed the Speaker button. "Hi, there."

"Hey, you guys about ready to begin work on the room again?"

Gavin shook his head. *Tell her no,* he mouthed. He wasn't sure what the next move should be, but they wouldn't pack up or take apart one more thing. *Why* did he start taking apart the house before waiting the amount of time they'd promised Sapphira?

His mom nodded at him. "No, sweetie. Something's come up, and we've decided to put that off for today."

"Good. Because I met a cyclist named Lou King. He said he knows you all and that Gavin can vouch for him."

Gavin nodded and gave a thumbs-up. Lou was a good guy. Gavin could say so himself, but if Tara knew he was home, she'd have questions about how things went with the lawyer and where things stood with Roy Ashe, and Gavin wasn't ready to answer any of that. Not yet. It was best to let her have a little time away while they adjusted to the news and he updated the lawyer.

"Yeah," his mom said, "on all accounts, Tara."

"Apparently he organizes bike rides on the island for visitors and residents alike. They're riding to Epworth in a few minutes and somewhere else after that. I ran into them at the big parking lot in Pier Village, and he introduced himself and asked if I wanted to join them. I thought maybe I'd ride with them for a few miles if you were still on a break."

Sue Beth leaned toward the phone. "That sounds like fun, but before we let you go, I have a question. Since we've paused working on the painting room, I'm thinking about getting my hair done. Did I notice that you have a white streak of hair? And if so, is it natural or bleached?"

"You saw that?" Tara laughed. "Almost no one notices it since the rest of my hair is blond. Yeah, it's natural, so I have no suggestions for your stylist. But color is in, so go for it."

"Thanks, sweetie," Sue Beth said.

"Listen, Tara. It's Julep again. You should go for the whole ride. It's a good day for biking. Really hot, though, so drink lots of water."

Gavin looked at his mamas. Apparently they wanted to give Tara one fun day before her world was rocked—again. And give themselves a day to adjust to the new reality regarding the debt hanging over their heads.

"Are you okay, Julep?" Tara asked. "You sound like something's wrong."

"No, I'm good. We're all good. Enjoy your ride." She ended the call.

If only he could offer them some encouragement, but he was fresh out. What were they going to do? He drew a steadying breath. His first step had to be calling the lawyer back.

At least Tara's—no, Siobhan's—inheritance would eventually make a positive difference in her life. That thought was the only balm to the ache in his heart.

32

T ara tilted her head back, letting the evening air toss her sweaty hair as she coasted toward Julep's driveway. What a refreshing outing. Grief still lined every thought, but she'd found moments of respite throughout the day. Brief and fleeting moments, but welcome—as though golden rays of hope were trying to break though. She slowed the bike and turned onto the short driveway. A fire was burning in the pit, and the whole gang was sitting in chairs in Julep's backyard, doing absolutely nothing.

She rang the bike bell, hopped off, and walked to the sitting area. "Hey." She set the bike against a tree, noticing all the fixings for a meal near the blazing fire pit. "Gavin Burnside, you're not on duty, eating, or working on the house. What's with *that*?" She took a seat. "How'd things go today with the lawyer and Roy Ashe?"

"Good. Roy wasn't happy, but we'll get our money." Gavin was using his EMT voice again.

She chose to ignore it.

"Hungry?" Julep lifted a cover off a plate of hot dogs that looked as if they'd been cooked over the open fire.

"No thanks. The bike group had a late lunch in Brunswick and then stopped for ice cream less than an hour ago." She'd eaten both times while talking to people who knew nothing about her. She didn't mention her brothers, and it was nice to be with people who didn't feel sorry for her or awkward around her. "So what happened that all work on the painting room came to a halt?"

"Yeah, we need to talk about that." Gavin's voice softened even more as he rapped his thumbs in quick succession against the arms of the chair. "We need to talk." The rapping of his thumbs quickened as he repeated himself.

Nervous behavior wasn't typical for Gavin, was it?

Concern hit her. "Is everyone okay? Hadley, Elliott . . ."

"Oh, yeah, yeah, yeah. Nothing like that, sugar." Dell picked up a clear pitcher with icy water, poured some into a cup, and held it out. "And it's not bad news as much as unexpected and a bit shocking."

"Shocking?" She took the drink. That was a weird word to use unless it was coupled with bad news. "I'm listening."

"Should we all stay?" Julep asked. "I'm not sure Tara needs all of us staring at her while she's grasping the news."

"Oh, for land's sake"—Sue Beth sat up straight—"it's not bad news, not for her. Stop dawdling."

Tara used her thumbnail to pluck at a splinter of old wood on the arm of the Adirondack chair. "Then you should spit it out, Sue Beth."

The woman's face drained of color, and she looked at her friends. Then she got out of her chair and crouched in front of Tara. "Honey, remember the dream you told us about?"

"Of course. I told you this morning." Just how bad did they think her memory was?

Sue Beth put her hand over Tara's. "It wasn't a dream."

Tara's heart froze for a moment. Then she thought about who was telling her this. She looked at Gavin. He was levelheaded. "What is she trying to say?"

Gavin's eyes met hers as he stood. "Sapphira spent a lifetime looking for her granddaughter. She put ads in newspapers. One of those ads attracted Sean and Darryl to St. Simons because your birth date and Sapphira's granddaughter's birth date are the same."

Grief slammed against her, stealing her breath. Her brothers had loved her so fully. How would she live without that powerful source? But the birth dates matching meant nothing. "That's an interesting coincidence, but I dare say about ten thousand other babies were born on that same date in the US."

"Tara." Gavin stepped closer. "*I* was the kid you gave the snow cone to. You rolled the window down because you were in a car, not a room, and you begged people for money to buy the snow cone because your mom had locked us in the car in summertime, and I was overheated."

"My mom?" Her heart lurched. "You guys knew my mom?"

Sue Beth was kneeling now beside Tara, and she rubbed Tara's arm. "Yeah, sweetie."

Tara stood and plunked the glass of water on a table. "That can't be true. It's just all too crazy."

"It's true, Tara." Gavin rubbed his forehead. "We can run a DNA test if you like. Sapphira had her DNA results on file in case that was needed to verify someone who arrived in response to the ad in the paper, but I don't need any additional proof. Same birth date. Sapphira's daughter's name was Cassidy, same as your mom's name. Siobhan's hair had a white streak, a variance like a birthmark." He offered a smile, but it didn't make it to his eyes. "You have that very same streak. I know all I need to be assured you're Sapphira's granddaughter, the one for whom she put this home and property in escrow."

Her eyes filled with unwanted tears. "I . . . I had someone who loved me?" She faced the back of Sapphira's home. "All those years in foster care . . ." She'd battled every moment to cope with the heartache and loneliness. She'd gone through an emotional war to learn to care about herself and trust herself when no one else in her family cared about her. And now . . .

"I . . . I had someone?"

"Your nana, Sapphira O'Keefe." Julep stood.

"My . . . nana? Did she paint the picture I have, signed to Spunky Boo?"

The girls' reactions said it all. She was Spunky Boo.

"Spunky Boo, Sunshine, and Masterpiece were her favorite nicknames for you," Luella said.

"Sapphira was a remarkable woman," Julep said. "And she never stopped hoping and praying that you'd return home. You and Gavin were best buds, despite that you were two years older. But all of us knew and loved you, and we grieved when Cassidy disappeared with you. Sapphira never got past the loss. Never stopped praying that you would come back."

"And my dad? Did you know my dad?"

The Glynn Girls looked at each other, their hesitancy clear.

Julep brushed Tara's hair back, pinning it behind her ear. "No, sweetie. Your mama never did say. She was nineteen, and we think it was a visitor to the island, probably here for a month or two. Someone who swept her off her feet, seduced her, and returned home. It broke her heart. She'd fallen in love, and we believe he was the first guy she'd been with. She'd lost her dad, fell into a summer romance, and then had you. About the time you were born, she began using drugs to cope with her emotions."

Tara took a step back, her heart pounding. None of this was what she'd imagined over the years. She'd pictured her mom as being abused while growing up and turning to drugs to cope with all that baggage. So Tara was grateful to have been raised in a different kind of home from the one with her mom—in nonviolent homes, even if they were foster care. But . . .

None of what she'd believed was true?

"No. No. No. *No!*" She fisted her hands. "I'm not her. You're wrong." She paced. "I can't believe my mother grew up in a good home and just became a train wreck as an adult." Anger churned, and she didn't know what to do with herself. "She had the picture-perfect childhood, and then she destroyed mine? Was she crazy? Somebody tell me she was nuts and that's why she did that!" Tara pulled air into her lungs. "I held it together to raise Sean and Darryl, carrying my abandonment like an unbearable load because the princess didn't have it in her to be a decent human to her own daughter? Was she a narcissist?" She turned to the Glynn Girls, shaking all over. "Someone answer me!"

Julep folded her arms. "We don't have the answers you want. You aren't anything like her. We could see that from the time you were a little bitty thing. She was frail and needy, afraid of her own shadow. She was also a daddy's girl. She was seventeen when he died, and she was never the same after that. Looking back I can see now that her life slowly spiraled downward from that point."

How much more could her heart take? She stared at the home. It was like she was in a scene out of a dream.

All the old questions churned inside her again. She thought she'd put them to rest. Was God testing to see how much she could take? Why else would she learn these things when there was nothing of real value to gain from them? She didn't need a guardian, and Sapphira was gone, and she couldn't even celebrate discovering her roots with Sean or Darryl. For all intents and purposes, this was useless information. It felt as if God were mocking her.

She lifted her eyes heavenward. *Why?* She wanted to scream the question, but she refused to embarrass herself. "I'd like to be left alone now, and I'll stay in Sapphira's house tonight." Maybe it would hold a few answers for her.

"But"—Julep shook her head—"the only rooms with complete flooring are the painting room and its adjoining bathroom."

"Sapphira's painting room is the perfect place to stay—alone, please."

The Glynn Girls looked to Gavin.

Why were they looking at him? This was *her* home! "It's not a request." She walked toward the house.

"Come back to your room anytime," Julep said. "But in case you do choose to stay here for the night, I'll bring blankets for a pallet and a pillow."

Tara made herself stop, turn, and respond. "Thanks, Julep, and thanks to all of you. I know this isn't your fault. It isn't anyone's fault." Except her mom's. And God's. "Get some rest."

The looks on their faces and Gavin's face caused Tara to think for a moment, and their loss in all this dawned on her for the first time. But she had no strength or clarity to address it right now. Using her phone, Tara turned on the flashlight app. She went inside and walked across the subflooring to Sapphira's painting room.

At least the lighting fixture still worked in this room. She turned it on and started looking through watercolor paintings, sketches, and photographs. The work captured her mind and heart, and her anger faded a bit. The colors and images gave her a glimpse of Sapphira's soul, and a smile tugged at Tara's lips. Sapphira must have been whimsical and loving.

Tara opened a drawer and discovered a book filled with sketches. The top ones appeared to be done with charcoal and colored pencils. They were light and airy, and there was a little blond-headed girl in each one. Some had the girl and a little boy, probably Gavin and her, at various places on the island. She turned each page, but suddenly all color disappeared, and the girl was barely visible, as if she were moving farther and farther away. The last one had a woman about the age the Glynn Girls were now on a bench outside this home. The boy was beside her, and both were looking down the road.

The girl wasn't in the picture.

Tara crumbled to the floor. "God, she waited for me. She *loved* me. She prayed and planned for me to return. Why?" Tara pounded the floor with the flat of her hands. "Why?" She cried until she had no more tears, and then she turned off the light and lay on the floor, staring out the huge window.

As moonlight made the world outside look like silver and silhouettes, a new thought came to her as gently as a snowflake falling.

Look for love, not loss.

The words struck deep. She looked again at all she'd learned today.

Love had reached out to her when her mama abandoned her. What kind of childhood would she have had, going pillar to post, from one drug house to another, hardly attending school? Instead, she'd entered stable homes. In each of her three foster homes, love had taught her various skills and understandings that had guided her later on. Her foster parents had been vessels of love. They wanted nothing from her except to be allowed to help her be her best self. Every foster parent she'd had was a believer, and they all felt God's love and wanted to share it. Some had strict house rules and no-nonsense boundaries, but they were vessels of love. Until now she'd felt like a visitor in those homes, but love had welcomed her.

How had she not seen that before now?

Her friendship with Hadley and Elliott had begun inside their last foster home, and Tara's rapid bonding with them was stronger than anything her mother had been capable of. Had God been directing her steps all along, taking her toward love because her mother was more in love with drugs than life or God or even her own flesh and blood?

She drew a deep breath. *Show me more, God, please.*

Images of Sean and Darryl came to her, and her heart ached. She wouldn't have wanted to give up that time with them for anything, including growing up with Sapphira. If Sapphira had found her, Tara most likely wouldn't have been in North Carolina during that tiny window of time when the boys' grandmother knew where to find her. The boys would've been raised with strangers. From what she'd seen growing up, it was harder for boys to stay in the same home year in and year out. Their anger, impulsivity, and raging hormones too often got the best of them, and with each foster-care move, they risked going to rougher homes, where love was hard to find and frustration was easy.

What had Gavin said? *"Every crumb of love matters, and I'd dare say you gave a feast."*

Love surrounded her now, and she basked in it. Raising her brothers had been a long, beautiful lesson in letting go of her anger toward her mom.

Every time she had shared some tiny smidgen of truth with them, it grew inside her, and she understood it in ways that freed her. She needed that time with Sean and Darryl. She needed to fight for their right to enjoy their childhood, and in some ways it gave her a chance to relive her own while understanding more fully the stress of adulthood and parenthood. It'd given her new respect for her foster parents and new compassion for her mom.

Sapphira hadn't found her, but love had in many forms and through many people. Because of that, Tara had been able to give love just as she'd received it—not perfect or infallible as it worked its way across this fallen planet to reach its intended person, but sustaining, like an oasis in the desert.

The longer she basked in this God moment, the more she saw His great effort to bring vessels of love into her life.

"God," she whispered. "I'm sorry I accused you of using me like a science experiment."

Anger and hurt seemed to flush from her heart, and she felt holy arms of love wrap around her. For the first time since losing Sean and Darryl, she felt like a vessel for love.

There was a tap on the door. She got off the floor and opened the door. No one was there, only a stack of blankets, a pillow, several bottles of water, and a plate covered in foil with a beautiful ribbon on top.

Even here. This weird little family was also a vessel of love.

33

G avin."
A whispery voice tugged on him to wake, but he couldn't quite manage it.

"Come on, sleepyhead." Someone gently shook his shoulder.

He moaned, his neck and back too stiff to move. He pried his eyes open. Where was he? He blinked and tried to lift his head. Oh yeah, he was sitting outside Sapphira's painting room door, leaning against the wall. He stretched his neck and peered up to see Tara hovering over him. "Hey."

She smiled. "You're one of the good guys. Now get off your butt, and let's have some coffee. We have a lot to talk about."

Concern for her eased, and peace pushed aside his worst fears. Evidently he still hadn't grasped the power of her inner strength and resilience.

He tried to stretch his legs and arms. Gavin considered himself in good shape, but right now his body did not agree. Tara reached out her hand, and he took it and moaned as he stood.

She chuckled. "You're too big to hole up in this hallway to sleep."

He rubbed the back of his neck. "Yeah, I guess so."

"You were afraid I might slip out during the night, too upset to be responsible for my actions."

"Nah, I like sleeping in odd places regularly. It ups my skill set."

"At what, moaning and walking like a man three times your age?" Tara shooed him. "Go."

He hobbled out of the hallway. "Your strong suit isn't mercy, is it?"

She laughed. "It's not, actually." She went into the kitchen, to the coffee maker, and began making coffee. "My strong suit is motivating people to do as I tell them. Seems to me that since you were the first person I exercised that skill on—and a mere toddler at the time—you'd have that figured out by now."

Gavin sat on a stool at the bar, rubbing his face. "Seems like."

She snapped her fingers. "Why are you not already awake?"

"It takes me a while."

"Every day?"

"Yeah."

"That's odd. How do you manage that as a firefighter?"

"Training." He rubbed his eyes with the palms of his hands and yawned. "Lots and lots of training. When the station alarm goes off anytime during the night, I'm out of bed and dressed at least a full minute before my brain has stopped dreaming."

"I guess the solution to that is I need to get your mom one of those fire station alarms or a reasonably close facsimile." She set a cup of coffee in front of him.

He grabbed her wrist. "Don't." He deeply enjoyed her sense of humor—what little he got to see of it. "I beg you."

She laughed hard and pulled free. "It'll be under the tree come Christmas morn. But I won't be here to enjoy its merits." She poured herself a cup of coffee. "It's time for me to go home."

Gavin was wide awake now. His feelings for Tara were broad and varied, apparently spanning time from when he was in diapers until right now, and he was in no way ready for her to leave. "How soon?"

"In a few days, maybe a little longer. Some of the answer to that depends on things I don't yet know, like flights and other important stuff." She motioned from his mug to his mouth. "Drink. Get awake. We have stuff to talk about."

"I . . . I'm awake. Definitely awake." And deeply disappointed, but he knew this was coming at some point.

She made the same motion again, and they both sipped on their coffee for a few minutes—him sitting at the island, her standing behind it.

Tara set the cup on the island, keeping her fingers through the handle. "Before waking in the hospital, I saw and talked to my brothers in heaven." She pulled something out of her pocket, rested her arm on the island toward him, and opened her palm. "I've had this since I was eighteen." She shared the story of it, from the time Darryl tossed it on the porch and stood on it, saying he was rock climbing, until it came up missing and Darryl tried to find it for her.

"How did you find the rock?"

"I didn't. Maybe a friend did while going through the debris at the cabin while I was in the hospital unconscious. But no one has volunteered that information, and it seems they would. Still, the truth is I won't ask, and I've told no one else of the vision . . . or dream. I *need* to believe that maybe God gave me a miracle in the midst of the tragedy."

Gavin put his hand over hers, cradling the rock between their palms. "You hold tight to that possibility, Tara."

She studied their hands, and her eyes slowly moved to his. "You don't think it's wrong or maybe a bit crazy to hold so tightly to the hope that the rock is a miracle while knowing if I talked to friends about it, someone could tell me the real story?"

He traced the edge of the rock with his finger, touching her palm as he did. "However it got into your hand, it was love that brought it to you. Whether that love was from a friend who found it or from God Himself, love put it there."

She covered her face with her free hand. "Sometimes their deaths feel pointless. They weren't trying to save someone. They weren't in a war or rescuing people from fires. Nothing in anyone's life is any better for the loss, only worse. So very much worse." She drew a ragged breath and put the rock in her pocket. "Sorry." She shook her head. "Clearly I still have a lot of things about life and death to work through."

Gavin cradled his mug, unsure if he should go to her or reach across the island and take her hand. "Life is a breath, Tara. Even if their deaths were pointless, their lives weren't. Their lives changed you, and you're here to make a difference in others because of that change. Death can't be pointless unless we let it be."

She stared at the granite island. "The span of our years is as nothing before Him," she whispered. "Every one is but a breath. Our time is but a breath, so we better breathe it. Our life is like the morning fog. We were made to live and love and know Him, but on this earth we will not stay long. In Him, we win even when we lose, so choose to be strong. Faith, hope, and love are living gifts inside us, though their appearance may change as life marches on, but do not let any battle steal your victory song. Strength and light and love must go on." She lifted her head.

"That's beautiful."

"Yeah, and I'd forgotten about it. Thank you." She drew a breath and smiled. "It's something Sean and Darryl and I came up with and would recite at the end of a hard day." She chuckled. "It's a mishmash and para-phrasing of a few Bible verses and some words from the 'C. S. Lewis Song,' and we made it our own." She took a few deep breaths and slowly released them through pursed lips. "Okay, then. I'm fine again for at least the next sixty seconds."

He ached when he thought about the roller coaster she was on, but he couldn't free her of it. No one could. They sipped coffee in silence.

She went to the coffee pot and grabbed the carafe. "By the way"—she refilled his mug—"the house and property are yours."

"What? No. Absolutely not. That's not what Sapphira intended."

"You're keeping the house and land. Finish taking the house apart, de-molish it, and divide the land. The whole nine yards."

"I just covered this two sentences ago, Tara. The answer is no." Were they going to move from sharing heartfelt, deep things to arguing?

"I have news for you, bud. The house and property are legally yours, and you can't make me take possession of them."

Apparently they were going to argue.

His mind was made up, and she wasn't winning this one. "Fine. It's all mine, and when I'm finished with all the necessary steps, I'll put the money in your account."

"Giving me large sums of money that I've asked you not to is flirting with stalking or some other law I don't know about. I have the right to remain poor if I so choose, not that I'm actually poor. But that aside, my right to be poor is in the Constitution . . . or not. But I'm not allowing you to give me the money."

Heavens to Betsy, she was spellbinding—whether addled, grieving, or perky. He fought to hear her words as her countenance held a light he didn't want to take his eyes off of.

"No, Tara. I don't want those things that Sapphira intended for you to have. And it's not against any law." At least he didn't think it was. Who knew? "It definitely doesn't make me a stalker."

"It makes you a bit . . . loopy, for sure. Giving me the money makes no sense, Gavin. You're going to ignore my wishes, plunk it into an account for me anyway, and then you'll go bankrupt, and your mom will lose her place and possibly her business. Forget stalking charges. I'll be able to have you committed." She folded her arms and rested them on the island, leaning in. "Look, I get how you feel. You have ethics, and I'm messing with your sense of fair play. But you have no legal rights to win this one. I know what I know, even when I'm too confused to know anything." She frowned. "What did I just say?" she whispered and shook her head.

"Your playfulness is much appreciated, but the answer is no."

"Wrong. As it turns out, everything became yours legally yesterday. Sapphira and God deemed it so. It's yours, and you can't make me take it. I hold the power in this situation, not you. So the answer is whatever I want it to be. I say you're keeping everything. You can't win, so drop it and be happy."

Ire ran through his veins. He stood. "You don't fight fair."

She came around the island. "But I banked on the fact that you would." She tiptoed and kissed him on the cheek.

The power of the kiss entered his body and spread, reaching inside every sleeping hope and awakening it. He longed to pull her into his arms and kiss her. But that would be a huge mistake. She didn't have any of those feelings for him. Even the kiss was from her to a friend, one she'd learned was connected to her childhood. She was just now able to feel anything other than misery. Still, he wrestled with his desire, won, and then plunked onto a barstool. "It's good to see you doing so well."

"Thanks. I had a God moment last night. I think it lasted about three hours. I know I'll grieve the rest of my life, sometimes unbearably hard, but I'm a vessel again, ready to figure out life and walk in love toward those who are still on this earth." She sat on a barstool. "I'd like to keep everything from the painting room, including the shiplap, to use on a project yet to be determined, but I have nowhere to store it right now. Can you store it for me?"

"That would be the absolute least I could do for you." He ran a finger around the mouth of the mug, wishing it wasn't too soon for her to step outside of her grief so they could see where this relationship could land. "You don't have to go. There's a place for you here in our lives."

"Thanks, but no. This is your life, and mine is in North Carolina. But I may take you up on that one day."

His heart about ruptured, and he was glad to be sitting down. "Seriously?"

"I think anything is a possibility right now. I need to tend to things, and as I do, I'll know what the next step is, just like I knew I needed to stay here rather than go home with Hadley and Elliott, even if I stayed because I imagined a young man whispering *stay*. Maybe it wasn't my imagination. What do I know? Seriously, the answer to that is I know it's almost time for me to go. Learning my identity was the unfinished business, the reason I couldn't leave earlier."

"I'm not sure we can figure out who we are through any single incident."

"True. And I'm not sure what I'm supposed to do with my life. I need to figure it out. Can I cope with living in the cabin? I have to try. But not right away. I'm going to wander for a bit first, maybe stay with different friends as I work up the courage to live in the cabin again."

"Sounds smart."

"Necessary, I think. And I like the idea of starting a nonprofit of some sort to honor Sean and Darryl, but I'm not sure I'd be very good at pulling it together."

"I've never thought this of anyone before, but I believe you can do anything you set your mind to."

She seemed unsure. "My brain doesn't feel clear or powerful like it used to, but thanks. On a different topic you need to make those firemen buddies of yours pay for their antics the night I came to the station."

She'd grabbed his attention anew, as if she didn't already fully have it. He scratched his head. "What?"

She cupped both hands around her mouth and made eerie ghost sounds. "Maaaarrrrryyyy."

"You knew?"

"I knew something weird was going on, but it took a few days for it to dawn on me that they were harassing you about me, or rather Mary. How'd they know?"

"The only thing they knew is that I'd chased a supposed ghost down the beach, and they dubbed you Mary because of the ghost folklore on the island. But I think the Glynn Girls set them straight the night we talked at the fire station. If they'd known the real story, they wouldn't have—"

"No explanation needed. Save your breath for plotting to get even."

"Tara." He mocked complete shock.

She chuckled. "Am I telling you my idea or not?"

Amusement at her asking a similar question to one he'd voiced during their first real conversation made his heart flutter. "You are." For the first time in his life, he second-guessed his decision to be a fireman. Even if inklings of feelings for him ever stirred in her, she wouldn't allow them to grow. He was sure of it. She wouldn't choose someone with a career of going into burning buildings. She'd lost too many loved ones to willingly enter a relationship with someone whose career was hazardous.

She raised a brow. "Use their teasing and my leaving to your advantage."

"How?"

"Seriously?" She tapped the island with her fingers. "You need help to make your balloon payment on time, and the news from yesterday threw everything off schedule. Since I'm leaving the island soon and you need help, tell them I was your childhood friend who returned to the island with a head injury and their antics ran me off. Then let them know you need help with Sapphira's house."

He broke into laughter. "That's mean."

"Yeah, so much meaner than wagging a ghost costume out a window and playing that music while I'm sitting on a bike in front of the firehouse."

"You've got a point."

"Changing subjects, you were right about my need to do something positive concerning my loss. Since Sean and Darryl aren't here to continue their lives, I need to find a way to continue something in honor of them. I don't have any idea what that is right now. But if God can pull beauty out of ashes, there's something He wants to do in my life. I'm in search of what that is."

"I'm really going to miss you." Was he saying too much?

Curiosity reflected in her eyes, and she started to say something, but his mamas burst inside carrying plates of food while shushing one another.

"Oh." Dell's eyes grew wide. "You're up."

"I am." Tara smiled. "And I woke up sleepyhead too. We've had coffee, shared secrets, talked shop, argued, and made up. Now the food has arrived."

"Argued?" Julep asked. "What could you possibly have to argue about?"

"Uh." Tara rubbed her chin. "Before we reveal that, just remember I've won, and it's not open for debate."

"Sounds ominous . . . and interesting." Luella set a covered serving plate on the counter.

Gavin told them what was going on, and the four mamas stood there like granite.

Tara raised a brow. "Done deal." She spread her opened palms at them. "Breathe and move on. Not Sean nor Darryl nor I had any desire to uncover money when we planned this trip. Thanks to each of you, I got what my brothers wanted me to find here—to understand my roots, to learn how I came to be and why things played out in such a confusing way, and to find out if I had any family." Tara's eyes misted. "And apparently I do."

His mamas' stances went from rigid to mush as they enveloped her in a group hug. Gavin put his arms around all of them, and they stayed that way for a bit, enjoying the gift of knowing Tara. Her brothers should be here as the ones who introduced her into their lives, but despite the circumstances they had come to know her.

"Okay." Gavin stepped away and clapped his hands. "Food. Why are we hugging when there is food?"

Sue Beth picked up a plate from the stack she'd brought in. She put food on it and held it out to Tara.

"Oh, no way." She took it and held it out to Gavin. "I'd like a plate with less than half that amount."

Luella poured coffee into a row of mugs. "So what's the plan, Tara?"

"I know I'm ready to see my church family and small group. And I'm sure Sean's and Darryl's many friends could use a hug and someone who really cares about their loss and confusion to listen to them. I'm ready to step out in love, wherever it takes me." She looked out a window, suddenly seeming far away. "So I head back to North Carolina in a few days. I'm not sure I'm ready to stay at the cabin yet, but I'll do some out-of-the-way mountain climbing and visit friends, and"—she shrugged—"figure it out as I go."

Luella's gaze seemed fixed on Tara. "You know good places to climb in North Carolina that are outside of the highly publicized ones?"

"Definitely. Mountains, small towns, B&Bs. Western North Carolina is home, and I know it well."

"How would you feel about having some company?"

"Company?"

"My publisher would love for me to write a travel guide about rock climbing in western North Carolina—although I doubt I could climb a rock, much less a mountain."

"You could. It might be a bunny slope, but you could do it. The real thrill would be rappelling down a huge mountain. Come with me if you want."

"I'll swanee." Luella gasped. "I never thought I'd get to do a travel guide like this. I'll drive. When do we leave?"

"Lu." Gavin gave her a look. "I'm trying to assure her she has a place here, and you're trying to get her to pack before breakfast is over."

"I know there's a place for me here." Tara made a sweeping gesture at the lot of them. "And I thank you, but I need to find my place in *my* world, the new one that doesn't include Sean or Darryl. Since we don't need plane tickets, I'd like to leave in a few days. Doable, Lu?"

"One hundred percent. Dropping everything spur of the moment to travel is what my life is built around, and my publisher will be excited to hear about this venture."

"I hate to ask." Sue Beth licked frosting from the cinnamon roll off her fingers. "But what about Sapphira's art room?"

All eyes turned to Tara.

"Well, then"—Tara pursed her lips and squinted her eyes—"I think our next step is to deal with the art room. Gavin needs to make new arrange-ments to get help removing the brick from the outside of the house. The rest of us—whoever is available—work on packing up the art room."

"Knowing what today might hold,"—his mom took a pinch off a bacon strip and ate it—"I called Ellen last night and asked her to fill in for me. She's the one who kept the shop yesterday, and she runs Blue Sails for me when none of us can be there. So Luella and I are free. Dell has a few pho-tography appointments that couldn't be rescheduled, and Sue Beth is teach-ing some art lessons later this afternoon but is free all morning."

"Then we have a plan for packing up Sapphira's—my nana's—art room. And unlike yesterday, when you start talking about the stories behind the more interesting pieces in the room, I'll stop work and actually listen."

<hr />

Luella stepped up, up, up the metal spiral stairs of the lighthouse, her left hand gripping the skinny, round handrail. She looked over her shoulder and grinned. "Hurry up, Chuck." She had only an hour before she and Tara were supposed to leave, but she had to squeeze in one last outing.

Charles was at least ten steps behind her and looked quite at ease with his right hand in a pocket as he stepped at a slower pace.

"I can't believe you already went up this tower twice today, Luella."

He didn't sound out of breath at all. The rat.

She turned around to face forward and willed her own breathing to slow. She always felt a little claustrophobic as the tower narrowed. They were almost to the next landing. The sign ahead said there were only forty-one more steps to the top. "I told you I'm training to do rock and mountain climbing with Tara. I'm so accustomed to the flat land of South Georgia I'm afraid I'm going to be left in the dust."

"I don't know how much good this training is going to do on the day you're leaving. Seems to me you're going to end up with legs that feel like Jell-O by the time you actually get to a mountain."

She stopped. He might be right. "Well, in any case let's slow the pace." She caught her breath and took it easy going up the next flight. They stepped through the metal door to the lighthouse deck and into the bright afternoon sun. She loved the feel of sea breezes in her hair from the top of the lighthouse.

"So what do you think?"

"Very nice. But it was nice on the ground too, and I don't mean the lighthouse." He was grinning at her.

She smiled back but shook her head. It was hard to push past her first instinct to decline a compliment.

He walked along the circular deck, taking in the view, spreading his hands on the black rail. "This was a good idea. I've been so busy with the hotel and other properties that I haven't come up here. I can't believe this is my first time at the top of this thing."

Luella came up beside him and leaned an elbow on the railing, looking at him. "I know. Especially someone like you, who enjoys travel and culture. A large part of your hotel's attraction is this lighthouse and the fact that people can walk across the street to it."

They went around the small, round balcony to look over at the hotel. He gestured to it with a hand wave. "And its haunted back stairway, according to a certain travel guide I know."

She held her hands up. "I've never personally verified the ghostly footsteps going up and down the stairs."

"Maybe if you slept on the stairs by yourself, you'd hear mysterious sounds and then . . . you moaning, 'What am I doing here and why?'"

She laughed and poked his chest. "I think *you* should attempt that one, seeing as you're the manager."

"You're the keeper of the ghost stories. I think the verification is on you."

She studied him. He was smiling, looking out over the island, and the late afternoon sun made the laugh lines around his eyes stand out. She had no doubt he'd put a lot of effort into making sure his children had as good a childhood as he could give them. But she'd bet he wasn't a pushover or someone who ignored the harder parts of parenting. A good man. What would it have been like had they met when they were younger? But that was a foolish line of thinking. At least they could enjoy each other now.

"What is it?" He looked at her, tilting his head.

"Oh, nothing. I'm just going to miss you."

"Yeah." He smiled. "I'll miss you too. St. Simons will be far less interesting with one fewer Glynn Girl. What about your tours?"

"My ghost tour protégé—Dell's grown daughter, Maggie—will take over for me until I get back. She's been fascinated with all the stories since she was a little kid." She ran her finger over the smooth black paint of the railing. She wasn't one hundred percent packed, and Tara hoped to leave the island for Asheville within the hour. Dinner was at Hadley's place tonight at seven. But it wouldn't be fair to Charles to cut his first lighthouse-lookout time short.

He clucked his tongue. "Telling ghost stories to a young child. Bad influence."

"I like to think of it as being the cool 'aunt.'"

They should go back down. It would take her at least ten minutes to make it back to her apartment, fifteen to finish packing, and then another ten to get to Julep's to pick up Tara. But . . .

Why was it so hard to leave this time? Being the "aunt" to all her friends' children had always been enough for her as far as family went. It wasn't as though she and Charles were superserious. They had been on just a handful of dates, for Pete's sake, and she was fifty-two.

"Luella."

His soft voice made her look up. He leaned in and kissed her, making her breath catch. The soft sensation of his lips on hers eclipsed the pleasantness of even the sea breezes.

He pulled back enough to look in her eyes. "A kiss on the top of a lighthouse. That's a first for me."

She smiled. "And me."

She longed to lean in and kiss him as if there were no tomorrow. How silly was that? It made no logical sense to want to get serious about this relationship. She'd made it this far in life without needing to have or be a significant other, and she really didn't want to give that up now. She just needed to start her trip. Then her drive for adventure and travel would take over, and she'd feel more rational again.

34

Tara stepped over a crumbling, fallen log on the trail. Birds chattered from the tall trees around her. The morning sun streamed through the woods, hinting that it would be a hot afternoon. A group ahead of them was laughing and talking loudly.

Was Luella ready for her first time to rappel? Hopefully she'd love it. She'd been an even-keeled traveler since they began almost two weeks ago. According to Luella, her research for the next travel guide was going well. They'd stayed in five different places since leaving St. Simons. Luella had booked the stays as they went, finding unique bed-and-breakfasts and insisting on paying because she could deduct the expenses as part of her writing business. The excitement of travel had made facing each new day easier, but it also had chiseled a deep ache in Tara's heart. She hadn't had the money to travel like this with Sean and Darryl. But because they'd had breaks a lot of families didn't get, like not having a mortgage payment, they'd enjoyed outdoor activities together in ways most poor families couldn't.

Once again a recurring idea of late sprang to mind. Could she make a difference by starting a nonprofit and helping underprivileged families?

The wind carried the strong scent of her mountains, and her brothers seemed to fill the air around her. She ached for them to be with her on this hike.

Webb, her former boss and today's instructor, topped a knoll, facing them. He smiled and waved and turned back. Apparently he was just checking to be sure they were still back here. She'd told him earlier this week that she wouldn't return to work at the outfitter store, but she appreciated his willingness to hold her job open for her. She'd also had lunch with her boss at the grocery store and let her know the same thing. Why was she burning bridges when she had no other source of income? But she couldn't return to either job. Something else was calling to her. She just wasn't sure what that was yet.

"Did I see you wave at someone?" Luella asked.

"The instructor was checking on us."

They'd joined an adventure group billed for beginners, and Webb had been clear that he didn't mind the slower pace. Today's program was only a half-day one, and it would give them a taste of several things: hiking, climbing, rappelling, and wading through creeks.

"My goodness." Luella went off the path and closer to the edge of the mountain, looking out at the view. "I can see why you love these mountains." She closed her eyes and breathed deep. "It just smells and *tastes* like life and freshness."

Tara smiled. "It does." The sweet smell of mountain laurel brought back many amazing moments of being in the woods with her boys.

They were nearing the end of the trail to Cove Creek Falls, and once there they would gear up and rappel from it.

"Webb seems disappointed you're leaving the store for good."

"Yeah, that place was a big part of our family life. I worked there to afford gear. Sean and Darryl worked in the bike-repair shop from an early age and branched out to the main floor once they were sixteen. But I can't go back."

Sadness nagged at her, undermining her strength for starting a nonprofit. But what about all the underprivileged boys and girls who never got a weekend of camping or mountain climbing or rappelling because of the lack of money? That thought made her heart ache. As painful as they were, she was so grateful for the memories she had of being outdoors, having adventures with her boys.

She'd used the evenings, when Luella was busy on her computer writing about the day's adventures and searching for the next one, to research her fledgling idea—to start a fund that would allow underprivileged families to rent or buy things like camping equipment and climbing gear. There wasn't a better, happier place for a family than outdoors.

Once the idea had become a little clearer in her mind, she'd called Gavin. He'd sounded excited at the prospect for her and encouraged her to keep moving forward and to reach out to other people in the industry. Webb was one of those people.

Luella headed back to the path. "Are you ready for tonight?"

Tara followed. "As ready as I'll ever be, I suppose." They would stay in *her* cabin tonight. Her and her boys' home. But odd as it seemed, it felt right. Could her brothers feel any closer than now as she hiked this winding trail? The first rock climb they'd done as a family had taken place here. "Now, the real question is, Are *you* ready to go out on the rope?"

Luella laughed. "You're putting a middle-aged woman from an island at sea level on a rope hanging off a cliff near a waterfall. What do you think?"

Tara patted her shoulder. Even though the constant ache of accepting that Sean and Darryl were gone forever was a tough opponent, Luella's sense of humor had made being in the mountains of North Carolina these many days bearable. "Having you rappel like this seems a bit mean of me. But in my defense, it's what you said you wanted."

"One can't write a proper guide without experiencing the adventure for oneself. But ask me again when we're hanging off the wet, rocky cliff if it's still what I want."

"You'll love it. Lots of people say rappelling is the fun part. It's the reward after your muscles are burning from the climb."

"But you enjoy it all."

"I do. I've missed climbing." The sunlight sparkled between the green, rustling leaves of the trees. "And everything about this area."

They continued the hike in silence, and before long they were in a circle with the group, listening to the instructor.

"Oh, Tara." Webb waved her over. "I got a text from a friend a few minutes ago. He'd already heard about Sean and Darryl, and he personally knows someone on the board of REI. He ran your idea past her, and she wasn't against it. She said it's a mammoth undertaking, but if you follow through and pull all the info together, you can send her the details in an email. If she likes it, she'll take it to the board. I'll forward her email address as soon as he sends it."

Her heart leaped. "That's great. Thanks."

The loss of Sean and Darryl seemed to have shaken everyone who heard about it, especially those in the climbing community of Western North Carolina. Maybe it was selfish of her, but it helped to know that people cared, that her loss was also a loss to them.

"We're no REI, but my wife and I will be fully on board to help."

Tara could see Sean and Darryl smiling, and her heart was warmed by Webb's support. "I . . . I don't know anything to say except thank you."

"That's plenty." He eyed his group. "Okay, gather up." As the group listened to the rappelling instructions, Tara started strapping on her own trusty seat harness and helmet. When she'd signed up for this outing, she'd asked if she and Luella could go down at the same time, and Webb said he'd have an instructor set up two anchors at the top of the falls. They'd also go down first so that as they waited for the rest of the group to reach the bottom of the falls, Luella could take notes and have questions ready for the guide.

She tightened all her straps and started checking her carabiners and belay equipment. This was her third climb since returning to the mountains, giving her a way to connect with many of her rock-climbing buddies. There had been tears aplenty, but then they shook off the sadness and did what they do best—climb high and have one another's backs.

While traveling she'd also spent an evening with Pastor Mike, his wife,

Patti, and their kids. Pastor Mike asked her to consider speaking to the church one Sunday morning. She didn't mind the idea, but when he asked if she'd do it in five weeks, she'd felt sick to her stomach. That would be just shy of three months after her brothers died, and it wasn't a large church, about three hundred. Could she do it without falling apart? She hoped so because she'd told him yes.

With her gear ready she attached her double-link sling to the anchor and started rigging her rope for her descent. She made sure she was redundant on all counts and tested her system. Everything was good. But it looked as if she'd be waiting awhile for Luella to be done with the instruction. Leaving herself attached to the anchor, she sat on the edge of the waterfall and let her feet dangle.

She took a deep breath. Luella was right. The air tasted like life. She imagined Sean and Darryl being here with her. They felt so close, as if their physical presence was all around her, but even if they were here, straight from the other world, she couldn't see or feel or talk with them. How could joy and grief be so tightly interwoven, tighter than the weave of the thick climbing ropes?

Her mind drifted to when she woke in the hospital with the rock in her hand. She could still hear the heavenly singing. Had the experience been a dream? She could also hear Gavin's voice from two weeks ago when they were in the kitchen at Sapphira's house, sorting out which of them the property belonged to. *I've never thought this of anyone before, but I believe you can do anything you set your mind to.*

Was that true? If it was, she had the strength to hear the truth about the rock from Elliott and Hadley. The fact was, she'd put it off long enough.

"All right, I think we're ready." Webb's voice shook her out of her thoughts. "We've gone over everything and practiced a few times. Let's get Luella set up to rappel."

Tara gave him a thumbs-up.

They walked Luella through attaching to the anchor, and then Tara attached herself to her rope while Luella mimicked her steps on her own rope. Webb double-checked Luella's ropes. Within a few minutes they were ready to begin the descent.

"On 'rappel'!" Luella shouted, readying the instructor.

"On 'rappel.'" Tara echoed, smiling at her.

Stepping down the side of the rock sent a surge of energy through her. It was amazing every time. But what was Luella thinking? Was she still nervous? "You good?"

"Yep. I think so." Luella looked focused, which was a good sign. Many people concentrate on climbing technique and forget that rappelling is going down—and inherently more dangerous.

"Take your time. No one is in a hurry. Actually, hold on." Tara locked herself in place and pulled out her phone.

Luella froze, holding her rope still. "Better not drop that thing down the waterfall."

"Thanks, *Mom*." Tara winked at her. "I won't." Using the front camera, she snapped a picture of Luella and herself on the rock face with the waterfall in the background. "Just gotta send this to Gavin, and then we'll get back at it."

Before she could put her phone away, she got the response.

Do I need to get my big ladder?

She laughed and tucked the device back in her deep shirt pocket and unlocked herself to continue the rappel.

"So, of all the people you could send that text to, why Gavin?" Luella stayed focused on the ropes and her descent.

"Hmm?" Tara's mind raced. "Oh, you know, there's no waterfall in St. Simons." And he was her friend. Why else?

"Not Julep, Sue Beth, or Dell." Luella's breathing was a bit rapid and shallow.

Was a simple text a big deal? "Well, I . . ."

"Ignore me. I'm just teasing you, sweetie."

"It's all right. Glad I seem well enough to tease now." *Well enough.* She was functional, as opposed to being broken beyond repair, but the zest she'd felt for life would be forever out of reach. No more "life is amazing." But rather just "enough."

Bouncing her feet off the rock, she finished her rappel and then started unfastening. She helped Webb belay other newbies while Luella made her notes.

"Tara, I was thinking . . ." Luella trailed off as Tara helped her unfasten.

"Are you ready to head back to St. Simons *now,* never to leave the flatness of your island again?"

"Not yet, no." Luella laughed. "I hope you don't mind my saying this, but it hit me so hard just a minute ago that if your mom could see you—whether it's now or a decade ago—she would be amazed by you, proud of who you are, grateful to the moon and back that you aren't like her."

"Yeah? That's interesting, I guess. I've never thought about it, and I don't allow thoughts of her to roost. It's exhausting and unhelpful. Was she that powerless to stop the addiction that she'd throw me away for a fix? And later do the same to Sean and Darryl? I can't understand that, especially in light of knowing she had good parents."

Luella nodded. "I'm sure we'll never understand what makes some people turn their backs on everything and pursue drugs, but it's like a plague across this country right now. Maybe you should consider writing your story—about surviving despite having an addict for a mom—and encourage other women not to take that same path."

"Have you lost your mind?" Tara immediately regretted her scoff. "Sorry. But you think drug-addicted women read motivational or self-improvement books?"

"You have a story to tell, Tara. And, yeah, I think it would empower you and others if you shared it, whether through speaking or writing or both."

"I told Pastor Mike I'd share my story at church five weeks from now. I'm hoping I can get through that successfully, but either way, when it's over, I think I'm forever done, Lu."

Luella got a pocket-size notebook and a pen out of her backpack. "Do me a favor. Between now and then, when ideas come to you, jot them down. After that, if you still think you have nothing else to share besides what you'll talk about that Sunday morning, then I'm good with it."

When she put it that way, how could Tara argue? She took the small leather-bound notebook and tucked it into her pocket.

35

Gavin took his phone off silent as he came out of the courthouse. The much-needed permits felt like golden tickets in his hands. Even with the many contacts he had within the local government, it'd taken a lot of hoop jumping to get these permits within two weeks. After he divided the property, the two plots sold within forty-eight hours of being on the market. He'd gone to closing already, because people with money to buy those lots didn't want to chance Gavin's changing his mind.

The balloon note was paid in full, and his mom, Dell, and Sue Beth had been busy getting new stock and doing a store makeover to draw more customers. They hoped if they could somehow make a big splash with summer sales, Seaside Properties would award them the rental rights to the Home Décor building. Gavin felt that was a lost cause, but it'd been nice that the girls were so occupied that he'd been left alone to carry out his plan in private. Of course, they'd see the start of his handiwork by tonight, but he'd been able to keep it a secret so far.

His heart hopped about like a flying squirrel going tree to tree. Tara had won the argument about the inheritance. That was true, and he would always be grateful to her for that. But in the three weeks since she left, he'd set in motion a way to give her something she couldn't refuse.

It was taking some gymnastics, both physically and financially, to pull off this plan. But odd as it seemed, he was thrilled to take out a loan for it. How was that possible? He headed for his truck. Finally it was time to execute the second phase of his plan. His mom would be thrilled when she learned of it this evening. But there was a lot of work to do between now and then. His two crews were probably already on the property, and one guy was a structural engineer. Gavin was antsy to be there. Too bad it'd taken longer at the courthouse than expected.

His phone rang, and Tara flashed through his mind. Calls from her made his day, whether she needed to talk about heavy or hopeful things. But this time the screen said *Jimmy*.

"Hey, Jimmy."

"Where are you?"

"Courthouse." He got into his truck.

"You've got to come to Sapphira's ASAP."

"What's the problem?"

"We can't jack up what's left of the house to move it. One guess why, Gavin, just one."

"The Glynn Girls?" He sighed. Well, they were without Luella, which often led to some rather overemotional decisions on their part. Maybe he should've informed them of his plan rather than trying to surprise his mom. He started the truck and backed out of the parking spot. "What are they doing?" It'd taken him two weeks to coordinate today. What were they thinking?

"They're having a sit-in, even made a few picket signs."

"What? Are you serious?"

"I couldn't make this stuff up, Gavin. My imagination isn't that good. Are you sure we're the ones who ran off Mary?"

"Tara."

"You say tomato. I say too-mat-o."

Guilt nibbled at him. The men would've come today regardless, because Gavin needed them, but he'd told them they'd run off Tara just to get under their skin a bit. It was time to come clean. "No one ran her off. Her home is North Carolina."

Jimmy gasped. "You lied?" His theatrics were clear. "Guys," he yelled, "listen to this. Gavin lied when he said we ran off Mary."

"Tara," Gavin repeated.

"Yeah, whatever. You like that one, don't you?"

Leave it to Jimmy to see truth and be so blunt it hurt. "I do."

"I thought so. I hate mush, so let's stop this topic right now and talk logistics. Are you going to stop sitting in the air-conditioning, eating bonbons, and get here, or what?"

"Don't leave, okay? I need you."

"See, if you'd talked to Mary like that, she might still be around."

"Jimmy!" If Gavin could invent a Stop button that worked on firemen, he'd sell it to half a million firefighters like himself and be really rich.

"No need to yell. We're here for you, mostly because we want to see in living color how you're going to break up this act your mamas have going on."

"Thanks." It took him fifteen minutes to get to the causeway, but once across it, he was pulling onto Sapphira's street in three minutes. As soon as he turned the corner, he saw the three women sitting on a bench just outside the doorway to what was left of the house, and they were arm in arm. There appeared to be a poster on his mom's lap.

His buddies from the station were under a shade tree, looking relaxed and maybe gaining fodder to harass Gavin. He might need to talk to Tara to figure out a way to spin this back on the guys. She seemed to have both the knack and guts to carry out her payback plans.

Gavin put the truck in Park and studied the chaotic scene. "Good Lord in heaven, give me patience, because she's my mom. Actually all three of them are, plus Luella, and I'm grateful for my mamas." He looked heavenward. "Right?" There were people all across the world who longed for another minute with their moms, and he had four women who loved him even when they were upset with him for wrongs or perceived wrongs he'd done. He grabbed the bottle of water from its holder. Amusement got the better of him, and by the time he opened his truck door, he was laughing. "Mamas, what are you doing?"

"We're protesting." His mom slapped the blank poster on her lap. "We're staying right here. No food or water until you listen."

"Is this a challenge?" Gavin rubbed his chin, feigning being thoughtful. "Because I think I could win this one." He shook the water bottle.

His mom studied him. "We're serious. Aren't we, girls? Save the art room."

Dell and Sue Beth released a loud yell that sounded more like a happy cheer than a determined chant.

Gavin rubbed the water bottle against his forehead. "Can you tell me what you think you're protesting?" He lowered the bottle. "Or is that a secret to be revealed after your emotions settle or Luella reasons with you— whichever comes first?"

"Julep's pretty wired." Dell slapped a pink-coated paintbrush against her stained white pants. "All three of us are."

"I can see that. The question on my mind is why."

Dell shrugged, looking a bit less ornery. "It could have something to do with our having the first energy drinks of our lives before we talked and decided we needed to take action."

"We tried calling you." Sue Beth huffed. "But you didn't pick up."

"My phone was on silent while I was at the courthouse. And what I'm hearing is you're exhausted from the weeks of long, hard hours at the shop, and you decided to have energy drinks while you talked among yourselves about this. Is that a fair assessment?"

"Oh, hush your mouth," his mom said. "This isn't about what we drank." His mom narrowed her eyes. "We found out this morning that you sold the remaining part of Sapphira's house, Tara's shiplap and all, to the Historical Society. And we won't stand for it!" She lifted the poster, and Dell and Sue Beth each grabbed a corner of it. In pink letters it read "Save this tart room."

Gavin stifled a laugh. "Someone misspelled *art.*"

"What?" His mom stood and jerked the sign so she could see it. "How on earth . . ." Her face mirrored disbelief before she lowered the sign, looking resolute again. "However it's spelled—"

"That would be *a-r-t.*" Gavin elongated each letter.

Sue Beth looked at the sign. "We were rushing around to make this, and that's not a *t* in front of *art.* It's a wispy dollop of paint that looks like one."

"Okay," Gavin elongated the word.

"This isn't funny." Mom shook her finger again. "Most of Sapphira's house is gone, and there's nothing any of us can do about that. But to sell what's left to the Historical Society without even getting the shiplap, doors, light fixtures, crown molding, or anything else possible out of it for Siobhan is wrong. It's just flat-out wrong."

Something much deeper than what his mom was complaining about was bothering her, and fresh guilt pressed in on him. Had Tara let all of them off the hook too easily?

Jimmy walked up nonchalantly, arms folded, movements slow—classic Jimmy. "So . . . who's Siobhan?"

Gavin shoved his shoulder, not that Jimmy budged. Gavin focused on his mom. He could blurt out the truth about his plans, but his mamas clearly had some stuff to work through. "Go on. I'm here to listen."

"You promised you would save the shiplap and wood flooring and anything else salvageable for Tara, but you haven't."

Jimmy leaned in. "Just how many women were staying under this roofless wonder, apparently known as a bachelor pad, as you demolished it?"

"One." Gavin shooed him, knowing Jimmy wasn't going to step out of hearing range, but couldn't he at least back away a few steps?

Mom sat on the bench and looked up at him. "What are you thinking, Son? This past week I kept waiting on you to remove the goods for Tara, but you didn't. Then while I was at the shop this morning, the mayor's wife came into the store looking for furniture, and she said you'd sold the art room to the Historical Society. I'm so disappointed and angry I don't even know where to begin, Gavin. I can't be a part of stealing one more thing from Tara, not one more blessed thing."

And there it was, the real issue digging at his mom's soul—anger at herself and him for taking Sapphira's home apart before it was legally theirs, before Tara could claim it.

"Mom,"—Gavin put a hand on her shoulder—"I'm not sure where to begin. First, I was wrong to start divvying up Saffy's house before time, but Tara forgave me, and you need to forgive me too. And yourself. If it helps, she's convinced if she'd known sooner or if she and her brothers had arrived here on time, they would've helped me deconstruct the house while we got to know each other. Okay?"

His mom buried her face in her hands. His poor mom. She meant well. Gavin sat beside her. "And, second, either the mayor's wife is mistaken, or you misunderstood her. I didn't sell anything. I gave them artwork, not the art room. I also gave them pieces of shiplap, flooring, and such to use as part of the display, all of which I talked to Tara about beforehand."

"Why didn't you tell me?" His mom stood.

"Because I'm moving what's left of this house to the small lot near your home, and when the time is right, I'll give it to Tara to use as a vacation spot or whatever she wants. I was going to surprise you with that plan when you came home from work tonight."

Jimmy scratched his head. "So two women, right? Not three. Siobhan and Tara stayed here, because Tara and Mary are one and the same."

Gavin ignored Jimmy and put his arms around his mom and hugged her.

She broke into sobs. "I hate this planet sometimes. Too much loss. Just too much. Poor Tara."

"I know, but if life didn't keep on keeping on, people meant to be born wouldn't be. So we take our losses with our gains and let love bring us joy and break our hearts."

Dell and Sue Beth moved in, and they had a group hug. He stayed there until his mamas' emotions calmed and tears subsided. All of them had spent years hoping that Cassidy had pulled her life together after leaving the island and that Siobhan had been given a reasonably sound, happy childhood. That bitter disappointment and the settling in of that heartbreak was also part of the reason for this sit-in. And overwrought emotions.

"We good?" Gavin released them.

The women nodded.

"Uh," Jimmy said, "and while questions are being answered, how many girls is Gavin chasing after, and are the others as good at running from him as Mary?"

"Apparently all three of them are expert sprinters," Gavin said.

Jimmy laughed. "Who is this Tara person?"

"You know about her," his mom said. "She's Sapphira's Siobhan."

Jimmy went slack-jawed. "No way." He grew serious. "I . . . I'm sorry, Gavin. If our pranks and nonsense did anything to upset her . . ."

Images of Tara in Saffy's house plotting this moment of revenge sprang to his mind. He smiled. "They didn't."

"So what's the plan?" Dell gestured at the remaining part of Sapphira's home.

"I have permits to move this portion of the house and dry it in—repair the roof and make the building watertight. But after that it'll sit there for a while. It'll take time to get documentation to set it up with electricity and all the other utilities a house needs to have." His effort to save a portion of the home for Tara had put him weeks behind on the schedule as far as clearing the land and removing all the debris, but he'd put that stipulation in the contract when selling the land.

Each of his mamas hugged him again.

"I'm still confused," Jimmy said. "Siobhan returned, and you chased her down the beach as she tried to get away. Now you're putting one-fourth of a house you demolished on a lot next to your mom—may I repeat, next door to your mom—in hopes it'll entice her. Is that the plan, Gavin?"

Gavin sighed. "Close enough."

"Okay, I like this plan!" Jimmy clapped his hands together and rubbed. "I'll have fodder to rib you for decades."

"Thanks."

Jimmy slapped Gavin on the back. "Anytime, buddy."

36

Luella drove toward church as Tara fidgeted with the notes to her speech.

Tara slapped the thin leather binder into her lap, leaned against the headrest, and sighed. "What was I thinking? I can't do this. I couldn't sleep last night. I feel sick, and my head is killing me."

Luella had assured her a dozen times she'd do great. What else could she say? "Call Hadley or Elliott."

"No. They can't fix this."

But in the seven weeks since they'd left St. Simons, Luella had seen much proof of how close the three of them were. "Come on. Give them a call."

"No. They have enough to deal with as they drive here."

Luella tucked a stray curl behind her ear as she kept her eyes on the road. No sense arguing. Tara had a stubborn streak the size of Texas. But it was actually a gift from God to get her through life with more than just her sanity still intact. She inspired people. Saved lives. And apparently hated public speaking.

Tara closed her eyes. "But as much as I detest getting in front of a crowd, I have discovered it feels really good to write. I'm on my third notebook."

Luella thought Tara had been writing a fair amount, but she'd been rather private about it, even as they shared hotel or B&B rooms. "I'd like to read them, and if you're interested in trying your hand at being published, I'll do what I can. My editor doesn't acquire that kind of manuscript, but she may know some who do."

Tara sat up. "Maybe someday." She shrugged. "Right now it's just thera-peutic, and my real work is getting the nonprofit established."

While Luella worked on the tedious aspects of her research, Tara stopped at outfitter stores and talked to owners or managers. Almost every store was willing to consider donating to the cause once Tara had nonprofit status.

Luella turned into the parking lot. It had a sea of cars, and Tara gasped.

"This many people can't have come to hear me." Tara pulled her phone out and texted someone. A moment later her phone pinged. "Pastor Mike said he hadn't expected this kind of turnout either." Tara opened and closed the snap on her leather binder. "What was I thinking? Oh, he said they have a parking space reserved for us with orange cones. My guess is it'll be in that area." She pointed. "Near where his office is."

"Okay." Luella slowed, looking for a set of cones.

Tara fiddled with her phone. Was she texting someone else? A moment later she put it to her ear.

"Hey, Tara." It was Gavin's voice. "What's up?"

There was no such thing as a private phone call in a shared vehicle. The person on the other phone was easily heard. Luella broke into a big smile. Was their friendship deepening? Luella had spent enough time with Tara to believe with her whole heart that Gavin and Tara could have a great and lasting friendship, one that met emotional needs for each of them. If Julep had a clue these two were texting and talking the way they were, she'd be beside herself with hopes and dreams for Gavin, Tara, and future grand-children. But Luella knew most guy-girl relationships weren't destined to end in marriage.

She spotted the orange cones and Pastor Mike and his wife on the side-walk waving at her. He removed the cones and gestured for her to pull in.

"I'm a basket case." Tara's voice trembled. "The parking lot is full twenty minutes before start time, and . . ." She trailed off.

Luella pulled in and then reached over and squeezed Tara's hand. As Luella got out, she smiled at them. "Hey, good to see you again."

"How goes the research?" He glanced through the windshield at Tara. "Everything okay?"

"Some jitters, but she'll be fine." Luella hoped that was true. Tara got out, a huge grin on her face. She spoke to Mike and Patti, and soon Luella and Tara were walking behind them down the sidewalk.

"You look better," Luella whispered.

"Gavin said I should run like the wind and never look back." She rolled her eyes. "He's a mess. He offered to head my way and find me and said we'd putter off into the sunset, never to be heard from again." Tara chuckled.

"There's a reason he has four mamas."

"Yeah?" They went inside and down a long hallway.

"I didn't pseudoadopt any of Dell's or Sue Beth's children. And they didn't adopt each other's either, but at one time or another when Gavin was young, we each adopted him. He's different—vulnerable, tender, tough as nails."

"Is this a sales pitch?"

"No, honey. Not from me. I believe in staying single if that's what you want. I'm simply saying I'm proud of him and telling you why he has four mamas."

"I need to get the microphone headsets." Pastor Mike and his wife went into his office.

Luella stopped and turned Tara by the shoulders to look her in the eyes. "When you're behind the pulpit, remember that these people love you. Many are weary of the battle. Others are scared of what life could bring their way. But you've survived their worst nightmares, and they're hoping you tell them they can too. That's all. It doesn't have to be perfect, only real and honest."

"You're pretty good at this Mom stuff." Tara smiled. "Thanks."

There was shuffling in the hallway ahead of them, and soon Hadley and Elliott were engulfing Tara.

"I think all twenty of your mountain-hiking and rock-climbing crew are here." Hadley removed a hair from Tara's dress.

"James too?"

"The leader of the pack," Elliott said.

"Good. I need to talk to him." Tara turned to Luella. "I don't see him a lot, but he gives good dad-type advice, and I need a bit of that. I'll invite him, his wife, and the rock-climbing gang to the cabin, and we'll get the fire pit roaring and make an afternoon of it. You mind?"

"Sounds perfect, but we're not prepared to feed a crowd."

"It'll be easy. I've pulled these things off last minute a dozen times over the years."

Tara focused on her friends and opened her hand. The small rock she kept with her rested in her palm. "Was this in my hand when I woke in the hospital?"

Hadley and Elliott glanced at each other. Hadley nodded. "Yeah."

"It was missing before the house was hit with the storm. Who found it and brought it to me?"

Hadley put one hand under Tara's and one over the rock. "We don't know how it got in your hand, Tara. One of us was with you around the clock. It makes no sense that you had it in your hand."

Tara stumbled backward until she was against the wall. A broad, beautiful smile spread across her face. She clutched the rock tight, her eyes closed as if she was praying. She hugged her friends, but no one said another word about the incident, as if it was too precious to question or analyze or gab about.

Pastor Mike and Patti came out of the office.

"Let me help you get this on and show you how it works." Patti held up a headset and body pack.

Pastor Mike put his set on. "Tara, you sit on a pew in the front, and I'll invite you up when it's time."

"Sure."

"We have a seat for you." Hadley motioned to Luella, and she followed them. Luella had been to this church a few times since leaving St. Simons, but it'd never been this full.

When Tara stepped onto the platform, she looked calm and comfortable. She told several funny stories about Sean, Darryl, and her. People laughed, some while wiping tears. She was hitting hearts, and Luella knew most of the people here would never be the same, not because Tara's words were more profound than anything they'd heard before, but because most knew her or knew of her. She was a part of them, and she was sharing from a vulnerable place, not quite three months after her brothers died.

She quickly recapped going to St. Simons Island, falling asleep on the plane, and dreaming and believing that Sean and Darryl were still alive. She shared about the text messages from Darryl, the day her time at the hotel was up, and her losing her phone, credit cards, and cash in the rising tide. The crowd was clearly mesmerized.

Walking to the other side of the platform, she began again. "You all look horrified, but you shouldn't, because while I was in the state of Georgia, I found my cabin. You know the one that sits not too far from here in the mountains of North Carolina. Yeah, I found it there, so in my thinking I had only two problems at that time. I couldn't manage to connect with Sean and Darryl, and there was this roofer guy who kept coming inside *my* house and taking it apart."

Her delivery of the sentences and her vivacious animations were perfect. People laughed despite the subject matter. She didn't mention Gavin's name, but she described him as a really bad guy, a force of evil, and she continued to add humor and make faces as she told of their various encounters. The crowd could see the scenario from Gavin's point of view, and they laughed at her insistence of what a horrible person he was.

She paused and took a drink from a water bottle sitting on the podium. "So let's circle back and talk about God. Sometimes our view of life and God are similar to the view I had of *my* St. Simons house and roofer guy—

distorted and incomplete. I kept trying to squeeze what I needed to be true into my reality. It didn't fit. I told roofer guy he was the worst repairman ever. He didn't tell me the truth—that I was mentally incapable of grasping his level of understanding.

"When I think of how he handled that situation, I'm reminded of God—silent when we say ridiculous things that He knows aren't true. Patient. Kind. And protective.

"A friend helped me see that we are all vessels. We will carry something to everyone we come in contact with. Let's choose to be vessels of love, patience, hope, and faith. When it's all said and done, whether you're the one in the ground or a loved one is, the times you won't regret are the times you loved deeply with patience and kindness and sacrifice."

She paused, scanning the listeners. "And love never dies . . ."

Luella couldn't stop thinking about Tara back when she was called Siobhan. What a journey she'd been on.

How could she embrace what Tara was saying and be a vessel of love in her own life? Her heart turned a little flip, and butterflies settled in her stomach. It was time to go home. And time to stop running from her feelings for Chuck.

37

Tara drove up the long gravel driveway toward home. Loneliness clung tight, making her chest ache. Luella had gone home three days ago. Tara stopped in front of the cabin, turned off the car, and got out. She wriggled Darryl's rock out of her jeans pocket and eased into the rocking chair on the porch. The now familiar sentiments of grief and gratefulness wrapped around her anew. "Ah . . . home."

The quietness settled over her. Green leaves swayed, ducks on the pond quacked, and she longed to go back to the time when Sean and Darryl would be home soon, hungry and with smelly gym clothes and a need to talk and laugh and watch a show together.

Coming home was a mixed bag. "I miss you."

Nothing.

The breeze didn't pick up. The ducks didn't flap about.

Nothing.

They had a life, and so did she, and the two wouldn't meet again until she died. But she'd been given a sign to last her a lifetime. She clutched the rock tightly. God loved her. The air around her teemed with the feeling of their presence, but maybe that was because they were in her mind and heart. She cried a lot at night, but morning never failed to come, and she showered, dressed, and focused on making Sean's and Darryl's lives matter now and hopefully a hundred years from now.

She'd applied for nonprofit status, but until it came through, probably in the next three to six months, all her time was spent on preliminary work—getting the plan out there for store owners and managers of outfitter stores, making contact with potential contributors, setting up protocols for how families could get training and equipment for outings, and starting all sorts of social media landing pages.

She was also writing a nonfiction book. Luella suggested she write the first five chapters and a cover letter and pitch it to a few agents. Maybe she'd get a contract. Maybe not. But she needed to write. In many ways writing from her life experiences felt like talking directly to Sean and Darryl.

Her phone beeped with Julep's tune. She pulled her phone out of her pocket and glanced at the list of texts from each Glynn Girl, asking if she'd eaten, slept, was home yet, had plans for the evening, remembered to put gas in her car.

Good grief, I've inherited four mamas.

She sent quick answers and went into the cabin. When she turned on the lights, a light bulb flickered, and she looked up, once again noticing the new paneled ceiling. She took a picture of it and sent it to Gavin.

A few seconds later she received a response.

Hey, T. What am I looking at?

This was their first text for the day, but they texted and talked a few times each week.

You're looking at the ceiling in the cabin, the end results when a man knows how to repair a roof.

Ha! I have no apologies to give. You got in front of your church and said . . .

She chuckled. He'd texted those same lines earlier in the week, never saying anything after the word *said*. Did he mean that she'd told everyone he was a horrible roofer so he had nothing left to apologize for or that she'd said his responses reminded her of God—patient, kind, and protective?

The social media guy at the church had uploaded her talk, and apparently Gavin had watched it—he and about two thousand other people, which seemed a lot to her since she'd spoken less than two weeks ago.

She'd shared a lot that Sunday morning, maybe too much. On the other hand, being vulnerable, encouraging, and honest had freed and strengthened her in ways she'd never imagined.

Ready to hear Gavin's voice, she navigated to Favorites and touched his name.

"Hey." He sounded out of breath. "I had something I needed to tell you, but, first, how was your last meeting?"

What were they doing? Even if there was a spark between them, and she was beginning to think there was, it was too soon. Years too soon. She was an emotional wreck, and he wasn't a first-aid kit. That wouldn't be good or healthy for either of them.

"Good." She went to the car to get her suitcase. "Another store is on board."

"You must be an incredible salesperson."

"The people I've met are the incredible ones, so very ready to give a hand to help children and families bond and have fun. I never imagined strangers having hearts this big."

"You have to be wiped out. How much sleep have you had since Elliott had the baby Monday?"

"After being there for the birth, I ran most of the week on sheer adrenaline. But I've not had a lot of sleep, and I'm starting to feel it." She'd been in the room when Aiden was born, and she'd never experienced anything like it. She'd had appointments Tuesday through today, and then she kept Aiden half the night, giving the new parents a bit of sleep, although Elliott got up twice to nurse him. "Elliott and Trent are so in love they literally glow."

"Since no one is sleeping at night anyway"—he groaned and huffed—"it's bound to make for two good night-lights."

She used to like the idea of marriage and babies. She'd hoped that one day she'd fall in love and the rest would follow, but now the whole concept made her feel overwhelmed and nauseated. "What are you doing?"

"Ah, just another project around the house."

"I should let you go."

"No." He sounded forceful. "Uh, I mean, please don't."

Maybe he felt sorry for her, or maybe he liked the friendship as much as she did. How could she know?

"Okay."

Once in a while the desire crept into her heart to go to St. Simons Island and spend time with Gavin. How would she and Gavin know if there could be more between them if they didn't date? But that sounded like a really bad idea. If she and Gavin dated and it didn't work out, everything would be awkward between her and the Glynn Girls—and they were like family now, especially Luella.

"Oh, Tara . . ." Gavin sang her name. "Did you get caught up reading an email?"

"Sorry. The thing I got caught up in was my own thoughts." She couldn't tell him what was on her mind, so she searched for something they could talk about. "I heard on the news today there's a chance that a Category Five hurricane in the Caribbean could turn east. Any chance it'll affect St. Simons?"

"It's too soon to tell. We'll probably know in a few days, maybe a week, but if it comes this way, we'll get as prepared for it as possible."

Her heart clenched. "That doesn't sound promising or safe." The line was quiet for a bit. "Gavin?"

"I'm a rescue worker, T." He paused. "We'll make sure our family and friends pack up and go two or three hours inland days before it hits. But a lot of people will refuse to go until the last minute, and public safety workers will continue helping people evacuate until we're made to pull out. Even then we won't go far. When the worst is over, we'll begin search and rescue."

She couldn't really imagine what all he did to help people year in and year out. Her heart warmed at the thought.

"Tara, you got quiet again."

"Your job suits you, Gavin."

"I agree. Does it bother you—my job?"

"It's disconcerting. How could it not be? But it seems as if we're on this planet to help those in our path the best way we know how. It's what we do. What I hope we always do."

He released a deep breath. "I like that answer, a lot."

"You sound relieved." Had she missed something?

"Yeah, well, sometimes people can't handle an aspect of a friend's life, and they pull away."

"Makes sense."

Regardless of her stray thoughts about being attracted to Gavin—and apparently he had them for her too—she would take Pastor Mike's advice and not do anything but heal for a full year: no dating, no selling the cabin, no making expensive purchases, no skydiving, no swimming with sharks, or anything similar.

If Gavin wasn't seeing anyone else in a year or so, and if she still had an ounce or two of romantic notions about him after traveling the US and getting the nonprofit set up, then she'd consider returning to St. Simons. What if her interest in Gavin was connected to her grief and maybe her gratefulness to him for helping her when she was so broken? Maybe she should stop texting and calling so often and let him return to his normal life.

"You rethinking your answer, Tara?"

"Huh?" She gathered her thoughts. "No, not that. Other things."

"About?"

"Uh, well." Should she tell him? She told him *everything* else. "Us."

"Oh." He coughed as if he'd been drinking something and choked. "Is there something you want to cover about us?"

"No . . . yes . . . maybe."

He chuckled. "Well now that we've cleared that up, what else can I help you with?"

She smiled, and it felt odd to smile when one's chest throbbed with grief. "I think that's everything."

"Tara?" Gavin cleared his throat. "Don't overthink us, okay? There is no need to 'get in' or 'get out.' You save all that superpower thinking for the nonprofit and the book."

She'd been given an out for this conversation, and since she didn't know what to say to him, she'd take it. "Yeah, you're right."

It seemed as if they were clearing the air without admitting to it. She should tell him her yearlong plans. "I'm thinking of working with a mentor who's had success helping other nonprofits get a solid start. The process is daunting."

"I think that's a good idea. Any ideas who?"

"Hadley knows a guy. I've talked with him via phone, and he seems well versed in the process. He's willing to mentor me, and I'm supposed to let him know within the week."

"Sounds like a good plan, and if Hadley trusts him to help you, that says a lot."

"It does. But he feels strongly that I should spend the next year traveling, talking face-to-face with potential contributors, making myself available to speak to churches and organizations, and giving PowerPoint presentations to the board of any company that will listen." Between the donations given when her brothers died and the money Gavin put in her account from the sale of the shiplap, she had the money to pursue the plan.

"I hope all that traveling also means hiking and rock climbing new mountains and camping out in states you've never visited before. I expect at least one picture a week, Tara."

His support warmed her, and the unbearable pain in her chest eased a bit.

38

L uella adjusted the sleeping mask covering her eyes as the car went over a small bump. Where were they going? "You know, Chuck, if I'd had any idea returning to the island included whatever shenanigan this is, I might have stayed in North Carolina."

"You're fine and no peeking." Charles's deep voice made her heart thump like a schoolgirl's. "Are you peeking?"

She'd been home three weeks, and he'd made every outing interesting, but he was really going over the top for this.

"No. I was simply adjusting it so the elastic didn't pull my hair. But I don't need to peek to know exactly where we are." She reached over and squeezed his hand on the car's gearshift.

"Really, now?"

"Yep, but it's an interesting way to spend a Sunday afternoon drive."

The car stopped.

Luella nodded, not needing to take the mask off. "We're at Fort Frederica."

He laughed. "How on earth . . ."

"When you're born and raised on a seventeen-square-mile island, you get to know the place." The car was moving again. She sat in silence for a moment, feeling its movements. "And now you're just driving in circles."

A drawn-out sigh came from the vicinity of the driver's seat.

The next thirty minutes were filled with twists and turns and Charles driving who-knows-where through neighborhoods and up and down driveways.

"Having fun?" Luella asked.

"Are you here with me?"

"I am."

"Then I'm having fun. Ever hear the one about . . ." He told silly jokes, making her laugh entirely too easily. She did her best to tell equally funny jokes.

Finally they stopped.

Luella reached for the mask. "Okay, okay. You got me. I don't know where we are. Can I take this mask off now? Is this place the surprise?"

"Yep. Go ahead."

Luella's eyes adjusted to the brightness of the day. Straight ahead was Blue Sails. "The store?" Why would he go to all this trouble? She tilted her head. "I'm confused."

He nodded, saying nothing further.

She narrowed her eyes. Was that *it*? "I've been thinking Tara could be the fifth Glynn Girl, but I've changed my mind. *You* could be it, pulling a prank like this. You know that?"

"Maybe that's my goal."

She studied him for a few seconds.

"Okay, okay." He pointed at the tie-dyed beachwear shop that shared the building with Blue Sails Casual Living. "That's the surprise."

"Dye Hard is the surprise? I hate to break it to you, but Sue Beth already gifted me with a full set of monogrammed tie-dyed beach towels. I'm not sure my apartment has room for more."

"You're funny. What if I told you that Dye Hard is moving their shop over to the newly built shopping center at Jekyll Island, vacating this space? They just turned in their notice a few days ago."

Was he saying—

"And," he continued, "the property manager," he pointed to himself with a thumb, "wants to get their shop filled as soon as possible before the summer ends, and fall begins in eight days And his boss authorized him to rent it at a discounted rate."

A grin spread across her face. "Oh really?"

Charles pulled her hand into his. "It's not the building you wanted. That one's already spoken for. But it would give Blue Sails Casual Living the footage you wanted to spread out, both downstairs in the shop and upstairs with additional room for Sue Beth's studio, and it'll do it at minimal cost. It makes your building part of the much-desired corner lot. You girls had good business all summer, despite everything that was going on. I believe this expansion would help your business grow even more."

Luella looked at the building, trying to imagine their spreading out to take over the whole thing. It would give Sue Beth a separate entrance for her art classes. And they could compartmentalize the store better, maybe even designating a room for small events.

"That sounds *amazing*! We'll have to talk numbers with Julep, but I like this plan even better. We don't have to pack up and move, just put in a couple of double-wide doorways between our store and Dye Hard's and spread out. This was very thoughtful. Thank you." She got out of the car and started walking toward the shop. She couldn't wait to tell everyone. They'd be thrilled.

Charles closed his door and stepped onto the sidewalk with her, grabbing her hand to stop her. "Wait. There's one more surprise. I think you'll be happy."

She stopped and turned to face him. "Yes?" She was already pleased as punch. What else had he planned?

He held both of her hands. "When I came to this island, I thought I would stay only a year, maybe two, and I'd told the owners of Seaside Properties my plan. But I've revised it, and I'm staying on the island in a permanent position based out of the hotel. I'm too intrigued by you to be willing to move away. There's nowhere else I'd rather be, whether you want to stay single forever or not."

Her heart threatened to burst, and her smile was so big it almost hurt. "I find my position on *that* particular point is shifting quicker than the incoming tide."

"That fast."

"Every bit. I'm finding the idea of marriage doesn't seem so bad anymore, provided it's to someone like you."

"Someone *like* me?"

"Okay, just you."

He leaned down and kissed her.

She leaned back, her heart going crazy. "Well, hello, darlin'."

He laughed.

She took him by the hand. "Chuck, sweetheart, would you marry me?"

He blinked.

"Should I take that as a yes?"

He leaned in and kissed her on the cheek. "For better or worse, with Glynn Girls stopping by and calling all times of the day and night, I would consider it an honor above all honors if you, Luella Demere Ward, would marry me."

She wanted to say something quippy and cute, but all she could think was that this felt as much like a miracle as Siobhan finding her way home again. "So this is love?"

Charles kissed her cheek again. "It is, and it'll continue growing like kudzu until death do us part. I promise."

39

The cool morning air carried the aroma of fall, campfire smoke, brewing coffee, and the murmurings of her hiking and rock-climbing buddies. Tara closed her eyes and soaked it in. Songbirds chirped loudly as sunlight made the autumn foliage even more spectacular. Thoughts of her brothers clung to her, even now, sixteen months after their deaths. But grief didn't own her.

Hope did.

Still, grief, with its ever-shifting size and weight and methods of torture, was a constant companion. But it was a quieter roommate as Tara pushed to keep her mind, soul, and body busy and productive.

She spread the ashes inside the fire ring and doused them one last time. She picked up her backpack.

"Hey." James, one of her longtime hiking and rock-climbing buddies, lumbered toward her, shoving a water bottle into his backpack. When she was in high school and he was her instructor, she'd thought he was really old. Funny, now that she was the same age as he'd been then, they both felt young to her.

He slung the straps to his backpack over his shoulders. "You ready?" He looked behind him at the rest of the hiking buddies. "Some will join in a few minutes. The rest will wait to begin the hike once we're back from the overlook."

She nodded. James and the others were thru-hiking—backpacking for eight days straight on the Appalachian Trail. But Tara was doing the same as she'd done for months—going to various outfitter stores along the Appalachian Trail for her nonprofit. Her usual method was to drive as close as possible to each AT outfitter store and either hike in or take a shuttle bus. But months ago her hiking and rock-climbing friends had plans to be here at this time, and she was scheduled to be in this general area now too. So five weeks ago they had arranged to meet at this campsite last night.

"Our first moments alone." James planted the end of his walking stick in the dark soil as he went. Walking sticks and long-distance hiking often went hand in hand, and Tara hoped that by the end of the day, she didn't regret not bringing hers. "Everyone was so excited when you could work it out to be here at the same time as we are."

"Thanks. I have tons of goals I'm working toward, but my actual schedule is very flexible."

She'd crisscrossed the US, meeting with store owners or managers and starting marketing campaigns. She'd spoken to dozens of churches and colleges, and she had a strong base of supporters.

Underprivileged families were already registering to have gear loaned to them without charge—gear for camping out, fishing, canoeing, and the like. And they could sign up for lessons and gear for mountain climbing and rappelling. The packages included a stipend for food and, when needed, transportation to the site location.

"How's the book writing going? Nonfiction, right?"

"Yeah, and I think it's going pretty well. I finished the first round of edits a few weeks back, and I have a few more editing rounds to go, but it'll hit store shelves this time next year."

"Hmm. Let me think about this." He angled his head and rubbed his chin. "Gavin was a first reader for you, because it definitely wasn't me or my wife."

She chuckled and nodded. "Should I apologize?"

"Nah. I'll forgive you and him."

James had met Gavin about six months ago when Tara invited him to North Carolina to rock climb and camp out with the group. Gavin came, and he'd been so much fun. He had seemed to really enjoy it too. He would probably come for another outing like that if she'd invite him. So why hadn't she?

He'd given her an open invitation to the island, but the only time she'd returned to the Golden Isles was for Luella's wedding, and even then she didn't go to St. Simons Island. Luella and Charles wed at the Jekyll Island Club Resort, and all Tara managed to do was fly in a few hours before it and leave a few hours after it was over.

James and she reached the overlook, moved to a jutted rock, and sat. The view was breathtaking. Looking at the fallen planet from this perspective was like a glimpse of heaven, and she was filled with gratefulness to God.

After taking a picture of the view with her iPhone, she sent it to Gavin. A longing to stop the constant traveling for the nonprofit and put down roots in St. Simons Island tugged at her once again. How else would she and Gavin ever figure out if they could be more than they were?

Tucking the phone away, she soaked in the view.

James propped his arm on her shoulder. "I'm sitting on this rock with you because my wife's back at camp, taping her feet for today's hike. Why are you here with me?"

He knew her well.

She shrugged. "I'm not ready. I don't know why."

But Tara missed Gavin. He felt the same, didn't he? They talked almost daily. At times it was simple chatter, but other times they laughed so hard it was difficult to breathe, and when her grief spilled over into tears, he listened, neither assuring her it would be fine nor rushing her to change the topic.

She'd fallen in love, and she had a constant desire for a life teeming with love and chaos—one that included being near four rather dramatic mamas, a firehouse filled with pranksters, a quiver full of his babies—or at least two or three along with a foster child or two—or gobs of helping the Boys and Girls Clubs of America. And most of all, one quiet, stalwart, gripping, patient, and tender man.

James shifted. "It's bound to be terrifying. You grew up without the ones you loved. You later loved and lost. Is that it?"

"Maybe." Did he have to be so direct?

Gavin and she didn't talk about their relationship, not even when she'd invited him to hike and camp with her friends or when she'd invited him and his mamas to North Carolina a few times. All of them had slept in the cabin a couple of nights, hiked, and camped out a few nights. Only she and Gavin had rock climbed and rappelled, laughing and talking until love felt tangible.

He and the Glynn Girls as well as Hadley and Elliot and their families had helped her survive every first without Sean and Darryl—Thanksgiving, Christmas, New Year's, and the worst of all, the anniversary of the day they died. Much of that was done via texts and phone calls, but he never forgot to be there for her, even when he was exhausted after a day of saving people from burning buildings.

Her insides quaked at the thought of giving her barely healed heart away again.

Her phone pinged with Gavin's tone. A text. She was sick of texting and phone calls and too little real contact. Weary of avoiding the topic of what she felt for him. At the very same time, she couldn't wait thirty seconds to see what he'd written, and she moved at breakneck speed to answer his calls. If he was off this morning, she'd FaceTime him and show him a live view of the overlook. They'd drink their coffees and talk as if sitting across the table from each other.

What was she doing traipsing the countryside, thinking about him all the time? She pulled her phone out and read the text.

Good morning! That's gorgeous. You still making rounds in Virginia?

Yeah. With James at overlook. Group still at campsite. Have a ten
o'clock appointment with next outfitter store on AT.

That sounds like all good stuff. The fire station alarm just went off,
so I gotta go. Talk later, okay?

Absolutely. Be safe.

James tapped his stick against the rock. "He's waiting for you, Tara. You
know that, right?"

Gavin's actions did say that . . . didn't they?

The desire to find a place on the island to live had started months ago,
and it continued to grow. Gavin had deep roots there and a career he was
good at, one that often allowed him to help those he cared about. With
hundreds of pieces of the nonprofit now in place, she could travel less often.
If Gavin wanted to, and he would, he could take time off here and there and
go with her.

"I don't want to sell or abandon the cabin." But she knew she could let
underprivileged families stay there for weekends or a week at a time, and
then she could return at will. Was she getting ahead of herself? She had no
experience with men and dating.

"That's your excuse, T? And you believe it?"

She didn't respond. They both knew she didn't believe it.

Fog hovered in the valley, rising in patches like swirling snow and dis-
sipating into thin air. That was life—beautiful, mysterious, and gone.

James scratched his scraggly five-day beard. "I can't imagine how you
feel, but love is the beginning and ending of everything good. Everything,
T. You can't stop love. But you can waste it. I know Pastor Mike said to
wait a year, but you're three months past that and procrastinating. That's
fine. It's your life. But be honest with yourself about what you're doing and
why."

"If Gavin and I date and it doesn't work out, everything will be awkward between me and the Glynn Girls, and they are like family now."

James said nothing, but he knew what she was just now realizing—when it came to her and Gavin, fear had taken on many forms and excuses.

She missed him. "I don't think there's another man for me like Gavin."

"I've known you since you were a teen, and I agree. And yet you're living in a cabin six hours from him, and your days are spent sending pictures and texts."

She mulled that over. Love, however fleeting, was never wasted. Didn't she know that by now? Love and legacy didn't disappear. It broke off into tiny pieces, like seeds on fertile soil. She couldn't stop it from growing. All she could do was let its fruit rot on the vine.

"Yeah." Her whisper echoed back to her. "What's with me living like that?"

40

G avin breathed in the cool ocean air through his nose and blew it out through his mouth as his feet hit the ground four times. He repeated the cadence again and again. Finding a rhythm came naturally these days, even when running long distances. It was nice when time and tides aligned to let him jog on the hard sand of low tide before the day got hot. He checked his smartwatch. His hunch was right: he'd run almost three miles. And, according to the device, he'd apparently missed a text from his mom too.

Could you come on back to the house now?

He didn't know what she needed a hand with, but he imagined it was something she'd made for the addition to the store. Even though it had been a year since they got the additional space, the Glynn Girls were still redesigning and staging it to be exactly how they wanted it. She didn't interrupt his workout time often, so it must be important. He pulled his phone from his pocket to text a quick reply.

K.

He ran through a cluster of gulls, making them scatter and squawk. What was Tara doing right now? Maybe she was running too. On some mornings when they had shared text messages, he'd noticed they had the same routine of jogging before the busyness of the day settled in. She was like his running buddy, except for the hundreds, sometimes thousands, of miles that separated them. He'd love to hop in his car and drive the six-plus hours to visit her, but she hadn't asked that recently, and he wouldn't suggest the idea. Besides, she wasn't at the cabin right now. Was she still in Virginia?

She was doing a fantastic job of working through everything her own way without anyone pulling or pushing on her. And the success of her nonprofit and the power of her yet-to-be-published nonfiction book were proof of it.

His mamas had invited her to come to the island anytime, and he'd assured her it was an open invite. She'd declined without any hesitation.

St. Simons was a perfect place for jogging most all year—flat, warm, with a nice breeze coming off the ocean and wide-open expanses of sand. Yeah. Come here to jog on the beach. Never mind that she was in the land of crisp mountain air, thousands of miles of trails, and rocks for climbing. He longed for her to see the new cottage. But if he told her about it, she might feel some obligation or guilt to use it, and he didn't want that. No, she had to want to come to St. Simons again for her own sake. Then he'd show her the place and let her know it was hers to use whenever it suited her.

He was coming up on Gould's Inlet, where he'd started running on the beach. It was still early enough that the popular spot was almost empty. There were a few people casting their nets into the tidal stream for crabs. It looked like another runner was headed his way.

What is that? He skidded to a stop in the sand so his vision wasn't impaired. *No way.* He rubbed his eyes. The glaring light of the still-rising sun was making him see things.

The vision came closer.

Tara? His heart leaped, but his feet wouldn't move.

She ran until she melted into his embrace. The feeling was heaven. He wrapped his arms around her and held tight, breathing in the sweet scent of her hair and feeling the steady beat of her heart. Her ear was on his chest.

His own heart had to be going a mile a minute. The mere sight of her was more exhilarating than any physical exercise.

She pulled back enough to look at him. A dazzling grin spread across her face. "Hey, you."

She was here. Really here. "Hey." *Smooth one.* He'd often rehearsed what he would say to her if she returned like this, but none of those words were coming to mind. How on earth could he tell her how she lived in his mind and heart every moment of the day, regardless of however many miles separated them?

With her fingers splayed she combed her long hair from her face. "Maybe I should've told you I was coming, but I wanted to surprise you." She chuckled. "Based on the look on your face, I can't tell if you're happy or uncomfortable or—"

Her lips drew him in, a magnetism too strong to ignore, and he stopped her words with a kiss. He couldn't help it. But she didn't pull away. Was she caught up in the moment too? He put his hand on the back of her head and ran his fingers through her hair. Its softness reminded him of silk.

She broke the kiss. "Wow." Her breathing was fast. "That's"—she touched her fingers to her lips—"quite the welcome."

Did she feel for him some of what he felt for her? If only they could have been rooted in the same town. They should've had a childhood together. She would've been his best friend. Maybe much more.

He put his arms around her waist. "You know, just hoping you'll feel welcome to visit again." Would visits always have to be enough? How would she respond to the cottage? He was positive his mom didn't tell her that place was hers. If Tara gave it only a quick glance, she'd think it was a home someone built on that third piece of property. Tara's arrival had to be the reason his mom had texted him to head home.

"Gavin, I was thinking we should date."

He grinned. "Me too."

"But here's the problem with that. I'm going to be one of those women you hear about who talk of marriage on the first date."

"I'm happy to join in on that conversation."

Her beautiful brown eyes bore into him. "I don't want to be anywhere else but with you. In your life. In your arms."

Was this for real? Of all the surprises he'd had in life, this was the best by far. Actually, nothing else compared. "You do?" He had to be grinning like an absolute fool.

He leaned in and kissed her again. When he pulled back, he glanced down at her feet. "I see you wore your running shoes. Let's run back to Mom's house. I have something to show you."

Holding hands, they ran across the expanse of hard sand, jumped over the tidal stream that flowed along the dunes, and stepped onto the pavement of the East Beach neighborhood. They walked hand in hand.

Tara pointed toward his mom's house. "Your mom told me where to find you. I just pulled into her driveway less than twenty minutes ago."

He grinned. "So you *drove* and you just got to the island?"

She shrugged and smiled. "I had to wrap up my appointments along the AT in Virginia yesterday. Headed this way twelve hours ago."

"You drove all night to see me?" No one had ever done something like that for him.

"Yeah, and if my brothers can see me, I know they're laughing. Me driving all night. Me running down the beach into your arms." She giggled.

They turned the corner off Bruce Drive, and about four hundred feet later, they were walking up his mom's driveway. "This way." He led her past the entrance to his mom's house and to the separate shell-and-gravel driveway that went to the new white-clapboard-and-brick cottage.

She pointed at it. "I saw this when I arrived. It's so cute and looks great. Your land buyers haven't wasted any time getting houses built." She gestured across the three lots. "The one closest to your mom's house is my fav.

On stilts, elevated like your mom's, but so inviting with lots of curb appeal. They have good taste."

The flying squirrel inside him jumped and flew about. "I'm glad you like it. I've been using my carpentry skills on this one, and I happen to have a key. Let's go inside."

She paused, her fingertips gently lifting the leaves of the jasmine he'd uprooted from Sapphira's and replanted. She inhaled it and smiled before they walked up the wooden steps and onto the front porch that was as wide as the small cottage.

She touched the face of the brick cottage. "This looks like Sapphira's brick."

"It is her brick." He held the door open for her, and she walked inside.

Her jaw dropped. He chuckled, put a finger under her chin, and closed her mouth.

She pulled away. "It's . . . part of Sapphira's home, a piece of the living area, right?"

He nodded.

She meandered into the next room and gasped. "The art room. The easels, the paintings, everything. Even the lighting is right."

He found it hard to speak as he watched her excitement. "I tried to recreate everything as close as I could. I moved all the reclaimed materials that would still work. I called in that big favor from the squad and hired some professionals too. There's a bathroom, a kitchenette, and a twin bed in the nook over there."

She went to the staircase and peered toward the ceiling. "And a roof."

He laughed. "I hired someone to do that—ceiling and roof. Up those stairs is space enough that you could build a nice large bedroom or two and a small full bathroom."

"Wait. And by 'you could,' you mean the owners could."

"I mean you."

Her eyes bore into his. "Me?" She turned a circle. "This is for me?"

"It is. I wanted a place for you to stay anytime you wanted but with no obligations."

She squealed and stomped her feet as if running in place. Was there something wrong?

"Are you okay?" Had he overstepped?

She hurried back to him, stood on her toes, and wrapped her arms around his neck. "Yes. I love it. It's home. I . . . I'm inside a room where someone loved me and prayed for me all my life. I'm home."

He embraced her. Love already permeated every space of the small house, and he knew it would for the rest of their lives and into the next generations.

Epilogue

The following spring . . .

Tara slung her strappy, white lace heels over her shoulder as she walked through the soft, cool grass of the lighthouse lawn. *Phew.* The reception had been two hours of dancing, singing, and laughing—so much laughing—under the huge live oaks in the park.

The wedding—Gavin's and her wedding—had been perfection. She couldn't believe it. She turned to look once more at the place she and Gavin had said their vows: on the boardwalk to the beach across from the lighthouse, near the spot where he'd first chased her.

Dell and Sue Beth had decorated the plain wooden boards with a carpet of fresh flower petals, and had wrapped countless fragrant jasmine vines around the handrail and over the antique metal arch they'd set up for Gavin and Tara to stand under. They used the same white jasmine flowers that used to bloom around Sapphira's trellis in her front yard and now grew up the rails of Tara's house.

She lifted the hem of her long, white satin dress and hurried around the keeper's quarters at the bottom of the lighthouse, heading toward the Historical Society building they'd rented for the day. She'd danced and celebrated a little longer than she should have, and her traveling outfit waited in the changing room.

All the firemen were here with the trucks. That way if a call came in during the wedding, they could take off, but no call came in. The firemen and their families were now her family too, and she'd bonded with them over the months, knowing it was the beginning of a lifetime of having family.

A few stray rose petals stirred from the grass in the breeze. Tara smiled as she stepped on one with her bare toes. Hadley's little girls had been the flower girls, and her little boy, along with Elliott's, were the cutest ring bearers ever. Hadley, Elliott, and their families had arrived on the island a few days ago to help set up the wedding. They and the Glynn Girls had thrown Tara the most fun prewedding "girls party" at Tidal Creek Grill, complete with off-key karaoke.

Thoughts of Gavin and her beginning their honeymoon journey to Oahu in an hour thrilled the deepest parts of her. First they'd fly to Atlanta and stay the night at the Renaissance near the airport, and tomorrow morning they'd board the long flight to Hawaii. They'd chosen Oahu because it had mountains and beach, and they would rock climb while there.

"Wait for us!" Julep called.

Tara turned to see all four "mamas" in their Sunday best hurrying across the lawn after her. Oh boy.

Dell beamed at her. "You'll *definitely* need our help getting out of that dress, sugar."

Sue Beth nodded in agreement.

There was a long string of small buttons going down the back of her lace-and-chiffon bodice. That would be hard to undo by herself, but she'd wanted a breather from the uproar of the day's festivities. Still, she hadn't considered that she'd need their help.

"Good thinking."

Luella shrugged. "Might as well accept it. Married or single, you're not getting rid of any of us. I should know."

"Good." Tara winked at Luella.

She and Luella had something special, maybe because Luella didn't have any children of her own and Tara had no mother. But all of them were close.

The Glynn Girls, Gavin, and Tara would return to the cabin in North Carolina from time to time. They were planning to spend a long weekend there in two months on the second anniversary of Sean's and Darryl's deaths, hiking and rappelling, although only Tara, Gavin, and Luella would rock climb. They'd hold a vigil around a campfire at the cabin. Tara was both looking forward to and bracing herself for the anniversary. The weekend was sure to be filled with sharing memories that would make her cry and laugh and cry some more. Would she need that time each year?

The Glynn Girls and Tara entered the Historical Society building, went down the hall to the room they'd designated the "bridal changing room," and closed the door behind them.

"Before we undo all this perfection, I want to look at you one more time." Sue Beth clasped her hands together, looking at Tara up and down.

Julep rolled her eyes, looking at Sue Beth. "You know that Dell took like ten thousand pictures of both of them, right?"

"That I did." Dell put the tripod in the corner and set up the camera. "I'm not finished yet either."

"A picture is different than experiencing it firsthand." Sue Beth punctuated her statement with a huff. "And *you* promised to be nicer to me, Julep Burnside."

"And how many times over the past two years have you reminded me of that? I was simply making a statement, and, Dell, you can't take pictures of her undressing."

"Sure I can. She's not stripping naked, only changing into traveling clothes." Dell took Tara by the shoulders and eased her to standing in front of the full-length mirror. "I've set up the camera to snap a shot automatically every ten seconds, and I'll keep them very private."

Tara rubbed a temple. "Mamas, please. I'm supposed to be at the airport in an hour."

They all laughed, chortling and giggling.

Dell clapped her hands. "She already sounds like Gavin!"

Tara turned, looking over her shoulder at Luella. "Can you help me out?"

Luella moved behind Tara. "You know, it's really Dell's fault that you're in this predicament. The vintage dress is stunning, but there are two feet of tiny buttons. She tried to get me to choose a complicated dress like that, and when I refused, she said that she would soon have another wedding to help plan and *someone* would wear such a dress."

"And who was right?" Dell grinned at Tara. "You look divine in that dress."

"Thank you." Tara loved this dress, or she wouldn't be wearing it, but how could changing out of it be such a complicated ordeal? "Now help me out of it."

Luella brushed Tara's hair to the side and unbuttoned the top button on the nape of her neck. "Did you remember to grab the silk scarf off the dresser?"

"Yeah, thanks."

"Here's a good question. Do you and Gavin have . . . uh . . . protection?" Sue Beth asked.

"Hush up," Julep said. "That's too personal a question."

"Oh, you're not fooling us, Julep Burnside." Dell adjusted the mirror, apparently still thinking of what would work best for pictures. "You just want grandchildren as soon as possible."

Julep plunked a chair near Tara. "You might as well sit down. This is going to take a while."

It'd been so fun and exciting getting into the dress with the Glynn Girls fussing about, but now Tara needed a minute. Just one tiny minute without all four of them.

Dell touched her shoulder. "Don't slouch or the dress's beading could catch on the chair's fabric."

Sue Beth laughed. "Don't be so fussy. It's not like you'd let anyone else wear this dress!"

Luella undid another button. "You never know. In twenty-something years Tara and Gavin's daughter may want to wear it or maybe in forty-something years a granddaughter."

Good grief. Gavin was right. Their personalities really were too big for one small island to hold. "Could someone pass me my phone?" She wasn't sure where it was, but one of the girls had slid it into her purse to keep for Tara until after the wedding.

"Sure thing." Sue Beth pulled it out and gave it to her. It was time to text for backup.

> Dear husband, I'm being smothered by YOUR mamas. Couldn't you call at least one of them to help you for a little bit?

She watched the bubbles dance on the small screen. His reply came a few seconds later.

> My dear, sweet, beautiful wife, the love of my life, I certainly could . . .

She read it and waited for one of the mamas' phones to ring. But then the bubbles danced again.

> I'm not going to, but I do possess the ability.

Ugh. Really? She tapped her finger on the side of the device, plotting how to get what she wanted. An idea struck, and she had to bite her lips to keep from laughing.

> Dear husband, you do know, YOU could've chosen to be the one, the only one, helping me out of this wedding dress. We are married now.

Bubbles again. Then they disappeared. She waited a few more seconds.

A knock at the door caused Julep to unlock it and open it a crack. "Tara, it's your husband."

Gavin eased the door open and pushed past his mom. "Out mamas. Out now." He winked at Tara. She covered her mouth to keep from bursting out in laughter. He held the door as all four women exited, each griping a bit under her breath.

Tara stood, her heart quickening at the sight of him, now changed out of his tuxedo and in a lightweight button-up shirt and jeans. "You sure were quick on that rescue."

He closed the door, locked it, and smiled as he slowly crossed the room. "Anything for my wife."

"I like how that sounds."

"Me too." He tilted her chin up and pressed his lips to hers. A delicious feeling of fire ran the length of her body. He deepened the kiss, and after several moments they were both left breathless.

"Um . . . the buttons begin here." She turned, facing the mirror.

He hesitated.

"Gavin?"

"I'm analyzing the situation." He looked up, seeing her in the mirror. He traced a finger down the side of her neck and kissed the other side. He ran his hands down her arms until his fingers were intertwined with hers. "I can't believe we're married . . . or how much I love you."

She felt the same, but all she could manage was to squeeze his fingers.

He bent his elbows, causing her to bend hers, and he held her, gazing at her in the mirror. "I could stay like this for at least another thirty seconds, but the clock is ticking, and I think we should call in one mom."

"Fine," she grumbled. "You can rescue strangers from burning buildings but can't manage to rescue your wife from this dress."

He kissed her neck again before holding up his hands in the mirror. "Huge hands. Tiny satin buttons surrounded by delicate material." He lowered his hands to her shoulders. "I refuse for the story told of these few minutes to be that I ripped you out of the wedding dress."

She laughed. "That would be the story, wouldn't it?"

"Yep, and it wouldn't stay on the island. Oh no, not with the social-media following my wife has."

She turned to face him. "I love you, now and forever. For richer or poorer . . ." She kissed him and lowered her head until his lips were on her forehead. "But I want that honeymoon in Hawaii, so skedaddle and send in Luella and Julep. You find something you need Dell and Sue Beth to help you with."

"Done." He winked and strode to the door.

In the moment of quiet, she could feel Sean and Darryl all around her. Her joy seemed to mingle with theirs . . . for they had a life, and so did she.

Reader's Guide

1. In the novel we discover that the Glynn Girls met at camp at a young age. What do you think they did to hold their friendships together over the years? Do you have friendships that have lasted for multiple decades? If you have that kind of friendship, how have you maintained it? Do you believe that it is easier or more difficult for women today to make those kinds of friendships? Why?

2. The Glynn Girls approve of Gavin's dismantling Sapphira's house before the ownership fully transfers. How did you feel about that and Gavin's decision to forge ahead with selling the house in pieces? Was it over the line, or was he doing what he had to do?

3 As Tara's close friends, Hadley and Elliott are in the delicate position of determining how to handle Tara's grief over losing her brothers. They must decide if they should help her more because of her injury or give her the space she is requesting. Have you ever had someone close to you experience a terrible loss and not known how best to be a good friend? What did you do?

4. Charles McKenzie makes a terrible first impression on Luella. Describe an experience when you learned to care deeply about someone even though initially you thought you would not become friends. What made the difference?

5. Luella embraces her life as a single adult, a traveler, and a writer. She tells Chuck that she loves her life this way and can't imagine changing her lifestyle, but she does come around to wanting a life with him. What does she sacrifice in embracing marriage? What do you think she gains?

6. Sapphira's daughter, Cassidy, left St. Simons for good, taking her daughter with her. Sapphira clearly mourned that loss with her Glynn Girls family, but none of the women could change the bad path Cassidy had chosen to take. Have you ever had to let go of a loved one who seemed beyond help? How did you deal with that process?

7. St. Simons Island is a tourist destination in Georgia, and living in a tourist town can have a number of funny quirks and challenges. Do you live, or have you lived, in a tourist destination? If you could pick a tourist town to live in, which one would it be?

8. Gavin has multiple run-ins with Tara while she is still disoriented and unsure of her surroundings. He treats her very respectfully, showing her kindness and compassion. Do you think his traits are typical among male believers? Explain your answer.

9. The Glynn Girls are very connected to Sidney Lanier's poem describing St. Simons, "The Marshes of Glynn." Is there a particular artistic expression—a song, a book, a poem, or a painting—that always makes you think of your home or another location that you especially love? Describe it and how often you interact with it.

10. Tara identifies with the psalmist in Psalm 31, recalling verses nine and ten over and over: "Be gracious to me. O LORD, for I am in distress; my eye is wasted from grief; my soul and my body also. For my life is spent with sorrow, and my years with sighing; my strength fails." Is there a particular psalm that you have clung to during hard times? Or one that you use to turn mourning into joy? What is that psalm?

Acknowledgments

A very special thank-you to my grandmother by marriage, Joyce Ference. Thank you for the years of loving me, for the visits to your beautiful Brunswick home, for your delightful company and many delicious meals, and for the crucial information about the Golden Isles that made this book possible.

And a thank-you to my dad, Russ Rainwater. What amazing memories we've made in the Golden Isles over the years! Cindy and I greatly appreciate your meeting us in St. Simons and introducing us to the world of Glynn County firemen and EMTs.

—*Erin*

To Al Thomas, retired Glynn County Fire Chief—A heartfelt thank-you because without you this book would not have been possible.

To WaterBrook Multnomah—Thank you for embracing our desire to write this Southern novel.

To Shannon Marchese, Executive Editor, and Carol Bartley, the line editor—We would not want to write a novel without you!

To Jamie Lapeyrolerie—Thank you for your encouragement and expertise.

To our Woodsmall family—Thank you for your endless support and patience.

To the workers at REI, Buford, Georgia—Thank you for sharing your knowledge and experience with us!

—*Cindy and Erin*

THE AMISH *of* SUMMER GROVE SERIES

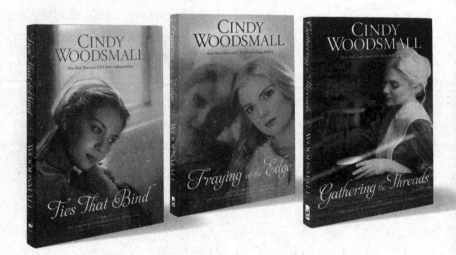

Ariana's comfortable Old Order Amish world is about
to unravel. Will holding tightly to the cords of family
keep them together—or simply tear them apart?

Do you love WaterBrook & Multnomah Fiction?

Be the first to know about upcoming releases, insider news and all kinds of fiction fun!

Sign up for our Fiction Reads newsletter at
wmbooks.com/WaterBrookMultnomahFiction

Join our Fiction Only Facebook Page!
www.facebook.com/waterbrookmultnomahfiction

waterbrookmultnomah.com